# LYCANTHROPY AND OTHER CHRONIC ILLNESSES

# LYCANTHROPY

## AND OTHER CHRONIC

# ILLNESSES

## KRISTEN O'NEAL

QUIRK BOOKS
PHILADELPHIA

Copyright © 2021 by Kristen O'Neal

ISBN: 978-1-68369-232-4

Printed in the United States of America

Typeset in Bembo & Avenir

Designed by Ryan Hayes
Cover illustration by Rik Lee

Production management by John J. McGurk

Quirk Books
215 Church Street
Philadelphia, PA 19106
quirkbooks.com

10 9 8 7 6 5 4 3 2 1

**For anyone who doesn't feel at home in their body**

-------

**1**

**Ticks don't actually have teeth. I looked it up afterward, scrolling** through photos with that same kind of sick fascination of watching someone pop a pimple. They've got this horrible ridged capitulum that opens up into three parts like the monster from *Stranger Things*, sinks into your skin, and holds on just long enough to derail the course of your entire life.

I don't know what time it is when I wake up. This time last year, I would have known the second I heard my alarm trilling: 7:30 a.m. on a Monday, enough time to hit snooze once, slip out of bed, turn on the coffee pot my roommate and I weren't allowed to have in our dorm, and get ready to leave for Bio at 8:40. Enough time to sit and drink it, knees to my chest, as she slept, scrolling through my email or my blog. I was a well-oiled machine. I was pre-med at Stanford and I had made it out of New Jersey. I was ready for anything.

It must have happened when I was home for the summer, trudging through the tall grass with my high school friends, cutting across a field to get to town. Or maybe it was down by the Amtrak tracks with the climbing plants as Jadie roped me into "acting" for one of her film projects. I don't know. I'll never know. The only thing I know is that when I got back to California last fall, I got sick. Really sick.

I don't set an alarm anymore. I know I've slept too long—my internal clock won't wake me when it's supposed to. It's sluggish now, constantly running low on battery, and so am I.

I take a quick inventory, staring up at the same crack in my ceiling that I've stared up at since I was five years old. My head is stuffed with cotton. I feel heavy, like something is pinning me to the mattress. And my joints *hurt*, a throbbing pain that will only get worse as I move. It feels like a handful of fevers scattered around my body, a dozen hungry black-hole stomachs—my left knuckles, my ankle, my knee, my hips, my wrist.

Sometimes it feels like coals being stoked hotter and hotter until I can't move. Sometimes it feels like a fist clenched tight, tight, tight, until I think that my bones are going to break. Sometimes it feels like each segment of my body is floating away from the others like Pangea, a strange, electric humming that separates all of my bones.

Sometimes it doesn't feel like anything at all. Sometimes it just hurts.

Today will be okay, probably. But when the weather's about to change, I can roll over and feel every point where my bones connect to each other. Last week I landed wrong when I walked down the steps to the car, and my swollen knee remembers this as well as I do.

I hear my door creak open before it's pulled shut again with a soft *click*. I don't make a sound.

"Let me just check if she needs anything," comes my mom's voice. She doesn't know how to whisper, so her version of a hushed tone cuts right through the door. "She hasn't been to church with us in so long."

My dad replies in Tamil, mostly. "Let the girl sleep. She needs to rest. You talked with the doctor yourself, didn't you?"

"And what does he know?" I can *see* my mom waving her hand. Then, a little louder: "Priya—"

My dad shushes her. "You are shouting—"

"I am *not* shouting, you are—"

"I'll stay back in case she needs me. Okay?"

There's a pause. Then, my dad's voice again: "She's going to be just fine."

My mom's: "We should be going to church as a family."

"We will, I promise."

"Okay."

The door opens again, and I let my eyes close. I hear my mom pad over to my bed, sit on the side. She smooths back my hair and kisses me on the forehead, gentler than she usually is with me.

I think about pretending I'm still asleep, but a soft-edged affection tugs at my heart and I pretend, instead, that she's woken me up.

"How are you feeling?" she asks.

"Pretty good," I lie. It's worth it for the grin that makes its way across her face, and she pats me on the cheek.

"Don't tell your father I woke you up," she says. "He'll get mad at me."

I smile back at her. "Have fun at church."

"I always put you in the prayer requests," she says. I know it's meant to be comforting, but the thought of everyone talking about me and my illness makes me want to stay in the house forever and never show my face in public again.

"Say hello to God for me," I joke. Her face turns severe.

"Say hello yourself!" she says. "You're being silly. Okay, go back to sleep. Don't tell your father."

"I won't."

I mean to wake up then, to pull open my closet and put on something other than sweatpants. I mean to go downstairs and eat breakfast with my dad, or maybe even flag down my mom and brother and sister, tell them I'm coming to church with them after all. But instead my eyes close, and I'm pulled back under before I even reach over and click the Tumblr app on my phone.

-------

**It takes me a few seconds to realize that the buzzing is coming** from my bedside table, but I'm not quick enough. My phone shimmies its way off the table and falls to the floor with a *thud* that's muffled by the thin, yellowing carpet. I pull it up by the charger like the world's worst fisherman.

*bigforkhands sent you a message*, the screen says, right underneath *11:53, February 2*. I try to be gracious with myself, but seeing the time still shoots a spike of adrenaline right through me. *You've wasted your day*, says a voice in my head. *What's a day when you've wasted the whole year?* says another.

The phone buzzes again. I should be rolling my eyes, but instead, I feel a smile spreading across my face. I open up my messages, scrolling up to the top.

**bigforkhands:**

hey did you know that during one of the battles in the civil war a bunch of soldiers just started.

uh. glowing in the dark

like

they were stuck in the mud for like two days and they looked down and were like "oh cool, sweet, my wounds are glowing blue"

thisisfine.jpg

and

AND!!!!!!

the soldiers with glowing wounds actually got better faster than the other ones??

**bigforkhands:**

listen some teens DID solve this mystery (as teens always do) and they found out that all these factors came together to make these nasty nasty wounds the perfect home for this bioluminescent bacteria

which... somehow heals you? idk I haven't quite figured that part out

you're the scientist, you tell me, doc

anyway

could you IMAGINE. what that would be like with this like, 19th century nothing knowledge

like. god. what must they have been thinking was happening to them?

**bigforkhands:**

ok I read more and they called it "angel's glow" which fucking slaps

it must have looked like a miracle, huh. like. i can't even imagine what that would be like. emotionally i mean.

do people still believe in miracles? do you?

**bigforkhands:**

priya wake up

Before I can even finish reading, my phone buzzes again, and I scroll down to type out a quick message.

**paranormaldetective:**
> Brigid!!!

**bigforkhands:**
> oh sweet you're up
> rise and shine, sweet cheeks

**paranormaldetective:**
> HATED that.

**bigforkhands:**
> stop using periods at the end of your sentences dude
> you sound ilke a serial killer
> you gotta be cool and fun... how do you spell lazey faire

**paranormaldetective:**
> Yeah I think that was right

**bigforkhands:**
> :)))

**paranormaldetective:**
> Okay, let me scroll back up.

**bigforkhands:**
> NO PERIODS!!!
> coincidentally that also describes my body

**paranormaldetective:**
> Are you okay

**bigforkhands:**
> absolutely not, thank you for asking

I scroll back up. She's sent me a post that reads, "Send Your Fol-lowers a Box of Toads to Demonstrate Your Undying Affection." Under this, there's another message from Brigid:

**bigforkhands:**
> hey what's your address
> for no particular reason

**paranormaldetective:**
> Brigid you LITERALLY just sent me a post threatening to mail me toads

**bigforkhands:**

i don't know what you're talking about

**paranormaldetective:**

Mmhmm.

**bigforkhands:**

was it a threat or a promise

**paranormaldetective:**

I'm not giving you my address

**bigforkhands:**

ughhh you're always so much cagier on the internet than i am

it's like you actually learned the lesson you were supposed to learn instead of telling strangers your name and a bunch of information about yourself and also your deepest darkest secrets

**paranormaldetective:**

Consider it an honor that you know my name

**bigforkhands:**

oh i do, trust me

okay, I'll give you MY address

**paranormaldetective:**

Knock yourself out!

Not literally please

**bigforkhands:**

too late

This is exactly the way that Brigid and I became . . . well, friends. At first that was just the word I used to explain our conversations to my parents—*one of my friends was telling me about this. No, you don't know her, she goes to another school.* I was lying, in more ways than one; even though we messaged every day, *friend* didn't seem like the right word for someone on the other side of a computer screen, someone made up of pixels and words and images, whose blog description said "i'm bridge, i'm 20, and i'm not sure what's happening here either." It didn't seem like the right word until, suddenly, it was.

Here's what I see when I scroll through her blog: A meme about Victor Frankenstein. An extremely cursed text post I refuse to repeat even to myself. A gifset from *True or False*, the mid-2000s USA Network TV show that we bonded over watching a decade too late. A post that just says "I saw a snake on my way home from work!!" followed by a digital illustration she's done of a grinning cartoon snake with a braided, crosshatch design on its back. It's captioned "funky little dude!" She's got such a distinct style that I always know when I see one of her drawings—her tag is "doodles," and they're made to look effortless, but she's really talented.

I can never quite tell how etiquette translates to talking to people on the internet. How many posts do you have to reblog from each other before it's okay to send them a message? How many comments do you have to leave before you become friends?

But I didn't actually have to worry. A few weeks into following each other, she sent me a message that said "i LOVE your blog and upon deliberation, i have decided that we are going to be friends!"

And that was it. She spoke it into existence like God creating the universe.

We've been chatting on and off for two years now, whenever she felt like popping into my inbox. But we've been talking almost nonstop since I've been back in Jersey. I keep up with a handful of college friends, but no one knows what to say to me. *Sorry you had to drop out of school for the rest of the year. Sorry you had to move back home in shame.*

With Brigid it's easy. We talk about movies or religion or celebrity crushes or yearning, she sends me memes, and she doesn't feel sorry for me.

My phone buzzes again, and I swing myself out of bed, trying to stand. I forget my knee until it buckles, and I have to catch myself on the bed. The giddy bubble of brightness from Brigid's messages pops.

I take a couple of breaths to stop myself from crying. I cry more now than I ever used to. I hate it. When I'd gotten back from the hospital, the sight of my own clean, white sheets had twisted something in my chest, and I'd wanted to ask my mother to change them to something colorful, but I was embarrassed I couldn't change them myself, and exhausted from the trip home, so I'd just burst into tears instead.

**bigforkhands:**
6969 cool street
...ok but actually, no mcelroyisms:

> 11 Natalis Road
> Bellows, PA 19508
> we're pen pals now, the contract has been signed

I cannot believe it.

**paranormaldetective:**
> ...Oh my God

**bigforkhands:**
> what??

**paranormaldetective:**
> You literally live like, an hour away from me

**bigforkhands:**
> whAT!!!!!!!!!!!!!!!!!!!!!!!!!!!!!!!!!!!!!!!!!!!!!!!!!!!!!!!!!!!!!
> YOU'RE KIDDING ME
> we are NEIGHBORS, PRACTICALLY

**paranormaldetective:**
> !!!!!!!!!

**bigforkhands:**
> holy shit holy shit holy shti

**paranormaldetective:**
> This is so crazy!!!!

**bigforkhands:**
> come visit
> slumber party
> hiking trip
> rob a bank with me
> ...i'm kidding, sorry for being weird haha

**paranormaldetective:**
> No, I don't mind

**bigforkhands:**
> you never seem to, and i cherish that about our
> friendship

I smile.

**paranormaldetective:**
Me too <3

**bigforkhands:**
:')

**paranormaldetective:**
Is that his nose

**bigforkhands:**
no! he's shedding a happy tear!
or she
do smileys have gender

**paranormaldetective:**
No

**bigforkhands:**
yeah of course they don't

**paranormaldetective:**
So... Bioluminescence?

**bigforkhands:**
love of my life... i thought you'd never ask

# 2

**Whenever we go to the doctor, my mom comes into the room**
with me. It's an embarrassment and a relief. I should be able to do this
myself; I'm glad that I don't have to.

This is the second doctor I've seen. Well, that's not exactly true. In
California, I went to the school clinic first, after I realized I couldn't
keep ignoring how exhausted I was all the time—how my heart
skipped beats and my head fogged and my whole body hurt, from
my joints to my skin. The first thing that every professor said in our
premed classes was "do *not* diagnose yourself or your friends," but I
was doing it anyway. Was it my thyroid? Chronic fatigue syndrome?
Arthritis, lupus, heart failure, cancer?

The doctor at the clinic eyed me when I listed my symptoms.

"It feels a little bit like the flu?" I tried. "But there's more stuff, and
it's just been getting worse since September."

"You've been feeling like this for . . . two months?"

I nodded.

"Then it's not the flu. Honestly, I know every kid hates to hear
this, but you probably have mono."

"I don't have a sore throat."

"Are you sexually active?"

"No."

He put down his clipboard and raised his eyebrows.

"Really?"

I frowned. "Yes, really."

"Oral counts as—"

"I know what sexually active means!" I said, my face heating. He was still waiting. "No, I've never had sex."

"I'll run a few tests and we'll let you know," he said. Then, glancing back up at me from his clipboard: "You look okay, though."

The next doctor I saw was the one at the emergency room, after my heart slowed, my muscles twitched, and I passed out during finals week.

I am sitting on the examination table of New Jersey Doctor #2, tapping my thumb in a slow rhythm while my mom highlights sections of the hundreds of printouts she brought with us. New Jersey Doctor #1 diagnosed me with Lyme a month ago but made a mistake with my antibiotic dosage and was promptly discarded.

"The first thing you have to remember," my mother says, looking up at me, "is that doctors don't know everything."

"I'm studying to become a doctor, Mom," I say. *Was*, I think. It puts down roots in my throat. *You were.*

"Doctors are very smart," she says. "But they have so much to remember that sometimes you have to help them along. And sometimes they don't care."

Today's a bad day. If I hadn't had my mom to drive me, I would not have made it to the office. She'll help explain my symptoms, too. *She had to take off work today*, I think, guiltily. I feel like I'm hovering just a few inches above my body. I don't stay on any one thought for long, except for when my mind clamps down on a single line from a song and replays it over, and over, and over, and over.

I've decided that today is a bad day, and that February is a bad month. The worst month. The coldest and grayest and most miserable month, bleak, naked stick trees jutting their arms out toward the gray sky, ice slicking over every single road in my miserable neighborhood. When was the last time I drove somewhere on my own? I can't remember. Not California. The cold is sinking into my bones.

I close my eyes, and when I open them back up, the doctor is in the room with us.

"Hi, Priya, how are you feeling today?" he asks. His voice is gentle. I am swimming in it.

I shake my head no, once back and forth. It makes me dizzy. I see him frown.

"I'd hoped that things would have started to calm down by this point, but you had one of the nastier cases of Lyme I've seen. I'm not surprised there are still some lasting symptoms, especially since it's only been about three weeks since you went off the antibiotics."

"Had?" my mom asks.

"Hm?" The doctor turns to face her. I realize I can't remember what his name is.

"She *had* one of the nastier cases?" my mom repeats. She is laser focused. Thank God.

He nods. "We'll take more blood today, but the bacterium itself should be gone."

My mom shuffles her papers. "But the damage has already been done. The joint pain could continue for the rest of her life."

"On and off," the doctor says. What was his *name*? "It's likely, yes."

I close my eyes again until the doctor touches my shoulder. "I'm sorry I caught you on a brain-fog kind of day, Priya." I feel guilty that he knows my name and I do not know his, because he has so many patients and I only have one Lyme doctor. There's another name for that, too, a bigger name than that one.

"Me too," I say, trying to smile, and he smiles back at me. I am grateful that my mother has her list of questions, and that I don't have to ask them, because I can't remember what any of them are.

The nurse comes to take my blood. I'm already lightheaded; I hardly feel the needle. I close my eyes. I hover over my body. I ache.

-------

**paranormaldetective:**
> I've been thinking a lot about quantum physics lately
> Even though I've always been more of a biology girl
> This is about to get cheesy, I'm about to pull a you

**bigforkhands:**
> TELL ME EVERYTHING!!!
> im so sorry, you sent me this like two days ago

i've been

mm

well to be perfectly honest i was a little incapacitated

**paranormaldetective:**

I

Just can't today

I'm sorry

**bigforkhands:**

oh no :/

is it that bad?

**paranormaldetective:**

Brain fog

**bigforkhands:**

dang

sorry, that wasn't like, a super empathetic response

**paranormaldetective:**

It's okay

Are you feeling better

**bigforkhands:**

yeah, i'm okay, just real tired

poppin those iron pills

looks like we just missed each other

**paranormaldetective:**

:/

**bigforkhands:**

go watch a movie you've seen a million times, it'll help

**paranormaldetective:**

Do you get this too

**bigforkhands:**

uhh... kind of? i mean, no. mine's different

it like, ebbs and flows over the month

**paranormaldetective:**

Okay

**bigforkhands:**

talk when you feel better?

**paranormaldetective:**
| Course
**bigforkhands:**
| okay, tell me what you end up watching
**paranormaldetective:**
| Shoot
| Dr hegazy
**bigforkhands:**
| ??
| is that one of those old russian ones
**paranormaldetective:**
| No, not a movie
| Nevermind
**bigforkhands:**
| neverminded
| <3

- - - - - - -

**bigforkhands:**

having a body is overrated. 2/10. would like to become a ghost, specter, or phantasm.

**127 notes**

paranormaldetective reblogged bigforkhands: "having a body is overrated. 2/ . . ."

- - - - - - -

**paranormaldetective:**
| Hi, how are you feeling!
**bigforkhands:**
| priya my love!! you return to me!
**paranormaldetective:**
| In victory! Lol

**bigforkhands:**
i'm so glad you're feeling at least a little better

**paranormaldetective:**
And?? How are you?

**bigforkhands:**
haha i'm awesome!!! feelin a little sore but in a good way
what movie did you watch?

**paranormaldetective:**
I watched Singin' in the Rain with my mom
Well, sort of
I lied on the couch and watched Singin' in the Rain while my mom got up every 13 seconds to do something else
She has enough energy for both of us

**bigforkhands:**
lmao

**paranormaldetective:**
And when my brother and sister got home we watched the low road

**bigforkhands:**
SWEET
what season are you on again

**paranormaldetective:**
Two

**bigforkhands:**
ah so they're still very stupid and a little bit selfish

**paranormaldetective:**
Do they get less stupid...?

**bigforkhands:**
oh absolutely not
but they get better and kinder

**paranormaldetective:**
:')

**bigforkhands:**
wait what were you saying about pulling a me though

something about physics?

i was so bummed that i missed it

**paranormaldetective:**

Oh man haha

Idk, it seems dumb and overdramatic now

That was more of an 11pm kind of conversation

Like a, I'm alone in my room and it's late and dark and I'm feeling sorry for myself, sort of conversation

**bigforkhands:**

there's always time to feel sorry for yourself

**paranormaldetective:**

BRIGID

**bigforkhands:**

pleaseeeeeeee

**paranormaldetective:**

Okay but don't laugh at me

**bigforkhands:**

if i do you will never know because i will lie and tell you i didn't

**paranormaldetective:**

Great, thanks

**bigforkhands:**

i am a banner friend

who is patiently waiting

[CHINHANDS.GIF]

**paranormaldetective:**

Okay, okay

So you know about the multiverse theory, right?

**bigforkhands:**

of course

the theory is that multiverses exist, right

**paranormaldetective:**

Well, yeah

It's the concept that there are infinite universes of possible permutations of history and just, life

And that any decision or like, tiny moment could have turned out a little bit differently, and that different version exists, somewhere, parallel to us

**bigforkhands:**

i'm on the wikipedia page

**paranormaldetective:**

Shocker

**bigforkhands:**

i live here

wikipedia is my home

shelter me in your minimalist design, wikipedia

...go on

**paranormaldetective:**

There are a lot of TV shows and movies that use this but they have every single thing about the world be exactly the same, even though just one different decision would ripple out to everything else

Like, everything

**bigforkhands:**

like a butterfly effect kind of thing

**paranormaldetective:**

Right

And I used to think that the whole idea was really, really stupid

And I still kind of do on like, a scientific level

But... what if there really is just that one thing?

That one thing that derails your entire life

And you can see the life that you were supposed to be living running parallel to this one but you can't get to it

So what if that one tick bite was. It.

...this is so dumb, I feel dumb

**bigforkhands:**

IT'S NOT DUMB!!!!!!!!!!!!!!!!

oh my god, you're not allowed to say it's dumb

i'm really sorry that this has happened to you

**paranormaldetective:**
| Yeah it kind of sucks, haha

**bigforkhands:**
| sorry if this is invasive but you have lyme, right?

**paranormaldetective:**
| Oh!! Omg no, not invasive

**bigforkhands:**
| or some other kind of tick thing
| tick sickness

**paranormaldetective:**
| I completely forgot I didn't tell you

**bigforkhands:**
| tickness

**paranormaldetective:**
| Yeah, I've got Lyme disease
| ...that was your worst portmanteau yet

**bigforkhands:**
| what the fuck is a portmanteau

**paranormaldetective:**
| You just did it??

**bigforkhands:**
| how dare you accuse me of such a thing

**paranormaldetective:**
| It's when you smash two words together haha

**bigforkhands:**
| oh lol
| i thought that was just a funny pun
| punny

**paranormaldetective:**
| THAT'S LITERALLY A PORTMANTEAU

**bigforkhands:**
| portman-whoa

**paranormaldetective:**
| I'm logging off

**bigforkhands:**
hahahahahhaa
i'm sorry, i'm sorry, i'm bad at being serious
there's not just one thing, priya. i promise

**paranormaldetective:**
Thanks

**bigforkhands:**
and maybe there are alternate universes, and maybe there's another you somewhere who's feeling fine right now and living a whole different life
but a shitty thing happened to you in this one
and you just have to find a way to keep going with it

**paranormaldetective:**
You're not bad at being serious, Brigid
That was pretty damn good.

**bigforkhands:**
you're gonna ruin my reputation

**paranormaldetective:**
Can I ask what your thing is

**bigforkhands:**
my thing?

**paranormaldetective:**
What makes you sick

**bigforkhands:**
oh i'm not sick

**paranormaldetective:**
Oh I thought...
Didn't you just say you felt so horrible that you couldn't function for several days?

**bigforkhands:**
mmhmm

**paranormaldetective:**
And this isn't the first time this has happened

**bigforkhands:**
nope

**paranormaldetective:**
And it's the same thing that keeps hurting your body

**bigforkhands:**
yeah, pretty much every month

**paranormaldetective:**
...that's like, the dictionary definition of a chronic illness

**bigforkhands:**
.........................................h m

**paranormaldetective:**
An illness... that happens chronically...

**bigforkhands:**
but like
most of the time i feel really good and really healthy

**paranormaldetective:**
But sometimes you don't

**bigforkhands:**
right

**paranormaldetective:**
I don't want to define things for you or anything, but you're allowed to be chronically ill even if someone else seems sicker than you
It's not a contest

**bigforkhands:**
thanks, priya

**paranormaldetective:**
Wait I'm sorry
Are we good
Did I overstep?
I can't read your tone

**bigforkhands:**
no we're good!!! i'm just feeling some feelings!
genuinely, thank you
you... might be right

**paranormaldetective:**
<3

**bigforkhands:**
<3

**paranormaldetective:**
I've gotta go eat lunch
Thanks for getting real with me

**bigforkhands:**
ugh. feelings

**paranormaldetective:**
Hahaha
I'll drag them out of you

**bigforkhands:**
anytime, dude
literally anytime

# 3

**My brother swings open the back door, groaning loudly enough** for everyone in the house to hear him. He drops his backpack on the floor and makes his way to the couch.

"Ugh, move, Priya, you're blocking my dramatic collapse," he says. I roll my eyes at him. He flops down beside me in a swoon and puts his awful, stinky sock feet in my lap. I gag, but I don't have the energy to shove him off.

"Good date, Suresh?" I ask.

He glares daggers at me.

"Close the door or Mom is going to kill you," I say.

"Oh, like I'm afraid of Mom," he scoffs.

"Suresh?" Her voice comes shouting from the other room. "Is that you?"

He's off the couch in a second, slamming the door shut and kicking his backpack under the couch.

"Yes, *amma*!" he shouts.

"Smooth criminal," I say.

"What are you watching?" he asks me, grabbing the remote.

"Nothing. Why did your date suck so bad?"

"Just because you're back home doesn't mean you get to grill me," he says.

I cringe. He looks at me sideways, purses his mouth. "If I tell you, will you promise not to make fun of me?"

"I promise," I lie.

"She didn't even *realize* it was supposed to be a *date*," he says. "Where's Kiki?"

"Play practice," I say.

"Oh, right."

"She'll make fun of you later."

"No one is allowed to make fun of me in my own house," he says. "Especially not you two nerds."

"I'm waiting to hear about your horrible not-a-date," I say.

"Okay so," he starts, "I asked her if she wanted to come with me to check out the new ice rink over on Hudson, and she said yes."

"Ice skating?" I say, my resolve already wobbling.

"No. Making fun. Of me." He jabs his finger at my face, and I lift my hands in surrender.

"Anyway, we get Starbucks first because I thought that would be like, *nice*, and I pay for hers, and she looks really surprised. But I'm trying to be, like, a gentleman."

"Of course," I say. He's scrolling through Netflix with quick, irritated clicks.

"And we get to the skating rink and I offer to pay for her skates, too, but she says she's got it, and I ask if she's sure, and she says she's sure, so we start going around the rink. And we're having a pretty good time and, like, talking about different stuff that's going on at school, and so I kind of, like, reach out to take her hand?"

"Respectable," I say.

"Well I thought so, I was feeling out the moment."

"And how'd the moment feel?"

"Great! I *thought*," he says darkly. He scrolls back through the comedy section for a second time.

"So I brush her fingers and she kind of laughs, and stops skating, and says—and I'm quoting her here—she says 'Wait, oh my God . . . this isn't a *date*, is it?'"

"Oof," I say.

"This isn't a date!" He drops the remote on the floor. "Is it!"

"What did you do?" I ask.

"I pretended that I'd lost my balance and that that's why I had *accidentally* grabbed her hand," he says. "And then I actually *did* lose my balance and fell down and she laughed at me so hard she snorted a little bit." He pushes himself up to grab his guitar and sits back down cross-legged on the floor in front of me. "Even *that* was cute. Which isn't fair at all."

"Buddy," I say.

He sighs, picking out a couple of notes. "Maybe I'll write about it."

I smile, and he immediately frowns.

"Stop!"

"No, don't worry, S," I say. "I won't make fun of you for being sensitive."

"Oh my God, stoppp." He groans.

"My sweet baby brother!" I grin. "The songwriter!"

"Stop! You're being so embarrassing!" he says. "I'm leaving."

He doesn't. We sit in companionable silence as he strums. My phone buzzes, and I'm surprised to see that it's a Facebook message.

I'm trying to avoid social media. I don't want to see everyone in California going to parties and having movie nights and late-night fast food runs and road trips. I'm even jealous of the staged studying pictures. I haven't posted anything on Instagram since October. "Finally off IV antibiotics!!!!" or "Gained weight and had to steal a pair of my dad's sweatpants because my jeans don't fit me anymore!" don't seem like they'd fit the general mood.

The message is from Nick. I'm instantly embarrassed by the way my heart picks up. We took Chem 31A together last year, struggling over the same concepts. Study hangouts gave way to regular hangouts. We became friends, and then something else, tenuous and undefined, that I could feel like a thread pulled taut between us.

**Nickolas Bower:**

Hey, I'm so sorry I never replied, I've been super busy

And I literally never check Facebook haha

**Priya Radhakrishnan:**

It's okay!

**Nickolas Bower:**

How are you feeling?

The premed crew misses you :(

**Priya Radhakrishnan:**

Aw!!

I'm actually feeling better, yeah. Kind of slow going though

> My life is really boring right now, tell me what you're up to!

**Nickolas Bower:**

> I mean, idk? I've got more time now that we're offseason, been to a couple of parties
> OChem is kicking my ass

**Priya Radhakrishnan:**

> Oh, I bet haha

**Nickolas Bower:**

> What else
> Went to this weird indie concert with Alanna
> You know her, right?

**Priya Radhakrishnan:**

> Alanna from nerd camp?

**Nickolas Bower:**

> Yeah!

**Priya Radhakrishnan:**

> Not like, super well, but yes!

**Nickolas Bower:**

> Haha yeah, she dragged me along with her
> Uhhh... I'm also rewatching Parks & Rec?

**Priya Radhakrishnan:**

> Great show!

There's a lag. I can see him start typing, then stop again. My face suddenly feels hot with embarrassment. I'm not a part of this anymore.

**Nickolas Bower:**

> I actually have to go to class rn, but I hope you're taking care of yourself.
> Are you really doing better? Like, seriously?

**Priya Radhakrishnan:**

> I am, really.

I pause. Why am I not just telling him the truth? I take a breath and start typing.

> I mean, I am better than I was when I was in the hospital, but it's actually been really hard. Having to stay back

The green dot disappears, and I realize he's gone offline. I erase the message, lock my phone, and drop it on the floor next to the couch.

The door bangs open and shut again, and a piercing soprano rendition of "Do You Hear the People Sing?" shakes the whole house. Suresh and I hold eye contact, wincing, and he plugs his headphones into the jack of his guitar.

"Hey, kiddo," I call.

"I am a *freshman*," she says. I hear her clanging around the kitchen, still singing.

"Ugh, Kiki!" Suresh shouts. She sticks her head into the living room in time to see him put his headphones over his ears to drown out her singing.

"I saw that, Suresh!"

"Chill for a second, you're just in the chorus."

"*Just* in the chorus? We are the *backbone* of this musical, Suresh."

"Whatever," he says.

Kiki emerges with an apple and an entire block of cheese, taking a bite of each.

"I thought dairy was bad for your vocal cords," I say.

She shrugs. "Eh, I'm just in the chorus."

"Oh, come on!" Suresh says.

She grins, settling herself onto the couch. I put my legs across her lap and she pats them gently. I try not to wince when she hits my knee. The swelling still hasn't gone down. I'm starting to think it never will.

"So we're watching *The Low Road* again, right?" Kiki asks. It's her favorite animated series. An unlikely group of characters—a close-up magician who doesn't know his fake magic has turned real, a bard who's been kicked out of school, an anatomist who's a little too into blood magic, and a cat burglar running from her past—have to save the world, because they're the ones who accidentally awakened an ancient evil in the first place.

"Don't either of you have homework?" I ask. Suresh keeps playing his guitar.

"I did mine at rehearsal," Kiki says. It's probably a lie, but I'm not Mom. I motion to Suresh, who tosses me the remote, and I scroll back over to where we left off.

I feel Kiki's eyes on me, and I glance over to catch her looking at me.

"What?"

"Nothing," she says. Then, after a beat: "It's weird having you back."

From anyone else it might have stung, but I know what Kiki's trying to say. She ducks her head, smiling a secret smile, and edges just a little closer to me.

"It's weird to be back." I don't say anything else, because I don't want to break the moment. I push all thoughts of Stanford out of my head and hit PLAY.

Kiki scoops my phone off the ground before I can protest, clicking it open.

"Why don't you have a password on this bad boy?"

"Why is no one watching the show right now? Where's the sanctity of sibling movie night?"

"Not a movie," Suresh says distantly.

"I could reply to all of your texts right now," says Kiki.

"Okay, go ahead," I say coolly.

She frowns. "Maybe I will."

"Alright."

I see her sigh and click into another app. "Who is big fork hands? Is that supposed to be a person?"

"Wait, did she message me?"

"Yeah."

"Well, hand it over."

"I can't believe you're still on this dumb blog."

"You and me both."

"Are you still gonna be on it when you're, like, an adult? Paying your mortgage and looking at memes? In the retirement home posting thirsty gifsets of actors?"

"I don't post thirsty gifsets!"

"Uh-huh, okay, Priya." Kiki grins. She tosses the phone into my lap.

**bigforkhands:**
| dude
| do you follow sebastian?

**paranormaldetective:**
| Uhhhh

**bigforkhands:**
| sorry, his url is mereextravagancy
| used to be bardofblackfriars

**paranormaldetective:**
| I don't!

**bigforkhands:**
| omg okay wait one second, let me find his post

bigforkhands sent a post:

**mereextravagancy:**

okay this started as kind of a joke but after talking to a lot of my mutuals i actually got kind of excited about it? so...

does anyone wanna form a chronic illness support group?

**13 notes**

I click through to the comments, my heart in my throat.

**thorswagnarok:** oh this rules
**thorswagnarok** reblogged mereextravagancy: "okay this started as kind..."
**spookyspoony:** Yes!
**fyodorbrostoevsky:** yeah I'm in
**fyodorbrostoevsky:** also how was i not following you before?? shakespeare blog of my dreams?
**mereextravagancy:** uh 19th century literature obsessed angel... welcome...
**quintuplevampire:** I'm not chronically ill but I'm disabled, can I join?
**mereextravagancy:** of COURSE MAX!!!
**typhoonsss:** pick me!

I feel a sudden thrill go up my spine without really knowing why. I don't reply to Brigid until I'm back in my room, away from my siblings. This feels like a private thing, a thing that they wouldn't understand.

A thing that, maybe, the people commenting on this post would.

"She's going to look at porn," I hear my sister say.

"I AM NOT, KIKI!! DON'T BE GROSS!" I shout.

**paranormaldetective:**
| ...whoa

**bigforkhands:**
| yeah
| yeah
| sorry i didn't mean to type that twice
| i'm just

**paranormaldetective:**
| I know
| ...let's join

**bigforkhands:**
| you should!!

**paranormaldetective:**
| WHAT IS WITH THE SECOND PERSON HERE??

**bigforkhands:**
| i know! i'm sorry!!

**paranormaldetective:**
| You're sick, I'm sick

**bigforkhands:**
| yeah

**paranormaldetective:**
| I'll join if you join

**bigforkhands:**
| hhhhhhhhhhhhhhhhhhhhhhh

**paranormaldetective:**
| I'm not trying to pressure you

**bigforkhands:**
| i know
| i just feel like a liar?

**paranormaldetective:**
| You aren't!!

She doesn't respond. I go over to Sebastian's blog. There's another post.

**mereextravagancy**

"i am interested but my situation is kind of strange and i'm not sure if i'm sick enough" @ bigforkhands I do NOT accept the idea that there is some sort of barrier to this support group! I am the king! If you are struggling with the things your body is doing to you you are WELCOME HERE!!!

**3 notes**

I click the comment bubble.

**thorswagnarok:** all hail king seb
**fyodorbrostoevsky:** long may he reign

I scroll back down to the original post. My cursor blinks. I look at the ramshackle collection of bizarre urls and try to imagine each of the people behind them.

**paranormaldetective:** can I join too?

I get a notification seconds later.

**mereextravagancy: @paranormaldetective** yes!!!
**mereextravagancy** started following paranormaldetective.
**FOLLOW BACK?**

I click the button.

# 4

When the doctor calls with the results, my mom picks up the receiver in another room, listening in for anything I might miss. The *Borrelia burgdorferi* is officially out of my body; I am bacteria free. My mom lets out a little whoop. She's always ready to celebrate the small victories, but I just keep listening silently. We knew the antibiotics would kill the bacteria. The damage has already been done.

After the doctor hangs up, my mother keeps talking.

"We are going to have a family dinner tonight," she says in a mix of Tamil and English, "and I'm going to make a nice masala dosa, with rice and fish—all gluten free, you know. Priya? Are you there?"

"I'm here, Mom," I say. "I'm just in the kitchen, I can hear you in the next room."

"I was reading online that sometimes diet changes help with the inflammation," she continues. "It's different for different people, but we can see what works for you. Let's start with the wheat."

"*Amma*, no—"

She clicks her tongue. "You might also have a leaky gut."

"That sounds like something you just made up."

"I did not!"

"Uh huh."

"It is real, Priya! I bought you some acidophilus."

"Okay."

I watch as she comes into the kitchen, still talking to me through the cordless phone. She rummages through the fridge, squinting to read a bottle she takes out of the side of the door.

"It has ten billion colony-forming units, Priya."

"Mom, we are in the same room. I'm hanging up the phone."

She smiles at me. "Good, because I need to call your auntie. Where are you going? You have to take your pills. The antibiotics broke your gut, we have to fix it."

She gets me a glass of water, and I dutifully gulp down two of the probiotics. She beams at me.

"You are getting stronger every day, and we are going to get you all the way better, okay?"

"Maybe," I say. She looks at me sternly, and I feel my chin start to wobble.

"No," she says. "You are getting better."

She believes it so hard that I tell myself I do, too. I'm going to get better. I'm going to go back to school, and play soccer again, and become a doctor.

"Now shoo," she says. "I have to start cooking before I pick up your sister. She can't get a ride from that other family today."

"The Goldsteins?"

"Sure."

"I can pick her up," I say, in spite of myself. My mother turns and gives me a look that says *I know you need help walking over ice, and you haven't driven in months, there is no way you can handle this.*

"You can ride along," she says. "Maybe you can start driving again later."

"Please, let me try," I say. I'm going crazy trapped at home. I feel like I'm under house arrest. "It's such a quick drive, and there's no snow today."

The pause lasts centuries.

"Maybe tomorrow," she says. "But I will be sitting in the front next to you. Just in case."

I think about being a high school sophomore with a learner's permit and my mother screaming instructions from the passenger side, or my father slowly unfolding his newspaper to read the articles out loud to me while I white-knuckled the steering wheel. I am officially fifteen years old again. My shameful return is complete.

-------

**mereextravagancy** mentioned you in a post: let's make a group chat!

**typhoonsss:**

hello! i went ahead and made a discord server so all of us could start talking – figured it'd be easier than endless debate over which app to use

anyway, here's the link!

https://discord.gg/FPGn2h

**paranormaldetective:**

Ah, thank you so much!

**typhoonsss:**

no problem at all, dear! xx

I log into the server, nervous like the first day of school. There are already four other people online, with usernames I don't recognize. The server is called "chronic illness support group." Boring, but effective.

I'm not totally sure how to find my way around the interface, so I just sit back and watch.

**Rat King Kong:**

This was the best idea

**old soft pretzel that is now hard:**

*worst

**peebrain:**

i started crying at an episode of h2o: just add water today

**I II II L:**

the australian children's series?

**peebrain:**

yeah

**old soft pretzel that is now hard:**

was it a sad episode?

**peebrain:**

no

i just started like. crying

**Rat King Kong:**

> That's kind of a mood

**I II II L:**

> God's honest mood
>
> chopped really gets me sometimes

**old soft pretzel that is now hard:**

> i started crying yesterday because i thought about becoming a parent and loving your kids so much and having to say goodbye to them when they move out of the house
>
> i am poor and gay and have endo so children are not in my near future
>
> but, still

**peebrain:**

> that is way more profound than mine

**Rat King Kong:**

> I'm crying right now

**I II II L:**

> same

**peebrain:**

> me as well

**Spook (spookyspoony):**

> whose username is f*cking loss

**I II II IL:**

> i'm valid

**peebrain:**

> hey, why does chopped get you,
>
> ...I don't know who you are

**I II II IL:**

> who really knows who anyone is

**Spook (spookyspoony):**

> I cannot take this anymore
>
> Okay kids, listen up

**Rat King Kong:**

> yes mom

**Spook (spookyspoony):**
| Who is even here right now?

**paranormaldetective:**
| Sorry, I've been lurking!

**peebrain:**
| PRIYA!!!!! <3 <3 <3

**paranormaldetective:**
| ...brigid?

**peebrain:**
| DUH

**Spook (spookyspoony):**
| Okay

**paranormaldetective:**
| Why

**Spook (spookyspoony):**
| This isn't my first rodeo, so I'm going to help you all out
| on the logistical side of things here.
| First off:
| Everyone change their usernames so we can see your
| name / whatever you want to be called, followed by your
| blog url

**peebrain** changed their name to **bridge (bigforkhands).**
**Rat King Kong** changed their name to **Seb (mereextravagancy).**
**paranormaldetective** changed their name to **Priya (paranormal-detective).**
**old soft pretzel that is now hard** changed their name to **lee (typhoonsss).**

**I II II L:**
| someone give me a good ~dramatic quote~ to go out
| on

**Seb (mereextravagancy):**
| now cracks a noble heart
| goodnight, sweet prince

**I II II L:**
| thanks nerd

**I II II L** changed their name to **al (thorswagnarok).**

**Spook (spookyspoony):**
| That's better.

**bridge (bigforkhands):**
| IS it though?

**al (thorswagnarok):**
| pour one out for pure anarchy and chaos, boys

**Priya (paranormaldetective):**
| I for one am relieved to actually know who everyone is

**Seb (mereextravagancy):**
| Yeah, same
| bridge and al, you guys are chaotic neutral

**Priya (paranormaldetective):**
| Chaotic chaotic

**bridge (bigforkhands):**
| hey! chaotic good!!

**al (thorswagnarok):**
| yeah

**Priya (paranormaldetective):**
| Should we wait for everyone to get online before we do
| introductions, etc?

**Spook (spookyspoony):**
| We should probably set up a time
| I've been in a couple of groups, and we generally
| meet once a week, at a specific time, to make sure that
| everyone's online

**Priya (paranormaldetective):**
| Ah

**al (thorswagnarok):**
| makes sense

**bridge (bigforkhands):**
| we're still gonna goof off on the chat between meetings
| though, right

**Spook (spookyspoony):**
| I cannot stop you

**Seb (mereextravagancy):**
> You wish you could!!
> Your pronouns are she/her, right?

**Spook (spookyspoony):**
> She/they!

**Seb (mereextravagancy):**
> Ah ok, glad I checked! We can make a pinned for pronouns

**Spook (spookyspoony):**
> Thank you for asking

**lee (typhoonsss):**
> when are we sorting out schedules for the weekly chat?
> i'm in the UK so I'm slightly worried about finding a good time :/

**al (thorswagnarok):**
> o m g
> do you pronounce it like shej-yulls

**Seb (mereextravagancy):**
> Oh my god

**lee (typhoonsss):**
> here we go haha

**bridge (bigforkhands):**
> i'm going to say something i have never said in my entire life, al:
> don't make this weird

**lee (typhoonsss):**
> thank you, bridge

**Seb (mereextravagancy):**
> Yeah I'm in the pacific northwest so that sure is... A Time Difference

**al (thorswagnarok):**
> please don't make me do math

**lee (typhoonsss):**
> 8 hours!

**katie (fyodorbrostoevsky):**
HEY, GUYS!!!!

**lee (typhoonsss):**
hi, katie!

**Priya (paranormaldetective):**
Hi katie!

**Seb (mereextravagancy):**
Hello and heart eyes emoji, dear katie

**katie (fyodorbrostoevsky):**
Very forward, seb

**Seb (mereextravagancy):**
All about society's progress, kat

**al (thorswagnarok):**
hiiiiii

**bridge (bigforkhands):**
HI!!!!

**lee (typhoonsss):**
do you want to try to get ahold of max, spook?
i think he's the last one who commented on seb's post

**Spook (spookyspoony):**
Brb

**Seb (mereextravagancy):**
I feel like someone should be playing elevator music
while we wait

**al (thorswagnarok):**
https://www.youtube.com/watch?v=dQw4w9WgXcQ

**katie (fyodorbrostoevsky):**
oh what a great song, al thorswagnarok

**Priya (paranormaldetective):**
I can't believe we are still doing this

**bridge (bigforkhands):**
groovy

**lee (typhoonsss):**
NO!!!

**Priya (paranormaldetective):**
In the year of our lord 2019

**Seb (mereextravagancy):**
I'll Kill You

**al (thorswagnarok):**
you can try

**Spook (spookyspoony):**
Ok, Max is on his way to the dr and can't talk, but we'll do introductions once we set a time

**katie (fyodorbrostoevsky):**
I'll make a whenisgood

**Seb (mereextravagancy):**
What is it, 2012

**katie (fyodorbrostoevsky):**
Maybe

**al (thorswagnarok):**
the world ended but we just didn't get the message

**Priya (paranormaldetective):**
Kind of rude of the world to not loop us in

**katie (fyodorbrostoevsky):**
I know, what's that about

**bridge (bigforkhands):**
ooh I think that's my fault guys, I said some pretty rude things to the world at that party last week

**lee (typhoons):**
dammit, bridge

**bridge (bigforkhands):**
¯\_(ツ)_/¯

**Spook (spookyspoony):**
Something something global warming

**al (thorswagnarok):**
clenched teeth emoji

**katie (fyodorbrostoevsky):**
http://whenisgood.net/zfp4rxk

**Priya (paranormaldetective):**
> Thanks, katie!

**Spook (spookyspoony):**
> Filled out!

**lee (typhoonsss):**
> me as well!

**Seb (mereextravagancy):**
> Wait, before everyone goes, I think we need a better
> name for our group chat

**Priya (paranormaldetective):**
> That's what I was just thinking!!

**Spook (spookyspoony):**
> Not a lot of puns about chronic illness

**lee (typhoonsss):**
> hm

**bridge (bigforkhands):**
> oh lol
> i've got it

bridge (bigforkhands) changed the server name to **oof ouch my bones**.

**katie (fyodorbrostoevsky):**
> alskjflsdfj

**Seb (mereextravagancy):**
> yes

**al (thorswagnarok):**
> feels good
> feels organic

**Priya (paranormaldetective):**
> It's perfect, Brigid

**bridge (bigforkhands):**
> :)

# 5

**It's my first time driving since last summer. For a second I'm** struck with a primal fear that I won't remember where my feet go, where my hands should grip the wheel. But it's muscle memory, one thing that my body has not actually forgotten how to do.

My mother sits at my right to make sure that any morsel of joy I'd glean is transformed directly into anxiety. "Watch out, Priya!" "Careful, slow down around the turn." "Can you turn the wheel?"

She yells in Tamil when I take the final turn too hard, and I put the car into park, feeling my wrist pop.

"Mom, just let me drive, okay? I know what I'm doing, I'm not a baby bird."

I turn to look at her and catch her staring at me. The worry is radiating from every part of her, forming a puddle of that exacting, overwhelming motherly love. As soon as she sees me looking, she schools her face into something more neutral. My annoyance with her ratchets up. I shouldn't be upset that she's looking at me with so much pity, especially after what Lee said in the group chat, about parents and children. But I am.

She places her scarf around my shoulders, turning the key and cranking the heat up. I sigh.

"I know," she says.

She's right, but I'll never admit it. Picking up Kiki takes its toll. By the time I get home I'm dead on my feet. I tell them I'm going to my room to finish the work from the class I had to take an incomplete in last quarter. I nap until dinner instead.

I don't tell my mom that the drive has been anything but fine. If I keep driving, I'll be able to take the car out by myself. It's my ticket to a space of my own, where I don't feel my family's eyes on me every second of every day. I'd forgotten the way it felt to be alone behind the wheel, music cranked up a little too loud, thumb tapping the wheel and lights zipping by you on the highway, warm and orange like fireflies.

The next day my pain feels like a radar pinging out from each central point, and my head is scrambled and heavy like I haven't just slept for ten hours. I pick Kiki up again; my mom comes again, too. I feel like a murderer in a '90s movie being transferred from one prison to another.

When Mom takes Kiki and Suresh to the strip mall, I have the house to myself. I know every inch of it; we've lived here longer than I've been alive. It's still got carpeted floors, linoleum in the kitchen. When I came back home, I was more surprised than anything to find that nothing had changed, no chair out of place or kitchen cupboard reorganized. The hunk of metal that used to be a swing set still sits rusting in the backyard, sunk into the grass.

I settle into my usual hollow in the living room, on the left side of the couch.

**paranormaldetective:**
Hey
I don't have any fun facts for you or anything, just wanted to see what you were up to
**bigforkhands:**
aw!!!
**paranormaldetective:**
Okay, okay
**bigforkhands:**
i am up to approximately nothing
bellows is boring as shit
i've seen (1) other person all shift and it was hattie lol
...sure you don't have anything for me?

**paranormaldetective:**
| Nah

**bigforkhands:**
| what have you been thinking about lately

**paranormaldetective:**
| I mean. My body

**bigforkhands:**
| yeah

**paranormaldetective:**
| I just. There's so much that I took for granted about
| being healthy and being able to run and exercise and
| just... function

**bigforkhands:**
| right

**paranormaldetective:**
| How long have you been sick?
| Or, well
| You know.

**bigforkhands:**
| i do know
| uhhhhhhhhhh
| fuck haha, this is weirdly hard to talk about

**paranormaldetective:**
| We could save it for the GC

**bigforkhands:**
| nah, this is good practice
| or whatever it is people say
| uh, so this has been happening since I was eleven

**paranormaldetective:**
| Like a puberty onset thing?

**bigforkhands:**
| idk
| it, uh

**paranormaldetective:**
| You don't have to tell me

**bigforkhands:**

no it's okay

it was really fucking scary at first?

when you're a kid you don't have a way to wrap your head around this, you know? like, you don't have a way to talk about the pain, and the uncertainty

my parents tried their best but they were terrified. i could like, physically feel their fear

**paranormaldetective:**

God. I'm so sorry

**bigforkhands:**

it's okay!!

**paranormaldetective:**

I mean, it's ok if it wasn't ok

That sounds really traumatic

**bigforkhands:**

yeah, i guess it was

i mean

you know, you get it

**paranormaldetective:**

Kind of

But that's a really long time to have to deal with something like this, and I'm sorry

**bigforkhands:**

thanks

sorry, we were talking about you

**paranormaldetective:**

Omg DON'T pull that! This is a conversation, it goes two ways!

**bigforkhands:**

<3

but: your body

**paranormaldetective:**

It hurts!! Haha

I'm trying to start driving again?

**bigforkhands:**
| that's good!

I hear the garage door rumble to life. A minute later my father shuffles into the room, sock-footed and yawning.

"Priya, how are you feeling today?" he asks.

"I'm good, Dad," I say.

"Are you sure? How long have you been sitting, do you need to get up and stretch?"

"No, I think I'm okay here. I picked up Kiki from school today."

"Where is she?"

"Shopping with Mom and Suresh."

"Oh no," he says. "She'll bring back shirts and make me try them on."

"You can give us all a fashion show!" I smile. He lets out a disapproving huff. "How was work?"

"It was work," he says, and that's all I'm going to get out of him, I suppose. I still don't quite understand what he does, other than the fact that he does it for an engineering company, and that he's weirdly popular there. We went to a Christmas party with him one year and everyone told us how funny he was. I guess to a bunch of engineers, my nerdy, soft-spoken father is the life of the party.

"Can I tell you a secret?" he says, leaning in and tapping his nose. I nod, feeling an echo of the way I felt when he'd ask me the same thing as a child. "I'm glad we have the house to ourselves." He nods. "A little peace and quiet never hurt anyone. Do you want to have a reading party?"

"Sounds good," I say. He's rifling through the papers on the table, peering underneath. He fishes out his latest biography, or maybe exposé. He'll tell me about it in about thirty seconds, and I'll forget in the next thirty.

"Priya!" he says. He has a hand on his hip, and his glasses are slipping down the bridge of his nose. "Where is your book!"

"It's up in my room, on the nightstand," I say. He nods, walking up the stairs to retrieve it for me.

"I can get it," I try, but he waves his hand, shaking his head. He reappears a few minutes later with a shabby book, dust cover ripped, and drops it in my lap.

"Don't you want to read something new?" he asks. "This is for kids, and you're a smart girl. You will finish this in five minutes, I'll time you."

I grab the book protectively. "You bought it for me!"

"Yes!" he says. "Ten years ago!"

"So it's time for a reread," I say. He just tuts, then sits down on the couch cushion directly next to mine, even though the whole couch is empty.

"*Appa*, scoot over," I say. He looks up at me and blinks, affronted. He does not scoot over. He opens his book and begins to read.

So I open mine, too. I know I'm probably gravitating toward the books I treasured most growing up because I'm looking for mental comfort food. My brain is as tired as the rest of me, but when I open these books, I feel like I'm exactly where I'm supposed to be.

PRIYA PATEL: PARANORMAL DETECTIVE, the cover reads. There's an Indian girl with a flashlight and a shocked expression on her face, nudging a closet door open in an old-timey Victorian house. A glowing tentacle reaches out from behind the door. The cover is purple, my favorite color growing up. My dad had seen it on the shelf at our local bookstore when he was browsing for his latest read and bought it for me right away.

"You should be reading up on your studies," my dad says. He's looking over my shoulder at the illustration for chapter three, Priya shaking hands with her neighbor, Justin (her Watson). There's a ghost watching them in the background, but neither of them have noticed her. "You don't want to get behind the others."

I clench my jaw, trying to keep my emotions level. "I'm already behind the others, Dad. I'm going to be at least two quarters behind the others, no matter what I do."

"You'll make it up," he says. It's the thing I don't want to hear right now. The deadline to register for summer classes is next week, and I haven't even been cleared by Dr. Hegazy, much less started on the paperwork. Even if I start in the fall again, I'll still be behind. Everyone will have moved on without me.

I wonder what they're saying about me. *Did you hear about that girl that had to go to the hospital? The girl who got so sick she had to drop out? Did she die? What happened to her?*

But I don't want to argue with my dad, so all I say through the tightness in my throat is, "Okay. Thank you."

He pats my knee and goes back to his book. I feel an uneasy buzzing start to build in my chest, in my head.

When the garage door rattles again I catch my dad's eye, making the same face he makes at me—the one that says, *well, that was nice while it lasted, huh?*

"Priyaaaaaa!" Kiki sings out. "Come see what we bouuught!"

"I will if you come show me," I say.

"We went to Marshalls *and* TJ Maxx," says Kiki.

"Lucky us," Suresh mutters, slouching in.

"Priya, I bought you new clothes too," my mom shouts. "The trousers should fit you better, you have to try them on. You're bigger than you used to be."

It's true. It's all in my hips and my thighs, a little in my stomach.

I'm used to her being this blunt. I am. But still.

The buzzing ticks itself up a little louder.

"I'm tired, Mom," I say, clenching my jaw.

"It'll only take a second—"

"Mom!" I say. It's too close to a shout. She raises an eyebrow, and she's going to say something about my *tone*, and I am going to burst into tears.

"Priya, come on," my mom pushes. "I have to find out what fits and what doesn't so I can go make returns. I don't want this to just sit in your closet."

I haul myself off the couch, grabbing the bag from her on the way to the bathroom. I'd heard the phrase *flesh prison* before, but I'd never understood it. My body was a vessel—ready to explore the world and learn and feel and focus. My body was for soccer, fists clenched and arms pumping and legs steady, blood pounding in my ears and sweat pooling at the small of my back and on my forehead and upper lip, air stinging my lungs as summer turned to fall turned to winter. It was for driving, tapping pedals and shifting gears and turning the wheel. For eyes burning when I stayed up too late studying and neck muscles bunching and synapses firing to store the Krebs cycle and World War II and Spanish conjugations, hopping from the cerebral cortex to the hippocampus. For linking arms with my friends and jumping into swimming pools and piling on them at sleepovers.

I turned food into energy, and my hemoglobin carried oxygen, and my heart pumped and my joints moved like they'd been oiled. I worked exactly the way I was supposed to.

Now I feel heavy, and it's not just the extra fifteen pounds, although I'm distinctly aware of them when I take off my pants and slide my legs into the new ones. After trying on the first pair I start to ache, and I have to sit down on the toilet seat to pull on the next pair. I look at myself in the mirror, and my eyes start to well with tears, which is just as embarrassing as everything else. The buzzing in my chest is a rickety hum now, like an electric generator. My skin feels tight and tender, and the thought of going back out to the rest of my family is suddenly unbearable.

The pants are two sizes bigger than everything else in my wardrobe. I shove them back into the bag without folding them and go back out.

"Well?" my mom asks. "You didn't show us, do they not fit?"

"They fit," I say, forcing a smile. "Thanks, Mom."

"Where are you going?"

"Just headed up to my room for a little bit. I'm tired."

"Okay. Love you."

"Love you too."

**bigforkhands:**
> did you know that Coco Chanel was a nazi
> ...you still there?

**paranormaldetective:**
> Yeah, sorry, I'm still here
> Had to try on some clothes my mom bought me
> I'm 19, I should start buying my own stuff

**bigforkhands:**
> no way, ride that grift out
> anything good?

**paranormaldetective:**
> No, haha

**bigforkhands:**
> sorry :/

**paranormaldetective:**
> I did not know Coco Chanel was a nazi

**bigforkhands:**

/i/ don't know why we're just kind of conveniently not talking about it

**paranormaldetective:**

Maybe it's not a conspiracy

**bigforkhands:**

WAKE UP, PRIYA

OF /COURSE/ IT'S A CONSPIRACY

**paranormaldetective:**

Honestly probably a PR one

**bigforkhands:**

yeah

**paranormaldetective:**

I'm sorry for cutting out on you

Can I be really honest?

**bigforkhands:**

yeah, of course

**paranormaldetective:**

Ugh, this is going to sound really dramatic

**bigforkhands:**

i don't mind

**paranormaldetective:**

It's not just the joint pain, or the brain fog, or anything else, right

I've gained weight since I've gotten sick, which – yeah, of course I have

But it's like I can't even hold on to one single thing about myself

There's no constant left

**bigforkhands:**

dang

**paranormaldetective:**

It's disorienting

**bigforkhands:**

i know... exactly what you mean

**paranormaldetective:**
| I thought you might

**bigforkhands:**
| like, EXACTLY exactly
| every fuckin month my whole ish gets upended

**paranormaldetective:**
| I'm sorry

**bigforkhands:**
| no, don't be
| it just means I take advantage of feeling good, you know
| i remind myself of how it feels to be out of control and then say, but look, i am IN control, and I am strong, and I can feel the sunlight on my face
| ...well it's like 8 degrees out but you know what I mean

**paranormaldetective:**
| There's still sun in the cold

**bigforkhands:**
| that's my new album name
| it's 45 minutes of spoken word poetry

**paranormaldetective:**
| It sounds great

**bigforkhands:**
| someone's playing a recorder in the background to really set the mood

**paranormaldetective:**
| What else

**bigforkhands:**
| hahaha i'm sorry i made fun, that was actually kinda uplifting

**paranormaldetective:**
| I try

**bigforkhands:**
| we should go on a road trip

**paranormaldetective:**
| Where'd that come from?

**bigforkhands:**

from me remembering how close we live and wanting to cheer us both up

**paranormaldetective:**

Yes, let's do it, where are we going

**bigforkhands:**

i'll start thinking on it

**paranormaldetective:**

We could meet in the middle

**bigforkhands:**

omg yes

what's the exact geographic midpoint of our houses

i promise i won't reverse engineer your address from that information

**paranormaldetective:**

I didn't think you would but now I'm not so sure

**bigforkhands:**

please, what do i look like, an engineer?

some sort of math, person?

a topographer?

**paranormaldetective:**

Do you mean cartographer?

**bigforkhands:**

how should I know?

**paranormaldetective:**

Hang on, let me find the website

Our exact midpoint looks like a town called Emmaus, PA

**bigforkhands:**

huh

**paranormaldetective:**

Yeah, huh

**bigforkhands:**

okay, idea number one, meet in Emmaus

**paranormaldetective:**

Maybe God's there

**bigforkhands:**
| lol
| nice catholic joke

**paranormaldetective:**
| He won't /seem/ like God though
| We won't realize it

**bigforkhands:**
| i feel like that's always the case, right?

**paranormaldetective:**
| I don't know
| I used to think God was another thing you'd know when you saw
| I used to be really sure of everything

**bigforkhands:**
| i've never been sure of anything in my life

**paranormaldetective:**
| Well I'm coming your way

**bigforkhands:**
| i hope literally
| i've got to track down some scenic attractions
| you'd better be on the lookout too, priya

**paranormaldetective:**
| Scout's honor

**bigforkhands:**
| haha okay, i've gotta go
| talk to you soon?
| ps, i'm sure you look really great

**paranormaldetective:**
| You're sweet
| Talk to you soon

The night is not good to me, or to the hum in my chest. I check Instagram, even though I know I'll regret it. I look at my own pictures, pictures of a girl I recognize. The one in the mirror is strange and unfamiliar to me.

I was so worried about what everyone was saying about me, but now, as I look at so many shiny, grinning faces, I wonder if they're saying anything at all. My face heats in shame at the thought that any of them would still be thinking about me now that I'm gone. It seems self-centered and ridiculous.

*It's like I was never even there in the first place.* The thought is worse to me than any rumor mill would have been. It's like I don't exist. And the Priya in the pictures doesn't, not anymore. She's not the same. My body is a landscape I don't recognize.

The humming in my chest takes on weight in the dark. I struggle to make my breathing even as I lie in bed, sheets pulled up to my chin.

*I don't exist. I don't exist. I don't exist.*

I close my eyes until it's true.

# 6

**We settle on Tuesday, at 6 p.m. my time (and Brigid's).**

oof ouch my bones (ONLINE – 8)

**Seb (mereextravagancy):**
| Welcome to our very first meeting!

**katie (fyodorbrostoevsky):**
| doot doo doo!
| That was supposed to be like
| A trumpet noise

**lee (typhoonsss):**
| we're tracking, hon

**al (thorswagnarok):**
| speak for yourself, lee

**bridge (bigforkhands):**
| i gotcha katie

**Spook (spookyspoony):**
| Ok we should all introduce ourselves – we can talk about
| our conditions, pronouns, and maybe a fun fact?

**bridge (bigforkhands):**
| please don't make me do a fun fact
| the second I hear those words my brain wipes itself clean
| and i've suddenly never done anything in my life

**Priya (paranormaldetective):**
You send me fun facts literally 24/7

**bridge (bigforkhands):**
about other people! not about me!!

**Seb (mereextravagancy):**
I get that, bridge

**bridge (bigforkhands):**
did you guys know coco chanel was a nazi

**lee (typhoonsss):**
SERIOUSLY??

**Max (quintuplevampire):**
Yikes

**katie (fyodorbrostoevsky):**
actually I did know that!

**al (thorswagnarok):**
smarty pants

**katie (fyodorbrostoevsky):**
yeah she literally ran away to switzerland so she wouldn't
be arrested for being a nazi spy

**al (thorswagnarok):**
rest in pieces, coco

**Seb (mereextravagancy):**
Cheers, i'll drink to that, bro

**Spook (spookyspoony):**
Is it going to be like this every time

**bridge (bigforkhands):**
yeah, probably

**Spook (spookyspoony):**
Ok nevermind on the fun fact, we can just do pronouns

**Priya (paranormaldetective):**
So condition, pronouns?

**Spook (spookyspoony):**
Thank you Priya, haha
I can start? We'll just feel it out
I'm Spook, which is obviously not my given name

...I can see you all typing and if anyone makes the "hi, spook" support group joke I am kicking you out of the server

**bridge (bigforkhands):**

hi, spook

**Seb (mereextravagancy):**

Hi, spook

**katie (fyodorbrostoevsky):**

hi, spook

**al (thorswagnarok):**

i am spartacus

**Spook (spookyspoony):**

I am leaving

**Seb (mereextravagancy):**

NO WE LOVE YOU

**bridge (bigforkhands):**

WE'RE SORRY

**Spook (spookyspoony):**

...alright haha

I'm Spook, she/they, I've got fibromyalgia

I was diagnosed... four years ago, now? Doesn't seem like that long

Lately I've been dealing with worse fatigue than usual, and it's miserably cold in Ontario, which is only making the pain worse tbh

**al (thorswagnarok):**

:/

**katie (fyodorbrostoevsky):**

<3

**Spook (spookyspoony):**

But ANYWAY. Who's next

**Seb (mereextravagancy):**

I'll go!

I'm Sebastian, I've got Ehlers-Danlos

that is the only time I will be typing that out, it's EDS from here on out a lot of people don't know what it is, but basically I am very flexible. In fact, too flexible.

it's a connective tissue disorder haha

so basically I have a whole magnificent constellation of symptoms but the big ones are joint pain/dislocation/ weirdness, and my hearing is not fantastic

...I feel like that was a lot of info

**katie (fyodorbrostoevsky):**

No!! I learned a lot already!

**bridge (bigforkhands):**

hi, sebastian

**Seb (mereextravagancy):**

oh yeah and my pronouns are he/him

lol hi bridge

**Max (quintuplevampire):**

Joint pain Buddies!

**Priya (paranormaldetective):**

Joint pain buddies!!!!

**Seb (mereextravagancy):**

We all do a cool three way high five and hurt our elbows and wrists lmao

**Priya (paranormaldetective):**

Hahaha

**bridge (bigforkhands):**

hey would you say all of us are

.................................... pain pals

**Spook (spookyspoony):**

HA

**al (thorswagnarok):**

...

**lee (typhoonsss):**

that was so bad!!

**bridge (bigforkhands):**

it's like

like pen pals

**katie (fyodorbrostoevsky):**
BIG SHUT UP

**Seb (mereextravagancy):**
Alsjdflaksdjfasdfj

**Priya (paranormaldetective):**
Brigid......

**Max (quintuplevampire):**
Can I go next?

**Spook (spookyspoony):**
Yeah, shoot

**Max (quintuplevampire):**
So I'm actually not chronically ill

I have cerebral palsy

And I know that

Feeling pretty okay most of the time but having mobility issues and people treating me differently because of the way I look might be sort of the opposite of what you guys deal with

I use a wheelchair by the way

**Spook (spookyspoony):**
I use a wheelchair sometimes and I am definitely treated differently when I'm using one vs when I'm not :/

**Max (quintuplevampire):**
But I do have to deal with joint stiffness tremors and assholes who constantly assume I'm mentally disabled or tell me what an inspiration I am to them

**Seb (mereextravagancy):**
Lmao ugh

**Max (quintuplevampire):**
Plus I thought it would be neat to hang out with some people who understand what it's like to not have a quote unquote normal body

**al (thorswagnarok):**
hell yeah

**Max (quintuplevampire):**
Oh yeah and I'm a dude

He slash him

**lee (typhoonsss):**
| we are happy to have you! xx

**Max (quintuplevampire):**
| Thanks!

**Spook (spookyspoony):**
| Lee, wanna go?

**lee (typhoonsss):**
| sure!

| i'm lee, she/her, and i've got endometriosis (and associated ibs), which is very not fun

| i've also got anxiety, so i think about the fact that people with endometriosis are at a much higher risk for certain cancers... a whole lot

| i'm sorry, that was a bit much for session number one!

**bridge (bigforkhands):**
| DON'T APOLOGIZE <3 <3

**Seb (mereextravagancy):**
| We are sending love across the ocean

**katie (fyodorbrostoevsky):**
| Whoosh

**Seb (mereextravagancy):**
| Can you feel it??

**lee (typhoonsss):**
| i think i can!! wow!

| nice and warm

| and... sticky? which of you children did this

**al (thorswagnarok):**
| sorry, im eating a popsackle

**lee (typhoonsss):**
| that's okay, dear

**Seb (mereextravagancy):**
| Ok I remember calling spook "mom" before but I'm officially rescinding that

| Lee, you're our mom

| Spook, you have tangible dad energy

**Spook (spookyspoony):**
Oh, that checks out

**bridge (bigforkhands):**
seems right

**katie (fyodorbrostoevsky):**
Yes

**lee (typhoonsss):**
i would be HONOURED to be your collective mum

**al (thorswagnarok):**
MUM

**katie (fyodorbrostoevsky):**
HONOURED

**Priya (paranormaldetective):**
Here we go again

**lee (typhoonsss):**
why do americans get this way about people from the uk??

you'd see a chav blowing smoke outside a kebab shop in bristol and be like "wow... it's mr. darcy..."

**bridge (bigforkhands):**
what does that say in english

**Max (quintuplevampire):**
Can someone translate

**katie (fyodorbrostoevsky):**
Yes I speak British

Ahem

I believe she is saying "Americans will see a dirtbag from cleveland who smokes outside b dubs and be like "wow, it's brad pitt""

**Seb (mereextravagancy):**
Katie, that was kind of a masterpiece

**Priya (paranormaldetective):**
Absolutely

The one flaw is that I don't think anyone has ever considered an American accent to be a turn on

**lee (typhoonsss):**
| that's correct
| no offence

**bridge (bigforkhands):**
| none taken

**Seb (mereextravagancy):**
| We know America sucks

**Priya (paranormaldetective):**
| Well actually, are some British people into southern
| accents?

**lee (typhoonsss):**
| oh excellently spotted, priya
| that is true for some of my friends
| aaaaanyway
| who is next!?

**al (thorswagnarok):**
| i'll go
| you can call me al

**Seb (mereextravagancy):**
| OH come ON

**Priya (paranormaldetective):**
| You have GOT TO BE KIDDING ME

**katie (fyodorbrostoevsky):**
| I don't get it

**Spook (spookyspoony):**
| Did you pick that for your online name just to make that
| joke

**al (thorswagnarok):**
| i would never
| ((whispering behind my hand: yes))

**Spook (spookyspoony):**
| @katie (fyodorbrostoevsky) - https://www.youtube.com/
| watch?v=uq-gYOrU8bA

**katie (fyodorbrostoevsky):**
| LOL

**al (thorswagnarok):**

so i'm al

i use any pronouns you wanna toss at me
(i'm nonbinary), and my head hurts (i get migraines with
~aura~)

**Max (quintuplevampire):**

What does that mean

**al (thorswagnarok):**

oh basically my brain glitches out

everything looks wild and wacky for a little bit, like
looking through dirty glasses or a kaleidoscope

but also i get super nauseous and numb

and one time i tried to talk but my words got all
scrambled up

**Priya (paranormaldetective):**

Aphasia??

**al (thorswagnarok):**

that's the one

**katie (fyodorbrostoevsky):**

Ok that's really scary!

**lee (typhoonsss):**

:/

is looking at the screen okay for you?

**al (thorswagnarok):**

i'm ok for now

i... have special tinted glasses lolol

they are piss-yellow and make me look like a dad at a ski
resort

**bridge (bigforkhands):**

.......................please show us

**Seb (mereextravagancy):**

AL

OH MY GOD AL PLEASE

**al (thorswagnarok):**

you'll have to use your imagination for now lol, my
laptop camera is broken as shit

**Priya (paranormaldetective):**

You did paint us a pretty vivid word picture

**al (thorswagnarok):**

thank you priya

all in all it's pretty okay, but i have had to stop seeing movies on the big screen lately, which kind of sucks, that was a big thing for me

**katie (fyodorbrostoevsky):**

Oh no, that's the worst :^(

**al (thorswagnarok):**

yeah, i realized that I was getting a migraine every single time

i think it's the mix between a dark room and a bright screen, idk

**Priya (paranormaldetective):**

I haven't seen a movie in theaters in forever, but it was such a communal thing when I was a kid

**al (thorswagnarok):**

yeah, exactly

**lee (typhoonsss):**

oh... we should have a movie night...

**Seb (mereextravagancy):**

YES

**bridge (bigforkhands):**

HELL YEAH

**Priya (paranormaldetective):**

That sounds so fun!

**Spook (spookyspoony):**

Like we all click play on something at the same time?

**Max (quintuplevampire):**

We could try one of the chrome extensions?

**al (thorswagnarok):**

PLEASE!??!

ok im done, who's next

**katie (fyodorbrostoevsky):**

I can go!

I'm katie, she/her, and I have not been diagnosed with anything yet but I have had the worst year haha

**Seb (mereextravagancy):**

:(

**katie (fyodorbrostoevsky):**

I've been having a lot of digestive issues, and feeling super fatigued all the time, and my skin has been a nightmare on top of everything else

I'm super glad it's winter because I haven't actually been able to shave my legs

The eczema is out of control

...this seems like oversharing haha

**Spook (spookyspoony):**

No such thing in this group, that's the point

**lee (typhoonsss):**

totally xx

**bridge (bigforkhands):**

i haven't shaved my legs in years dude

solidarity

**katie (fyodorbrostoevsky):**

that's cool! I still feel really weird about going out in public without having shaved them?

I feel like everyone is judging me

But I also feel like they're judging the awful ugly red patches so I think I'll just wear jeans for the rest of my life haha

**Priya (paranormaldetective):**

So you've got a system-wide thing going?

**bridge (bigforkhands):**

ooh yes, ask Priya, she's premed!

**Priya (paranormaldetective):**

Oh no please don't, I'm not a doctor haha

**Spook (spookyspoony):**

Yeah, we shouldn't be trying to diagnose each other

**Seb (mereextravagancy):**

Counterpoint: doctors can be totally useless

**Max (quintuplevampire):**
| We can talk about things she could ask her doctor about

**lee (typhoonsss):**
| ^^^

| have you looked into crohn's?

**katie (fyodorbrostoevsky):**
| Maybe? It's kind of a blur tbh

| I spent my winter break just going to different drs but they haven't figured anything out yet, and now I'm back at school

**Priya (paranormaldetective):**
| Have you had any autoimmune tests?

**katie (fyodorbrostoevsky):**
| Texting my mom about that right now

| I got an endoscopy at the end of December and they didn't really say much about the results, I don't think they found anything

| So, that's me right now! the not knowing sucks

| And I just

| I feel like no one believes me?

**Spook (spookyspoony):**
| Ah, yep. Join the club

**katie (fyodorbrostoevsky):**
| I don't want to haha

**lee (typhoonsss):**
| it took me YEARS to get diagnosed

| because i'm a woman, and my disease involves uterine tissue

| no one took it seriously when i said i was in pain

**katie (fyodorbrostoevsky):**
| that's so horrible, lee

| I would say something like "that's the worst part of this" except that's... not true

| The worst part is feeling like hot, wet garbage and waking up and puking at 5 in the am

**bridge (bigforkhands):**
i feel you :/
people don't even believe my thing exists

**Priya (paranormaldetective):**
Same.

**lee (typhoonsss):**
me too, love
i'm sorry you don't know what's wrong yet <3
keeping a sick journal is a good idea in the meantime! it's a pain in the arse but it's really, really useful when you're going to doctors

**bridge (bigforkhands):**
what is a sick journal?

**lee (typhoonsss):**
it's just a place where you can write down different symptoms you're having on different days, or around different things
i suppose it's more like a log?
so you can write down what you ate, what you did, how you felt
you may notice patterns yourself, but you can also pull it out to talk about your symptoms at the doctor

**katie (fyodorbrostoevsky):**
thank you!!!

**Priya (paranormaldetective):**
Keep us posted!

**katie (fyodorbrostoevsky):**
I will!
Okay who's next, priya or bridge?

**bridge (bigforkhands):**
not it

**Priya (paranormaldetective):**
Brigid you can't just say not it

**bridge (bigforkhands):**
i don't know what i want yet
waiter take priya's order first

**Priya (paranormaldetective):**

Okay, I'll go haha

I'm Priya, I'm a she, and I am technically Lyme-disease free as of last week but am still very much dealing with the fallout

Aka, joint pain/swelling, brain fog, and fatigue

It has been... a bad few months

I've been feeling bad since last fall, but things really got drastic at the end of last year, and I actually ended up having to take a medical leave of absence from school and move back home

**lee (typhoonsss):**

oh, that is so hard xx

**Seb (mereextravagancy):**

Is your home life okay?

...sorry, you don't have to answer that

**Spook (spookyspoony):**

I was wondering the same thing

**Priya (paranormaldetective):**

No, it's fine! My home life is really wonderful, actually. My parents are supportive, my siblings are the same as ever.

It actually makes me feel really guilty? You know?

Like, I know not everyone has that kind of support system, but even with that, I'm still having such a hard time

**Max (quintuplevampire):**

There's no qualifier with that stuff though you know

**Priya (paranormaldetective):**

Yeah

**Max (quintuplevampire):**

Your body hurts and that's hard

And you had to take a leave and that's hard too

**Spook (spookyspoony):**

All of us are dealing with what we have the best way that we know how, so there's no use in comparing ourselves to other people

Or to each other

**Seb (mereextravagancy):**

We're here for you, kiddo

**Priya (paranormaldetective):**

Thanks, everyone!

That really means a lot

...alright, brigid, it's all you

**bridge (bigforkhands):**

ughghhghghghhghghh

**al (thorswagnarok):**

lol

**bridge (bigforkhands):**

sup guys, I'm bridge, short for brigid

she/her

my thing is actually really hard to explain, and i'd rather not get into the weeds with it if that's okay

**lee (typhoonsss):**

of course

**Spook (spookyspoony):**

You can say as little or as much as you like

**bridge (bigforkhands):**

thanks

yeah, so basically it gets really bad once a month, and i get really anemic and get these weird bruises, then i'm exhausted

there are a couple of other small things, but that's the main thing

**lee (typhoonsss):**

i'm tracking

if you ever want to message me directly, feel free! i know exactly what that's like

**Seb (mereextravagancy):**

Is it your period?

...shit sorry, you just said you didn't want to talk about it

I'm an asshole

**katie (fyodorbrostoevsky):**

| no, Seb, she's a werewolf

**bridge (bigforkhands):**

| h a !

| ha  ha h ah hah h hahh ahha  hah ah a h a

| ha a a a a a a  a

| you're fine, seb

| yeah, it's my period, plus some other stuff

**Seb (mereextravagancy):**

| haha sorry

**Spook (spookyspoony):**

| Tonight /is/ a full moon

**katie (fyodorbrostoevsky):**

| the image of a werewolf on a laptop is very funny to me

**bridge (bigforkhands):**

| ac t u a l l  y

**al (thorswagnarok):**

| ?????

**Priya (paranormaldetective):**

| I think she's trying to restrain herself from delving
| into the kind of facts you would find in the bowels of
| Wikipedia

**bridge (bigforkhands):**

| You know me so well :')

**Priya (paranormaldetective):**

| Hahaha

**Seb (mereextravagancy):**

| UM, don't restrain yourself

**lee (typhoonsss):**

| yeah, we want to know!

**bridge (bigforkhands):**

| sweet

| so, actually

| the association of werewolves with the full moon is really
| modern

there was a movie in 1943 that used that trope and people have assumed it was part of the old legends ever since!

**Max (quintuplevampire):**

Classical Hollywood

*old Hollywood

**katie (fyodorbrostoevsky):**

So there aren't any old moon myths?

**Seb (mereextravagancy):**

This isn't just ANY old moon myth

**katie (fyodorbrostoevsky):**

Lol

**bridge (bigforkhands):**

i think there might have been one from france about a full moon being a component of turning you /into/ a werewolf for the first time

**Spook (spookyspoony):**

Huh

**bridge (bigforkhands):**

...anyway, i might tell you guys more later

about my thing, i mean

but thank you for listening for now

**lee (typhoonsss):**

any time!

on that note, i'm going to be late for work tomorrow if i stay up any longer

so this is where i leave you lovelies

but i'm excited about this, you all seem wonderful

**Seb (mereextravagancy):**

That's what YOU think

(just kidding, I love everyone in this group chat)

**katie (fyodorbrostoevsky):**

Night, lee!

**al (thorswagnarok):**

goodnight mum

**lee (typhoonsss):**
| ha!
| night, children xx

**Max (quintuplevampire):**
| It's dinner time so I am actually out too
| Nice to meet ya'll!

Max (quintuplevampire) is offline.

lee (typhoonsss) is offline.

**Spook (spookyspoony):**
| Should we just disband until next week, then?

**katie (fyodorbrostoevsky):**
| Aw X(
| Yeah, alright!

Spook (spookyspoony) is offline.

**Seb (mereextravagancy):**
| Oh I will be blowing up your phones WAY before then
| ;)

**katie (fyodorbrostoevsky):**
| ;)

**bridge (bigforkhands):**
| ;)

**Priya (paranormaldetective):**
| Oh God, it's spreading

**al (thorswagnarok):**
| ;)

**bridge (bigforkhands):**
| well?!?!??!
| ;)

**Priya (paranormaldetective):**
| Ugh

**al (thorswagnarok):**
| peer pressure

| ;)

**Priya (paranormaldetective):**
| This is so dumb lol
| ;)

**bridge (bigforkhands):**
| YES

**Seb (mereextravagancy):**
| Oh wow, Priya, are you flirting with us?

**katie (fyodorbrostoevsky):**
| Yeah, what's with the winky face?

**al (thorswagnarok):**
| god priya, we're in public

**Priya (paranormaldetective):**
| You guys are the worst lol
| Bye for now

**bridge (bigforkhands):**
| ;)

Priya (paranormaldetective) is offline.

# 7

**I pull into the Abramses' driveway, putting the car in park. My** pain today is in my right wrist and hip, with that same twinge in my knee that I think is here to stay. I'm glad it's the left knee instead of the right, because I can stretch it out under the dashboard when I drive instead of having to hit the gas or the brakes. Today the pain is a haze, a steady ache that I almost find comforting. That's not quite the right word for the thing I am feeling, but today is a good day. I am starting to realize that a good day doesn't mean no pain, anymore; it means that the pain is small enough to manage, a dog with its own leash.

I can hear them playing a slower song I haven't heard from Suresh before. He's literally in a garage band. They used to be a basement band until Mr. Abrams got sick of the noise and banished them from the house. Frankly, I can't see how the garage would be quieter, but I'm just grateful they aren't at *our* house.

When the music stops and I hear the squeal of a jack being pulled, I zip up my puffy down coat, flip the hood over my frizzy curls, and rap on the garage door with the car key fob. The door slowly ticks up, revealing Jersey's hottest band, Big Little Fries—aka my brother and four of his friends. Or, five, now—it looks like someone is there with a trumpet, too. The last time I heard them play, last summer, there were only three members. They're multiplying.

"Hey, Priya," says Jenny Abrams with a soft smile, putting her bass into its case. I wave. Suresh gives me one of those cool-guy head nods that I find completely insufferable.

"You ready to go, S?" I ask.

"Oh, I didn't know you were coming," he says. "I was gonna call Mom in a little while." He pauses like he's expecting me to say something like "I'll come back later!" or "I'll just hang out with you and your friends for a while," but the end-of-February cold is ticking the pain in my knee up higher until it starts to throb, and I didn't drive out here just to turn back around and go home brotherless.

"She sent me to come get you," I say, even though it's obvious. "So . . ."

He caves, clicking his guitar case shut and grabbing one of the other kids to help him hoist the amp into the trunk.

"Priya?" I hear. I turn toward the door to the house. It's Mr. Abrams, wearing slippers, a comically large cardigan, and a longer beard than the last time I'd seen him.

"Hi, Mr. Abrams," I say, shoving my hands into my pockets. I see the confusion on his face and silently beg him not to ask the question I know he's about to ask. *Don't make me talk about this. Don't make me shine a floodlight on my shame.*

"What are you doing back home?"

There it is.

He keeps going. "I thought Rachel told me you landed at Stanford?"

My tongue sticks to the roof of my mouth, and I force it to move. "I did." The furrow in his brow digs itself deeper. "I, uh. I had to take this semester off." *No, now he'll think I flunked out.* "I got sick, I'm on medical leave."

"I'm so sorry to hear that," he says. The pity is rolling off him in waves. I look at myself from the outside and see the dark circles behind my smudged glasses, the Marshalls sweatpants tucked haphazardly into my snow boots.

"Are you feeling any better?" he asks. I shouldn't be this mortified. I shouldn't be embarrassed to take up space in my own life. I take another look at his face. His concern is genuine. He is offering niceties. I force myself to nod, push my mouth into a smile.

Suresh comes to my rescue, slinging a gentle arm around my shoulder. "Okay, let's bounce."

"I hope you get well soon." Mr. Abrams nods. Static hums in my chest.

"Thanks, Mr. Abrams," I say.

"Oh yeah, thanks for letting us practice here, Mr. Abrams," Suresh adds hastily.

"Anytime," he smiles.

I am quiet in the car. Suresh doesn't notice. I know it's not his job to, and that if I started talking about what I was feeling, he would listen. He's not a bad brother. But I wish I didn't have to offer it up. I wish I could let my discomfort show on my face, that someone would see it and ask me if I was okay.

I know that this is the imbalance between adult and child, the idea that you live your own life and your parents appear at its edges in the morning and at night. It's why your parents say "what did you do today?" and you tell them and don't think to ask what they did. Adults always had so many questions for me—*How's school going? Where are you studying? What's your major?*—and when I'd finish answering them, I'd stand there wanting to ask them questions back but not knowing what to say to a real grown-up.

I am this person now, the one who asks questions instead of answering them.

I am okay. It's just easier to listen to Suresh than to talk, now that I'm the person he doesn't know what to talk about with.

-------

**oof ouch my bones (ONLINE – 5)**

**Seb (mereextravagancy):**
| Sebastian is trans!!

**katie (fyodorbrostoevsky):**
| Yeah!

**Priya (paranormaldetective):**
| Why is Seb talking about himself in the third person

**bridge (bigforkhands):**
| It makes him feel important

**Seb (mereextravagancy):**
| OUCH

**katie (fyodorbrostoevsky):**
you ARE important, Sebastian

**Seb (mereextravagancy):**
THANK YOU for CARING, darling katie

**katie (fyodorbrostoevsky):**
<3 <3 <3

**al (thorswagnarok):**
gross stop flirting

**bridge (bigforkhands):**
katie no, you're giving him a big head

**katie (fyodorbrostoevsky):**
is that dangerous

**al (thorswagnarok):**
you don't know HOW dangerous

**bridge (bigforkhands):**
you haven't seen the things we've seen

**Priya (paranormaldetective):**
Were you guys talking about something, or...

**al (thorswagnarok):**
Saint Priya, keepin us on track

**katie (fyodorbrostoevsky):**
patron saint of being a good listener

**Seb (mereextravagancy):**
Patron saint of practical advice

**bridge (bigforkhands):**
patron saint of my heart

**Priya (paranormaldetective):**
You guys!!!!
I know we just had our first meeting but I love you all already

**bridge (bigforkhands):**
<3

**al (thorswagnarok):**
but seb WAS talking about shakespeare or some nerd shit

**Seb (mereextravagancy):**

Sebastian! From twelfth night! Is trans!!

**al (thorswagnarok):**

is 12th night the one with the bear

**katie (fyodorbrostoevsky):**

no twelfth night is the one with the girl who dresses up like a guy and falls in love with a duke and then her identical twin brother shows up

**al (thorswagnarok):**

oh

you mean she's the man

**Seb (mereextravagancy):**

Softly: don't

**bridge (bigforkhands):**

whoa, they made a shakespeare play out of a classic 2000s romcom?

**katie (fyodorbrostoevsky):**

whoa that's so crazy, bridge

**bridge (bigforkhands):**

i know, crazy

**al (thorswagnarok):**

like a historical AU of she's the man, yeah

**bridge (bigforkhands):**

i'm shookspeare

**Seb (mereextravagancy):**

I will kill all three of you

**Priya (paranormaldetective):**

Hahahaha

**katie (fyodorbrostoevsky):**

Okay but realtalk, Seb

Everyone is always like, oh, shakespeare was so stupid, twins can't be identical if one is a girl and one is a boy

**al (thorswagnarok):**

yes... everyone...

**bridge (bigforkhands):**

everyone

**katie (fyodorbrostoevsky):**

> JOKE'S ON EVERYONE
> LOOPHOLE
> TRANS SEBASTIAN

**Seb (mereextravagancy):**

> THAnk you katie!!! As always you understand me like no one else does!!!
> The rest of you are heathens

**bridge (bigforkhands):**

> shakespeare was woke

**al (thorswagnarok):**

> wokespeare

**Seb (mereextravagancy):**

> I know you're joking but I feel like he kind of was, in a lot of ways
> Especially if we just conveniently ignore t*ming of the shr*w

**al (thorswagnarok):**

> seriously though, sebastian is a really dope name, dude

**Priya (paranormaldetective):**

> Yes!!

**bridge (bigforkhands):**

> thirded
> he's not in the play for that long though, is he?
> sebastian
> the character

**Seb (mereextravagancy):**

> He isn't, no
> But I really admire his dedication to taking "go with the flow" to the next level tbh

**katie (fyodorbrostoevsky):**

> shipwrecked? let's see what else is out there
> a woman I don't know seems to be in love with me? tight

**Seb (mereextravagancy):**

> But to be perfectly honest, mostly I just liked the sound of the name
> And how it felt on me, and how it made me feel

**al (thorswagnarok):**

ur so valid

**Seb (mereextravagancy):**

Thx

**al (thorswagnarok):**

honestly... same hat

this name started as a joke, because i didn't want people knowing my actual name on here

but as gender things have started to shift it's been like... really helpful to hold onto

y'know

**Seb (mereextravagancy):**

I absolutely know

same hat!!

**al (thorswagnarok):**

hoo boy

ok that was too much honesty for today, folks!!

someone give me something else to talk about

**katie (fyodorbrostoevsky):**

rare birds

**Seb (mereextravagancy):**

Worst marvel superhero

**Priya (paranormaldetective):**

The crushing weight of being alive

**bridge (bigforkhands):**

sexiest pokemon

**al (thorswagnarok):**

aaaaaand we have a winner!!! deeply cursed, thanks soul sister

**bridge (bigforkhands):**

anytime, soul sibling

**al (thorswagnarok):**

(..........................the worst marvel superhero is iron fist)

-------

**I can't sleep. Mom would say it's because I'm on my phone too** much, the light training my brain to keep me awake later. She might be right, but I am restless. It feels like something is sitting on my chest.

I pull on my sweatpants and make my way down the stairs and into the kitchen. I don't know what I'm looking for until I see the car keys on the kitchen counter, and I scoop them into my hand and put them into the front pouch of my hoodie. I tug on my boots, gritting my teeth as my hands start to throb with pain. I leave them untied and walk out to the car.

Kiki's Les Mis CD starts playing the second I turn the car on. I hit the knob so that I can only hear the hum of the engine underneath me. The roads are as quiet as the house was. I was worried about ice, but it hasn't snowed in two weeks, and most of what was left has melted. I come to a complete stop at the stop sign out of our neighborhood with its identical two-story houses with identical two-tree front yards, turn on my blinker to the right. I don't know why I do this when there's no one else around, but it feels safe. It makes me feel safe.

I guide the wheel over, make it past the patch of Victorian-style renovations, the overgrown front yard littered with plastic flamingos, the house that never gave out Halloween candy. I make it to the main road on autopilot and turn right again, past the Wawa and the tanning salon turned massage parlor turned GameStop. I pull into the CVS parking lot and slow to a stop. It's still open. I look at the clock in the car—1:14 a.m. I stare at the lights on the dashboard until the 4 turns into a 5.

I don't know what I'm doing here until I do. I turn off the car.

"This sucks," I say. One of the fluorescent lights in the parking lot blinks in and out above my head. "This sucks!" I repeat, a little louder.

"I hate this!" My voice bounces around the empty car. I'm yelling now. "I am so tired of feeling like this! Why did you do this to me? Why did you let this happen? It isn't fair! This wasn't the way it was supposed to go, okay? This wasn't part of the plan!"

I hit the steering wheel with the palm of my hand and it *hurts*, which I know I should have expected, but the pain explodes out into the joints of my fingers and I feel every single one of them start to ache. The heaviness on my chest loosens like phlegm and my eyes prick with tears and I curl my hand into my stomach and begin to cry.

"Shit," I whisper. It's a really ugly cry, sniffling and heaving. I avoid my reflection in the rearview mirror.

I take a breath in: *this used to be so easy.* A breath out: *I'm never going to get better.* In: *it's okay.* Out: *it's okay, it's okay.* I lean back in the seat with my head against the headrest and close my eyes.

My phone buzzes. I sniff my snot up into my nose again, rooting around the center console. There are no tissues. Of course there aren't. I look up at the glowing red letters of the CVS in front of me and sigh. But first, I click my phone open.

**bigforkhands:**
> hey, everyone kind of just moved past your comment in the group chat today, and i really didn't mean to
>
> something about the crushing weight of life?
>
> and i know that's how every single person in gen z talks because we're all like, a /little/ bit depressed, but i just wanted to ask
>
> are you ok?

I start to cry again, letting out that wet sort of laugh–sob. My heart swells with affection for Brigid, still thinking about me from Pennsylvania.

She *noticed*.

I go into the CVS and buy a packet of Kleenexes, a book of stamps, and, on impulse, a children's birthday card with a frog on the front that says "Hip Hop Hooray, Today's Your Day!" The cashier smiles at me awkwardly as she rings me up and doesn't say anything, and I'm grateful to her for that. I pull the cap off my pen with my teeth once I'm back in the car and scrawl, "Hey, Brigid: thanks for being a good friend. Priya. P.S. I know the difference between toads and frogs, so don't @ me."

I lick the envelope shut and stare at that top left corner for a second. Before I can regret it, I write down my return address and slide the card into the mailbox.

I drive home and crawl back into my bed, pulling my blanket up to my chin.

**paranormaldetective:**
> Brigid!!!!!!

Ugh, you're the best.

Yeah. Yeah, I'm okay

Thank you for asking if I wasn't

Goodnight <3

**bigforkhands:**

<3 <3

night, kiddo

tell me about it in the am

**I forget what day it is. I'm dimly aware of my siblings fighting** with each other downstairs, shouting back and forth about whose turn it is to take out the trash while my mom yells at both of them. I have no idea what she's saying, or how long it takes for her to come upstairs and fill up my bathtub, shake shake shake Epsom salt into the water, add coconut oil, and stir it up with her hand. It's going to make me smell like a curry, but I lower myself in, pushing my curls back and pressing my cheek against the cool of the tub wall.

I finally check my phone and, oh, *oh*, it's *Tuesday*, and that means something again.

oof ouch my bones (ONLINE – 8)

**al (thorswagnarok):**
| maybe we should just start?

**lee (typhoonsss):**
| it is late for me :/

**bridge (bigforkhands):**
| Give her a sec!
| PRIYA
| PRIYA PRIYA PRIYA

**Max (quintuplevampire):**
| I am not sure that's going to work

**Spook (spookyspoony):**
| It won't, you have to @ her

**Priya (paranormaldetective):**
| Hi, hello, I am here!

**bridge (bigforkhands):**
| :)))))))))))))

**al (thorswagnarok):**
| HOW

**katie (fyodorbrostoevsky):**
| WTF

**bridge (bigforkhands):**
| i summoned her :)

**Priya (paranormaldetective):**
| We're connected

**bridge (bigforkhands):**
| yeah

**Seb (mereextravagancy):**
| Ok then, welcome back, crew!!
| How is everyone feeling this week?
| How are the Denizens of the Discord?
| The citizens of Oof Ouch, My Bones?

**katie (fyodorbrostoevsky):**
| oof ouch, population us

**bridge (bigforkhands):**
| PEOPLE
| OF
| THE BONE ZONE

**Seb (mereextravagancy):**
| _NO_

**al (thorswagnarok):**
| boners

**Seb (mereextravagancy):**
| NO!!!!!!!!!!!!!!!

**katie (fyodorbrostoevsky):**
| alksjflksjfsflsjkdfj

**bridge (bigforkhands):**
> genius, pal
> (p)al

**lee (typhoonsss):**
> HAHA

**Spook (spookyspoony):**
> Why are you all like this

**Max (quintuplevampire):**
> Buckwild. You guys are the worst Haha

al (thorswagnarok) changed the server name to **THE BONE ZONE**

**Seb (mereextravagancy):**
> Scream

**Priya (paranormaldetective):**
> I appreciate the joke here but I do not want people to
> think I am part of some kind of weird sex thing whenever
> I get a notification from this group

**katie (fyodorbrostoevsky):**
> lmao YEAH

**bridge (bigforkhands):**
> i... literally didn't think about that alskjfls

**Spook (spookyspoony):**
> WHAT DID YOU MEAN, THEN?

**bridge (bigforkhands):**
> a zone for bones!!!
> skeleton central!

**Max (quintuplevampire):**
> Sure

lee (typhoonsss) changed the server name to **oof ouch my bones**

**Seb (mereextravagancy):**
> Balance is restored to the kingdom

**lee (typhoonsss):**
> while I'm at it, let me change the preferences so only i
> control the group name

**bridge (bigforkhands):**
| you don't TRUST US??

**al (thorswagnarok):**
| you know.............. that's fair

**Spook (spookyspoony):**
| Does anyone have anything they're dying to talk about?
| Anything they need to vent

**Seb (mereextravagancy):**
| Oh... I've got a great one

**Priya (paranormaldetective):**
| I have one
| Oh Seb, you can go first

**Seb (mereextravagancy):**
| Thanks, kiddo

**Priya (paranormaldetective):**
| I'm probably older than you

**Seb (mereextravagancy):**
| No way, I'm ancient
| I am twenty and one-half

**Priya (paranormaldetective):**
| Dang it, you actually are older than me >:(

**lee (typhoonsss):**
| oh no WONDER you all call me mum
| i'm a RELIC
| ...i need to get off this website

**Spook (spookyspoony):**
| Same, lee
| I am in grad school
| I am a scientist. I have a job

**lee (typhoonsss):**
| yeah

**bridge (bigforkhands):**
| i also have a job

**Spook (spookyspoony):**
| How old are you

**bridge (bigforkhands):**
20

**katie (fyodorbrostoevsky):**
Are you guys in college too??
(I'm 19)

**Priya (paranormaldetective):**
I'm also 19!

**lee (typhoonsss):**
i am TWENTY SIX i can feel my corpse just withering away

**bridge (bigforkhands):**
Yeah, I'm at the community college one town over!
Working part time at this weird-ass antique place

**Seb (mereextravagancy):**
Yep! I'm doing online courses right now

**al (thorswagnarok):**
i'm 18 but still in high school

**Spook (spookyspoony):**
Oh God

**Max (quintuplevampire):**
I'm also in high school

**lee (typhoonsss):**
you are infants

**Spook (spookyspoony):**
Children

**katie (fyodorbrostoevsky):**
Wee babes

**Spook (spookyspoony):**
No no, you're not a part of this
You belong with the teens
Bridge and Sebastian are on thin ice

**lee (typhoonsss):**
ahaha

**Seb (mereextravagancy):**
>:(

**Priya (paranormaldetective):**
Not to be the organized one again but
**katie (fyodorbrostoevsky):**
oh right lol
**bridge (bigforkhands):**
we love you for it
**Seb (mereextravagancy):**
Oh right we meet in this group for a reason
The chat for chronic illness
The chronic illness chat
**bridge (bigforkhands):**
The discord created specifically to talk about chronic illness
**Priya (paranormaldetective):**
Hahaha
**Seb (mereextravagancy):**
But gather 'round, everyone, because yesterday I heard those five little words
Can you guess?
**Spook (spookyspoony):**
"Wait, you won't get better?"
**Lee (typhoonsss):**
"but you don't look sick!"
**Priya (paranormaldetective):**
"You should just sleep more."
**Max (quintuplevampire):**
Hey what's wrong with you?
**Seb (mereextravagancy):**
Oh my GOD
Uhhhhh, mood
**al (thorswagnarok):**
oof ouch my feelings
**Seb (mereextravagancy):**
It was none of the above, drumroll PLEASE

**katie (fyodorbrostoevsky):**
rrrrrrrrrrrrrrrrrrr

**bridge (bigforkhands):**
buhh duh duhh duh buh duh duh buh duh

**al (thorswagnarok):**
rat a tat tat a tat tat

**bridge (bigforkhands):**
haha nice

**al (thorswagnarok):**
lmao

**Spook (spookyspoony):**
Just spit it out

**Seb (mereextravagancy):**
"Have you tried essential oils?"

**lee (typhoonsss):**
NOOOOOOOOOOOOO

**Max (quintuplevampire):**
No!

**Seb (mereextravagancy):**
Essential oils?? Why no, girl who went to my high school who is now married and neck-deep in an MLM scheme! Why did I not think to rub my flesh in peppermint or bathe in eucalyptus so I could burst forth like a newborn bäbë, fully healed and smelling like a god?

**al (thorswagnarok):**
oh dang :/

someone told me that they would fix my migraines, i was gonna try it

were they just full of it

**Seb (mereextravagancy):**
Oh, kiddo :/

the people selling them do try to prey on people with chronic illnesses

**lee (typhoonsss):**
it's a person to person thing but sometimes strong smells actually make headaches/migraines worse, so

**al (thorswagnarok):**
| wait yeah, that happens with perfume for me
| >:(

**Priya (paranormaldetective):**
| Seb I kid you not
| Someone my family knows from church stopped to "check in on me" a few days ago
| AND TRIED TO SELL US ESSENTIAL OILS

**Seb (mereextravagancy):**
| OH MY GOD!

**Priya (paranormaldetective):**
| I have Lyme disease!! There were literal bacteria attacking my body!

**Seb (mereextravagancy):**
| No, but Priya
| You don't understand
| The Plant Juice Will Fix You

**katie (fyodorbrostoevsky):**
| drag em!!!!

**Priya (paranormaldetective):**
| Yeah the lady who came over pulled the whole "but you don't look sick!" thing also

**lee (typhoonsss):**
| you've almost got BINGO, priya

**Seb (mereextravagancy):**
| Don't you want to get better? Are you even trying?*
| *is a literal, actual thing she said to me!!!

**katie (fyodorbrostoevsky):**
| *kill bill sirens*

**al (thorswagnarok):**
| not to curse
| but that's very not cool

**bridge (bigforkhands):**
| that person fuckin sucks

**Spook (spookyspoony):**

I mean I do actually use essential oils

For stress, but CBD oil has helped my fibro, a little bit

Mostly for falling asleep

**Seb (mereextravagancy):**

Oh shoot, sorry

I wasn't trying to say anything bad about you, whatever works

I guess I was more talking about people who lie to sell it, or abled people who believe those lies

You know?

**Spook (spookyspoony):**

I know!

Just to offer another opinion

**Seb (mereextravagancy):**

Totally

**Max (quintuplevampire):**

Not to be that guy but am I the only one who doesn't know what an MLM is

**bridge (bigforkhands):**

I WAS GONNA ASK SKDFJFLSFK

**al (thorswagnarok):**

i was just good to roll with "men loving men scheme"

not sure what that says about me

**Seb (mereextravagancy):**

SCREAM

Men loving men? Now THAT'S a scheme I could get into!

**lee (typhoonsss):**

where is the wlw scheme

**katie (fyodorbrostoevsky):**

you tell us

**Seb (mereextravagancy):**

To clarify, I'm mostly into girls

...mostly

**bridge (bigforkhands):**
| is anyone really straight though

**Seb (mereextravagancy):**
| No

**Priya (paranormaldetective):**
| Yes

**Max (quintuplevampire):**
| I am

**Spook (spookyspoony):**
| Hate to say this but "everyone has gay thoughts, right"
| does tend to translate into "I have gay thoughts"

**bridge (bigforkhands):**
| oh obviously i have gay thoughts

**lee (typhoonsss):**
| me as well

**al (thorswagnarok):**
| ¯\_(ツ)_/¯

**katie (fyodorbrostoevsky):**
| Sexuality is kind of a moving target anyway, tbh

**Max (quintuplevampire):**
| Yeah I still don't know what an MLM is

**Seb (mereextravagancy):**
| Multi-level marketing
| ^^
| Like a pyramid scheme

**al (thorswagnarok):**
| omg so it's like that always sunny episode
| where mac and dennis buy a timeshare

**bridge (bigforkhands):**
| have you been to florida?

**Priya (paranormaldetective):**
| Not physically

**al (thorswagnarok):**
| ahaha

**bridge (bigforkhands):**
> YES

**Priya (paranormaldetective):**
> Speaking as someone who is/was premed, essential oils aren't gonna fix your underlying problem and they're not a certified treatment plan for anything other than "I want my place to smell good"

> Speaking as a sick person, you know what's best for you because you're the only person inside your body

**lee (typhoonsss):**
> and of course all of us want to get better

> no one wants to continue to be in pain

> but sometimes that's the way it is, and that's the thing that we have to deal with

> not that you won't figure out your diagnosis, katie, i am sure you will

**Spook (spookyspoony):**
> Yeah, it's so offensive to say something like "don't you want to get better" because it like... assumes that wanting it is all that we have to do to make it happen

**lee (typhoonsss):**
> exactly

**Max (quintuplevampire):**
> It's just life baby

**Priya (paranormaldetective):**
> Forever seems like a really long time right now

**bridge (bigforkhands):**
> woof.

**katie (fyodorbrostoevsky):**
> <3

**Spook (spookyspoony):**
> Yeah, it does, sometimes

> And some days are way worse than others

> But hey, it's better than the alternative

**lee (typhoonsss):**
> and truthfully it does get easier

you've just been diagnosed, priya, but you'll start to figure out... well, everything

you'll put up safeguards and find out your limits and suss out what helps and what hurts

**al (thorswagnarok):**

really??

**lee (typhoonsss):**

really really

**Spook (spookyspoony):**

Really really!

You know what I like to say

in my head

**Max (quintuplevampire):**

What

**Spook (spookyspoony):**

I'm still here, bitch

I'm not sure who the "bitch" is, exactly

**Seb (mereextravagancy):**

This bitch of an earth

**katie (fyodorbrostoevsky):**

that's how it is on this bitch of an earth

:o

**Seb (mereextravagancy):**

Angel

**bridge (bigforkhands):**

I'M STILL HERE, BITCH!!

**al (thorswagnarok):**

we're still here, bitch!!!!

**Priya (paranormaldetective):**

We're still here!!

# 9

**It's March, now, and this snowstorm is going to be the last one of**
the year. When I say "I can feel it in my bones," I mean it in a way I've
never meant it before. When the sky opens itself up, all of my joints
take a deep breath and let go of the pain they've been holding on to
all week. It's the biggest relief I've felt in months. The pressure in the
air has always existed, but now I've become a divining rod, tuned into
something that I can't see or hear—something that I hadn't been able
to sense before now.

Kiki and Suresh have been hoping for a snow day, but by Sunday
night the snow has almost completely melted. I've been watching their
faces fall all day.

"Suresh, go tell your sister it's time for dinner," my mother says as
though I cannot hear her.

"Priya!" Suresh screams from downstairs. "It's time for dinner!"

"Yeah, give me a second!" I yell back, pausing Netflix and opening
my blog. I have, as usual, a message from Brigid, sent a few hours ago.

> **bigforkhands:**
> hey
> this is kinda wild, and you probably aren't going to
> believe me
> but before i lose my nerve i have something to tell you

My heart hammers in my chest. Before she loses her nerve?

**paranormaldetective:**

Yeah, shoot

You can tell me anything

"PRIYA!" It's Kiki's voice this time, and I leave my laptop but bring my phone, waiting for the telltale buzz. The five of us hold hands as Dad says a quick prayer over the food, Kiki leaning bodily across the solid wood table to put her hand in mine.

"Do you want to hear about church this morning, Priya?" my mother asks. She's caught me with my fork in my mouth, so I just nod, even though I don't really want a play-by-play.

"The sermon was—" she starts.

"Mrs. Solomon yelled at one of the kids in Sunday school today and everyone lost it," Kiki bursts out, grinning.

"Kalika!" Mom says sternly.

"Don't interrupt your mother," Dad says, less sternly.

I slide my phone out of my pocket under the table, checking for notifications. There's one from Instagram, and I click it despite my better judgment. It's a meme from one of my high school friends that isn't particularly funny, so I go back to the home screen and start scrolling down aimlessly.

I let my eyes blur until I get caught on one image. It's a selfie that Nick's posted. With Alanna. It looks like they're off campus; I can see a fuzzy string of bulb lights glowing orange behind them, the canopy of a tree. His nose is pink and his smile is wide, and she's leaning on him and grinning. She's looking at him, not the camera. They're probably listening to a local band outdoors, splitting a pizza. It looks like the kind of place undergrads take someone they're trying to impress. The kind of place you take someone on a date. An ugly feeling starts to ferment in my gut.

I click the comments. There's a string of heart emojis, a "y'all are the cutest!" Someone's posted the eyes emoji, and Nick's replied with a smug smile.

"Priya, are you listening?" My mom says, and I clench my jaw.

"I'm listening," I lie.

"She's on her phone," says Kiki, narrowing her eyes. I glare at her across the table, mouthing "traitor." Suresh would never sell me out like this, but that's mostly because he's also pocket-scrolling.

"Priya." Mom's voice is disappointed, and she holds out her hand.

"I'm not giving you my cell phone, Mom," I say.

"Not at the dinner table. You know this."

I put my phone under my leg and hold my hands up. "Okay, okay, I've put it away." But I check the Tumblr app, quickly, to see if Brigid's replied.

She hasn't. I know that if she has something to tell me, she'll tell me. That's the way it works between us. But for some reason, the world feels a little off-kilter without her.

-------

**I spend Monday avoiding the work I still have to finish from my** incomplete class, Human Biology, after my dad mentions it to me for the fourteenth time. I spend Tuesday waiting for Brigid to reply to me.

I don't realize how much I've gotten used to talking to her until I'm not. For the past few months we've been carrying on one lazy, never-ending conversation. I don't realize that she's become my go-to person until I can't go to her.

It's not like her to go offline for this long without mentioning it first. I check the app again, but it remains stubbornly blank. I type out another message.

**paranormaldetective:**
> Hey, just wanted to say that you don't have to tell me anything if you don't want to
>
> If you've changed your mind, it's fine!

I'm grateful when 6 p.m. rolls around; I'm one of the first people in the chat, which makes me feel like the world's biggest loser.

**oof ouch my bones (ONLINE – 2)**

**Priya (paranormaldetective):**
> Hey katie!

**katie (fyodorbrostoevsky):**
> Priya! you're early

**Priya (paranormaldetective):**
So are you haha

**katie (fyodorbrostoevsky):**
[SP-POINTING-98G.JPG]
how are you doing?

**Priya (paranormaldetective):**
I'm... okay?
That was vague, haha

**katie (fyodorbrostoevsky):**
no, i get it
you just got diagnosed, right?

**Priya (paranormaldetective):**
Yeah, back in January
But I was sick all fall and had no idea what was happening to me

**katie (fyodorbrostoevsky):**
I know that feeling

**Priya (paranormaldetective):**
Yeah, I'm so sorry

**katie (fyodorbrostoevsky):**
no, don't be
I think both of us are just... new at being sick

**Seb (mereextravagancy):**
Hey, you two!

**katie (fyodorbrostoevsky):**
Seb!! What's up!

**Priya (paranormaldetective):**
Hey!

**Seb (mereextravagancy):**
Not much, might ask Spook and Max a few Qs about wheelchairs when they get here

**katie (fyodorbrostoevsky):**
Oooooh

**Seb (mereextravagancy):**
Priya, is bridge ok? I know you two are close

**Priya (paranormaldetective):**

> ...I actually haven't talked to her for a few days, why do you ask

**Seb (mereextravagancy):**

> Did you not see her post??
>
> I sent her a message, but I wasn't super worried about it
>
> ...although, now I might be

**Priya (paranormaldetective):**

> I didn't see it

I can feel my pulse in my throat as I navigate over to Brigid's blog. I'd missed the post from Sunday night, late.

## bigforkhands

.

#honestly? #i'm so sick of everything #i'm just so tired #i hate this #i hate feeling like this #i want it to be fucking over #like is this gonna be the rest of my life?? #what kind of fucking life is that #god ok this is embarrassing #don't look at me #i'm fine #i promise #but sometimes #suddenly #i am really really not fine #lmao #you guys don't even know. #ugh #delete later

**11 notes**
**worm-punks:** are you okay ?
**mereextravagancy:** lmk if you need to talk, babe
**thorswagnarok:** :/
**scatmanz0z0:** i'm sorry :(

I realize now that Brigid hasn't been online since then. I tell myself she's probably just taking a break, but looking at her post makes my chest feel like it's filling up with water.

**oof ouch my bones (ONLINE – 7)**

**Priya (paranormaldetective):**

> Do you guys think she's alright?

**Seb (mereextravagancy):**

> Yes, absolutely.
>
> Probably

**katie (fyodorbrostoevsky):**
Seb.

**lee (typhoonsss):**
hey, love
i really wouldn't worry too much

**Priya (paranormaldetective):**
Yeah?

**lee (typhoonsss):**
i really wouldn't. it's totally normal for people to log off for a few days when they need a bit of a detox, yeah?

**Priya (paranormaldetective):**
Yes, totally.

**Max (quintuplevampires):**
What did I miss

**al (thorswagnarok):**
yeah, did we already get started?

**Spook (spookyspoony):**
Are we all here?

**Seb (mereextravagancy):**
Sort of

**Priya (paranormaldetective):**
I just haven't talked to brigid in a few days
It's probably nothing

**Spook (spookyspoony):**
Should we get started without her...?

**Priya (paranormaldetective):**
Probably?

**katie (fyodorbrostoevsky):**
she can join us in a couple of minutes, she's probably just late!

**lee (typhoonsss):**
do you have her phone number, priya?

**Priya (paranormaldetective):**
No, we just talk in the app :/

**lee (typhoonsss):**
| i suppose all you can do is wait for her to reply, then

**al (thorswagnarok):**
| oh right, i saw her post :(
| i think she's sick right now, right?
| i mean we're all sick, that's sort of the point here
| but like, that's what her post sounded like to me

**Priya (paranormaldetective):**
| Yeah

**katie (fyodorbrostoevsky):**
| yes, totally

**al (thorswagnarok):**
| sick of being sick

**Spook (spookyspoony):**
| Ain't that the way.

**Priya (paranormaldetective):**
| You guys aren't worried, then?

**lee (typhoonsss):**
| i'm not!

**Spook (spookyspoony):**
| Me neither.

**katie (fyodorbrostoevsky):**
| I wouldn't worry!

**Priya (paranormaldetective):**
| Yeah, let's just get started, then

Seb tells us about his upcoming wheelchair evaluation for part-time use with his EDS, and how he's worried about people judging him for standing in public. Spook and Max reply, but I can't focus. It doesn't feel right without Brigid cracking jokes or making fun of Al's taste in movies or Seb and Katie's flirting. Her absence is a hole punched right in the middle of the conversation.

# *10*

**typhoonsss:**
hear anything from bridge today?

**paranormaldetective:**
No, nothing :/
I know I shouldn't be worried but there's something about the post that really freaks me out, you know?

**typhoonsss:**
yeah. yeah, i do know
but i'm sure it's ok
she's ok

-------

**mereextravagancy:**
Hey, you don't know where bridge works, right?
I figured if anyone would know it'd be you

**paranormaldetective:**
No, I wish
All I know is that it's some sort of weird novelty antique shop in the next town over from her, and that her boss is eccentric and lets her take a lot of sick days

**mereextravagancy:**
| Sounds great, haha

**paranormaldetective:**
| Yeah, totally
| Were you gonna call?

**mereextravagancy:**
| Yeah, I was thinking about it

**paranormaldetective:**
| They probably aren't allowed to tell us if she's working
| anyway
| Isn't there some kind of law about that?

**mereextravagancy:**
| Probably
| Well, thanks anyway, priya

**paranormaldetective:**
| Yeah, of course

**mereextravagancy:**
| Tell us when you hear from her?

**paranormaldetective:**
| I will

-------

**thorswagnarok:**
| bridge update?

**paranormaldetective:**
| no :/

-------

**"Priya, the mail,"** says my mother. It's after dinnertime on Wednesday, and I push my glasses back up the bridge of my nose to frown better at her.

"Sorry, I'm going," I say. I know she gives me small chores because she's worried I don't have a sense of purpose, but carrying the mail from the driveway to the kitchen isn't exactly Hannibal crossing the Alps. I pull on my snow boots; even though everything has melted, it's still wet. I don't see a single elephant on my way to the mailbox.

I drop the pile of mail on the kitchen counter, but before I retreat to my room, I notice a postcard peeking out from the bills. On the front, there's a creepy black-and-white photo of a beardy, old-fashioned white man using a pointer to gesture at some kind of skeleton, but flayed out into hundreds of tiny, thin strands. It looks like something straight out of a '50s horror movie, an evil brain that belongs in a tank of bubbling goo. HARRIET COLE'S NERVOUS SYSTEM, it says underneath, in block letters.

I flip it over. It's from Brigid, postmarked Saturday. I read it in my room.

Dear Priya,

Did you know that in the 19th century a cleaning lady named Harriet Cole donated her body to Drexel and they took out all her nerves, one at a time? It took months (obv.). No one had ever seen anything like it before. It rules. I would have loved to be at the world's fair when everyone flipped their shit over it.

Anyway. Trying to write small here but I'm outta space. They looked at me weird when I asked if they had a postcard of her so I just printed this on cardstock from my mom's office. Made me think of you, I guess.

Thanks for being a good friend too.

~~Love~~ Love, Brigid

I laugh once, sharp and quick and mostly out of surprise. It's so bizarre, and so completely her. I stare at the letters, taking in her cramped, uneven spider-scrawl, the way that each line angles upward. It feels like being haunted. Her postcard has reached me but she hasn't. *Why not?*

I dig my thumbnail into the cardstock on the right of the card, where she's written out my address. And then, above it in tiny block letters:

11 Natalis Road / Bellows, PA 19508

Sebastian was right: we don't know where she works. And Lee was right: no one has her phone number. No one has any way to contact her at all. But Lee was wrong about one thing. Waiting isn't the only thing to do. Not really.

I type the address into Google Maps on my phone and watch the blue line snake between my location and Brigid's house: *1 hr 7 min*, it says.

That's it. An hour and seven minutes. And just like that, I feel my head clear for the first time in months.

It's nothing. It's an episode of a podcast. Three episodes of a sitcom without the commercials. The time it takes to bake a potato or wait in the waiting room of a behind-schedule doctor or soak in an Epsom salt bath or take a nap.

I push myself out of my bed and walk down the stairs to the now-empty kitchen. I put one arm into my coat, and then the other. I shove my sweatpants down into my boots, and I pull the hood of my hoodie over my head, and I grab the keys off the counter, put them into my pocket along with my wallet and my phone. I get into the car and open the garage door, check my mirrors, and pull out.

I drive.

**"**

I can hear my phone vibrating against the cupholder of the car, but I ignore it. The lights on I-78 pass overhead every few seconds and I count them in a rhythm. I'd rather be lit completely by their orange glow, mostly in shadow, but the lights from the other cars on the road cast a harsher brightness onto my console.

I pass a diner on the right with glowing red letters and chrome trim. I don't read the name on the sign. I just listen to the hum of the wheels below me, look ahead at the way the highway curves. I can't see what's around the corner. I can't see past the shadows on either side of the road. This stretch of asphalt is the only place in the world that exists, the rumble of the bridge below me. It's like I've been plucked off the earth.

Until my phone buzzes again. I tip it back with my middle finger to read the display, sigh, and punch ACCEPT.

"Hey," I say, before I realize I can't hear a response. I hit the speakerphone button. "Sorry, I didn't have it on speaker."

"I *said*, where are you, Priya?" Suresh's voice is tinny and too loud. "Did you take the car?"

"Yeah, sorry. I just have to do something."

"Okay well, are you bringing it back soon? I'm supposed to go over to AJ's in like, negative five minutes."

"Welcome to Pennsylvania," Google Maps says.

"*What was that?*" Suresh hisses. I can hear him moving, fabric rustling and a door closing.

"What was what?" I say, as though Google Maps has not just snitched on me.

"Oh my God, Priya," Suresh says. "Oh my God. Why are you *crossing state lines*?"

I merge into the left lane and weigh my options. I could lie. I could come to my senses and take the next exit, go back home, and give Suresh the car.

"Okay, I'm not a federal criminal," I say. "It's twenty minutes away."

"Are you insane?" he scream-whispers. "Like, have you lost your mind?"

"Not sure yet," I say.

"It's like ten p.m., Priya!"

"I know, I'm sorry."

"So, what, when are you coming back?"

"I haven't thought that far ahead."

"Ohhh my God," he says. "Oh my GOD, Mom and Dad are going to kill you—"

"No!" I cut him off. "No, they aren't, because you are going to cover for me."

"Yeah, right."

"May I remind you who was still awake when you got home at three in the morning last month? Or who did not tell our parents that you and your band took an unsupervised trip to NYC last year instead of practicing at the Abramses'?"

There's a pause, and I hear him huff.

"Okay?"

"Okay, okay," he says. "But you'd better get home as soon as you physically can. Never mind AJ's. Even though you knew it was my turn to have the car tonight."

"I forgot."

"Yeah, whatever, dude. I can only cover for so long. You're dead meat if they wake up and you aren't here."

"No, I'm not gonna be gone that long," I say. "The drive's only an hour. Less than an hour, now."

"Kay," he says. "Have fun like, running drugs or meeting a secret boyfriend for sexual favors or whatever. I'm assuming you're doing one of those two things."

"Yeah, you know me."

"Well, I thought I did."

"It's—I think my friend needs me," I say. There's a pause.

"Alright," Suresh finally says. "I trust you."

"Bye, S."

"Bye, jerkface."

I hear the three end tones and push the phone back down, letting the quiet dark swallow me up again. I watch the exit signs pass overhead, the numbers ticking up. My frenetic certainty starts to peter out. I come back to myself.

Oh. Oh, this was a mistake.

What do I think is going to be waiting at Brigid's for me? I imagine walking up to her front door, ringing the doorbell. Having to explain to her parents what I'm doing there. *Oh, I'm a friend of your daughter's, from the internet. She didn't text me back, so I drove to your house. Can I come in?* Or worse, having to explain it to Brigid. *Hey, what's up? I got really paranoid that something had happened to you so I thought I'd show up on your doorstep, like a psychopath. Oh, you want me to leave? Yeah, that tracks.*

But when Google Maps tells me to take the next exit, I realize I'm closer to Brigid's than I am to my own house.

*You can still turn around,* my brain tells me. *It's not a sunk cost.*

I take the exit.

The road to Bellows is much slower going than the highway. I brake as I hug a tight, terrifying curve around what I think is an offshoot of the Delaware, or the Lehigh. When the moon peeks out from behind the clouds that have been covering it all night, I see the river's snakelike sprawl, glittering ink waiting to swallow the trees, then the road, then my car.

I pass through a small town with a two-stoplight main drag, then turn back into the forest. This road is darker than anything I've been on all night. There are no streetlights. I can only see the handful of feet that my headlights splash out ahead of me, and I'm walled in by trees on both sides, some evergreen and some stripped bare. There's fog tonight. I didn't notice it on the highway, but now I can see it every time my car goes into a dip in the road. I turn off my high beams and feel even smaller than before.

The highway was familiar territory. I've driven on it for the past three years, and before that I watched my parents drive it, sat in the backseat trying not to fall asleep as they told me it was illegal to turn on the overhead light when I tried to read in the dark. But now that I'm on a strange road in a strange town, my thoughts start to shift. On the highway, I'd been worried about looking ridiculous in front of Brigid, or creepy, or weird. But here on the rural Pennsylvania backroads, my thoughts start to turn darker.

What if something really *is* wrong? What if she's not okay? What if she's really sick, or hurt, or—

I swallow. Or, worse.

"In one mile, turn right on Nells Church Road, then keep left," says Google Maps. I jump at the sound.

My heartbeat picks up. I did not think this through. I did not think about what I might find when I got to Brigid's. I didn't think about what I might have to recover.

"Your destination is on your right," says Google Maps. I pull up to the curb, slow to a stop, and look.

Unlike my house, 11 Natalis Road isn't in the middle of suburbia, separated from the neighbors by a narrow strip of grass and a fence. It's a quarter of a mile to the nearest house, which I passed on my way up.

The house is painted slate gray, with a dark roof and small windows. It's built unevenly, a two-story pointed roof on the right sloping down into a one-story rectangle on the left. There's an overhang above the porch, a rocking chair out front that's moving back and forth in the wind. I hate it. The lights upstairs are off, but the windows in the front are glowing yellow, dimly illuminating the porch.

It's sitting at the top of an incline too small to be called a hill, but the gravel driveway curves up toward the house. There's an old car from the late '90s or early 2000s parked badly in the driveway, almost completely sideways, like someone was trying to drive it into the house. Its front wheels are denting the grass.

I don't want to get out of the car yet. Part of me still wants to turn around, even though I'm already sitting outside her house. I open the Tumblr app and navigate back to our conversation.

**paranormaldetective:**

Hey, I know this is a weird question but are you home right now?

I don't expect a response at this point, after three days of radio silence. I lean forward to squint at the side of the mailbox that's caught in my headlights to make sure it's the right house. The front flap is hanging open, and I can see the mail protruding from inside.

I get out of my car and let the door thud closed behind me. The sound seems loud out here. I can hear crickets chirping, and when I tilt my head up, I see more stars than I can see in New Jersey. It's colder here, too. All my joints are stiff from driving; my knees and hips hurt most, then my elbows and wrists. I try to shake them out, but that just makes them hurt more. My left knee starts throbbing again as I walk over to the mailbox, and I grit my teeth.

There's an 11 on it. There are also three wrapped newspapers piled at the base, three days' worth of mail inside. *Something is wrong*, I think, dimly. And when I look up at the car on the lawn from this angle, the sight sends a pang of fear right through my chest.

The driver's side door is hanging open.

*Something is wrong.*

I make my way up the driveway, gravel crunching under my feet. I step onto the porch, and a gash of yellow light casts itself across my boot. The front door of the house gapes at me.

It's wide open.

"Oh my God," I whisper to myself. "Oh, my God."

Priya Patel would see an open door as an invitation to investigate—a mandate, even. But Priya Radhakrishnan just wanted to make sure her friend was okay, and she's regretting ever getting into her car in the first place.

"Brigid?" I try to yell, but it comes out quiet. I clear my throat and try again. "Brigid, are you there?"

There's no response but the crickets.

I squeeze my eyes shut and take a deep breath in and out, counting the seconds. *Ten, fifteen, twenty.*

I shoot up a quick prayer and walk inside.

# 12

I shut the door behind me once I'm in the foyer. The house is still, but not empty. There's an inside-out T-shirt on the floor in front of me, next to a threadbare sports bra and a ring of keys. I bend to pick the keys up, wincing at the way my joints crack. I spot house keys and car keys, a library card fob and a rewards card from a taco restaurant. It's all held together with a beaded lizard keychain, green and blue and gold.

The lights are on in this room, but the rest of the house is in shadow. The rooms seem to branch out from this central hub, ahead of me and to my right. There's a door to my left with a heavy deadbolt screwed into it that doesn't match the rest of the house. It looks like it'd take two hands to close, but it isn't bolted.

My heart is hammering against my ribs now. I don't want to move outside the ring of warm light in the foyer.

"Stop being silly," I whisper. "It's just a house."

It's just a house.

"Brigid?" I yell again. I hear a distant *thump* and I nearly jump out of my skin.

I head forward instead, turning on every light I pass. There's a hallway stretching in either direction, what looks like a kitchen in front of me, a staircase to the second floor. Brigid's room is probably up there, but I don't go up.

Instead, I push open the doors I find along the hallway. There's a study, a living room, a bathroom at the end of the hall, where the hallway makes a right angle toward the garage. I clench my jaw as I fumble for the bathroom light, bracing myself, but it's empty too, the shower curtain pulled back. I can see the moon through the tiny window above the toilet.

I go back to the kitchen and turn on the lights. They flicker, once, before staying lit. There's a round breakfast table at the far end in front of tall, looming windows that face the backyard. One of the lights above the table has burned out. I can see my reflection in the window, but I can't see anything outside but the darkness. It makes me feel uneasy, like I'm dreaming and don't know it.

There's a smell coming from the fridge, sweet and putrid. I open the door and I'm hit with a wave of stench that makes bile rise in my throat. I put my nose into the crook of my elbow to tamp down my gag reflex.

The fridge is, frankly, disgusting. There are only four things inside: a handful of ketchup packets in the door, a half-gnawed block of cheese that's gone hard at the exposed edge, a six-pack of energy drinks, and, in Ziploc bags filling up two full shelves, half a dozen raw, defrosted steaks. There's blood pooling in the bottom of the bags. A bag on the second shelf is leaking, the juice dripping down to the bottom shelf where it has coagulated, dark and tacky.

I slam the door shut. "What the hell," I whisper.

I should leave. I should go home.

There's another *thump*. This one's closer, and I hear the plates rattle in the kitchen cabinets, feel it in my joints. I realize with a jolt that it's coming from below me, underneath the floor.

"Hello?" I shout, louder this time. I hear something moving, and then the creak of stairs, the shifting of weight.

"Who's there?"

Another *thump*. It's not below me anymore. I walk slowly back toward the front door and stand across the foyer, staring at the door with the deadbolt. I realize now that it must be the door to the basement.

"Brigid?" I call.

Something slams into the basement door from the other side, rattling it. I jump back. There's another thud, then another. I hear a long, low growl start to build. On the next slam it takes a sharp turn into a yelp, high-pitched and desperate.

There's a dog locked in the basement—a dog that, judging from the state of everything else around the house, hasn't been fed in three days.

"Hey, it's okay," I call out in what I hope is a soothing voice. "It's okay, I'll get you some food."

I realize two things, now, in the following order.

First: I probably shouldn't open the door to a dog that hasn't eaten in three days, one that's slamming itself against the door in an attempt to get out of the basement. It sounds big—person-sized. I slide my phone out of the pocket of my hoodie and google "will a hungry dog attack you." All the results are about pets eating the bodies of their dead owners, which wasn't really what I was trying to ask.

I realize the second thing when the door shakes again, so hard that I hear a *crack*. I realize that I lied to myself when I said there was a dog locked in the basement, because the door in front of me isn't locked at all.

I turn to go back to the kitchen to check the pantry for dog treats, or maybe just go out the back door. But I hear a growl behind me that freezes me in place, see an enormous blur of motion out the corner of my eye.

When I turn around to face the foyer again, the door to the basement is swinging on its hinges, splintered at the doorframe.

I've made a mistake. I've made a series of mistakes that all led up to this particular mistake, here in a strange house in middle-of-nowhere Pennsylvania.

I hear a low sound behind me. The blood rushes in my ears. This can't be happening. I am not about to be attacked by some kind of feral, door-breaking dog. I take a shaky breath in before I turn, but when I do, there's nothing behind me but a series of dark gashes in the white carpet.

I have to get out of here.

I edge backward until the wall hits my back so I can see into the hallway, the one that goes toward the bathroom. The one that seems a lot longer now than it did before.

The one that now has a series of faint tracks leading down it.

I breathe in silently through my mouth, staring down that corridor. The overhead lights flicker as I feel a quiet thud, a careful step. I see a paw with five toes step around the corner and into my line of sight, then a snout, another paw. I remind myself to keep breathing as it comes around the corner.

It's big. Its shoulders come up past the crown molding on the panels that reach halfway up the walls, up past my waist. It's tight with muscle but it's thin, all too-sharp angles and jutting limbs. It's covered in dark brown fur, with patches of black, and its pointed ears lie flat against its head before twitching forward, twice.

I still can't quite see it. The light from the bathroom casts its shadow down the hallway as it makes its way slowly toward me. All the component parts I'm looking at are telling my brain *dog*, but there's something wrong about what I'm seeing, a wrongness that makes my palms itch.

And then it lifts its front paw, pulls its back leg in, shifts its weight, and stands on its hind legs.

It's not a dog.

I don't know what I'm looking at anymore. My brain tries to turn the picture over once, twice, three times, but it can't make sense of it. It sniffs the air. My breath hisses as I try to stifle a gasp, but I can't.

It isn't a dog.

It turns its head and looks me dead in the eye.

I watch the muscles in its back legs bunch. And then I turn and run for the front door.

I don't make it. My left knee buckles underneath me. I feel the creature behind me, hear its claws skitter on the foyer's wood floor as it launches itself toward me. I push myself up and stagger into the darkened room next to me, grab a chair and toss it in front of me. I can see the kitchen through the hallway, and I pray for my brain to clear enough to formulate some kind of plan.

The creature swipes the chair away into the wall. One of the legs breaks off. I try to roll under what I realize is the dining room table but instead I feel my shoulders hit the ground, knocking the air out of my lungs. I gasp, breathe through the pain. My ears ring. It's on top of me. Its weight is pinning me to the ground and I scream, trying to kick. Its snout sniffs me curiously. My ear is wet with it. I gag.

*I'm going to die*, I think.

Then: *not yet.*

I pull my phone out of my hoodie pocket, swipe up as quickly as I can, and hit the flashlight button. I squint against the bright light that hits the creature square in the face and watch its pupils dilate before it recoils.

I drag myself under the table, across the room, to the hallway. My joints are protesting, but I crawl as fast as I can. My shoulder pops and I grit my teeth, pushing myself up and limping back into the warm light of the kitchen. Damn it. Damn it, damn it, damn it. I'm going to die in this house, and when someone else finds me, they are going to find two bodies, mine and Brigid's. What if she's upstairs? What if she's already dead? What if this thing eats our corpses? Why didn't I read the Google search results?

I steady myself on the kitchen sink, hold myself up by one arm. This can't be real. This can't be happening. I hear it behind me again. There's a plate in one side of the sink, a cast-iron pan in the other. I hiss as I grab the pan by the handle with both hands, gripping as tightly as I can, and turn. The not-dog is lunging at me now, jaws open, red tongue lolling, sharp yellow-white teeth dripping with saliva. I shove the pan into its open mouth and it bites down. One of its canines breaks off, skittering across the floor. I hiss as a sharp pain hits my shoulder joint, slicing through like I've been stabbed.

I remember the fridge.

The fridge, across the room. Just a couple of steps.

Its jaws are locked around the pan and I know I don't stand a chance in a strength contest with this thing. I look into its eyes again, at its pupils and warm brown irises, trying to figure out what seems so wrong about them. It hits me in a second. It has human eyes.

The creature yelps when I let go of the pan, landing on the floor with a thud. I make a break for the fridge, pulling open the door. My shoulder hurts. I gag again at the smell but I rip open one of the plastic bags and toss it toward the thing.

I'm hoping for a baseball pitch, a perfect arc that lands as far away from me as possible, but the raw steak lands with a squish a few feet from where I'm standing. I toss another one, a little farther, and put the fridge door between me and the creature.

It perks its ears up and sniffs the air again. This time when it lunges, it's toward the meat, and it tears into it with gusto, swallowing it in three bites. It grabs the other steak now with its front paw, pulling it to its mouth and making little snuffling noises as it eats. Its tail, long and bushy like a German Shepherd's, begins to wag.

I wish I'd rolled up my sleeves before this. I feel a trickle of raw steak juice drip down the side of my hand and down my arm and feel bile burn my throat. I grab two more bags, making sure not to open them yet, and limp my way back to the hallway.

My shoulder pulses with pain and I yelp, dropping one bag too soon. The creature looks up and its gaze holds mine again, burrowing into me. It comes bounding toward me and I pick up my pace down the hallway.

I've grabbed the leaky bag by accident, and the blood drips steadily onto the white carpet. *I'm ruining this house*, I think nonsensically. The creature is gaining on me, and I can only walk at a limp. I'm either carrying its next meal or about to become it. Everything hurts. And all I can think is, *I'm ruining the carpet*.

I tear open the bag and click my tongue. The creature stands on its hind legs again. I force myself to look at it. I toss the steak into the bathroom, and it makes a slapping noise against the bottom of the tub. I open the bathroom door as far as it will go.

"Come on!" I yell. "In here! Come get it!"

I back down the bend in the hallway, waiting and hoping. All of my muscles are tensed. I can feel the terror from my jaw down my spine and into my calves. Every curse I know goes through my head, and then, after a split second of guilt, every prayer.

There's a blur of motion in front of me, a snout, four paws, that bushy tail, as it leaps forward through the door into the bathroom. I lurch forward and slam the bathroom door shut, leaning against it. I expect the creature to break down the door, throw itself against it again, but all I hear now are snuffling noises, loud chewing and meat tearing, then the metallic popping of a shower curtain being torn off its rings.

I sink to the floor, chest heaving. My hands are shaking, I notice. They're sticky. My sweatshirt is stained pink with steak blood. It stinks. I want to push my hair back but I don't want to get anything in it, so I just let it keep falling around my face.

I should block the door with something while it eats, I think, but I can't get up. I see a squat oak table down the hallway, but I know I'm not strong enough to move it in front of the bathroom door. Everything hurts. My head's swimming with pain, and I feel like I'm going to throw up again. I hear scratching on the door behind me, the kind that's probably leaving gouges in the wood.

"Shh," I say. I rest my head back against the door. "Shh."

The gouging stops, and I hear claws clicking on tile. I hear the thing let out a deep sigh. And then it's quiet.

I sit for a few minutes and wait for my head to clear. It doesn't. I push myself up anyway, even though it hurts. I wash my hands in the kitchen sink, check for Brigid's keys, ready to walk back out the front door.

I remember why I came here in the first place. *Brigid.*

If the thing gets out again, it might find Brigid. It might do something to her.

I sit at the breakfast table so I can see the hallway and the stairs at the same time, as well as the front door. I try to get comfortable in the chair, but it's wooden, and my joints are screaming. I still haven't found Brigid's room. I still can't go upstairs.

Instead, I pull my phone out. I open a new tab in the browser, search "Bellows PA animal control," and call the first number that pops up. A 911 operator transfers me, and I count the rings for what feels like hours. It's past 11 p.m., and I'm worried that no one will answer.

"Hey," says a voice on the other end.

"H-hi?" I say.

"Oh right, shit. I mean, dang it. Bellows County Animal Control, what's the nature of your problem?"

"I . . ."

"Ma'am?"

"Something attacked me, and I trapped it in the bathroom."

"What kind of a something?"

"Like—like a big dog," I say.

"Yeah, okay," he says. I hear muffled conversation, a quiet laugh. "I can do one more run before I go home. Where are you?"

"I'm at 11 Natalis Road."

"Alrighty, sit tight."

I look around me at the broken chair, the iron pan on the floor next to the thing's tooth, and the stained, torn-up hallway carpet. I sit tight.

# 13

**By the time I hear a quiet knock at the door, it's Thursday. I've** taken off my hoodie and tied it loosely around my waist, leaving me in a tank top. I'm cold, but I can't muster the energy to put it back on.

There's a glass panel in the middle of the front door, and I see movement behind it, someone waving. The presence of another person—a professional—makes me feel like I've just taken a breath from an oxygen mask. I can feel myself stabilizing. Someone else is here. That means it's going to be okay.

I open the door to the animal control officer, who's bouncing on his toes despite the heavy boots he's wearing. He doesn't look like he's that much older than I am—barely in his twenties. He's East Asian; his dark, unruly hair brushes his shirt collar, and he's got a few days' worth of short stubble on his chin and his upper lip. His short-sleeved olive-green uniform shirt is untucked.

He tips his pole at me in a "can I come in?" gesture and flashes a grin. The pole is taller than both of us, and I'm relieved at the thought of putting that much distance between me and the creature.

"Hi, thanks for coming so late," I say, stepping aside. I am immediately aware of how wrong it is that I'm inviting yet another stranger into a house that is not mine.

"Sorry it took so long, we're over in Echo Creek," he says, stepping in. I nod like I know where that is. The radio on his belt chirps, and he turns it off. "So how aggressive was this dog, on like a scale of one to ten?"

"Uh . . ." I say.

"Oh wait, are you okay? I, uh—I should have asked that first, huh."
He's new.

"I think I'm okay, yeah," I say. "A little shaken up."

"Yeah, of course," he says, nodding. "Did you get bit?"

*Did I?*

"No, I don't think so," I say.

He gestures at my bare arms, the blood on my sweatshirt. I hold
them out, and he reaches out with a gloved hand, turns my arm over
carefully.

"That's steak juice," I say, realizing how stupid that sounds the
second after I say it.

"Oh," he says. "Sure."

"So, it's in the bathroom," I say, walking over to the hall and
pointing ahead.

"You're limping," he says.

"Yeah, it knocked me down," I say. "But I've also got Lyme disease, so my joints are a mess right now."

"Oh shit," he says. "The nasty kind? My cousin had Lyme for a hot
second, but they caught it early, so she was fine."

"The nasty kind," I say.

"I'm really sorry, that's a bummer," he says. "Does the door open
in or out?"

"What?"

"The bathroom door."

"Oh, uh, out."

"Also a bummer, but let's give it a try. Wanna wait somewhere
else?"

I go back down the hallway and take my position around the bend,
several feet away. I nod at the animal control guy, and he nods back.

He kicks at the door with the toe of his boot. "Hey there, pup,"
he calls. It's quiet. He looks over at me. I shrug, and he makes a turtle
face.

"Maybe it's asleep?"

"It did eat three or four steaks."

"Yeah, that might do it," he says. "Alright, let's see what we're
dealing with."

He cracks the door open, bracing himself and grasping the pole with both hands. Nothing. He looks around the door slowly. Then he drops his pole, whips his head around, and shoots me the most judgmental look that I have ever been on the receiving end of, the kind of baffled, narrowed-eye, curled-upper-lip look that says *how many things, exactly, are wrong with you?*

"What?" I ask.

"Real question, no disrespect, but are you high right now?" he asks.

"No? Of course not?"

His eyebrows shoot up. "Like, I'm not even talking weed. Are you on shrooms? Did you and your friend go on, like, a peyote trip here?"

"I don't do drugs!" I shoot back. "What are you talking about?"

"C'mere," he says, pulling the door open wide. I hesitate before walking over and edging in beside him.

"So," he says, pointing with one of his gloves, "that's a human woman."

He's right.

The tub is smeared with pink. The shower curtain has been pulled down and slashed a few times. Almost every inch of the tile floor is covered with piles of dark brown hair. And slumped facedown in the middle of the floor, one arm flung into the tub and the remains of the shower curtain partially covering her body, is a completely naked girl.

"Oh my God," I say.

"So if you're not high," the animal control guy says, "is this a prank? I mean . . . it's not even that funny. I don't get it."

"I don't get it either."

I walk into the room in disbelief, gingerly turning the girl over. A trail of pasty white liquid has dribbled out the side of her mouth, caked into her chin-length brown hair and into the tile grout. She's breathing, her chest heaving, and I pull my sweatshirt from around my waist, wincing as my shoulder throbs.

"Definitely not a dog," the guy continues. "That's a pretty shitty thing to say about your friend, dude." He pauses. "Is she okay? What did you *do* to her?"

"What did *I*—can you just help me pull her up?" I say.

He steps into the bathroom, eyes fixed on the ceiling. When he helps me pull her into a sitting position, the shower curtain slides down her chest.

"Nope!" he says, squeezing his eyes shut.

I pull my hoodie over her head carefully and she stirs, groaning. She's tan, with freckles scattered across her face and purple circles under her eyes. Her bottom lip is split.

I recognize her from a handful of pictures posted on her blog, from the selfies she messaged me after she cut her own hair, flashing a peace sign and grinning a toothy smile.

"Hey, Brigid," I say softly.

"Pull her arms through so we can help her up," the animal control guy says. He's got one eye closed and is squinting through the other.

"Help me," I say. I can't bend my own arm quite right.

Brigid groans again as we maneuver her arms. It's hoarse and throaty, deeper than I would have expected.

"Sorry, sorry, sorry."

Her mouth works for a second before she spits more of the white paste onto the floor. She hisses, pulling her lips back, and my heart pounds in my throat.

Her left canine tooth is gone.

My brain churns, telling me that there are dots to connect, but I can't. I can't.

"She's not hurt, is she? Did she hit her head?"

I run my hands along it quickly, but I don't feel any bumps or cuts. There's no blood on the floor, just the pink smear in the tub from the steak. I shake my head.

"Okay, you ready?" I ask. The hoodie is big on her, makes her look even thinner than she already is.

"Yeah, let's try to walk her to one of the bedrooms," he says.

I wince. "I don't think I can."

"Can you get her feet if I carry most of the weight?"

"I can try."

"Sweet. Grab her feet and tell me where to go."

I have no idea where the bedroom is. I'm sure as hell not making it up the stairs, though, so I point down to the other end of the hallway.

"Okay, let's try this again," he says, hooking his arms underneath hers and letting her head loll back onto his shoulder. Her legs hang limp. I grab her feet, trying to ignore my pain.

"We good?" he asks, looking up at the ceiling again. "That hoodie riding up?"

"We're good," I say. We back down the hall in a straight line, and he uses his elbow to push open the door. It's the master bedroom; the bed is made.

"Bingo," I mutter.

"What?"

"Nothing."

We deposit her onto the bed. I pull the covers out from under her so I can put the blanket on top of her. The animal control guy and I stare at each other for about ten seconds. I have absolutely nothing I can say to defend myself.

"Well . . ." he says. "I guess I'll just . . . get my catchpole and go."

"Yeah," I say. "Yeah, I'm so sorry I dragged you out here."

There's another awkward pause. I'm desperate to explain myself. "There really was a dog. Or a wolf, or. Something."

"Yeah, alright," he says. I appreciate him not voicing the obvious question, the one I am completely unable to answer: *if there was a dog, then where is it now?*

I look over at Brigid, sprawled out on the bed. I swallow.

. . . *No.*

No, no, no, no, no.

"I'll just let myself out," the animal control guy calls from the foyer. I hadn't even noticed him leave the bedroom, but I shut the door behind me and walk out.

"Sorry again," I say.

"It's been weird, dude," he says. "See ya."

I stand in the foyer until my muscles can't take it anymore. Any adrenaline that had been fueling my body has seeped out by this point, leaving me hollow. I'm sick of putting weight on my feet, trying to avoid my messed-up knee. My hips ache. My shoulder throbs. Just thinking about getting behind the wheel makes my whole body hurt. Just thinking about climbing up the stairs to the second floor makes me want to die.

So I shuffle through the kitchen again. I open three cabinets until I find medication, shake out two ibuprofen and swallow them dry. I notice now that I can see a family room from the kitchen, through one of those cutouts in the wall. It's got a two-story ceiling, a TV, a coffee table, and an old leather sectional. I collapse there, pulling down the blanket spread across the back. I hook my glasses onto my bra strap and shift my weight to something as close to comfortable as I can manage. Sleeping on the couch isn't going to help my joints, but I'm going to wake up sore no matter what I do. I'm too tired to think about anything else.

I'm starting to drift off when I remember the group chat. I type out one last message for the night, timestamped 12:46 a.m.

**oof ouch my bones (ONLINE – 1)**

**Priya (paranormaldetective):**
Brigid's okay

I think it's true.
I hope it is.

# 14

**I wake up confused, my face pressed into cracked brown leather.**
There's light coming from somewhere. My head is floating, and when
I shift, I'm hit immediately with a wave of nausea. My mouth is dry.
I groan.

I take inventory. The pain in my joints is *radiating*: down my shoulder and into the fingers on my right hand; out from my hips; along my
left leg in both directions from my stupid knee. I don't need to roll up
my sweats to know that it's swollen. I can feel it.

I'm not at home. I remember now. I fumble for my glasses as
images from the night before flash in my brain—the fog on the road,
the car on the grass, the open door, the open maw of the creature
that attacked me. Now that it's daytime none of it seems real. I can't
see anything but the ceiling from here, the warm triangles of white
against shadow on the white popcorn ceiling and the fan in the middle
of the room and the railing to the second floor landing at the top of the
stairs. I can't see any evidence of anything that happened.

My first attempt at pushing myself into a sitting position fails completely. I am bone-tired, despite having slept for—

Oh, God.

I look at the ground, trying to calibrate myself. I should have
grabbed my phone before I sat up. Stupid.

Maybe I don't need to check it. Maybe I can just keep sitting here,
forever, until I wither away and rot, and someone eventually finds my
bones here on this couch.

I hear it buzz and see the screen light up with notifications. Panic catches in my chest.

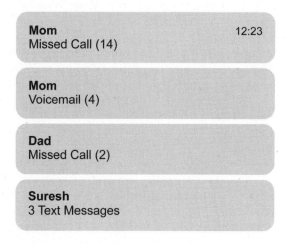

**Mom**      12:23
Missed Call (14)

**Mom**
Voicemail (4)

**Dad**
Missed Call (2)

**Suresh**
3 Text Messages

This is bad. This is worse than whatever happened last night. I'm not going to die on this couch. I'm going to die when I get home, because my parents are going to *kill* me.

I lie back down and scoop up my phone with my left hand. I really, really, *really* don't want to call my mom, but I know that if I text her, she'll just call again. And again.

I take a second to get my story straight: *I went over to a friend's and fell asleep.* Irresponsible. *I went over to a friend's but I wasn't feeling well so I decided to sleep over instead of driving.* I can hear my mother's voice: Which friend? Do we know her? *You don't know her, it's a friend from school.*

Before I can finish my train of thought, the phone begins to buzz again. I'd rather fight that thing from last night again than hear my mother's voice right now.

I hit ACCEPT.

"Hi, *amma*, I'm okay," I say, or I try to, before my mom screeches so loudly into the phone that I have to hold it away from my face.

"PRIYA! Priya, are you there?!"

Here we go.

"I don't know *what* you were thinking. Do you know how worried we have been? When we woke up this morning and realized you did not come back home last night? It has been *hours*. This house has been in chaos. We thought you were *dead*, Priya. Dead! We thought you had ended up in a ditch somewhere on the side of the road and *died*."

"I'm not dead," I croak.

"You had better have as good of an excuse, then!" she yells. "You don't ring your family, you aren't dead, what is wrong with you, hm? Your father was close to tears when he left for work this morning. Your brother and sister are worried sick. And I have been contacting everyone trying to find you!"

I cannot imagine anything more mortifying.

"*Where are you?*"

"I'm sorry, Mom," I say. This was not what I needed first thing in the morning. My head is starting to pound. I feel like I can't put the words together in a way that makes sense. "My friend was having an emergency so I drove over to her house, but then I felt too sick to drive home, so I decided to sleep over. I thought it would be the right thing to do."

"Which friend?"

"A friend from college," I say. "You don't know her."

"Then what is she doing here in the middle of March, hm?"

Oh no.

"Spring break," I lie. I hope desperately that she doesn't have a copy of the Stanford academic calendar.

"What is her name?"

"Brigid."

"I don't know a Brigid."

"I just said that."

"What do her parents do—"

"I don't know! I didn't ask them!"

"You should have told us you were going there." She sniffs. I can hear her getting choked up now, which is worse. "You should have texted us last night."

"I know, I'm sorry," I say. "I didn't want to wake you up."

"Did you say you weren't feeling well?"

"Yes, I'm going to take a bath here," I say. "I'll be home later tonight."

"Tonight? No, I'll come pick you up right now."

"Aren't you at work?"

There's a long pause. "Well. Yes. But I can take a sick day."

I feel myself start to sweat. I cannot tell her I drove to Pennsylvania right now.

"It's okay, *amma*," I say. "I might just go back to sleep. You can come get me tonight."

"I don't like it, Priya."

"I know."

"Are you sure?"

"I'm sure."

"Okay."

I exhale.

"Don't worry about work, Priya," she says softly. "If you need me, I will be there as fast as I can."

"I know."

"If you feel worse, you call me right away."

"I will."

"Or have your friend ring me."

"Okay."

"Okay. I'm still upset."

"I know."

"Don't ever do this ever again, okay?"

"I won't, I promise."

"We were worried sick."

"I know. See you later, Mom."

"Yes, you will. Tell your father you're okay, and text Kiki and Suresh."

"I will. Bye, Mom."

"Good-bye. Oh! And—"

I hang up and pretend that I didn't hear her keep talking. I put my phone into the pocket of my sweats, close my eyes, and let out a long groan.

I never do this. Whatever *this* is. Whatever driving to another state without telling anyone where you're going and breaking into a virtual friend's house is. I wonder if being sick has made me different, if the disease that went for my joints and my heart and my brain also went down into my cells and mutated them, like that CGI sequence in movies where it zooms into the character's bloodstream and you see each checker-red erythrocyte spasm and turn a color that doesn't belong on the inside of your body.

"Hey, uh . . . Two questions."

The voice comes from a few feet away, sending a jolt of panic through me. It's female, deep in the way that your voice gets deep when you get the flu, like two rocks scraping against each other.

My eyes fly open. There's Brigid, tired-eyed, that off-white paste still caked solid across the left side of her hair. She's wearing cutoff sweatpants that reveal thick, dark hair on her legs, and an orange T-shirt, about three sizes too big, that says DABSYLVANIA, with a tiny vampire dabbing on the front.

"Who are you and why are you in my house?"

I push myself up, wincing.

"You know," she continues. "Just out of curiosity."

"It's, uh. I can explain. Sort of." I feel like I've been caught breaking and entering, because I guess I have. "I'm Priya. Paranormaldetective. Wow, that feels dumb to say out loud."

"*Priya?*" she says, incredulous. I nod.

"I was—I was worried. We all were."

"Oh my God," she says. Then, softer, as she steps closer: "Oh, my *God*."

"Hey," I say. "Nice to meet you."

She's silent, staring at me with an expression I can't parse. I'm not used to seeing her in real time, the way her face moves around her thoughts. She's expressive, which I could have guessed. I start talking again.

"I know this is super weird. Like, really *really* weird, and kind of creepy, I am so sorry. I was just going to, like, ring the doorbell or something, but I saw that your front door was open so I—"

"Wait wait wait," she says. She closes the space between us, sitting on the couch by me. She moves gingerly, tentatively in the way you move when you know that it's going to hurt, but that you have to do it anyway. Her whole bearing has changed. She doesn't look as guarded as before, or as confused. She looks nervous.

"I left the door open? The front door?"

"Yeah."

"Shit," she says. "*Shit.* Oh that's. Hm. That's bad." She screws her eyes shut for a second, and I watch her face cycle again. She frowns, winces, lifts her eyebrows. "Oh man. There are a few things coming back to me here."

"What do you mean?"

She cracks open one eye, looks at me. My heart pounds. I *know* that eye. The last time I saw it this close was last night, in the kitchen, when it was ringed with short, dark fur.

"What do you think I mean?" she asks. "Because we'll just go with that."

I pull my right leg in, half a crisscross. I'm hit with another bout of nausea.

"Brigid," I say.

"Priya," she rasps.

"Where's the dog?"

"That *is* the question, isn't it."

"Where did the dog go, Brigid?"

"I don't have a dog." She leans her head back, eyes searching the ceiling, and chuckles. I can feel its rumble in my own chest, through the couch. I see her broken tooth again, that left canine. "Do you really want me to tell you the truth, Priya? I kind of want to tell you the truth. I'm really fucking tired of pretending I don't exist."

What's happening now feels dangerous. We're both sitting on Brigid's old sectional, but it feels like we're circling each other, tense and wary. Something about her tone makes the hair on the back of my arms prickle. I stare at her until she turns her head and meets my eyes.

"I don't know," I say.

She runs her tongue idly along the gap where her tooth used to be, then feels it with her thumb. "You got me good, dude."

I hate the way she says this, like it's not an admission from another dimension, like it doesn't change the entire list of things I have held as knowledge of the universe we live in.

"No way," I say. "There is literally no way."

"Listen," she says. "Okay, listen. I didn't lie to you or the group, exactly."

"I didn't say you did."

"I mean, I technically lied, but what was I supposed to say, you know?"

This cannot be happening.

"So when everyone just assumed it was a period thing I was like, yeah, of course that's what it is."

I hate this. I hate the direction this conversation is heading, a roller coaster detached from its tracks. Brigid's talking faster, like something has shaken loose in her.

"And, like, it kind of is. I mean, I don't bleed out, but it's a thing that happens once a month. And I lock myself in the basement and give her plenty of room to run around and enough food for a day. Give *me*, I guess. The pronouns start to get a little wacky when I think about turning."

Turning *what*?

"She thinks differently than I do. I think differently when I *am* her. And it's not a bad different, necessarily. Everything around it is bad. But the thing itself is just . . . different. It's actually kind of a relief, sometimes. Hey, are you okay?"

"Sure," I say. "Why not."

"I'm rambling. Anyway, I'm sorry."

"For what?" I hear myself say from whatever kind of dream world I must be trapped in, because I cannot be having this conversation right now.

"For knocking you down," she says. "And everything else I kind of remember doing. Probably for scaring the shit out of you. I didn't mean to." She pauses, waiting for me to say something. I don't. "I was hungry."

I stare at her for a long time. She blinks back with what looks like disinterest but is probably closer to exhaustion. When she shifts her legs, a clump of hair falls out and onto the floor, leaving a bald spot below her knee.

My brain wants to run out ahead of me, but I don't let it. I pull it back and sit in this moment. I count to five.

There is something inside of Brigid. And last night it got out.

"You don't have a dog," I say. She shakes her head.

My gears are turning, but every time my mind tries to walk through everything I've seen to that final conclusion, it stops short. It's impossible.

All of Priya Patel's cases were out of the ordinary. She always said that if all the clues pointed to something, it was probably true. You can't ignore the truth just because you don't like it. It's true whether or not you want it to be. It's true even if you think it's impossible.

"You don't have a dog," I repeat. "You *are* the dog."

"I'm a *person*." She pauses. "Most of the time."

I feel like I'm going to be sick. The thing's teeth flash white in my head. I feel its paws on my shoulders. I see the way it pulled itself upright, dark against the light from the bathroom, wrong in every way a thing can be wrong.

"You're not sick." I breathe. "You're a werewolf."

"Okay, screw you! Take a look at me! Do I look healthy to you?" she says. "You're the one who told me I was allowed to say I was chronically ill, Priya. You can't just take it back."

"I'm sorry," I say. "I'm sorry, I didn't mean it like that."

She narrows her eyes at me for a second, then they go wide. There's a sick sheen over them, too wet and glassy. She looks hurt.

"You're afraid of me."

I think of teeth snapping, muscles tensing under fur, hot breath on my skin and human eyes rolling back inside an animal's body.

"No, I'm not," I say, but I take too long to say it.

She pushes herself off the couch, padding slowly to the kitchen.

"Brigid."

She comes back with an energy drink in one hand and a jar of heavy-duty iron supplements in the other. She tosses back a handful of pills and washes the whole thing down in three gulps.

"I'm not a fucking monster, okay?" Her chest heaves. Her voice breaks when she says *monster*. "I'm *sick*."

We've stopped circling; this is a standoff. The truth is there between us, lying limp on the living room table. It's impossible. It's still the truth.

I push myself up a little farther, pulling the blanket into a ball on my lap. Making room.

"How are you feeling right now?" I ask her. She laughs wetly, brushes at her cheeks. I hadn't even noticed tears there.

"Like shit." She smiles, lopsided.

"Hey," I say. "Me too."

"I feel like I've been hit by a bus."

"Also me too."

Her grin widens and she comes to sit next to me. I let my arm brush her leg, hoping it communicates the thing I mean by it: *You're my friend. I'm not afraid of you.*

"I'm sorry," I say.

"*I'm* sorry!" She laughs. "I attacked you," she says. And then, as though it's not an *unbelievably* weird thing to say: "I didn't recognize your smell."

"Yuck," I say. "Well, *I'm* sorry I broke into your house and knocked your tooth out with a frying pan."

"Pobody's nerfect," she says, slurping the energy drink. A laugh bubbles out of me. She holds the drink out in my direction and I shake my head. "Hey also, the fridge is *rank*."

"That is definitely not my fault!" I say. "Why did you leave all those steaks in there to rot?"

"For today," she says. "I'm usually just out for like eighteen hours, maybe twenty-four. It burns a lot of calories. Like, all of them."

"You were gone for three days, Brigid."

"I know," she says softly. "I saw when I woke up. Not so good."

I cover my face with both hands, moaning. "This is so weird. You know how weird it is, right?"

"Yeah, I know. I'm meeting you in person. You're at my *house*."

"You're a werewolf!" I yell.

"I have lycanthropy," she corrects.

"Right, sorry, I don't know the terminology here," I say. "Are you not cool with that word?"

"Werewolf?"

I nod.

"Nah, it's fine. It's accurate," she says. She glances at me again. "Sometimes I think that I hold myself at arm's length from myself."

"Mm."

"I don't know, I don't even know what that means."

"I do. I think I do it, too."

"Yeah."

She motions at my legs and I lift them softly, let her scoot underneath and drape them over her lap. I feel a sudden burst of affection in my chest, bright like biting into an orange slice.

"Can we start over?" I laugh. "I didn't think meeting you in person would go quite like this."

"Road trip, right?"

"Right, exactly."

"Well, I'm starving," she says.

"Please don't eat the steak."

"Yeah, it's going in the dumpster."

". . . I did, uh. I did feed it to the—you—last night."

"You fed me the rancid steaks."

"Unfortunately."

"That would explain all the diarrhea this morning."

"Information I for sure needed and wanted."

"Ugh, I have so much stuff to clean up." She groans.

"Sorry," I say. "The carpet stains were all me."

"Oh, thanks."

"Anytime."

"So, in the spirit of starting over . . ." She raises her eyebrows at me, once, like she's too tired to give the expression any more space on her face than that. "Do you wanna order a pizza? Or twelve?"

"I will eat half a pizza, max."

"Rad, eight pizzas it is."

"That seems like a lot."

"I'll put it on my parents' credit card."

"Not what I meant."

"I mean, I told you I was hungry."

"You should make sure you pace yourself," I say. "I read somewhere that if you eat too much when you haven't eaten in a while, you'll make yourself sick."

"I'll take it under consideration, doc."

That one word ties her together now, the Brigid that lives inside my computer and the Brigid sitting right in front of me. She's my friend. I *know* her.

I try not to think too hard about the third Brigid right now.

"Do you have your phone?" she asks. "I really don't want to get up."

I unlock it and pass it in her direction. "Where's yours?"

"No idea," she says. "Dead somewhere. Did you see it in the foyer?"

"No, but I found your keys there," I say. "And your sports bra."

She nods. "Car, probably. I'll look later."

"Can I borrow a charger?"

"Yeah, totally." She makes a face at me. "Do I talk to a real person on the phone or just put in the online order?"

"Online," we both say in unison. We stare at each other for a second, and then break down into giggles.

Yeah. I know her.

**oof ouch my bones (ONLINE – 4)**

**katie (fyodorbrostoevsky):**
| Oh thank god!!!!!

**Seb (mereextravagancy):**
| She scared us!
| Bridge? Are you there? You scared us

**Spook (spookyspoony):**
| Awesome! I told you it'd be okay

**katie (fyodorbrostoevsky):**
| I don't think they're there

**al (thorswagnarok):**
| it's like 12:30 my time and I have school tomorrow so I should really go 2 bed
| but I just wanted to say:
| hell yeah

**Seb (mereextravagancy):**
| HELL yeah
| Night, al

**al (thorswagnarok):**
| love yall

**katie (fyodorbrostoevsky):**
| we love you too!

al (thorswagnarok) is offline.

Spook (spookyspoony) is offline.

**Seb (mereextravagancy):**
| They must be asleep

**katie (fyodorbrostoevsky):**
| they'll see it in the AM

**Seb (mereextravagancy):**
| Are you going to bed?

**katie (fyodorbrostoevsky):**
| no, having a bad night. knife to the intestines kinda

| night. not gonna sleep for a while
| you?

**Seb (mereextravagancy):**
| I could stay up
| For you? Easy.

**katie (fyodorbrostoevsky):**
| :)

**Seb (mereextravagancy):**
| :)

# 15

**Sometimes you just know when you click with someone, when**
you realize the two of you were meant to find your way to each other.
When they say something a little stupid when they introduce themselves, or make a joke about an obscure interest you have, too, or ask
you a question so thoughtful it tilts the axis of your world, just a little.
Sometimes you just look at someone in that moment and think, *yes,*
*they're going to be important to me. They're going to change the shape my life*
*takes. We're going to mean something to each other.*

This is the feeling I get as I watch Brigid try to fold an entire
meat-lover's pizza in half, give up, and stack four slices directly on top
of one another to shove them into her mouth.

"Oh my God," I say.

"What?" she says. Her hair falls into her face, a chunk of it still
caked solid with that white paste. It smacks into her cheek, and she
shakes her head back, annoyed.

"Are you going to unhinge your jaw, or . . . ?"

"I'm not a snake."

"No, that would be ridiculous."

"Da wmm wa sth?"

"I don't know what you're saying."

She swallows in a gulp, washing the pizza down with more of her
energy drink. She begins to stack the remaining four pieces. It's mes-
merizing and horrifying. "I said, do you wanna watch something?"

"Yeah, that sounds nice," I say. "You should probably find your phone first, though."

"Why?"

"I don't know, a lot of people were worried."

"Aw."

"Wait. Wait, hold on."

". . . What."

"Oh my God, is this what you were going to tell me on Sunday?"

"Yeah," she says. "In hindsight, I'm kind of glad I turned. You never would have believed me."

"I thought you were gonna . . . come out to me or something."

"I'm *already* out to you."

"Yeah, but I couldn't think of anything else."

"That's fair."

There's a pause. I press the issue. "Shouldn't you at least call your parents to let them know you're okay?"

Something in her face shutters. She shrugs. "Yeah, maybe."

"Where are they, by the way?" I wonder if it's a question I'm allowed to ask.

"Brazil," she says. "They're gonna be there until June."

I try to gauge her expression. "And they left you here alone?"

"I mean, I'm an adult," she says. I make a face, and she makes one back. "Technically. I still live here because everything's set up in the basement, but I'm fine on my own."

"Right," I say, but I can't make it sound convincing.

"Like, I—didn't get to move out for college, okay? And it was pretty fucking devastating, and I haven't been able to convince them to let me leave. I just want my own space. Like, my own little apartment with reinforced doors and basement access where I can go to work and classes and shit."

"The millennial dream," I say. "Wait. Zienniel? Zillennial?"

"What! That is not a thing!"

"I read it on Al's blog!"

"That doesn't make it real!"

"What are we, then?"

"Priya, my love, I've been waiting for you to ask me that."

I laugh, and Brigid cracks another lazy smile. I try to remember what we were talking about, wind my way back mentally to the conversation.

"Your own place," I say.

"My own place," she echoes. "I convinced my parents to give me a trial run. Three months."

"Right."

"It's a win-win," she says. "They get to go on their retirement trip. Vacation for the first time in a decade. I get the place to myself."

"So you're not calling your parents," I say, voice flat.

"I can do this. I've *been* doing this nine years running, so." Her hair falls into her face again, and she pushes it halfheartedly with the back of her hand. "I usually lock everything," she finishes. I know she means to sound assured, but she just sounds bone-tired.

I grab another slice of the pineapple pizza, which Brigid called "a crime against God and nature" when we ordered it. It's my second piece in the time it's taken her to eat a pizza and a half. The thought of that much dough in my stomach is making me a little sick.

"Nine years is a long time," I say.

"Yeah," she says. "But not as long as the rest of my life. Hopefully."

"Did you . . ." I try to think about how to word this question. "What happened then? When you were a kid."

"Nothing happened," she says. "Do you mean, did a wolf-man come running out of the moors and bite me, *American Werewolf in London* style?"

I nod.

"Not that I remember, no. I mean, I could have blocked it out? I remember getting really sick. And then it just started . . . happening."

"Do your parents . . . ?"

"Nope," she says. She opens the next pizza box and starts stacking slices. "I remember sitting up on that landing when I was twelve years old, listening to them argue. Listening to them going back and forth about who to blame for the thing that I turn into."

She pauses. This whole time she's been talking like she's describing something distant, something that happened to someone else. When she turns to face me, I see her shoulders relax. She seems to remember herself.

"You have questions," she says.

"I have about a billion," I say.

"Alright, hit me, baby."

"Really?"

"Yeah, why not? I'm a lore *expert*. AMA, rapid fire."

"Full moon?"

"Nothing to do with it. Sometimes it's a full moon when I turn, but that's just a coincidence."

"Silver bullet?" I pause. "Sorry."

"Would kill me," she says. "But like . . . It'd kill you too. It's a bullet."

"Are you really good at basketball and/or lacrosse?"

"I *was* on the field hockey team in high school until they kicked me off for missing too many games. But when I was thirteen my dad accidentally hit me in the face with a basketball when I wasn't paying attention. So . . . mixed bag on that one."

I laugh.

"What, that's all you've got?"

"Uh . . ." I think about what I want to know. "Okay, are there . . . other werewolves out there? There must be, right?"

She props her elbow up on the couch cushion, leaning onto her hand. "I've spent a long time trying to figure that out," she says. "There must be. I know there must be, but I haven't met any. Google has not helped me at all. I tried posting something about it on Reddit, but everyone thought I was joking and they removed my question because they said it was inappropriate for the subreddit."

"Which one were you posting on?"

"A medical issues subreddit." She groans. "I cannot believe not one fellow lycanthrope saw that post before it got taken down! Every culture in the *world* has legends and stories about this, did you know that?"

I shake my head. Her eyes light up, just a little, and she scoots in closer to me.

"I started with Irish because my mom's Irish—not, like, from Ireland Irish, but her ancestors. I worked my way through all of Western Europe, especially France and Germany, and went on to Russia."

She never gets to talk about this, I realize. She's kept everything locked inside her for a whole decade.

"I've looked at Asian culture, South American, Middle Eastern, Hebrew—"

"Okay," I interrupt. "I know there aren't werewolves in the Bible."

"A-ha! That's what you think, Priya!" She leans in. "According to a medieval rabbi, Benjamin was a werewolf."

"Benjamin? Twelve tribes of Israel, Benjamin?"

"Mmhmm."

"That's crazy," I hear myself say.

"Yeah, crazy," Brigid says. "Why else would they think it was unsafe for him to go to Egypt, huh? Travel's tough when you turn into a wolf every month."

"Makes sense to me."

"I mean, who knows. The rabbi also thought our feet grew between our shoulder blades and that we had to drink human blood in order to turn back, so, grain of salt."

"You don't?"

"No!"

"You could tell me anything and I'd believe you. I mean, I saw a werewolf last night, I'm in a believing mood."

She laughs for real this time, a loud, throaty rasp that ends with an honest-to-goodness snort. I instantly want to make her do it again.

"What?" I ask.

"Nothing, I just—" She looks at me again, but she can't hold my gaze without breaking into giggles. "Just, when you said, *I saw a werewolf last night*, my brain just went *you did??* And then I was like . . . oh. Me. You were talking about me."

"You haven't told anyone about this, have you?" I ask.

She looks up at me, shakes her head. "Not for real," she says. "We were in Philly before we moved out here. I actually told all of my friends at school there, but I was eleven, and kids say shit like that all the time. They homeschooled me until high school, here, because I was like, turning every month and they didn't know how it worked. But I also think that they were worried I was going to tell everyone. Like, hey guys, new kid here, what's Bellows like? Did you know we had to move here because I wouldn't stop turning into a werewolf? Wanna hang out?"

I laugh. Her eyes crinkle, clearly pleased that her joke landed.

"Is it . . ." She stops herself before she even starts, tearing off one of the pizza box's folded corners. "Is it weird that when I say it, I still kind of feel like I'm lying? Like, I've been lying for so long that actually saying it out loud feels wrong, too?"

I lean back. "I don't know," I say, honestly. "I don't think so. But

I'm glad you told me."

"Kinda had to," she says. "I don't trust you or anything, you just happened to break into my house."

"O-kay, first off—"

"Yes, Priya? First off?"

"There was no breaking! Just entering!"

"That'll hold up in court."

"What, are you gonna press charges now?"

"No way," she says. "You would do so badly in prison."

I laugh, covering my face with my hands.

"You'd straight-up die, dude."

"I can't defend myself," I say. "Let's just watch something."

She searches my face, still smiling. "I'm glad I told you, too," she says. She pulls up Netflix and tosses me the remote. "You pick."

"Something with werewolves?" I ask, starting to scroll.

"Absolutely the fuck not," she says. When the clump of hair falls into her face for a third time, she lets out a scream.

"Oh my God! This toothpaste! Okay, I can't take this anymore, I'll be right back."

"What?"

She hauls herself off the couch, wincing. "Don't worry about it." She shuffles down the hallway, toward the bathroom, and I hear her voice rasp. "Decide what we're gonna watch!"

I think back to one of the first messages I sent to Brigid instead of the other way around: "You watch ToF too!?" *True or False* was our mutual obsession when we were both in high school, a buddy detective dramedy where a straitlaced cop and a compulsively lying former grifter teamed up to solve cybercrimes. Brigid and I both knew that they were madly in love with each other. Obviously.

"Hey Brigid," I call. "Is *True or False* on Netflix?"

In reply, I hear the distant, low buzz of electric clippers, a sound I recognize from side-by-side haircuts with Suresh in my parents' bathroom.

I push myself slowly off the couch for the first time all day. The pain starts throbbing again, and I limp in the direction of the buzzing. I should find some ice packs, ask Brigid if she has any in her freezer. I'm starting to feel hot, so I go back to the cabinet and shake out another handful of ibuprofen. It won't touch the pain I'm feeling, but it'll prevent a fever, maybe stop the swelling from getting worse.

I hobble down that same hallway, toward that same bathroom. The door is open. I walk in just in time to see Brigid shearing a strip of hair off the side of her head with total disinterest. The clump of brown, caked with white, falls to the floor, adding to the pile of hair that's already covering it. It looks like someone tried to install shag carpeting.

"Hey," I say. "Whatcha doing."

"That wasn't gonna wash out," she says, pointing. "And now I have an undercut. The other queer haircut."

I stare.

"I mean, I think I actually had a bisexual bob already. I'm not sure. I guess hair doesn't make you queer, but it can be, like, a marker," she says. Her hair is mangled, shaved back in an unsteady line.

"Are you also trying to look like you got your hair caught in a garbage disposal?" I ask.

"Hey!" she says. She looks in the mirror again, considering. "Yeah this isn't an undercut, is it."

"It is not."

"Well, alright then," she says, turning the clippers on again and shaving off another line. My heart jumps into my throat in panic. I've had the same haircut for the last eight years, a blunt cut that falls to my chest when I leave it down, long enough to pull into a braid or a ponytail to keep it out of my face. We tried bangs when I was twelve, and it was the worst six months of my life. Well. Sort of.

"Oh my God," I say. "Stop, you're stressing me out."

"I'll just shave it," she says. Her breathing picks up. "But first I have to. Sit down."

She sways and starts to lower herself to the floor, gripping the sink, the edge of the tub.

"Whoa, whoa, whoa," I say, reaching out and switching the clippers off before she drops them.

She nods at me before screwing her eyes shut.

"Are you okay?"

"Yeah, dizzy," she says. She takes in a slow breath through her nose and lets it out her mouth. I put the toilet seat down and sit, too.

She looks at me without moving her head, out the corners of her eyes. "Did this freak you out more than the werewolf thing?"

I laugh. "About the same."

"It's just hair. It grows back."

"I guess you're right."

She leans back between my legs, lifting the clippers up toward me.

"What?"

"Wanna fix it for me?"

"I had bad hand-eye coordination before my hands got all shaky from Lyme," I say. "You really don't want me to."

"That's what that grate on the front is for," she says. "It's a fail-safe."

"No failure is safe from me."

"My arm's getting tired."

I take the clippers from her, feel the device's weight in my hands. The plastic guard has long teeth, a *2* etched into its plastic side. This is such a colossally bad idea. And there's something intimate about it, too, something that feels strange to do for someone I met in person a few hours ago.

"Are you sure?" I ask.

"Hell yeah, dude," she says. "Buzz me."

"Don't say it like that."

"Buzz me!"

"You're so weird."

She reaches up and turns the clippers on for me. And I decide right now that when it comes to Brigid, maybe it's best to just go along with her.

I put my left hand on her head, gingerly position the clippers at the base of her hair before chickening out. She gathers her hair and pulls it up so that I can see the nape of her neck. I take a deep breath, and I slide the clippers up. They really do sound like a garbage disposal. I'm sure I'm doing this wrong, but I'm left with a clump of chin-length hair in my hand.

"This is for you," I say, dropping it on her lap.

"Gross!" She laughs.

I take another swipe. It's kind of satisfying, watching the hair fall away. Brigid starts humming a song I don't recognize, and I find myself getting into a sort of rhythm.

"Hey, can you leave it a little longer up top? That might look kinda cool."

"Absolutely not," I say, buzzing the top. "I don't know how to do that."

The bathroom is already disgusting so I just keep dropping the hair on the floor, brushing it off my lap. I have to rest a couple of times, but Brigid is patient. I push her ear back, biting my lip, and hope that I don't cut it clean off, even though I know that's impossible with these things.

I nick her ear anyway, and she hisses.

"Sorry, sorry!"

"It's okay," she says. "Is it bleeding?"

"No, just red," I say. "Razor burn. Here, turn around so I can get the front."

She repositions herself slowly. When she's finally facing me, I can't stop myself from bursting out laughing.

"Okay, you can't do that! The person cutting my hair can't just start laughing when she sees how it looks!"

"I'm sorry," I say. I start laughing again. "Here, one second."

I pull my phone out of my pocket and snap a picture of her. Her hair is buzzed up to the crown of her head, where the rest of it hangs down into her face. I turn the phone so she can see it, and she presses her lips together. I can tell she's trying not to laugh.

"You look like a cyberpunk Leo DiCaprio trying to jam facial recognition software," I say. That does it. She bursts out laughing, too, covering her face with her hands.

"I look like Dimitri from *Anastasia* got into a fight with a lawn-mower," she howls. "And lost."

"Let me fix it," I say, pulling at her hands. She closes her eyes, schooling her face into a neutral expression, but the second I hit the button on the clippers, she lets out another peal of laughter. I start laughing, too.

"What's funny?!" I say.

"I don't know!" She laughs.

I push her hair back out of her eyes with my left hand, gently, and slide the clippers up past her widow's peak. My hands are sore, so I turn the clippers off again, put them in my lap while I rub a knuckle into my right palm, flex my fingers.

"Sorry," I say. "Give me a second."

She opens her eyes. "You say sorry too much."

"Sorry," I say automatically. She frowns at me sternly.

"I'm . . . not sorry?"

"No, you're not," she says. "You've got nothing to be sorry for."

"Yeah, I guess not," I say. I look at my hands, gauging if I'll be able to finish. When I glance up, Brigid is looking at me.

"What?" I say.

"You've got resting nice face," she says. "Contemplative."

"Resting what?"

"Do people ask you for directions a lot?"

"Yeah, they used to," I say. "I'm not really out and about these days."

"Right. Sorry."

I grin. "You've got nothing to be sorry for."

"You got me." She smiles. "Hey, do you need me to finish this?"

"No, I've got it," I say.

"Cool," she says. "And for the record, I knew you would."

"Would what?"

"Have resting nice face."

"Why?"

She closes her eyes, brings her arms around her knees. "Because you're nice."

I'm grateful she doesn't see the way my eyes tear up. It's embarrassing.

"We'll see how nice I am after I ruin your hair," I say, switching the clippers back on. She laughs.

"Do your worst, Priya."

"Oh, I am."

When I finish, I put the clippers down and brush the loose hairs away. I love the way a buzz cut feels against your hands when you skim them back and forth, bristly and ticklish.

"Tiger fur," I say out loud.

"Huh?" Brigid says.

"That's what we used to call it when we were little and my brother would get a buzz cut. My sister and I would rub his head until he yelled at us."

Brigid reaches up and travels the breadth of her skull with her fingers, rubs them back and forth. She grins, wide and awestruck.

"Oh, holy shit. This rules."

"Right?"

"It feels amazing. How does it look?"

"You're actually pulling it off."

"Yeah?"

I turn my camera to selfie mode and pass her my phone.

"Oh, I love this," she says. "Wow."

"You look like the girl from *Deadpool*," I say.

"That is literally the biggest compliment, thank you." She turns her back to me again, angles the phone.

"Say cheese," she says, grinning with her broken tooth on display.

"Wait, hold on—" I hear the shutter click.

"Well that one's not gonna look great," she says. It clicks again. I frown. Another click. I finally give in, brandishing the clippers, and smile.

"It's perfect," she says. "We should send it to the group."

**oof ouch my bones (ONLINE – 1)**

**Priya (paranormaldetective):**

Hi friends

[IMG_1703.JPEG]

Brigid squints at my phone. "You have a text," she says. "Someone named Suresh is asking if you also got diagnosed with dumb idiot disease this morning."

"That's nice."

"Your brother?"

"Unfortunately," I say. "So . . . should we clean up in here, or . . ."

"Nah. We should watch *True or False*," she says.

"They took it off Netflix," I say, disappointed. "A true cyber-crime."

"Oh no . . ." says Brigid. She stands, grabs my elbows to help me to my feet. "Good thing I've got all three seasons on iTunes."

"Not, like, Amazon?"

"And support evil overlord Jeff Bezos? Fat chance."

"iTunes is for old people."

"I'm literally one year older than you," she says.

"You're an old woman."

"Well, we're both hobbling over to the couch, so I'm not sure what to tell you."

"My joints hurt, you're getting winded from walking . . . I guess we're both grandmas."

"Correct. I need more pizza." She picks up an entire box and settles it on her lap.

"It's cold," I say.

"Duh," she says. "It's even better like that."

"You're insane. It's insane how wrong you are."

"Okay, pineapple psychopath."

She grabs the remote.

"Which episode are you thinking?" I ask. "I've been meaning to rewatch—"

"The one where Evie makes contact with her old friend from her con artist days for a case but gets sucked back in?" Brigid says excitedly.

"And Carlos has to remind her what they've been working toward during their whole partnership!" I finish.

"Because they're in love!"

"Obviously they're in love. They've been in love since day one," I say. "That is exactly the episode, how did you know?"

"You reblogged that gifset last week."

"Ugh, that moment," I say.

"He fixes her shirt collar!" she says. "It's so gentle!"

"Poetic cinema," I say. "Okay, season two, here we come."

"I should warn you that I'm a talker," she says.

I shrug. "We'll turn on the subtitles."

"Oh," she says. "Oh, we might really be soulmates."

I grin and hit PLAY.

# 16

**I get grounded.**

I shouldn't be surprised, and I guess I'm not. I'm furious. I never thought I'd have to deal with this again after I left home. I'd finally had the space to make my own rules.

My body's already had me under house arrest for months, and there's nowhere in town for me to go—no friends around to hang out with and no parties to miss. My adventure to Brigid's has left me feeling like I have the flu. I stared Suresh down when he and my dad picked me up, silently begging my brother to let me ride with him. Instead, I sat in silence with my father for an hour, watching the road signs tick by as my vision blurred. I'd hoped he would pick me up instead of Mom, but when he looked at me and said, "you really worried us, Priya," I realized that his quiet disappointment was much, much worse.

My mother knows I have nowhere to go, so she takes my laptop. It might be the cruelest thing she's ever done to me.

"You can't do that." I hate that it comes out as a whine, childish and unflattering.

The reading glasses slip down her nose as she lifts it off my lap, closing it so quickly that I flinch. "You can't go to Pennsylvania overnight without telling us."

"I'm an adult."

"You're under our roof, Priya," she says.

"What about my schoolwork?" I ask, getting desperate.

"What about it?"

"I have—I have an independent study for my incomplete class!" I lie.

"Then you can always ring people for research, can't you?"

"No one does that!"

"I'm sure you'll figure it out."

"Dad!" I call. It's a weak move.

"What?" he shouts from downstairs.

"Can you tell Mom I need my computer to do my homework?"

"She needs to study!" comes my father's voice. I point out my door.

"She is grounded! I am taking her computer away!"

"Use the kitchen desktop, Priya," he shouts. "Good try!"

Later that night, with my dad hovering over my shoulder and poking his finger at the screen, I print out everything I need to finish Human Biology. My dad gives me two enthusiastic thumbs up. I press my mouth into a thin line that might look like a smile if you squint. I hate that he watches me do this, as though I can't be trusted to actually finish my work on my own. I also hate that he's right.

Finishing this class feels like trying to hold on to something that's already slipped through my fingers. I think about med school's long hours and frantic pace, about standing on my feet or staying awake for days at a time. I know I can't do it. It used to be this future dream I could log hours in service of, but now it's out of my grasp completely. I can't visualize it anymore. It seems as ridiculous as saying, what if I could fly? What if, in three years, I became a chicken?

And besides, all I can think about when I look over the notes on cell makeup is Brigid. What changed her cells? Was this coded into her DNA, or did she contract it? What happened to her, or didn't happen?

I feel my phone start to vibrate and sneak a look at the screen, hoping that my mom doesn't remember that the internet *also* works on my phone. I smile. Speaking of impossible things.

It's Brigid. She's calling me, like an old person. I grit my teeth and hoist myself out of the chair, shuffling toward the living room.

"Hello?" I say.

"Shit. One second."

"Hey, you found your phone."

"Oh man, this is weird, isn't it." Brigid's voice is fuller than before, but the rasp is still there.

"It's a little weird, yeah."

"I didn't actually mean to call you, I was trying to text but I'm also cleaning the bathroom and I've got hair all over my fingers and—oh shit, I just." I hear spitting. "I got some in my mouth."

"You couldn't put the phone down for the fifteen minutes it'd take to clean your house?"

"No? Who does that?"

I hear a rattling noise. I'm not sure I want to know what she's doing.

"Listen, while you're here, have you ever done yoga?"

"I have not. Why . . . ?"

"I don't know. I was googling stuff that might help with muscle soreness in your entire body. Like—you know when you work out for the first time after you've been sitting on your ass for a couple of weeks?"

I think back to the first few days of soccer season. "Yeah, I know exactly that feeling."

"Yeah it's that, but twice as bad, and everywhere, and also in my bones."

"Oof," I say.

"Ouch," she says automatically. I hear the smile in her voice.

"You don't seem like a yoga kind of girl."

"I KNOW!" she says. "Yes, this is exactly why I've never tried it. I'm not an Instagram model, I'm a walking disaster."

"That should be the next generation of Instagram influencer. Insta stars: they're just like you!"

"Instagram stars: instead of having their period, their bodies forcibly shape-shift once a month and sometimes they eat things that aren't, strictly speaking, edible!"

"So universally relatable!"

"So . . . yoga?"

"Wait," I say, shifting the phone to my other ear. "Are you asking me if I want to do yoga? I can barely move."

"Well we could try, like, geriatric yoga."

"That's not something I particularly want to look up."

"I'll do it." Her voice sounds far away, echoing in the bathroom. "Gentle . . . yoga . . . for old . . . bones . . . that's what I'm googling. Hey sweet, sixteen million results, Priya. That's—oh *shit*—"

There's a loud clattering, followed by the "end call" tone.

*So that didn't sound good*, I text her.

I get a text back half an hour later.

everthing is ok

Ever thing?

no, everthing

everthing

aw shit

i think i broke the ke

I'd say that seems likely

oh God

am i one of those people who has to use "u" now

Yes

Hang on, do you have actual, physical keys on your phone?

mavbe!

How is that even possible??

You can't even buy those anymore!

with God all things are possible

so what's up

tell me u have better news than the horrible monster i have become

(someone who uses "u")

Nope

Just working on the bio stuff I didn't finish last semester

snoozetown

You're telling me

I'm stupid now

ur not stupid

My brain is really and truly broken

I'm not just like, saying that

I can't focus the way I used to

:/

ur still one of the smartest people i know

Thanks, pal

It just feels like I don't have...

Anything anymore

u mean u don't have external success markers

ouch

i'm being ur therapist

Please no

i mean... according to ur metric what do i have

u know

> i go to RCC, seb takes online classes

> what do any of us have

>> Well that's different

> how come?

>> ...because I'm only allowed to say mean things about myself

> bingo

I put the phone down on the counter. She's right. It is different when it's me because I've always thought of myself as smarter than other people. It's what I've clung to since elementary school, when they put me in the advanced class for the first time. I was so proud of it, and so proud of the way my parents' faces lit up when they found out.

But there are holes in my memory like swiss cheese now, an off-and-on fog in my mind, so maybe I'm not destined for anything at all. Maybe the high school honors didn't mean anything in the first place.

And maybe that's okay.

Maybe it's okay to just focus on being a person. Maybe that's enough.

My phone buzzes, and it's not my texts that light up. It's the Tumblr app.

**bigforkhands:**
i'm sorry, i couldn't take it anymore
i had to switch back to my laptop, i am not nearly chill enough to use "u" that many times in a row

**paranormaldetective:**
Honestly it feels more normal to be messaging you in the app

**bigforkhands:**
familiarity

**paranormaldetective:**
Yeah
But you're right. I know you're right. It just makes me feel like a bad person.

**bigforkhands:**

no, i get it

it's something i had to get over, too

**paranormaldetective:**

you are extremely smart

not saying anything about community college, but you are

**bigforkhands:**

thanks dude

so i

ugh

this is gonna get long

**paranormaldetective:**

I don't mind

**bigforkhands:**

you sure?

**paranormaldetective:**

Yeah, go ahead

Just do what you usually do: start typing without thinking

**bigforkhands:**

asshole!!!

**paranormaldetective:**

:)

**bigforkhands:**

yeah, ok

when i was 17 and everyone else was applying to college or figuring out trade school or the jobs they were gonna take

my parents did not say a word

i kept waiting for them to bring it up or imagining us taking that cute like, family bonding college tour of the east coast

where my dad took me to his alma mater and gushed over it and my mom took me to hers and shit-talked his or whatever

and we'd just road trip and drive up and down the coast

and go on boring campus tours and make jokes about how ugly the dorms were and talk to students about how they liked it there, whatever

i was really into animation or maybe like, graphic design? idk

it just got later and later and we just... did not talk about it

and i think i knew, then

i think deep down, i felt it

but i decided to apply on my own anyway? i sent stuff off to a bunch of programs and i got a portfolio together for this animation program at carnegie mellon

i didn't tell anyone. not my parents or my friends or my blog. i think i was scared i'd jinx it if i said anything out loud? so i didn't

and i got in

and i just... got this one fucking moment of pure joy that no one could take from me, for four and a half minutes

i got this huge packet in the mail from CM and i was biting my lip to stop myself from smiling because i was good enough, and ready to leave, and just like, humming with excitement

for those few minutes anything in the world was possible

so I took the packet to my parents and i just watched my dad's eyes fill up with tears

and my mom got real quiet

and she just slid the packet out of my hands and put it on the table and said "oh, brigid."

and i just started crying

**paranormaldetective:**

Oh Brigid

**bigforkhands:**

yeah, it was kinda like that

haha

CM isn't even that far, is the worst part, but it's far enough

**paranormaldetective:**

I'm really sorry

That's so, so hard

**bigforkhands:**

yeah, i guess

there isn't exactly an animation program anywhere in bellows county

but there are other things

it's not what i would have picked for myself, but it's home, i guess

**paranormaldetective:**

A dorm wouldn't exactly have a great place to transform

**bigforkhands:**

i wouldn't think so, haha

**paranormaldetective:**

If it helps it sucked sharing a room with a stranger

**bigforkhands:**

eh, I think i would have made it work

but there's no point in thinking about what ifs or trying to figure out why i am the way that i am

it's not gonna fix anything

**paranormaldetective:**

I'm still sorry

**bigforkhands:**

thanks, priya

yeah

i am too

-------

**When Tuesday rolls around, I weigh my options:** In general, Suresh is more likely to do me a favor, but after last week, I probably owe *him* one. But Kiki is easy to bribe, so I promise to buy her an extra-large jar of Nutella and listen to her sing her lines in exchange for an hour of laptop access. She throws herself onto the bed next to me, sighing loudly until I ask her what's wrong.

"Nothing," she says. A pause. "It's just my nemesis."

I try my hardest not to laugh at her, because she's completely serious. "You're fourteen," I say. "How can you already have a nemesis?"

"She's in the chorus with me too," she says, playing with her hair. "And she thinks she's *so* much better than me just because she has a solo. And because she's, like, got this perfect, swishy blonde hair and perfect skin, and stupid, perfect face. Like . . . she's not even playing a character with a name. Pretty much none of us are."

"Mmhmm," I say.

"And she's always, like, *staring* at me. I think it's an intimidation tactic because she always starts glaring at me when I look back. So maybe . . . *I'm* the one being intimidating!"

I glance at her. She's wide-eyed and wearing a sparkly choker. She rolls over onto her stomach, kicking her legs.

"So, what do you think?"

"What do I think about what?" I ask.

"PRIYA!" she screeches. "Were you even listening?"

"I don't get what the problem is!" I say. "The pretty girl in the chorus looks at you sometimes."

"But in a *judgy* way," she says. "To throw me off my game."

"So focus up on your game," I say. "The best revenge is doing a really good job, right?"

"Ugh," she says. "What's the fun in that?"

I shrug. It's five minutes to six, and I raise my eyebrows, motioning toward Kiki's laptop. She sighs, pushing it toward me.

"Fine," she says. "But that didn't help me at all."

"Let me know when she does something more heinous," I say.

"Are you making fun of me?"

"Like maybe giving you a really intimidating high-five," I say. "Or asking you about your history homework, but in an intimidating way."

She throws a pillow at my face. "Stop it!"

"Okay, okay." I laugh, pulling up the chat.

**oof ouch my bones (ONLINE – 8)**

> **Spook (spookyspoony):**
> Hi everyone!

**Priya (paranormaldetective):**
| Happy Tuesday!!

**lee (typhoonsss):**
| finally!

**bridge (bigforkhands):**
| so how is the crew feeling this fine afternoon/evening/
| night (depending on your time zone)?

**Spook (spookyspoony):**
| bad

**Priya (paranormaldetective):**
| Bad

**lee (typhoonsss):**
| not good

**katie (fyodorbrostoevsky):**
| I'm actually feeling pretty good this week!!

**Priya (paranormaldetective):**
| That's great, katie!

**lee (typhoonsss):**
| yes!

**Seb (mereextravagancy):**
| Feeling like I want to avenge my father's untimely death

**Spook (spookyspoony):**
| Ok, hamlet

**Max (quintuplevampire):**
| Hi everyone I'm also bad

**katie (fyodorbrostoevsky):**
| Max!!!!

**Max (quintuplevampire):**
| Katie!

**bridge (bigforkhands):**
| hi also bad, i'm dad

**al (thorswagnarok):**
| BWAHH BWAHH BWAHH

**Priya (paranormaldetective):**
| STOP

**katie (fyodorbrostoevsky):**

> my dad did that ALL THE TIME when I was a kid and I
> hated it EVERY SINGLE TIME

**Seb (mereextravagancy):**

> Can we kick Brigid out of the discord, or

**al (thorswagnarok):**

> she just got back!!! we missed her!!

**Spook (spookyspoony):**

> If anyone should be banished for their crimes it should
> be Seb

**lee (typhoonsss):**

> no banishment please

**katie (fyodorbrostoevsky):**

> Brigid and priya, how was your hangout??

**lee (typhoonsss):**

> yes!!

**Seb (mereextravagancy):**

> I am so profoundly jealous you live close by

**bridge (bigforkhands):**

> it was so rad!!!!

**Priya (paranormaldetective):**

> It was great! We mostly watched true or false and ate
> pizza

**Seb (mereextravagancy):**

> That show is SO CORNY

**bridge (bigforkhands):**

> it's extremely bad but then, on a deeper, more profound
> level, it's extremely good

**Spook (spookyspoony):**

> Oh my God I LOVED that show in high school
> They're in love

**Priya (paranormaldetective):**

> YES

**bridge (bigforkhands):**

> THANK YOU

**Max (quintuplevampire):**
| Embarrassing y'all

**katie (fyodorbrostoevsky):**
| Uh I've never even heard of this show

**Priya (paranormaldetective):**
| _join us_

**Spook (spookyspoony):**
| I should do a rewatch

**bridge (bigforkhands):**
| before we get into the weeds with TOF
| uh, I feel like I should say something?

**al (thorswagnarok):**
| shoot

**lee (typhoonsss):**
| go ahead, hon

**bridge (bigforkhands):**
| i'm really sorry I made you all worry!!
| i was just sick
| but sick in that way where you're really, really tired of being sick, you know
| and I couldn't get to my account to update anyone
| these are all excuses, what I really wanted to say was thank you
| for all the messages, and memes you sent to cheer me up
| i had like, 35 messages in my inbox when I logged back on
| it made me cry haha

**lee (typhoonsss):**
| oh, hon!

**Seb (mereextravagancy):**
| Bridge!!

**katie (fyodorbrostoevsky):**
| of course we care!! how could we not!!

**al (thorswagnarok):**
| you did freak us out though

> b/c we love you

**Priya (paranormaldetective):**
> We're always here for you

**Max (quintuplevampire):**
> Anytime dude

**Spook (spookyspoony):**
> ^^^

**Seb (mereextravagancy):**
> <3 <3 <3

**bridge (bigforkhands):**
> <3 <3 <3
> !!!

**lee (typhoonsss):**
> i know what you mean, though
> i'm so tired
> not because it's late here, it just gets so exhausting
> not to complain or anything

**Spook (spookyspoony):**
> That is literally what this group is for

**al (thorswagnarok):**
> you ok, mum?

**lee (typhoonsss):**
> aw
> um, sort of!
> it's just been a really hard week to hang in here
> i just would like to not be in pain for a solid day, you know?

**Spook (spookyspoony):**
> I almost can't remember what it was like, before
> Honestly

**Seb (mereextravagancy):**
> Yeah

**Max (quintuplevampire):**
> What before haha

**katie (fyodorbrostoevsky):**

I feel like the fed-up-ness is what gets you, you know

**Priya (paranormaldetective):**

Yes

**lee (typhoonsss):**

absolutely

**katie (fyodorbrostoevsky):**

the mental drain of making doctors appointments and dealing with insurance and doing like, basic freaking tasks when you feel like crap

**bridge (bigforkhands):**

where it feels like your brain's shorted out, yeah

**lee (typhoonsss):**

the pain just hits this limit at a certain point when you think, I cannot keep living like this

except... you do

**Seb (mereextravagancy):**

Yeah, it feels like water drip torture sometimes?

The pain, the doctors that don't listen to you, dealing with insurance, using a cane, having to stay home from yet another event

Any one of these things is annoying, but you think you should be able to handle it, because other people have it so much worse

But each drip is a little bit worse

**Priya (paranormaldetective):**

I feel like it shouldn't be this hard to keep yourself alive

**katie (fyodorbrostoevsky):**

or this expensive

**Max (quintuplevampire):**

Yes.

**Seb (mereextravagancy):**

Y E S

**Max (quintuplevampire):**

Do you know the Hoops we've had to jump through to get them to even consider getting me a new wheelchair

I've needed a new one for literally three years and I

obviously need a power wheelchair not a push one

But it's apparently not quote unquote medically necessary

**Seb (mereextravagancy):**

MEDICALLY NECESSARY

UGH, YES, MAX

**Max (quintuplevampire):**

You shouldn't have to be an expert to navigate this stuff but you have to be

It's like finding a Lara Croft secret tomb to figure out where to get funding for just existing

**katie (fyodorbrostoevsky):**

it's exhausting

but also like! i would love to know what's wrong with me!

i would love for the doctor to actually listen when i say there's a problem instead of ignoring me!

**Seb (mereextravagancy):**

Ugh!!!! :(

**katie (fyodorbrostoevsky):**

it's like you were saying about being an expert, max

drs keep losing my records so i have to be in charge of everything myself

it's like having a part time job on top of everything else, except i have to pay to do it, and i'm too exhausted to do it because i feel so bad

**lee (typhoonsss):**

oh, kids

I'm sorry

i am out of spoons lately, too, between the pain and the arguments with the NHS

**Max (quintuplevampire):**

What's up

**lee (typhoonsss):**

ah, yes

i want to get a hysterectomy

but i'm still "quite young," so they're being difficult about it

**Priya (paranormaldetective):**
| That sucks

**Seb (mereextravagancy):**
| Ugh

**Spook (spookyspoony):**
| As if you don't know by now what the right decision would be
| You're an adult

**lee (typhoonsss):**
| i am
| and it was a bit strange
| i thought i might feel differently, once i started the process?
| i was worried that i'd have to set aside time to mourn it
| but this uterus was never going to give me children
| all it's done is hurt me, and i want it out more than i've ever wanted biological children

**al (thorswagnarok):**
| i am... very sorry I called you mum just now
| :grimacing:

**lee (typhoonsss):**
| i don't mind one bit, al!
| you are all my children <3

**bridge (bigforkhands):**
| WE LOVE YOU MOM

**al (thorswagnarok):**
| 11/10, would die for you

**lee (typhoonsss):**
| i forbid that

**Spook (spookyspoony):**
| When are you seeing the doctor next?

**lee (typhoonsss):**
| urgh, i have to set the next appointment
| flora's been on my case about it
| ...rightfully, because she loves me
| (flora's my partner)

**katie (fyodorbrostoevsky):**
| Flora is such a cute name!!!

**lee (typhoonsss):**
| she's pretty cute herself!

**Seb (mereextravagancy):**
| AW

**Priya (paranormaldetective):**
| Keep us posted?

**lee (typhoonsss):**
| absolutely
| thank you all for letting me vent!

**Seb (mereextravagancy):**
| Thanks for letting US vent!

**bridge (bigforkhands):**
| now tell us about your LADY

**al (thorswagnarok):**
| is this a sleepover now

**katie (fyodorbrostoevsky):**
| yes

# 17

**Something near my leg buzzes, and I open my eyes groggily. The** pain I'd gone to sleep with is still here this morning, dull and throbbing.

My phone buzzes again. I fish around the blankets and see a text from Brigid.

what's up

Literally nothing, I'm still in bed

Really killing my Saturday

so... ur home

Yeah, why

no... reason...

Oh. No. No way.

ur neighborhood is like, real cute

suburbia, huh

BRIGID

what

I pull myself out of bed and pad over to the window. I see a beat-up, forest-green car coast to a stop in front of the house, a solid foot away from the curb. I go downstairs, making my way to the front door. Kiki is there already, her face pressed against the glass of the front window.

I peek out too and laugh. She would do this to me. Of course she would.

Brigid is slouched against the door of her car, looking down at her phone through oversized neon-orange sunglasses. She's wearing jean shorts and hiking boots, a thick, plaid flannel over a green T-shirt that says I'M AWESOME AND SO ARE MY TEETH. There is absolutely no context provided anywhere else on the shirt. Her hair has grown out faster than I'd expected, but it's still cropped close to her head.

"Oh, God." I say.

"Who is she?" Kiki breathes, rapt.

"That's Brigid." I sigh. Kiki finally tears her gaze away from the window, planting it on me. "What?" she screams. "You KNOW her?"

"Yeah. She got me grounded last week. One second."

I put on the first shoes I find by the door, my mom's hot-pink flip-flops. As soon as I open the door, Brigid looks up at me. Her face splits into a wide, genuine grin, made lopsided by her missing tooth.

"Priya!" she shouts, waving both her arms in the air. She shoves her phone into the back pocket of her shorts and jogs up the steps to meet me.

I'm taken aback by how different she is in just a week and a half. There's color in her cheeks now, bright spots of pink. She pushes her sunglasses to the top of her head, rubbing her neck. Her eyes are bright. For a second, I think I understand why Kiki was staring. She looks deeply alive.

"You look so healthy," I say, even though I know people hate that, and even though I know that looking healthy doesn't mean being healthy or feeling healthy.

"Yeah, you kinda caught me at a bad time before," she says. Her voice is higher now, still with a bit of a rasp, but nothing like the low growl I'd heard from her. "This is what I'm like most of the time."

We stare at each other.

"What are you doing here, Brigid?" I finally ask. She smiles again in a way that—unfortunately—can only really be described as wolfish.

"Returning the favor, pal."

"Yeah, of course, right," I say. "Because you couldn't have texted me first."

"I did, like five minutes ago."

"Oh my God."

"Cool PJs, by the way," she says, her eyes flicking down and then back up to my face. I look down at the pattern, kittens playing with little multicolored balls of yarn. "Is that what you're gonna wear out?"

"Out *where?*"

"Out anywhere! I don't know, I didn't think that far ahead. What is there to do around here? I passed like, a lot of outlet malls. Like, a really concerning number of outlet malls."

"That is pretty much what there is to do around here," I say. I blink twice, half expecting her to have vanished by the time I open my eyes again. "Sorry, so are we—are we hanging out today?"

"Yeah, get with the program, dude," she says. She glances behind me, spotting Kiki. She waves. Kiki looks embarrassed, vanishing from sight.

"Sister?" Brigid asks. I nod.

"I don't think she's ever seen a girl with a buzz cut before," I say. "Lots to process."

"Sure," Brigid laughs. "Anyway, are—are you feeling up for this? We could always just watch TV." She pauses, fidgeting with her keys. "Or I could go back home. This seemed like a really fun idea until, like, two minutes ago, and now I am realizing that I'm inviting myself over and forcibly stealing your whole Saturday, so."

"No!" I say. "No, I'm happy to see you. Really. I guess this is what I get for showing up in Pennsylvania."

"Tit for tat," she says. It's a *True or False* catchphrase. I grin.

"Yeah, come on in," I say. "Let me change. Kiki can keep you company."

"What?" Kiki squeaks.

Brigid just grins at her. "Hey, dude," she says. "Are chokers in again?"

I change as quickly as I can without exhausting myself, pulling my jeans on. I think about how different Brigid looks now, wonder about the way she turns, the thing that's twisted itself around her—because it must be inside her at this point, right? How do her bones stretch? How does her skin pull itself over them? How do her claws push their way out? How does she recover so quickly? And why does she turn in the first place?

When I get back downstairs, Brigid turns to me, spinning her keys. "Well? Where to, doc?"

I search her face for a second. She's real. She's real, and she's inside my house. Every time I see her in person she becomes a little more solid, reminds me that I didn't just dream the whole thing up.

"I don't know," I say. "Let's just drive."

-------

**"Okay, let's brainstorm, baby," Brigid says. The windows are** rolled down, and she's got her sunglasses back on like it's summer and not the end of March. Being in the passenger seat of a friend's car makes me remember that my hometown was filled with good things, too, bright and honest, like screaming the words to your favorite song with the people you love the most.

Brigid keeps driving, failing to turn her blinker on at any of the turns and asking me if there are any "backstories" to the sculptures on my neighbors' lawns.

"Amusement park," she says. I shake my head. "Okay . . . Thrift shopping? Playing on a playground and being really obnoxious to the actual children? Throwing rocks at trains? That's huge in Bellows. A real crowd-pleaser. That and getting wasted."

"As great as all those things sound . . ." I start.

She glances over at me. "You're not feeling up for it."

"I don't think so," I say. "I'm sorry."

"No, I get it!" she says. "I'm sorry I made you worse."

"No, it's not your fault," I say, even though it's almost entirely her fault. I pull my hair back so the wind doesn't blow it into my face, feeling a twinge in my shoulder. It's still sore, off and on.

Brigid rubs her hand along her scalp, furrowing her brow. "I can't believe I let you shave my head," she says.

"You? Can't believe you *let me*?"

She laughs.

"You shaved your own head and then forced me to fix it for you!"

"Tomato, tomato."

"It's tomato, tomahto. You can't just say tomato twice."

"Why not?" she asks.

"I don't know." I laugh. "I don't know."

She passes me her phone. It isn't a flip phone, but it's almost as ancient. The screen is cracked, to the point that it's hard to see it. "Here, you pick the music."

"You trust me with the aux cord?"

"Absolutely not, this is a test."

The silence starts to stretch as I scroll through her phone, but I don't mind it. I look at her hand on the wheel. I can see it shaking, just a little.

"Hey, are you sure you're okay to drive?" I ask.

"What's that supposed to mean?"

"Like, are you . . . I don't know how fast everything happens."

"Are you asking if I'm going to turn into a werewolf while I'm driving this car?"

"Maybe."

"Do you think I'm going to wrap us around a tree and kill us both? Or are you more worried I'm gonna eat you?"

"In my defense . . ." I hiss.

"Oh my God!"

"You did try to eat me a little bit!"

"Only a very, very little bit! A microscopic bit!"

I roll my eyes. "You have a lot of seventies music on here," I say, finally picking "Hooked on a Feeling." "Like, maybe too much seventies music."

"No such thing." She drums her fingers against the wheel to the ooga chakas, quick and nervous, and takes in a breath.

"I'm fine," she says. "I would know it was coming. You'd be okay."

"Would you?" I ask.

"Would I what."

"Brigid, what exactly would you do?"

"I'm not gonna turn!" she says. It's sharp, a little annoyed. "I turned last week. You were there. You saw. I'm good."

"You turn once a month, right?" I ask.

"I mean, usually, yeah," she says. "Last year I was turning like, every other. It was nice."

"Why?"

"Why was it nice?"

"No, why were you turning every other month?"

"How should I know?" she asks.

I stare at her profile. "You aren't even, like, a little interested in figuring out why this is happening to you?"

"Nope," she says, and I can see her tensing, her hands gripping the wheel tighter. She sighs after a second, when the silence stretches. "I mean. Like, of course I'd like to know. But I don't have any way to figure it out, so what's the point in worrying?"

Something is turning itself over in my head, between the way she called me *doc* and the way I lied to my parents about having an independent study for school. Maybe it wasn't a lie at all. Maybe I really do have something I can spend hours digging into. Someone to help.

"I mean, the way I see it," I say, slowly, "there are two options."

"Okay," she says. Her voice is tight. I can't stop myself.

"One, it's viral or bacterial—something bit you, like something bit me. Or you got sick and it ended up doing this."

"But you didn't get better when they got rid of your Lyme disease," Brigid says. "It didn't *matter*. The damage was done, right?"

"I guess so." I pause, but I keep going when she doesn't interject. "Two, it's genetic. So one or both of your parents are carriers and passed it down, and it was coded into your genes. And maybe something triggered it, like an autoimmune response."

"You've been thinking about this a lot," Brigid says.

"I mean, yeah," I say. "Yeah, of course I have. It's real. You're real. This is a medical issue, so there's got to be a medical explanation, right?"

"And what, you think you can crack the case? Gonna cut me open and run some experiments in your lab?"

I'm quiet. She's being sarcastic, biting, and I know it's because I couldn't stop myself from talking about this. Of course I couldn't. She's—

"I know you're trying to help," she says softly, "but not today, okay? I just want to be normal for a second. No werewolf shit."

"Okay," I say. "Yeah, okay."

"Okay so . . . we could see a movie?" she says.

"Yes! There's still a dollar theater open here. Well, more like a three-dollar theater, but you get it."

"The price is right!" She whoops. "It's settled. But I'm obviously not paying for snacks."

"Obviously not."

"Point me to the drugstore so we can smuggle 'em in."

"Take a right up here."

"Thanks."

I point across the street to the CVS, and she nods.

"Listen . . ." she starts. I wait. "I could live my entire life cooped up in that house, asking questions I can't answer. I could be . . . afraid of myself. But I can't live like that, you know? I woke up today feeling good, and I wanted to hang out with you. So that's what I decided I would do."

We pull into the parking lot, and she puts the car in park. I shift so I can look at her, and she pushes her sunglasses up. I see uncertainty on her face, just for a second, before she grins again. It's a little fragile. Brigid is a lot of things—strange and bold and funny—but I realize now that she's probably lonely, too. I match my grin to hers, and her face grows more sure of itself.

"I'm glad you're here," I tell her. "You absolute weirdo."

"Thanks for letting me kidnap you," she says.

"Anytime. You'd better have a plan for how we're gonna smuggle these snacks in."

"I always have a plan."

"You literally never have a plan. For anything."

"At least I'm consistent, then."

"Okay, but what if I want popcorn?"

"They sell that at the drugstore."

"They sell *cold* popcorn," I argue. We get out of the car, the locks chirping behind us. "Which is just not the same as movie theater popcorn with exactly one pump of butter over the top."

"I was prepared to argue with you, but you make a compelling point. God, that sounds good."

"Thank you."

"I'm still gonna get Junior Mints, though. And pretzels. Oh! Pop

Rocks?"

"Those are the loudest snacks in the universe. Everyone in the theater is going to hate you."

"What can I say? I'm very hateable."

"No you aren't!" I say. "That's a rude thing to say about my friend!"

She actually looks over her shoulder.

"I meant you, dummy!"

"Priya, we were joking! You just made it sweet and genuine!"

"I sure did!"

"I don't know how to deal with that."

"You say thank you."

"Hm. Maybe next time."

-------

**After the movie, Brigid uses the free refill on the popcorn and** just carries it out of the theater, to the bewilderment of the employees. She wedges the tub into the console between us and we sit parked there, munching on the kernels and watching the cars go by on the highway in front of us.

"That was not a good movie," Brigid says, and I start to laugh.

"No, it wasn't," I say. "But did you consider that a nonzero number of things exploded that cannot physically explode?"

"That's a good point."

"And some very intense staring?"

"At least everyone was pretty, right?"

I pop another kernel into my mouth. "But like, too pretty, you know?"

"Yes, totally. It's like an uncanny valley of hotness. You look like this and expect me to believe you're a hardened criminal? It's just not realistic."

"They were definitely aiming for realism, Brigid. You could tell from the scene with the CGI wolves."

"But they looked so real, Priya."

"*So* real."

Brigid grabs a handful of popcorn, shoving it all into her mouth at once. "I hate to say you were right, but this is so good. I can literally feel myself getting dehydrated, but it's worth it."

A truck rumbles past, scaring a flock of birds from their roadside perch. The trees have started growing leaves again. I can see time moving around me as spring starts to think about arriving.

"Did you know that movie theaters used to ban popcorn?" she asks, mouth full.

"I did not." I pause. "Why?"

"They thought it was too plebian," she says.

"Movie theaters were fancy?"

"Fancy as hell," she said. "They wanted everything to be super high-class. Didn't want the popcorn in the building because they were worried it'd ruin the décor, but people snuck it in anyway."

I shake a packet of M&Ms at her, our only remaining CVS snack. "Ironic."

"Yeah," she says, grabbing another handful of popcorn. It's so ordinary. All of this feels so ordinary that I've completely forgotten, for a second, the reason I'm back in New Jersey in the first place. I've forgotten the things I saw the night I met her, the reason her tooth is broken.

"Since you're all about fun facts," I say, "did you know this used to be a cemetery?"

Brigid sits up so quickly that her elbow hits the horn for half a second, startling a family walking into the theater. I wave at them apologetically. Brigid rolls down the window and yells "Don't see *Avalanche*! It sucked!" She looks at me staring at her. "What?"

"Nothing."

"Oh my God, right. Ghosts."

"That isn't what I said."

"Uh, you said *graveyard*. That means ghosts."

"There's a plaque over in that grassy area."

"So this parking lot is like . . . cursed."

"Well, hang on."

"I will not hang on! You brought me to a curséd movie theater!" She says *curséd* with two syllables, like she's an English archaeologist talking about an ancient Egyptian amulet. "It's almost definitely haunted!" She peers over the dashboard like she's looking for a ghost. "So they just bulldozed the headstones?"

"That's what I've heard."

"And paved over the bodies? Priya, are we parked on a bunch of dead dudes right now?"

I shrug.

"Oh my God," she says. "That's such bad luck."

"Then why do you look so happy about it?"

"I'm not!" she says, her mouth curving around the words. She can't keep a straight face. "So has anyone ever seen a ghost here before? Roaming the dollar theater bathrooms? Headed over to get their eyebrows threaded across the strip mall?"

I roll my eyes at her. "You can look if you want, I guess."

"For someone with the URL paranormaldetective, you don't seem to be very into ghost hunting."

She's got me there. "I don't think anyone's seen any ghosts here."

"Bummer."

I stare at the white lines and yellow curbs, trying to imagine what the parking lot would have looked like a hundred years ago—uneven rows of headstones, someone laying flowers at their mother's grave. The dark forest beyond the crest where the highway is now, before it was hacked back.

"It's kind of sad, isn't it?" I say.

"Explain," says Brigid.

"I don't know," I say. "I know that scientifically it's just bodies turning to dirt, but a graveyard is a place built specifically for the people who are left behind. It's something tangible. All these graves had someone's name on them. They kept remembering even when everyone left to remember was dead. But now they're lost, like . . . for good."

Brigid stares at me, huffing out a breath. "Shit."

"Sorry," I say.

"Are you kidding?" she says. "This is why you're one of my favorite people. I'm talking about going ghost hunting and you turn it into, like, a meditation on grief or some shit."

"Well, both of those things do involve the dead people underneath us."

Brigid is still for a second. "Hey," she says seriously.

"Yeah?"

"Someone's probably died in every spot on earth by now. We're probably all balls deep in ghosts twenty-four seven."

"GROSS," I say, shoving her. "Please never, *ever* say 'balls deep in ghosts' to anyone ever again. I feel like I need to wash out my mouth just for repeating it."

"What? What's wrong with that?"

"I don't really want to think about anyone having sex with a ghost."

"Who said anything about ghost sex?"

"You did, Brigid! Just now!"

"I didn't—oh wait. Oh no."

"What."

"Does 'balls deep' not mean you're standing in like, the shallow end of the pool, metaphorically. Like up to your balls in something."

"It does not," I whisper.

She puts her head in her hands. "I've said this wrong so many times," she whispers back. "Oh my God."

"You can't possibly have thought that's what it meant," I say.

She pauses, looking over at me. "I do think I'd be open to sex with a ghost."

"And on that note," I say, "it's time to go home."

"Just because I said that? Come on!"

"I'm eating the rest of this popcorn without you. You can think about what you've done on the drive back."

"You're shaming me."

"I'm definitely shaming you."

"It does sound kind of like the start of a joke, doesn't it?"

"What?"

"A ghost and a werewolf walk into a bar . . ."

"Start driving, Brigid."

# *18*

**Brigid calls me again the week after, when I'm in the parking lot** of the library after working on my "independent study." I hit ACCEPT and start talking.

"So is this, like, a thing we're doing now?" I say. "Talking on the phone?"

She doesn't answer. There's a loud clattering instead, a muffled groan. I sit up in my seat.

"Brigid . . . ?"

I hear a scream on the other end of the call, garbled and low through the phone. My ear rings. It doesn't sound like the animal I heard two weeks ago, but it doesn't sound like Brigid either. My stomach curdles.

"Brigid, where are you? What's happening?" I realize she can't hear me, so I shout. "Brigid!"

"Fuck!" I hear a voice scream, an octave too low. "I didn't mean to—" She breaks off into a hiss of pain.

"Where are you right now?"

"Car," I hear. "Don't—" I hear panting, the sound of something tearing. "Don't. Come."

She's turning. She's in her car, on a road somewhere, by herself, and she's turning.

"Brigid, I—"

I hear her scream pitch itself down another octave as it comes out of her mouth. There's a retching noise, then a faint pinging like buttons spilling onto a tablecloth. The next few sounds are incomprehensible, but when I hear an animal yip and a growl, I know that Brigid is gone, and the creature is back.

"It's okay, Brigid," I say. "It's okay."

I put the phone on speaker, grab one of the Subway napkins that Suresh left crammed into the cupholders of the car.

GOING BACK TO PENNSYLVANIA, I write across the top, then draw a line down the middle.

| Pro | Con |
|---|---|
| −Family still thinks I'm at the library, won't be home for 5 hours | −no plan |
| | −I find the car, I get attacked and hurt |
| −I find the car, I make sure she's safe | −She told me not to come |
| −She needs help | |

Now I remember the reason I've sworn off pro/con lists; I always end up with the same number of points on both sides of the list, more confused than when I started.

I hear a roar from my phone's speaker, loud and angry, followed by the unmistakable sound of shattering glass. Then it's silent.

I add "I'm the only person who knows there's a werewolf loose in Bellows" to the pro column. I sigh. And then I drive to Pennsylvania.

It's less than an hour to her house from the library, and I don't hit traffic. I don't expect to see her car there—it didn't sound like she'd made it home—but I'm doing what any good paranormal detective does: looking for clues.

Her house looks different in the daylight, less foreboding. The lights are off and the driveway is empty. I scroll back up to the start of our last conversation, remembering that she mentioned being at work.

**bigforkhands:**
i am BOREDDD
omg i can't write ur name
i need to nickname u

detective p

no that sounds too much like detective pikachu

pri-med

pri-destination

pri-on disease

best friend forever

i just sold an antique brooch to this woman because i told her it was haunted

it's not haunted at all

i'm such a fraud

call me a fox sister

**paranormaldetective:**

At the library

Wait what?

**bigforkhands:**

i'll tell u later

**paranormaldetective:**

How are you bored already, it's like 10 am

**bigforkhands:**

it is but hattie is late

hattie, who has named this place after herself but hasn't bothered to SHOW UP

(just kidding @hattie thank u for giving me $$$ show up whenever u want)

**paranormaldetective:**

Draw something!

Gotta go

**bigforkhands:**

oh good idea

what should I draw

eh i might just google spooky things

**bigforkhands:**

oh :/

i don't think angel's glow is actually real

i can't find the original legend anywhere

there's no miracle, is there

**bigforkhands:**

| ugh, i think i have food poisoning

I pull up Google Maps and type in everything that I know: "Hattie antique pa." The result pops up right away: Hattie's Antiques and Oddities Emporium in Bellows, Pennsylvania. It's fifteen minutes from here, right next to the spot on the map that says ECHO CREEK. I turn on the directions and start driving, slowly.

I pass through Bellows's downtown, with its two stoplights and smattering of tiny shops. I see a café, a library, a German restaurant, a hardware store, a funeral home, a palm reader, and an arts-and-crafts store. There are just enough people here that I feel confident someone would have noticed Brigid by now, but I stare down each corner I drive past.

I pass a car-repair garage as I turn off Main Street and know I've left Bellows proper. There's still no sign of Brigid, and after I pass a church and what might be a farm, my phone announces that Hattie's will be on my left.

I park the car and get out, wincing at the way my knees pop.

Hattie's Antiques and Oddities Emporium is in an old, small barn that looks more like a shack, with dark brown wood shingling the walls. The windows have been painted green, and there are only three other cars parked outside. I push open the front door and a bell tinkles. When I glance up, I see a bundle of dried herbs tied to it. My first thought is *mistletoe?*, but it's the beginning of April and that isn't what mistletoe looks like. The smell of dust fills my lungs immediately, and I cough. I can see the motes floating through the air where the sun hits. It's dark inside, yellowing bulbs doing a poor job of lighting each corner, and I don't see a single person.

From the outside, I'd thought that things might be spaced out, but Hattie's is a maze of shelves, stacks, and furniture. There's nothing anywhere that tells me the difference between an "antique" and an "oddity." A pile of multicolored crystals is for sale, and so is the old wooden shelf they're scattered across. I take a few steps farther into the shop, where a group of unsettling dolls with porcelain faces watches me from the top of an old piano. There's a taxidermied bat on the wall above them.

"Hello?" I call out. "Your sign said you were open?"

I turn the corner, picking my way between a rocking chair and a rolltop desk. Inside the desk is a cluster of keys poured into a bowl like mints, a row of perfume bottles that are still filled with some kind of murky liquid, and what I really, really hope isn't a human skull.

The absolute chaos that rules the shop is starting to get to me. There doesn't seem to be a single thought spared for organization or placement. I feel like I'm inside a "spot the difference" cartoon, except every single item in this shop is the difference.

"How do they find anything?" I mutter to myself.

"It's about the experience of looking," comes a voice from behind me. I jump, spinning to see a white woman in her sixties, gray hair frizzing out from her head in loose, wiry waves. She's dressed in high-waisted jeans and an oversized button-up shirt, somewhere between lumberjack and hippie. "I try to encourage customer browsing," she says matter-of-factly. "But you look like you're on a mission."

"I'm actually looking for someone," I say. "I think my friend Brigid works here?" I don't know why she'd pick working here over one of the shops in town. Brigid loves talking to people. I can't imagine her not going stir-crazy here.

The woman raises her eyebrows, smiling, like something's just clicked into place for her. "Any friend of Brigid's is a friend of mine. Are you Priya?" She reaches out for one of my hands, and I try not to pull away, unsettled. Either there aren't a lot of Indian people in Bellows, or Brigid doesn't have many friends here. Probably both. She's talked about me, in any case. More than I've talked about her.

"Are you Hattie?" I shoot back. She laughs.

"So she's mentioned me, too. She tells me about you. Don't make that face, all good things. You two seem like dear friends—like Anne Shirley and Diana Barry."

It's all very sweet, and I try to return her smile, but I can feel that humming in my chest creeping into my throat.

"Yeah, do you know where she went?" I ask, chewing on the inside of my cheek. Hattie stares at me for a beat too long, a second that has me narrowing my eyes and wondering if *she* knows about Brigid, if she's wondering the same thing about me right now.

"She wasn't feeling well, poor thing," Hattie says, sympathetic. "She had to take off early, but I'm calling my friend Sharon to cover for her. It's slow around here, though—it's always slow, but weekdays are worst for us—"

"So she just went home?" I say, rudely, desperately trying to steer the conversation.

"Yes, I think so," Hattie says.

"Do you know the road she would have taken?" I try. "She lives right—"

I sneeze, the dust overwhelming me.

"Gesundheit."

"Thanks. She lives on Natalis Road, up past the downtown area."

"I know," says Hattie. "I've been keeping an eye on her while her parents are out of town. Don't tell her that, though. She'd be furious."

"She would," I say, softly. I wait. Hattie raises her eyebrows.

"Oh, the route!"

"Please."

"The quickest way is to take the shortcut through the woods, up Ash Tree Road. Do you know where that is?"

"No," I say.

"It's easy."

I brace myself for something incomprehensible, like turning through a field at the biggest oak tree or the third fence post, but it is easy, after all.

"You go right outta the parking lot here, keep on for two minutes until you see the old Lutheran church, white clapboard, little steeple. That's where you go left. You hit the garage and you've gone too far."

I remember it. "Thank you so much, I've got to go."

"See you later, Diana," Hattie says. "Tell Brigid—"

But I let the door shut behind me before I can hear the message Hattie wanted me to deliver. I'm annoyed at having wasted so much time already, annoyed at being called Diana, annoyed at being annoyed. Of course Brigid would be Anne, wild-eyed and too loud and ready to swallow up the whole world.

I check the time. It's been almost two hours since Brigid called me. I think about calling the police, but I have no idea what I'd say to them. "Just wanted to let you know that you should probably keep an eye out for a werewolf, just in case she tries to eat anyone!" Then I think about a police officer shooting her while she's transformed, and I shut down that line of thought.

I take the turn on Ash Tree. It's harder to see into the forest now that the leaves have started growing back, but I keep an eye out anyway. As it turns out, I didn't need to look hard. Brigid's green car is pulled off the side of the road, the driver's door open and the brake lights on.

I take a breath in and let it out slowly. I feel a phantom itch. I don't like being near the woods anymore, not since I learned that Lyme disease isn't like chicken pox—you can get it again, and again, and again. I've just gotten the bacteria out of my body, so I'd really rather not put it back in.

I braid my hair back quickly, pull the hood of my hoodie over my head, and tuck my jeans into my socks. I wish I had bug spray, but this'll have to work for now.

The second I open my car door to investigate, I hear '70s music trickling out of Brigid's car. It's "Take a Chance on Me," and it fills me with more raw dread than ABBA ever has.

The driver's side mirror has been torn off, and I hear the door dinging when I get closer. The inside of the door has been scratched to pieces, and the rest of the car is worse off. I sit down gingerly on the edge of the driver's seat.

The seatbelt is shredded, and there are gouges in the roof and the seats. The passenger window is shattered, a few shards still clinging to the edges. She must have kicked through it. I wonder if her foot's okay.

I catch sight of something small and white on top of a notebook on the passenger seat, with a smear of rust across the bottom. It's shaped like a candy corn, catching light like a pearl, and I lean over and pick it up to take a closer look when I suddenly realize exactly what it is.

"Oh my God," I breathe, dropping it. I taste bile in my mouth. It lands with a *clink*, which isn't the sound the floor mat should make, so I lean over to look in the well of the passenger seat.

No. No, no, no. I cannot do this.

I push myself out of the car and stare at the sky, counting to ten and trying to tamp down the nausea.

The song switches to "Funkytown," which is enough to shock me out of my horror. Brigid *would* have this on her playlist. Brigid would torture me, even when she's not here, by forcing me to listen to "Funkytown." I tell myself that I have to go back into the car to turn off the song.

I pull the key from the ignition and slip it into my pocket, grab the notebook from the passenger seat, and close the door. I don't look into the seat well or the cupholder. I don't look at the teeth again. The pile of thirty-odd human teeth strewn lazily across the car, stark white against the gray, speckled with the rust red of Brigid's blood. But I can see them whenever I close my eyes, imagine Brigid spitting them out to make room for fangs. I swallow. I've literally had this nightmare.

I go back to my car, staring ahead at Brigid's license plate. I can't tell where she's gone from here, if she's run across the road or into the forest or back toward Bellows proper. I can't call the police.

The obvious answer presents itself to me, and I lay my head on the lip of my steering wheel and groan.

I look up the number for Bellows County Animal Control for the second time and dial.

# 19

**I go with "there's a wild animal on the loose" instead of "I lost my** dog" because it sounds more urgent. I open the notebook while I wait.

It's a sketchbook. Looking through the drawings reminds me how good Brigid is. There are day-in-the-life comics, sketches of people and items at the antiques store. I recognize a cartoon version of Hattie from her crazy hair. Her comics are funny, too. I've seen a handful of these redrawn digitally on her blog, or just scanned in.

Interspersed with these, though, I see other drawings that feel different, darker. A human mouth crowded with oversized wolf teeth. A face with its skin peeled back from the upper left corner to reveal a skull, a dark, empty eye socket with a tongue creeping its way out of the hole. There's a full-page sketch of a girl, blurry edged and in shadow; her eyes are dark, and her hands are fading into nothingness. Her torso floats above her legs, and you can see exposed ribs, a pelvic bone. In between these the darkness forms a mouth, yawning wide with hunger.

I flip through the blank pages to the back, where I see writing. I turn the sketchbook upside down and open it from the other side. It's a log. I skim the entries quickly.

# DEEP DARK THOUGHTS

## ~~SICK JOURNAL~~, BECAUSE LEE SAID IT WOULD HELP

I guess we'll find out

I'm hungry all the time. Fucking starving. I feel like that's normal, idk. I get these headaches where it feels like my brain's, like, making a fist. My whole body feels like it's making a fist. It never gets to rest.

-------

A big chunk of hair fell out of my head 2 days ago. I literally didn't even think about it until I was messing with my hair at Hattie's and she looked horrified when she saw how much came out. I guess that's something? But it'll grow back soon, in a major way.

-------

Okay so here's how I know it's coming—

I get more tired all month, and a day or two before I get tingling, leg cramping, and sometimes weird bruises? And I feel like, weak and sick. But when it's happening like. Buckle up.

First up, my stomach. I mean, it's not just my stomach, it's everything. I always end up throwing up because everything inside me starts to move. Your organs aren't supposed to move. That shit was supposed to be what like, idiot doctors thought happened to women in the middle ages. My brain doesn't like it.

Then the itching starts, all over my whole body, and from here things go pretty quick, so I head down to the basement. There's this headache, too, right behind my eyes. And my other teeth come in, and I taste blood, and it fucking hurts, and the world goes black.

Super fun, right?

Like. Just a regular ass party.

Except, here's the thing. It came a week early this time.

-------

At the end of last year I missed a couple of turns. Like I'm gonna fuckin complain about that.

-------

It's happening faster. In both ways. Like, it was only two FUCKING weeks, and I turned again, and I usually have some time when I start to feel it, right, but I barely made it home. I left the front door open. Priya found me. She found out. Can't stop thinking about the look on her face, like she didn't know what I was. I guess I don't know either.

If I'm being honest, it's kind of a relief that she knows. Like, why am I hiding this? Who gives a shit? Who gives a shit about anything?

-------

Sometimes I feel like I'm different every time I turn back. Like I'm one person, then I turn, and when I turn back I'm somebody else, just a little bit. Like that ship that they keep rebuilding until all the parts have been replaced. Is it the same ship anymore? Am I?

-------

*My muscles feel really weak, like they can't flex anymore. Couldn't open the jelly jar. Smashed the lid against the counter instead and cut myself. I had to scoop out the pieces of glass, but I got my fucking jelly.*

--------

*Happy April. I'm still tired. I miss mom throwing that tire chunk for me in the basement. I miss dad grilling steaks after.*

--------

*My gums started bleeding this morning. Fun and new. Really shakin' things up here.*

That's the last entry. My eyes well up.

A truck pulls up and parks on the other side of the road. It looks like a regular SUV in the front but with a trailer where the back seat should be. I clear my throat and get out of my car, raising my hand.

A familiar figure steps out of the truck, putting a pair of gloves into his back pocket. Longish hair, my height, Asian, stubble across his chin. He looks up and starts to return my wave until he gets a closer look at me. I grin uncomfortably.

"Uh, hi again," I say.

He spreads his hands in the universal *wtf* gesture, meets my eyes, and shouts across the road. "Are you KIDDING ME?"

# 20

**"I am not doing this today."**

"I promise I'm not crazy," I shout back. "Please don't leave!"

"Give me one good reason not to!"

"Just take a look at the car. Please."

He glances both ways before jogging across the road, stopping right next to me. He stares me in the eyes, and I stare back. His Adam's apple bobs. I'm not sure exactly what he's waiting for.

"Listen . . ." He gestures to me.

"Priya," I say.

"Listen, Priya," he says. "Are you screwing with me? Are you pranking Bellows County Animal Control? Did we wrong you in some way?"

"No, I—"

"Do you hate me, Priya?"

"I don't hate you . . ." I point back at him, raising my eyebrows expectantly.

He sighs, folding his arms. "Spencer."

"I don't hate you, Spencer. Please look at the car that's been destroyed by an animal."

He does. The second he peers in the window, he glances back at me, eyes wide.

"This your car?"

"No, it's my friend's," I say.

"So where's your friend?"

"She had to go to work," I lie, "so I came by to help."

He looks at me suspiciously but opens the door anyway, picking up the shredded seatbelt. He twists around to get a look at the roof, too, running his finger along the inside of the gouge that Brigid's claw made.

"Holy shit," he whispers. "Okay, there's definitely something you're not telling me, but there really was an animal here."

"Yeah, I told you."

"It looks like your *friend*," he says pointedly, "was in possession of a wolf hybrid." He gets out and walks to the other side of the car. "Which is definitely, totally illegal."

"No, you don't have to keep looking—"

"Nah, it's no problem."

"Can't you just start tracking it or something?"

He stares at me. "What do you think I am, a ranger? Like a full-on Dungeons and Dragons character?"

"You literally work for animal control."

"Okay, yeah," he says. "I do know what dog tracks look like, but I can't, like, follow its heat signature." He glances in the passenger side window, and I curse under my breath. "Hey, there's something spilled all over the car. What are those, Tic Tacs? Or—"

He turns slowly, putting his hands up. "Dude."

"Listen—" I start.

"Those are *teeth*."

"Yeah. My friend's an artist, they're for a project. She works at Hattie's."

"Oh my God, this is why you keep calling," Spencer says. "You're a serial killer."

"Come *on*."

"You're going to serial kill me and take my teeth out with a pair of pliers or something."

"Okay, first off, you can't 'serial kill' someone," I say.

His voice pitches up. "*That's how you're gonna convince me you're not a serial killer?*"

"I'm not a serial killer!"

"You can serial kill someone," he says. "If you've already killed other people."

"I have never and would never kill anyone," I say.

"Sounds like something a serial killer would say," he says.

"Oh my God."

"*Teeth*, Priya. There are *human teeth* in the car."

"Look, can we just look for the dog? Please?"

"I'm not sure I want to be in an enclosed space with you."

"What am I gonna kill you with, my cell phone? My Lyme disease?"

His radio beeps, and he unclips it from his belt. "Yeah, shoot," he says, holding down the side button.

A voice emerges, crackly and low, with a stronger version of the accent I've heard traces of in Hattie and Spencer. "Hey, Yi. Just got another call from Mrs. Johansen."

"What else is new?"

"Ha, I know. You're on that loose dog, right? I think she may have spotted it."

"Awesome."

"No worries. Said she saw something across the road from her in Bellows, near the supermarket. She's worried about her feral cat colony."

"I'll go take a look. Thanks, Marty."

"Thanks, pal. Before you go, wanna hear something funny?"

"Always, man."

"When she called? She told us she'd seen a werewolf."

My heart hammers in my throat.

Spencer laughs. "Fingers crossed. See ya."

"See ya."

I feel like I should tell him. Give him some sort of heads-up, or something. *Hey, Mrs. Johansen and her feral cats aren't so crazy after all.* But I don't know how I'd even start that conversation, so I just follow Spencer back to his truck. I linger by the passenger side door.

"So, can I come? Or are you afraid I'm going to strangle you with my hoodie drawstring?"

He huffs, and it *almost* sounds like a laugh. "Just get in the truck," he says.

-------

197

**I'm grateful the ride is short, because we don't really talk on the** way over. I want to ask him some kind of question about working at animal control, but I figure I've already harassed him enough for now.

"It's really pretty here," I try.

"Which part," he says, "the buildings that are abandoned or the ones that look like they should be?"

"The farms," I say. "The whole mountainy forest vibe."

The light coming through the trees sends gray, hole-punched shadows skittering across the dashboard. Spencer peers out. "Yeah, I guess that part is nice," he says.

We idle in front of the supermarket. My stomach rumbles.

"Geez," Spencer says.

I glare. "I didn't have time to eat lunch."

He rummages around in the back and tosses me a bag of chips.

"Thanks," I say.

"No worries," he says. His radio chirps again, and he clicks the button. "Yep."

"Another call from the supermarket," Marty's voice crackles. "Someone tried to take out the trash. Sounded scared outta their mind."

"I'll check out the back. Thanks, man."

"Yep."

Spencer pulls the truck around behind the supermarket. It's backed up to the woods, so I can see how she could have run through without anyone seeing her. *Maybe this'll be okay*, I think. And then we turn the corner.

Even though I'm braced for it, it takes my brain a few seconds to parse what I'm seeing, to put the pieces together in a way that makes sense.

Bushy tail? Check. Huge, six-foot-something wolf body? Check. Large royal blue T-shirt? Check.

The creature—well, Brigid, I guess—is rooting through the gar-bage bin behind the store. The lid is flipped up, and she's got both paws on the metal lip, tearing into something with her teeth. A pile of trash spills over the edge and hits the ground with a splat. Her tail wags, slowly. She's still wearing a T-shirt, which kind of takes the menace out of the whole situation. It can't be comfortable anymore; it's stretched tight across her back. I can see a couple of patches where her fur hasn't completely grown in, a bit mangy.

When she shifts her weight, I notice that she's favoring her right foot. I can see what looks like matted blood from here, maybe a cut. She must have sliced it open when it went through the car window.

"So, uh . . ." Spencer starts. I look over at him. His mouth opens and shuts like a fish. His eyes are fixed dead ahead of us. I wait for him to say something.

"You kept saying dog."

"Yeah."

"I feel like you don't know what a dog is," he says.

The back door of the supermarket edges open, and a woman wearing a green apron sticks her head outside. At the sound, the wolf's ears prick up and her head swivels to the woman. Spencer leans his forearm on the rolled-down window and sticks his head out of the car.

"Please go back inside, ma'am!" he yells. At his voice, the wolf hops down from the garbage bin, steps toward us, and pushes herself unsteadily onto her hind legs. Her T-shirt has a picture of a yellow cartoon school bus, captioned with the words THIS IS WHAT A GREAT BUS DRIVER LOOKS LIKE!

"*Is* that what a great bus driver looks like?" I whisper.

"Oh my God," Spencer says.

"Okay, so," I say, "what's the plan here? Because you cannot hurt her."

"That's not a dog," he says.

"No," I say. "It's not."

She drops back onto four legs like she's lost interest in us, sniffing around the trash on the ground again. I freeze, tracking her movement with my eyes.

"She might run, Spencer," I say. "We cannot let her run."

"Okay, so when you said dog," he says, "I was thinking we'd *find* the dog. And it'd be an illegal wolf hybrid sort of thing you didn't have a permit for. And I'd have to give you, like, a talking to, and maybe confiscate it. But you'd be able to like, call her over to you or something. I use the catchpole, we all go home happy."

He points. He's still staring at her. "I can't use a catchpole! On that thing!"

"She's not a thing," I say.

"Oh, I am not prepared for this. I cannot be the person who is supposed to fix this."

"So get your tranquilizer, or whatever!"

He finally snaps his eyes to mine. "I don't have any tranquilizers!"

"What?!"

"What do you mean, what?! I don't have those! I'm not cleared to use those, and they have to be, like, calibrated to the specific animals!"

"You're supposed to be the expert here!"

"I think we used to have a shotgun, but no one's seen it in a while. I think one of the others misplaced it."

"You guys *lost a shotgun?*"

"It's gonna turn up! That's not the point here!"

"What is the point, Spencer?"

"The point is that you've got to help me figure out what to do with *that*."

He points through the windshield to where a thrift-store-shirted werewolf was standing a minute ago. But she's gone now. And there's only an empty parking lot in front of us.

"Oh, Jesus Christ," Spencer says.

"Come on," I say.

# 21

**Panic starts to grip me at the thought of losing Brigid again, but**
Spencer grabs my wrist and whispers "there," pointing past the far
corner of the grocery store, just into the woods. I can see a bushy tail
behind a tree, a creature moving with an uneven gait.

"I see her," Spencer says, nodding at me. "It's okay. Really, I've
dealt with weirder."

"Have you?"

"Yeah, actually," he says. "Once. It involves a bunch of drug dealers
who taught their pet parrots some deeply disturbing tricks. Another
time. For now, I've got a small, very expensive piece of insurance we
could use."

He puts the truck in park, hops into the back, and starts rummag-
ing. The wolf takes another step into the tree line, and I roll down the
window, leaning my head out. I remind myself of who she really is,
hoping some part of her remembers, too.

"Brigid!" I call. "Remember me, Brigid?"

I watch her ears perk up, swiveling in my direction, and she steps
back onto the concrete.

"Hey, that's it!" I grin. "C'mere."

She watches me, frozen in place. I notice that the fur around her
mouth is also matted, sticky and dark. My stomach lurches. She's had
plenty of time for a snack. Spencer hauls himself back into the driver's
seat, looking pleased.

"Bingo!" he says, holding up a gun.

"Spencer!" I hiss. "You can't kill her!"

He pinches the bridge of his nose, taking a deep breath. "Priya," he says, "it's a dart gun. I'm not going to shoot her. What do you think is wrong with me."

He pops out the dart. It's longer than I'd expected, segmented into color-coded parts. "There's a tracker here," he says brightly. "In the middle part. It's really cool tech, unless the animal sits on it. It also costs a hundred and fifty dollars, so we only have, like, two of them. So you have to promise not to tell my boss that I'm about to do this."

"When would I be talking to your boss?" I ask.

"Yeah, alright," he says. "Since we don't have any tranqs on us, unless you're packing ketamine—are you packing ketamine, Priya?"

"I am not."

"Okay, so no tranqing. I *do* know a guy, but I'd get in a lot of trouble if anyone ever found out I was buying tranquilizers off the street."

"You're buying tranquilizers off the street?"

"Of course not! I've been trying to figure out how to confiscate this dealer's dog, so I don't exactly want to give him my business. If you tell my boss I even brought that up I'm burying you in the woods."

"Now who's the serial killer?"

"Shut up."

"What is the *plan*, Spencer."

"I'm working on it. I'm not wild about the idea of me using my catchpole, and calling in backup would take a while. So while we're here: want to try to lure her up into the truck?"

"I don't think she likes small spaces," I say.

"What does she like?" he asks. "We are right behind a grocery store."

I nod. "Okay. Yeah."

"I'll stay here and get this dart into her," he says. "You go grab some bait."

"Go team werewolf," I say, before realizing what's come out of my mouth. Spencer is staring at me like I've grown another head.

"Team *what*?" he squeaks.

I laugh nervously. "Bye, good luck!"

I walk into the grocery store as fast as I can manage. I hear my knee pop, but I keep going, "excuse me, sorry"-ing past white person after white person. I'm grateful it's a small store, and I grab two steaks, one beef tongue, and a jar of peanut butter. Who knows. I don't know.

The cashier eyes me as I dump all the items onto the checkout counter. "Huh," she says.

"Just really hungry," I say, with a weak attempt at a smile.

The sight that greets me behind the store is a doozy. Spencer's on the hood of his truck now, kicking Brigid's paw away and trying to maneuver the catchpole around her neck. Brigid is growling and trying to climb up after him, but it looks like her injured foot is stopping her.

"I was gone for five minutes!" I shout at him.

"Longest five minutes of my life!" he shouts back.

I have an inkling of an idea—completely dependent on how good Spencer happens to be at his job—so I cross my fingers and go back to the front of the store.

"Okay, see ya," I hear Spencer yell.

I walk around to the back from the other side of the building.

"Brigid!" I yell. I whistle at her, which I'm sure she'll hate later, if she remembers.

She turns, stepping toward me on two legs. The sight fills me with that convulsive horror again, the same way that seeing a cockroach skittering its flat body across kitchen tile does. I steel myself, stare into her brown, human eyes, try to figure out if there's some part of her that still knows me.

"C'mere," I choke out, even though I really, desperately do not want her to come any closer to me. I glance back at Spencer, who's fumbling with the dart gun.

I hold out my hand. I read that this is what you're supposed to do when a dog is suspicious of you, so it can smell your scent, but it feels like I'm offering up a snack.

Brigid drops down onto four paws again, inching toward me.

"It's okay," I say. To her, to myself. "It's okay."

I stand stock-still. As she gets closer, I look at the blood on her snout, the way her ears are positioned. Then I glance back up at Spencer, who shakes his head at me, frowning. I frown back.

"Priya, get back," he calls. "Get the hell out of there."

He's right. Of course he's right. But I'm frozen to the spot.

"*Go*, Priya."

I can't. I watch her snout nose forward, hear it snuffle toward my wrist. I think about how many veins live there, how many she could tear through in a second if she wanted to. But she doesn't. She just sniffs at my hand. Then she looks up at me, and I see her tail wag, once, just a little. And I exhale, feeling like something has clicked into place. A little piece of the wrongness I feel looking at her has been put right.

I toss her the beef tongue, too nervous to open the paper packaging. She sniffs it, curious, and I look up at Spencer and nod. Then I back away from Brigid. She watches me, unmoving, as I go back to the front of the store. I stare at her until I can't see her anymore, then hear a yelp, a crashing through the brush. *Damn it.*

I walk back behind the store. Brigid is gone again. Spencer slides down the hood of the truck, hopping down and looking at me in disbelief.

"Dude," he says. "That was so stupid."

"I know."

"Like, kind of baller. But also insanely stupid."

"I was waiting for you to take the shot!"

"This isn't an action movie! What if I shot her with the dart and she attacked you?"

"I didn't think about that."

"Hm!"

"Did you get her?"

A slow smile spreads across his face. "I sure did," he says. He bends, picking up a broken tracker from the ground. "Well, with the second one. The first one hit her in the hip and she just . . . stood up and, uh."

"And what."

"And took it out."

"Yeah."

"She has five toes, dude. Five toes on each paw."

"I know."

"Alright, let's get to her before she gets to anyone else. One sec." He hops back into the truck, grabs a device that looks like a satellite dish, stretched out like metal antlers. It pings when he turns it on, and we grin at each other.

"You navigate," he says, handing it to me. "But be careful." The device pings in my hands, and he leans over to look. "We've gotta stay within four thousand feet for this thing to work. It looks like she's headed northeast right now, maybe up the road from Bellows? It's hard to tell."

"Wait a minute," I say, putting in Brigid's address. I pull up Google Maps to show him, and we compare for a second. "Is she going this way?"

"Could be, yeah," he says.

"I think I know where she's headed," I say. He raises his eyebrows. "I think she's going home."

-------

**We follow the tracker up that winding forest road. There's a cem**etery to the left that I hadn't noticed when I'd driven here at night, a hand-painted sign inviting you to COME DOWN TO JIM'S FIREWORK BARN—100% LEGAL!

"Are you sure she remembers where you live?" Spencer asks.

"It's her house," I say, and he gives me a weird look.

I spot a smudge of bright blue out of the corner of my eye. "Pull over, pull over," I say. He slams on the brakes and something rattles in the back of the truck.

"I don't see her," he says.

"There, behind that car," I say. She's sniffing around behind a rusted-out shell of a car, but she loses interest and keeps moving. I roll down the window and whistle, twice, watching her ears swivel up and around.

"She's gotta see us," I say.

Spencer groans. "How's your knee?"

I'm surprised he remembered. "It's . . . fine."

"Fine, you drive. I'm not supposed to let you do that, so—"

"Don't tell your boss, I know. It's not like I'm gonna steal your radio."

I hop out of the truck as Spencer climbs into the back and pops open the door.

"Brigid!" I call, waving my arms. "Come over here!"

She stares at us.

I get into the driver's seat and Spencer rips open the first package of steak, sitting with his legs dangling off the edge of the truck.

"How are you going to get her into the cage?" I ask.

"Very carefully," he says.

"Come here, Brigid!" I call out the window. "We have food!"

She starts to run toward us. Spencer tosses her the steak, and she catches it, tearing into it gleefully. He grabs the second one, unwrapping it and shaking it in front of her. Her eyes follow it. He tosses it into the cage and slowly hops down, keeping the catchpole between him and Brigid.

"Go ahead, get it," he says. She eyes the space warily, frozen in place. Spencer comes toward her carefully with the catchpole, but she backs away from him, growling.

"It's okay, Brigid, jump in," I say.

Spencer peers down. "She's still favoring that foot," he says. "It's making her even more skittish."

"Try the peanut butter," I say.

He unscrews the top and she noses forward at the new smell. She puts her front paws on the edge of the truck, leaning in to try to grab the steak out of the cage without getting into it. When she can't, she limps away from the truck again, waiting.

"She's too smart for you, Spencer," I say.

"She's not a dog," he says. "But she's not *not* a dog. Hang on, I have an idea."

He hops into the back again, hooking the steak onto one of the chain leashes and holding it in his hands so it dangles off the edge of the truck.

"Drive," he says.

"You're kidding me."

"I mean, slowly. Maybe she'll think it's a game."

I route Google Maps back to Brigid's house. And then I start driving.

I catch Spencer in the rearview mirror, but I can't see much behind him. "Well?" I ask.

I hear him laugh. "Yeah, she's coming." There's a pause. "Oh no. Oh, she's running. I didn't think this through."

"Hold on to something," I say, speeding up. I see one of Brigid's neighbors pull into their driveway as we pass. I wave as our weird little caravan rolls by, and the neighbor raises her hand in shock.

"Do you have a backyard?" Spencer calls.

I think back to the house, try desperately to remember. I remember the sliding glass door outside the kitchen, the floodlights in the back. And then a tall, sturdy fence, a gate to the side.

"Yes," I say.

"Okay, pull around back," he says. "Can you back in?"

"I can try." I put the truck in reverse, watch Brigid approach through the windshield now. "I thought you said we weren't in an action movie."

"Oh, with your thousand-point turn here? How could we not be?"

I pull around to the garage, stopping in the driveway. There's a gate in the fence right outside the passenger door. I hear the truck door slam, then Spencer scrambles up front, carrying his awful steak-rope with him.

"That's disgusting."

"Give me one second," he says. He huffs out a breath, preparing himself, and sprints out the door, jumping onto the fence. I'm not *not* impressed.

Until his boot misses the cross board, and he slips, and Brigid hops onto the hood of the truck. "Oh my God," I say. "Oh my God."

I roll down the window. "Brigid, this way!" I shout. "Please don't attack our new friend!"

She lunges for Spencer's leg and I scream. I see her jaws start to close around his calf with a startling clarity. *No, no, no.*

"Spencer!" I shout.

He curses, kicking her away with his heavy boots. She lets out a quick whimper. Spencer pulls himself up to the top of the fence, straddling it. He looks okay, thank God, and she can't reach him anymore.

"This is way taller than I thought it was," he shouts at me. "Getting kinda dizzy up here."

"Are you okay?" I shout back.

"Yeah, I'll be fine, just unlock the gate," he yells.

I pull out Brigid's key ring, looking at each of the keys. Car key, front door key.

"Uh . . ."

"Do you not have the key?" he yells.

"Just jump!"

"I'm like ten feet up!"

"Dangle first!"

"Oh, right."

He disappears. I can see Brigid losing interest.

"She's gonna run again," I say.

"Hold your horses," he says. I hear a bolt unlock, and then the gate swings open. He rattles the chain, and Brigid's ears perk up.

"Go get it!" I hear him say. Brigid vaults through the open gate. A second later I see Spencer run out, limping a little, slamming the bolt behind him and breathing hard. I get out of the car, and we stare at each other for a second, shocked. Then I start to giggle, and he does too. It builds until he's doubled over laughing and I'm leaning against the car door, tears of relief in my eyes.

He sticks out his hand and I crinkle my nose. He slides off his glove, holding it in his left hand, and I shake his hand.

"Good work, dude," he says.

"You too." I laugh. "Thanks for not leaving."

"You should have a vet take a look at her foot," he says, nodding.

"Right," I say. "Yes."

"And can I use your bathroom?" he asks. "I've had to pee for like twenty minutes. I was a little worried about how that one was gonna turn out."

"Disgusting. But yeah, no problem."

I let him into Brigid's house for the second time, and I go straight to the kitchen. There's a view of the yard and beyond, the way the hill slopes down a little. The steak is gone, and Brigid is pacing the backyard. She glances up at me as I sit down at the kitchen table. I wave, and she goes back to sniffing the ground.

Spencer sits next to me, backward in the chair, and rests his chin on the back. We both stare out at her.

"You know I'm gonna have to confiscate her," he says.

I look at him. "What the hell are you talking about?"

"It's illegal to have a wolf hybrid without a permit," he says.

I scoff. "We both know she's not a wolf hybrid, Spencer," I say. "She—come on. You can't take her. You don't even have to put anything about this in your report, or whatever."

He nods, slowly.

"Come back in three days," I say. "If you still think you should take her then, you can."

"I mean, I don't want you to spread the word that I can be bribed," he says.

"Can you?" I ask.

"Eh, probably. I think this is a little bit of a gray area."

"Yeah."

"But I do need my tracker back," he says. "And I do want to make sure that she doesn't escape again."

"Alright."

His radio chirps, and I look at him. "Please. Just a few days."

"I'll wait to call backup until later tonight," he says. "Hey, Marty, that you?"

"Yep. Just checking in about the dog, you get it taken care of?"

"Yeah, all good, man."

"Great. Was it a wolf dog?"

He looks at me, pausing. Then he takes a breath. "Yeah, somethin' like that," he says. He turns back and takes a picture of her through the window with his phone.

"Mrs. Johansen called again to say one of the cats was missing. She feeds so many of those bastards I'm not sure how she can tell, but she swears there's blood everywhere. Thinks something terrible has happened to it."

I meet Spencer's eyes, then look over at the matted blood on Brigid's snout.

"I'll keep an eye out, thanks. Anything else for me?"

"Not right now, quiet day. Take your time."

"Alright, man. Hey also, grab me some antibiotics? She got me in the leg."

"Will do, buddy."

"She, uh," I choke out. "Spencer, she—she what?"

"You didn't notice?" he asks. I shake my head. "Wow, thanks a lot," he says, turning in his chair so that I can see his right side. There are gashes in his pant leg. Blood. *She broke the skin*, I think. *She bit him and she broke the skin*. He rolls the cuff up and I can see the gouge marks.

"Oh, this is not good," I mutter, pulling my chair in to look closer.

"I can wrap it up back at the station if it's freaking you out, but I washed it out in the sink. It's not even that deep. It's already stopped bleeding, for the most part. Ruined my pants, though."

"It sure did," I say, dazedly. *The thing inside her might be inside you, now, too,* I think.

He gets up, taking his keys out of his pocket. "See ya," he says.

"Wait, hold on, you're leaving?"

He looks between me and Brigid pacing the backyard. "No," he says, clearing his throat. "No, I'm just gonna clock out. I'm coming back. I want to keep an eye on her."

I text my parents when Spencer leaves: *Staying over at Brigid's tonight. I'll be back tomorrow, I know Suresh needs the car.* For once, it's not a question. *I'm an adult,* it feels like I'm saying.

I'm going to have to be to deal with this.

------

**Spencer comes back with his medication and food for both of us.**
*Is it bacteria? Maybe antibiotics can kill werewolf bacteria,* I think, watching him swallow the pills. Maybe I won't have to tell him what's happened to him here. If I'd taken antibiotics soon enough last year, I would have been cured. If I'd taken them, I'd be in California right now. For the first time all year, for some reason, the thought doesn't sting quite as much.

Spencer offers me weed, which I politely decline. I look in the basement for the tire Brigid wrote about in her journal, ignoring all the teeth scattered around the floor there, too. I unlock the door while Spencer tosses it out for her, and she runs after it happily, gnawing on the edge when we don't throw it again. Spencer plays a horrible B horror movie with buckets of fake blood. I fall asleep on the couch again. My last thought before I do is, *Brigid would love this. I wish she were here.*

Or, more accurately, *I wish she were herself.*

Spencer shakes me awake. "Sorry, sorry," I mutter. "What time is it?"

"Eleven-thirty," he says.

"Dude, why are you still here?" I groan. Then I catch the expression on his face, something between horror and awe and disgust.

"I . . . just saw something," he says, "that I will never be able to unsee."

I walk back to the kitchen. He's turned on the lights in the back-yard. At the edge of the pool of light, half in shadow, I see Brigid. Brigid-with-skin, Brigid. Brigid with her freckles across her round nose, wearing the GREAT BUS DRIVER T-shirt that now comes down to her thighs. Her hair is long enough to brush over her forehead now, the tips of her ears.

"You said werewolf earlier, didn't you?" Spencer says.

"Yeah."

"Yeah. That checks out." There's a long pause as I watch the gears turn in his head, watch him look down to his right leg and think about the bandage underneath his pants. "Oh *shit*."

# 22

**"So when do my werewolf powers come in?" Spencer asks from** the couch.

"Spencer, oh my *God*," Brigid rasps. "Can you just let me apologize again?"

"Nope," he says. "This is, by far, the coolest thing that's ever happened to me." He's grinning like any of this is normal. Last night he'd started chuckling before breaking down into hysterical, heaving laughter. I'd made him sit at the kitchen table and drink a glass of water before explaining everything that I knew.

"There aren't any powers, dude," Brigid says through a mouthful of hamburger meat. "It's pretty underwhelming."

"You are a werewolf!" Spencer whoops. "Werewolves are *real*! In freaking, like, shitty backwoods Bellows! There is nothing underwhelming about that at all!"

"How are you feeling, Spencer?" I ask. "I still don't get how you're not freaking out."

"You mean like, do I feel like howling at the moon? Like there's some sort of supervirus surfing around in my blood right now?"

I nod. Brigid raises an eyebrow.

"Nah, man." He laughs, stretching. "I literally feel exactly the same. I actually slept pretty well."

"That's probably a good sign," I say. I push myself off the couch with a hiss, padding toward the kitchen. "I'm making some tea, if anyone wants any."

"I'm okay," says Brigid.

"Oh wait, can you grab me my antibiotics?" Spencer shouts.

"Get them yourself," I say, but I grab them anyway, tossing them toward the couch.

"Maybe I should stop taking them. Really give this supervirus a chance."

"Really give an infection a chance," I say, sarcastically. "Really let that sepsis get in there."

I lean over the sink, my fingers working along my scalp before I duck my head fully into my hands. The metal edge is cool on my forearms. I can hear the fan ticking in the other room, the murmur of Brigid and Spencer's conversation. The pain in my knee is edging back up, and I feel myself getting hot. *More ibuprofen. That'll fix this.* The teakettle starts to whistle, and I'm gripped with the distinct, dizzying thought that I am a part of something I should not be, in possession of a knowledge I should never have known. I am in over my head, but the only thing left to do at this point is to start swimming.

I take two ibuprofen and pour the tea.

"Dude, we totally went to the same high school!" Spencer says as I shuffle back into the living room. "I thought she looked familiar, but I got kind of distracted by the whole 'Priya's a serial killer' thing."

"Pretty good theory," says Brigid.

"The human teeth kind of solidified that for me," he says.

"That was my bad," she says.

"Also, I was kind of a stoner then, so I wasn't paying much attention to anyone."

"I remember you. You had a ponytail." Brigid chuckles.

"I . . . did," he says, looking at me and wincing. "Come on, man, she didn't have to know that."

Brigid shrugs.

"I actually kinda miss that look," he says. "Not super practical, though."

"Fashion never is," Brigid says. She glances at me, like she can feel my eyes on her. She doesn't look good. The circles under her eyes are so dark they look like bruises, and she's paler than she was before. She eats slowly, mechanically. She seems far away from me.

"How do you feel about campy horror movies, B?" Spencer says. Of course.

"Uh, amazing," Brigid says. "Nothing better."

"Am I the only one who calls you by your actual name?" I ask.

She shrugs. "I like that you do," she says, smiling softly. "But do *you* want a nickname, Pri?"

"B and Pri!" Spencer says, grinning. I groan.

"Okay, Spence," I say.

He shrugs. "You can call me anything you want, girl."

Brigid laughs for the first time all day, and I blink in surprise. Her teeth form an unbroken row, white and shiny.

"Your tooth is back," I say.

"Told you it wasn't a big deal," she says. "They fall out every time."

"Metal," says Spencer.

She raises her eyebrows at him, smiling tiredly. She's acting like it's nothing. But all I can picture is her hunched over the passenger side of her car, gums bleeding, as sharp teeth force out human ones.

She catches my eye and her smile fades. I try to coax my expression into something less concerned, but it's too late.

"What?" she says. Her tone is a little bit frayed at the edges of her voice.

"Nothing," I say.

"Don't look at me like that. You of all people should know why that sucks."

"Brigid—"

"Don't."

Spencer's gaze darts between the two of us. "What, what's going on?"

"We don't have to talk about this—" Brigid starts.

"We do, Brigid. It's only been two weeks since the last time you turned, and you turned again *yesterday*."

"How long is it supposed to be?" asks Spencer.

I see Brigid's jaw work. "Once a month."

"She's getting worse," I say softly. I look back at her, the defensiveness in her glare masking fear. "You're getting *worse*, Brigid. We can't just ignore it."

"I'm dealing with it," she croaks.

"Are you?"

"Yeah!"

"Spencer and I had to track you down at the supermarket, Brigid.

People *saw* you."

"Maybe that isn't a bad thing," she says. "She likes the fresh air. I missed getting to run like that."

"You got loose in town! You bit Spencer! You ate—" I swallow the rest of the sentence. Spencer shakes his head.

Brigid looks between the two of us. "What. What did I eat."

"Well," Spencer says quietly. "I got a call about a missing cat."

"Oh no," she says, looking queasy. She pulls a throw pillow over her face. "Oh, God. No. I didn't want to know. Oh my God."

"Brigid . . ." I pull the pillow back. Her eyes screw shut.

"Oh my *God*. I ate a fucking cat," she wails.

"Has this happened before?" I finally ask.

She looks at me. "No, Priya, I don't think I've ever eaten a live cat before."

"I meant the transformations."

She closes her eyes again. "No," she says. "Not like this. Something's, uh. Something's wrong."

I reach for her hand and squeeze it gently, once. She rubs my thumb with hers. "Then we've gotta figure out what," I say.

"Hell yes," Spencer says. "I'm in."

"Yeah, you sort of have to be, now," Brigid says, tight. "Sorry."

"Stop!" he says. "Nothing left to do but wait and see how it shakes out for team werewolf."

"Team werewolf?" Brigid laughs, hollow. "Do we have a hashtag?"

"Yeah," he says. "It's all over Twitter. You, me, Priya. Hashtag team werewolf. You're the only team in the league, and everyone's on your side."

"He's fun," Brigid says to me. Spencer laughs as Brigid pulls her mouth into a grin. He doesn't notice that it doesn't reach her eyes.

-------

**oof ouch my bones (ONLINE – 8)**

**Seb (mereextravagancy):**

> So, has it been as bad a week for anyone else as it's been for me?

> Not to start off on a bummer or anything

**al (thorswagnarok):**
yeah

**Spook (spookyspoony):**
I've had better. Everything hurts
At least they let me sit down at the lab

**bridge (bigforkhands):**
i'm, uh
i'm coping?
...sort of

**katie (fyodorbrostoevsky):**
<3

**lee (typhoonsss):**
i'm the same physically, ok emotionally!

**katie (fyodorbrostoevsky):**
any news on the hysterectomy, lee?

**lee (typhoonsss):**
not yet!
i went to that appointment with the new doctor and it went pretty well
she's open to it, so i'm going in for another scan this week

**Priya (paranormaldetective):**
That's good!

**lee (typhoonsss):**
yes! here's hoping
how's it going, katie? and seb, how's your chair stuff?

**katie (fyodorbrostoevsky):**
it's going :/
i'm getting another round of testing soon
no idea how I'm paying but that's a later problem

**Priya (paranormaldetective):**
Keep us posted

**katie (fyodorbrostoevsky):**
I will, I will

**Seb (mereextravagancy):**

> Still waiting on the chair! It's gonna be at least 2 months, so I'm still making use of the cane
>
> [IMG_4377.JPEG]

**katie (fyodorbrostoevsky):**

> you look very handsome in that picture, Sebastian

**Seb (mereextravagancy):**

> Thank you, Katherine :)

**al (thorswagnarok):**

> STOP
>
> FLIRTING

**Priya (paranormaldetective):**

> I don't think they can help themselves

**bridge (bigforkhands):**

> get a room

**al (thorswagnarok):**

> yeah, get a room

**Seb (mereextravagancy):**

> A virtual room?
>
> Like, DMs?

**Spook (spookyspoony):**

> Haha

**katie (fyodorbrostoevsky):**

> ¯\_(ツ)_/¯

**bridge (bigforkhands):**

> are you doing ok, spook?
>
> what's up

**Spook (spookyspoony):**

> Oh, we don't have to get totally into it
>
> Depression is just kind of kicking my ass right now

**lee (typhoonsss):**

> :/

**Spook (spookyspoony):**

> No, it's okay, I'm just tired of this
>
> I'm not suicidal or anything, I don't want to die

But I also don't want to keep living in this body that is in pain 24/7

I'm never not hurting

It's like I'm carrying an invisible monster on my back, you know?

**bridge (bigforkhands):**

yes

**Spook (spookyspoony):**

But I called my therapist and we're gonna go back to meeting once a week, over the phone

She might take a look at my medication, too

**lee (typhoonsss):**

i'm so glad you're on top of it

in that regard

**bridge (bigforkhands):**

do you ever

hold on, let me think about how to say this

**Priya (paranormaldetective):**

Take your time

**bridge (bigforkhands):**

with your body, it's like you're in this apartment, and it's a shitty ass apartment

the ceiling is caving in, and it's infested with rats, and you have to step around like, holes in the floor or whatever

and other people have like, beautiful perfect houses

and all you want to do is move, but you can't

**Spook (spookyspoony):**

Yeah

**Max (quintuplevampire):**

Not yet

**katie (fyodorbrostoevsky):**

max WHAT

that's SO ominous

**Max (quintuplevampire):**

One day body hopping technology will exist

But then who decides which bodies to transfer to ?

There is some cyberpunk dystopia just waiting here I'm telling you

**Seb (mereextravagancy):**

ok mood

**bridge (bigforkhands):**

i

i don't want to be dead, really

i just want to be like, briefly not-alive

**lee (typhoonsss):**

hon

**bridge (bigforkhands):**

no, no, I'm ok, that's not what I meant exactly

you ever just want to take a quick coma

like, maybe for a month

just to recuperate

**Priya (paranormaldetective):**

I get that

Sort of

**katie (fyodorbrostoevsky):**

I absolutely get it

Like, a sleeping beauty or snow white situation

**Seb (mereextravagancy):**

Yes

As long as you don't want to be dead

**bridge (bigforkhands):**

no, I don't

I promise

**al (thorswagnarok)**

i do

sometimes

want to be dead

There's a few seconds where no one sends any messages. No one knows what to say.

**katie (fyodorbrostoevsky):**

oh, al.

**lee (typhoonsss):**

i'm turning on the voice chat

**Seb (mereextravagancy):**

Me too.

"Al?" A voice with an English accent comes through the speaker. "It's Lee. You don't have to turn yours on if you don't want to. I just want you to know I'm here, in a tangible way, and I want you to hear what I'm going to say instead of just reading it. Alright?"

There's a long pause, and then I see Al's voice chat turn on. "I love your accent!" they say, and I hear a couple of people laugh.

"That's it," says Lee. "Alright then. We love you so much. You are so funny, and you're a great friend, and every single one of us is here for you, any time you need us."

"Absolutely." Seb's name lights up in the chat. "It's Seb. I always look forward to this chat, but you, specifically, make it a better place. Really and truly."

"It's Katie, we love you!"

"Bridge here. You're my sibling in arms, kid."

"It's Priya, I'm so sorry you're feeling like this. We love you."

"It's Max, and—and you know I care about you . . . because you're hearing . . . my voice right now."

"Max, it is so good to hear your voice."

"Thank you."

"Chat dad here with a virtual pat on the back. Lee can take the advice."

It's so surreal to hear everyone's voice. No one sounds like I'd imagined, because I hadn't even imagined anyone fully. I can feel my chest filling with warmth.

Al's voice chat turns off again.

"You okay, pal?" asks Brigid.

"You still there?"

**al (thorswagnarok):**

still here

i just don't want all of you to hear me ugly crying right now

"Turn it back on!"

"We want to hear you!"

There's a sniffle behind a mic, a deep intake of breath. "I'm here, guys," says Al, wobbly.

We all cheer, and I hear a muffled sound that makes me tear up, too.

"I don't have a joke to crack," they say.

"You don't always have to crack jokes," says Spook.

"But I thought that was what coping was," says Brigid.

"Okay," Lee says. "Al."

"I'm here."

"You've had thoughts about dying. Have you thought about killing yourself?"

It's quiet. "Y-yes."

"Okay. Like what?"

"Like, it would be easier to just be dead. Or—or, I wish I'd get hit by a car. Or, no one would really care if I was gone."

"Do you have any kind of plan?"

"No, no plan. Just these thoughts that won't stop popping into my head."

"That's good," Lee says. "That's great, honey. If those thoughts ever turn into something with a plan, I need you to walk straight to the ER. Promise me?"

"Yes. I promise."

"And you can DM any of us, but we can't do anything to help you from England or Oregon or Canada, okay? You have to get a system in place where you are."

"Right."

"Al?" Max says. "We . . . we would care. We would care . . . a lot."

"We'd be . . . we'd be devastated, Al," says Katie.

"We're a team, okay?" I chime in. "We're a crew. And it just wouldn't be the same without you in it."

"Yes."

"Absolutely."

"But you need to start going to therapy."

"Seb."

"What, it's true. Have you seen someone about this, Al?"

"No," they say. "I, uh. I never even admitted it to anyone until now. But I'm . . . I'm not okay. Everything feels so impossible. That was actually really scary, even though I feel like it's normal for everyone our age to talk about how much they want to die."

"It was really brave!"

"Would you be okay with seeing a therapist?"

"It's helped me a lot," says Spook. "It's kept me alive."

"I'm nervous about talking to my parents about it," they say. "My dad doesn't think depression is real."

"Oof."

"What about your mom?"

"She tends to go along with my dad, so I don't know. She never talks about things like this."

"I think it's important to tell her," I say.

"What if they won't help me?" they whisper.

"Can you . . . talk . . . to your school? Do you h–have a school psychologist? Or . . . guidance counselor?"

"I didn't think about that," Al says.

"Can you talk to them tomorrow?"

"Yeah. Yes. Sorry, I was nodding, I forgot you couldn't see me."

"They can . . . help you talk . . . to y–your parents," Max says.

"That's really smart. Thanks, dude," Al says.

"Anytime," says Max.

"Thank you for trusting us enough to let us know, Al," Lee says.

I hear them start to cry again.

"I love you guys so much," they say. "I'm so glad I know you."

I realize that I'm not as alone as I'd been imagining myself to be. I have my family. I have Brigid. But I also have Seb, Katie, Spook, Lee, Max, and Al. My body has tried its best to isolate me from everyone, but it hasn't won.

I have.

# 23

**It takes me a few minutes before I psych myself up to message**
Spook directly. I've never talked to her one-on-one before, and she
feels like a real adult, a little intimidating. I hit ENTER before I can
second-guess myself.

> **paranormaldetective:**
> Hey! I just wanted to ask – you're in grad school for
> medical research, right? Could I ask you a few questions
> about that? I was pre-med at school but I feel like that
> might not pan out anymore
>
> So, uh... I'd love to talk to you about your program? Or
> what you do?

> **spookyspoony:**
> Hi, Priya! Yeah, totally. I'm actually headed home right
> now, so I'll message you in about 40 minutes.

My computer chimes again in exactly thirty-eight minutes. It's
uncanny.

> **spookyspoony:**
> Okay, I'm doing an MS in molecular biology, with a focus
> in genetics, with the possibility of going into a PhD
> program after I'm finished.
>
> But frankly, the MS has taken me long enough (with the
> chronic illness stuff), so I may just start working in a lab

I'm doing rotations now to figure out which kind of lab work I like best

Any more questions?

**paranormaldetective:**

That is extremely cool

**spookyspoony:**

Thanks!

**paranormaldetective:**

Yeah, uh, I had a couple specific ones

I'm doing an independent study

**spookyspoony:**

Oh cool

**paranormaldetective:**

Yeah

Okay so, is there a way to figure out if someone's illness is genetic, or if it's bacterial or viral?

Clinically speaking

**spookyspoony:**

Well sure

Hang on, do you mean like, a whole new disease? Are you making scientific discoveries in your spare time?

**paranormaldetective:**

Haha

...yeah theoretically, a new disease

**spookyspoony:**

Okay, hold on

Let me break it down by each of the things you've mentioned

**paranormaldetective:**

Please

**spookyspoony:**

Viruses are really difficult to study, and an unknown virus especially would be almost impossible to identify

Bacteria are much easier to isolate

It's hard to prove, one hundred percent, that a disease is genetic, but there are definitely things to look for

For all these things you'd look at symptoms first, to see what triggered the onset – something bacterial or viral would have symptoms of an infection, probably

BUT symptoms don't have to be present throughout someone's entire life for a disease to have a genetic component. It might be triggered by something like puberty, or stress

**paranormaldetective:**

Okay

**spookyspoony:**

Am I making sense?

**paranormaldetective:**

Yeah, I think so

Look at symptoms first, start making connections?

**spookyspoony:**

Right, exactly

For an actual infection at a site you could do a culture

For genetics, looking at a family tree is a good start, too, to see if you can find similar symptoms and start connecting the dots that way

**paranormaldetective:**

Okay, gotcha

I think, haha

**spookyspoony:**

You can ask me more questions later, don't worry

So you're thinking about doing research instead of med school?

**paranormaldetective:**

Uh, I might be? I hadn't thought about it before now

**spookyspoony:**

I mean it's different from being a doctor, obviously research puts the focus on a different set of skills

So I wouldn't recommend using it as a consolation prize if you decide not to go to med school

Sorry, that's blunt, I'm trying to work on that

**paranormaldetective:**

No, I'm trying to figure out if it's something I'd enjoy

**spookyspoony:**

Oh cool

You could always look into an internship?

I really love it, I'm planning on researching the genetic component to fibromyalgia

**paranormaldetective:**

Oh wow

I didn't even think about trying to like... study yourself?

I didn't know people even did that

**spookyspoony:**

I mean, of course they do

Medical research needs sick people

Who's more invested in that research than you?

**paranormaldetective:**

I guess that's true

**spookyspoony:**

A lot of chronic illnesses are considered female illnesses, which is honestly why we don't know enough about them

Women are just expected to live with their pain

I was actually talking to Lee about this recently, you know what she said?

**paranormaldetective:**

What?

**spookyspoony:**

She said that being a woman means that everyone hates your body, and your body hates you

**paranormaldetective:**

That's. Yeah

That's really heavy

**spookyspoony:**

Unfortunately that sort of carries over to clinical research, too

Historically

I mean, you could definitely dig into Lyme research

There's still a ton we don't know about Lyme disease or

| why it affects people the way that it does

**paranormaldetective:**

| Yeah, a lot of people don't even think chronic lyme exists

**spookyspoony:**

| Exactly
| You could try to solve your own mystery
| Right there in your username, huh

**paranormaldetective:**

| Yeah, I guess it is

**spookyspoony:**

| Alright, I've gotta go, but let me know if you have any
| follow up questions
| Good luck on your independent study

**paranormaldetective:**

| Thanks, Spook!

**spookyspoony:**

| Yeah, anytime.
| Oh before I go, you're checking in on Al tonight, right?

**paranormaldetective:**

| Yep, they talked to their counselor and I think it went
| well! So I am following up on that

**spookyspoony:**

| That's great, I'll message tomorrow
| Later

**paranormaldetective:**

| Later!

It's overwhelming, but Spook's given me somewhere to start, at least—questions to ask Brigid, things to look for in Spencer. I hadn't really been thinking about research at all, not even as a second choice.

But there's something about it that's tugging at the back of my brain now, something I might be able to get excited about. It *is* like solving a mystery, but Spook was only half right. I don't want to solve myself. I don't want to think about myself long enough to put my body, or my mind, under the microscope.

I want to solve Brigid.

-------

Are there any other lycanthropes in your family?

hello to u too

Still haven't fixed your phone?

what's wrong with it

Oh my God

and totally, we all talk about it at reunions

no dude lmao

idk anyone else

if there is someone they're keeping it to themselves

Maybe someone in your extended family?

gotta send a mass email out

subject line: u a werewolf? Please respond

Fantastic idea

no, ur right, that's nuts

i've gotta do individual emails

add that personal touch

Hahaha

i'll think abt it

i mean

we are estranged from my gran

Ok, now we're talking

so svmpathetic lol

...Sorry

<3 ?

obviouslv <3

How long has it been since you've talked to her

like... 8 or 9

...years?

mmhmm

...oh shit

Maybe you should talk to her

yeah probably

i don't have her number though

oh Spencer says he's mad at u

What??

Are you guys hanging out?

he wants to know why u aren't using the

hashtag team werewolf group chat

Oh my God

he made it for a reason, Pri

Yes. To vex me

My phone starts buzzing, because I'm being FaceTimed. I hit ACCEPT. Brigid's face takes up most of the screen, and she grins lazily at me from behind those oversized neon sunglasses. Spencer is hovering near her shoulder, holding the phone. He waves at me with his other hand. It looks like they're in Brigid's backyard, squinting into the sunlight.

Their expressions are infectious, and I feel myself smiling back at them. "Hey guys!"

"Priya!" they crow.

"Hello from your two favorite werewolves," Spencer says.

"Potential werewolf." Brigid frowns.

"Pre-werewolf," Spencer tries.

"Thanks for hanging out without me," I say.

Spencer rolls his eyes. "You're in Jersey, dude."

And I'm stuck here. Suresh has been giving me the cold shoulder since I'd stayed out with the car again last week. He'd stuck a piece of paper to the back of the door that said OFFICIAL CAR SCHEDULE FOR PEOPLE WHO JUST KEEP TAKING IT WITHOUT ASKING IF THAT'S OKAY WITH THEIR BROTHER. He'd claimed it for today as soon as he got home from school.

"Excuses, excuses," I say. "How are you feeling, Brigid?" I ask.

She smiles at me, but it's tight around the corners of her mouth. "Oh, you know," she says.

I don't, but I let it slide with Spencer there.

"Spencer? How's the open wound?"

"Great," he says. "We're shooting the shit."

Brigid toasts me with an energy drink. "Literally. He brought over BB guns. We're trying to shoot the empty cans."

"How's that going?" I ask.

Brigid grabs the phone, twists it around to show a line of cans on a cardboard box. There's only one space missing.

"Shouldn't Spencer be a better shot?" I ask.

"After last week," he says, pulling the phone back, "I thought it might be a good idea to do a little target practice."

"We wish you were here," says Brigid. "Even though I know you don't like guns."

"At least they aren't real guns. Also, Spencer, why are you not at work? It's the middle of the day."

"For your information, I'm on the night shift today," he says. "Man, you're all over my ass."

"You wish she was!" Brigid says. Spencer and I groan.

"Tell us the biology intel," Spencer says.

"Oh, right," I say. "So there's no special one-stop-shop kind of test. Spencer, keep an eye on your leg and let me know if it gets red or oozing or anything like that."

"Aye aye, captain."

"There might be some kind of blood test we could do," I say. "Maybe compare samples from both of you? I don't know where we'd have access to a microscope, though."

"Oh," says Spencer. "Oh, I do, actually."

"Good to know. We should also be paying attention to Brigid's extended family, in case it's genetic," I say authoritatively. It feels good to lay everything out step-by-step.

Brigid pushes her sunglasses up, pushing back her new swoop of hair, and squints into the camera. "We? Am I gonna be your test subject, doc?"

"I mean, I wouldn't put it that way," I hedge.

"I was joking," she says, her smile dimming.

"Brigid, I—" I huff out a breath, working through my words in my head first. "I just want to help."

"Yeah, yeah, I get it," she says.

"This could be a chance to finally figure some stuff out, you know?"

Spencer turns to study her. "Yeah, like, if your heartbeat gets above a certain rate, do you turn into a werewolf?"

"No," she says.

"But if you run around the backyard for a little while and we write down what happens, then it's *science*," he says, raising his eyebrows. He looks into the camera. "Right, Priya?"

"Yeah, actually," I say. Brigid leans back in her seat. "I was actually looking up angel's glow, since you messaged me about it again," I say.

She doesn't ask me why I'm bringing it up. "The bioluminescent bacteria that magically heals you? The story's probably just made up," she says. "An urban legend."

"Well, that thing about the Civil War soldiers might be an urban legend, but the bacteria's real," I say. "The *science* is real. It's beautiful and impossible and it lights up like a glowstick, and . . ." I pause. "Maybe the fact that it exists in the first place is the miracle."

*Do you understand what I'm saying, Brigid?* I think through the screen. *I don't want to say it, but I don't think I have to.*

"But we don't have to do anything if you don't want to, Brigid," I say, softly. I want to push, but I don't.

She squirms in her chair. "We could really get up to some mad-scientist kind of shit here, huh," she says finally. I smile. "And I might, like—I mean, I might actually figure some stuff out."

"Hell yeah," I say. She grins at me, getting a glint in her eye. I feel myself settle. For the first time since that last transformation, she looks hopeful.

"Maybe there's something in the myths, too," she says, tapping her fingers on the table. "I can dig back into some of the stuff at Hattie's."

"Yes!" I say.

"Hashtag! Team! Wuh-wuh-werewolf!" Spencer whoops like he's at a monster truck rally, and Brigid laughs alongside him.

"Alright." She grins, bright like the sun. "Yeah, alright. Let's fucking do this."

# 24

**"We're ... done ... with ... God, give me ... give me a second."**
Brigid runs a hand through her sweaty hair, heaving in her breaths, and
rests her arms on her knees. "Nope," she says, pitching over entirely,
flopping facedown onto the grass, head pillowed on her forearm.

"What's the monitor say, Priya?" Spencer calls over. He's also
panting. They've been running sprints across Brigid's backyard for the
past fifteen minutes. I'm taking notes from the back porch, for once
glad to have an excuse not to run with them.

I check the phone. "147 bpm," I call back.

Brigid groans.

"So I think we can probably cross 'elevated heart rate' off the list,"
I say, writing down the numbers.

"Thank God," Brigid says from the ground.

"Sorry, how is this helping, again?" I ask.

Brigid and Spencer have plunged themselves wholeheartedly into
what we're calling *experiments* but that look suspiciously like *screwing
around*. Spencer touched her arm with a silver chain to see if she'd get
some kind of rash (she didn't); he'd tried shouting at her to make her
angry to see if she'd "hulk out" ("Spencer, I've been angry before."
"But are you angry *now*?" "I'm sure getting there!")

"Maybe adrenaline could play a part in all this," I say when we're
all around the table.

"Maybe," Brigid says.

"So what, we try to scare her?" Spencer asks.

"Guys, I don't think we should be trying to get her to turn," I say. "I feel like we've lost the thread here."

"What thread?" Brigid asks. Spencer points to her, raising his eyebrows.

"We could scare you," Spencer says, as though I haven't said anything.

"Impossible," Brigid says. "I'm not afraid of anything."

"Hm," he says. He pulls out his phone. I can see him googling "how to cause an adrenaline spike." "Hey, Brigid, stand up for a second," he says.

She pulls herself up.

"No, back up a little more," he says. She walks out onto the grass again, shrugging at him. He reaches for the BB gun that he left the last time they hung out and points it toward her, squinting through one eye.

"Oh my God, Spencer," I say. "Absolutely not."

"It won't even break the skin," he says. Brigid widens her stance, folding her arms across her chest and smirking.

"Do it, Yi," she taunts. "I fucking dare you."

"You know that means I have to," he says.

She spreads her arms like a starfish. "I saw you with those cans," she says. "No way you're going to hit me."

I take a long, slow sip from my lemonade. The straw gurgles.

Spencer pulls the trigger, and Brigid doubles over, cursing for a solid twenty seconds.

"You *asshole*!" she shouts.

"You dared me!" Spencer says. "Well, are you turning?"

"I'm going to kill you," she growls, shaking out her leg and lunging toward him. He shrieks, pushing himself out of the chair, but he's too slow. She slaps at his hands and I try not to laugh as he twists away from her, shouting. She yanks the BB gun out of his hands, pulls back, and throws it as hard as she can, chest heaving. I hear it clatter on the roof above me.

"We're even, we're even!" he cries.

Her eyes narrow. "I *knew* you were mad that I bit you," she says.

"I'm not mad," he says.

"You're allowed to be mad," she says, a little raw. He just shakes his head.

"Brigid," I say. They both look at me. "How are you feeling?"

She pauses, thinking. "Kind of tired. Pretty sore. But I don't think I'm turning, if that's what you're asking."

"That is what I'm asking," I say, opening the notebook to a new page. "Can we consider this experiment failed and move on?"

"Yeah, let's take a look at our blood," says Spencer. "I can draw some from both of us, I've done it before."

"On . . . people?" I ask.

"I mean, no," he says. "But it's not like either of you have any more experience with that."

"Yeah, works for me," Brigid says. "*Take my blood awayyyy . . .*" she croons, gesturing at me and Spencer. I laugh, despite myself.

"You ready to break into your office?" I ask.

"It's not breaking in," he says. "I have keys."

"It's not *not* breaking in," Brigid says.

He checks his watch. "Yeah, let's see what the vet left behind."

-------

**It's late by the time we get to Bellows County Animal Control.** There's a small shelter along with an office space in the back with hideous wood paneling and ancient, bulky computers.

"Don't tell—" Spencer starts.

"If you tell us not to tell your boss one more time, I am going to riot, Spencer," I say.

A dog starts yapping from the pound, then another, and another, until every animal in the building is rattling their cages. I turn and see Brigid with her hand through the bars as one of the dogs sniffs excitedly at her hand. She glances up at us, sheepish.

"I feel like he knows we're here at this point," I say. A fiftysome-thing man with gray hair, wearing the same uniform as Spencer, opens the door to the pound, glaring.

"Yi, can you get them to shut up," he drawls. "Not you ladies," he corrects, nodding.

"Sorry, Marty," Spencer says.

"Sorry, Marty," Brigid echoes, standing and wiping her hand on her shorts.

"Oh, Miss Brigid!" he says, surprised. "What are you doing around here?"

"Oh, you know . . ." she says. I make uneasy eye contact with her. "Hanging out. Running some top-secret blood tests. The usual."

Marty bursts into wheezing laughter. "You never change, do you, girl?" he says.

"That's what you think," Brigid says, pointing finger guns at him.

"And who's this?" he asks.

"Oh," I say. "I'm Priya. Brigid's friend."

"Hey," Spencer says, offended.

"Priya," Marty says, shaking my hand vigorously. "You new?"

"No, I'm over in New Jersey," I say.

"God help ya," he fires back.

"It is what it is." I smile. I suddenly feel like an entirely different person, someone well versed in folksy charm. I'm a stranger to everyone in this town. I can be whoever I want to be to them, and they would never know the difference. It feels . . . liberating.

On the other side of the door a phone starts ringing, and Marty waves a hand at the three of us, vanishing into the back office again. "Stay out of trouble!" he calls. "And don't be late to your shift again, I can't hold down the fort by myself here."

I look at Spencer. "That's it?"

He shrugs.

"How do you know him, Brigid?" I ask.

"He and Hattie are close. He swings by sometimes," she says.

"Oh, of course he does."

"This town has a population of, like, three thousand," she says. "I don't know what you expected."

"Come on," Spencer says. "Follow me. It's blood time."

Sure enough, there's an old microscope in the back. He's halfway through attaching a needle to one of the vials, looking suspiciously at the veins in the crook of his own elbow, before I stop him.

"We don't need that much, Spencer," I say. "You can just prick your finger and get a few drops on the slide that way."

"Oh." He blinks. "Yeah, let's do it your way."

He winces as he squeezes a drop out onto the slide, and Brigid does the same thing onto another without flinching. I lean forward to look into the microscope, both of them leaning in on either side. I can hear them breathing over my shoulder, suddenly nervous.

It's not until I look at the slide that I realize, with mounting horror, that I actually have no idea what I'm looking at.

Sure, I can see the faded orange circles of the red blood cells, spot the divot in the middle of a few of them. I can see a handful of fainter, larger white blood cell blobs and some tiny platelets. But when I scan across Brigid's blood sample, I don't notice anything out of the ordinary. I swap it out for Spencer's, scanning for similarities or differences, but it's just blood. It's just blood, and I am just a nineteen-year-old college kid feeling stupider by the second.

"Well?" Spencer says in my ear.

"What do you see, Priya?" Brigid says in the other.

I turn to face them, feeling awkward. "Okay, so . . . listen . . ." I start. Spencer's face goes slack, and I remember myself. "No, no, it's not bad! It's not really anything, I just . . . I just realized that I don't actually know what I'm supposed to be looking for."

"What do you mean," Spencer says slowly.

"I can't see anything in these samples, I don't know what I'm doing!"

"Oh my God," Brigid says. She lets out a wheezing kind of laugh. "Oh my God, Priya."

"Don't say anything!" I groan.

She's laughing so hard now that she has to grip onto the side of the metal table to hold herself upright. She's trying to talk, but she can't get anything out. Spencer rubs his hand across his face and starts to chuckle, too.

"Cool," he says. "Extremely cool."

"I can't believe we just believed you!" Brigid chokes out. "Like when you told us you could see if there was anything in our blood I was just like . . . yeah, of course, Priya can do anything."

My heart squeezes a little bit at that. "Aw. That's funny, because I can't actually do anything."

Brigid shoots me a look.

"You were so confident about it!" Spencer says.

"Please stop laughing." I sigh. "I get it, this is what hubris feels like."

"I thought hubris was that chickpea dip," says Spencer.

"Are you serious," I say. "Are you serious or are you doing a bit right now."

Brigid's eyes light up. "No, that's hummus," she says. "Hubris is when you're a baby and your skin turns yellow and they have to put you in the windowsill to get sunlight on you."

"What?" Spencer laughs.

"Brigid, are you—do you mean jaundice?"

"Priya!" she whines. "That's not how the bit works, you're supposed to say, 'no, that's jaundice,' and then come up with another wrong word to describe hubris."

"No, you win," I say. I look between the two of them. "I think we need another plan of attack."

-------

**paranormaldetective:**

> Quick question – is there a certain blood test you can have a doctor do to check for a bacterial infection?

**spookyspoony:**

> Oh God, no
> I mean
> Yes
> But if you've got bacteria actually INSIDE your blood that's sepsis and you're gonna be at death's door
> like, 75% chance you're going to die

**paranormaldetective:**

> ...ah
> Yeah I just realized that I don't actually know much about the practical, day-to-day parts of research

**spookyspoony:**

> You should check to see if a local lab is offering internships or shadowing opportunities!
> And I can talk on the phone about it a little later, if you'd be down for that?

**paranormaldetective:**
| That would be really great, actually

**spookyspoony:**
| Cool, lemme know when

**paranormaldetective:**
| Will do!

# 25

Brigid's got a shift at Hattie's the next morning, but she invites me and Spencer along, too. "Hattie won't mind," she says, navigating the lower level like she could find her way with her eyes closed. She plucks books off shelves and out from under table legs, stacking a pile under her chin. "She keeps all these weird, old-timey occult books around here."

"Okay, I'm not looking at those," I say, glancing at Spencer. "Be careful."

She chuckles. "What, do you believe in that stuff?"

"You are literally a werewolf."

"Yeah, exactly. What else could happen to me at this point? Nothing matters!"

"That was a very dark thing you said very cheerfully."

We end up sprawled on the upper landing, looking over the railing to the rest of the shop. We're up by the rafters here, dark wood and cobwebs, and it's hot enough that we have to take our jackets off, but we settle into a pleasant, muggy kind of silence, flipping through books and scrolling on Brigid's laptop. Brigid points Spencer to the bathroom a few hours in, and he stretches, heading down the stairs.

I'm reading *The Werewolf in Lore and Legend* by Montague Summers but I'm not getting anywhere. I forget the words as soon as I read them; I've been on the same page for fifteen minutes, reading the same line over and over: *but they are thirsty, and their legs have incurable ulcerations from frequent falls. Such are the marks of the disease. You must know that lycanthropia—*

If I start thinking about the way my brain works now, like Wi-Fi trying to connect with a patchy signal, I'll start crying, so I don't. Instead, I watch Brigid flopped on her stomach, kicking her legs in the air as she scans two separate books at once. *My body's trying to kill me,* she'd told me earlier, before Spencer got here. *And I just have to live with it.* Is she okay? Really?

I know she'd snap at me if she could hear what I was thinking. But I can't help it; sometimes, when I look at her, it feels like I've spun out on the road over black ice.

She clicks around on her laptop for a second, frowning, then rifles back through one of the books again. We're looking through myths this time—her self-taught wheelhouse.

"What is it?" I ask, raising my eyebrows at her. She meets my eyes across the landing, raising hers right back. "Did you find something?"

"I mean, it's a lot of the usual stuff," she says distractedly. "Like, yelling my Christian name three times doesn't seem like it would help turn me back. Or cure me for good."

"Brigid! Brigid! Brigid!" I hear Spencer call from the bottom of the stairs.

"While I'm transformed, dummy," she calls back.

"Yeah, I can't see that being useful as a medical cure," I say. "This is physiological. Brigid isn't, like, doing magic."

"That you know of," she says, winking at me.

I roll my eyes.

"That bathroom is absolutely terrifying, Brigid," Spencer says, sitting down with us again. "You didn't want to warn me?"

She grins. "Warn you about what?"

"You know what!" he yells. "I'm talking about the taxidermied boar head over the toilet that stares you directly in the eyes as you take a leak!"

"Oh," she says calmly. "That's Boris."

"It's WORSE that he has a name! That's so much worse!" Spencer says. "And why is he wearing a hat?"

"It's festive!" Brigid says.

"It's April," says Spencer. "Anyway. Horror show aside, what were you guys talking about?"

"I think I have a lead," Brigid says, that furrow back in her brow.

"I keep finding references to wolfsbane in these books. It's the common thread between all these myths."

"That's literally poison," I say.

"Yeah, I know," Brigid says. "That's why I don't think they mean, like, taking a big bite out of one of those purple flowers and dying on the spot. I think it's some kind of compound. Like, an old-timey version of a drug."

"What is it supposed to do?" I ask.

"Well, that's what I'm trying to figure out," she says. "Some of these myths say that witches used to make salves out of, like, baby fat, so that they could turn *into* a werewolf."

Spencer makes a choked sort of sound.

"But I've found a couple of things that talk about using wolfsbane to stop the transformations completely. To turn . . . human," she says softly. I can tell just by looking at her that her brain has gone somewhere else completely. She looks like she's on the brink of tears. I think about all the times we've messaged each other late at night, talking about everything and nothing, saying *I wish I was there to give you a hug right now.* I motion to Spencer to help pull me to my feet and shuffle over to her, sitting hip to hip.

"Hey," I say.

"I think we're fooling ourselves," she says, all in a rush. "I can't control this. I can't—I can't stop it. I don't know why it's happening like this. And in medieval myths werewolves transformed, like, every week, or every single night, so maybe that's what's going to end up happening, you know? Maybe it's just going to get faster and faster and faster until—"

"Brigid—" I say.

"All I'm seeing here," she says, tossing one of the books across the landing, "is the best way for someone to kill me. To unmake me. I'm getting really fucking tired of watching myself die."

I put my arm around her, and I feel her head hit my shoulder. Spencer scoots in on her other side, kicking her foot with his.

"Maybe I'm not supposed to be a person anymore," she says.

"Hey," says Spencer. "What the hell is that supposed to mean?"

"I don't know," she says.

"You're our *friend*, Brigid," I say. "Okay?" She looks at me, finally, and I'm relieved to see that there aren't any tears in her clear, brown eyes, just something shy of panic. I will it to subside. Everything else in my life seems big and loud, getting caught in a riptide or falling through a rotted floorboard in an abandoned house. But this? I can fix this.

"Okay," she finally says, looking away. She threads her right arm through the crook of mine, then the left through Spencer's.

"This is very *Wizard of Oz*," he says, and she finally laughs, leaning her head back against the railing.

"We've gotta find my Gran," she says. "She might have some actual fucking answers."

"You don't know where she is?" I ask.

"Nope," she says, popping the *p*. "I could go down the phone book for every eighty-year-old Maggie Leahy in the country. Start making calls."

"I mean . . ." I say. "Wild idea: you could ask your mom."

"Oh, that'd go over just great," Brigid says. "Hey, Mom, I know you hate *your* mom for being cold and distant and mean and haven't talked to her in almost a decade. But can I go hang out with her? Everything is totally fine, I'm not asking for any particular reason."

"You've never asked to see her before?"

"I stopped asking myself why she hated me when I was a kid," Brigid says. "It's not like wondering was gonna fix it."

"I'm sorry," I say. She shakes her head.

"Alright, can we be done with this?" she asks. "I'm researched out."

"Yeah, dude," Spencer says. The shop bell jingles, and I glance over in surprise. There hasn't been a single customer the whole time we've been here. I'd forgotten that Hattie's was even open.

"Sorry, we're haunted!" Brigid yells down.

"Haunted's right up my alley!" a woman's voice yells back. "Do I have the pleasure of speaking beyond the veil right now?"

Brigid grins as the steps creak. "Absolutely," she says. "One hundred percent certified deceased. It's ghost city up here in the rafters."

Hattie sticks her head of frizzy hair up, spotting the three of us tucked together, and presses her lips together in a fond smile. "Oh! Just look at you three! Don't move a single muscle."

Brigid groans. "Hattie!"

Hattie doesn't listen. She slides her phone out of the pocket of her billowy, oversized pants, lines us up, and takes several shots.

"I'm sending these to you," she says. I smile for the camera on instinct. "Hi again, Diana," she says.

"Hi again, Hattie," I say.

"Her name is Priya," Brigid says.

"I know," says Hattie. "We're doing a bit. Spencer, I didn't know you and Brigid were friends now," she continues, snapping another shot.

"BFFs," he says. "Blood brothers."

"Does your BFF know she should be downstairs at the counter right now?" Hattie says. Spencer lets out an "ooh." Brigid stacks the books and stands, and Hattie lets out a deep sigh.

"Brigid."

"What?" she asks, the picture of innocence.

"Your shirt."

She glances down. It's another thrift store monstrosity. This one's gray, with enormous rainbow letters that read I DON'T NEED GOOGLE—MY WIFE'S BOYFRIEND KNOWS EVERYTHING.

Hattie sighs. "Put on one of the aprons if Mrs. Carlton comes in. I don't understand you, darling, but I feel like you're very funny." She nods at me and Spencer. "You can stick around, but maybe make your way downstairs?"

"Will do, Hattie," says Spencer.

"I love you!" Brigid calls. I hear Hattie laugh from the stairs.

"What *is* with your shirts?" Spencer asks.

"Oh," Brigid says. "I kept getting bummed that I was ruining my favorite clothes so I started buying the ugliest thrift store shirts I could find. The manager texts me pictures now when the worst ones come in." She glances down at her shirt mournfully. "Kind of backfired, though. I love them all."

"Should we get out of your hair?" I ask.

"Up to you," says Brigid. She fixes me with a look. "You good to drive, Priya?"

"I'm good," I say.

"*Yeah* you are." She smiles. I roll my eyes, but fondness pools in my chest.

I slip one of the books into my backpack after asking Hattie if it's okay to take it. She looks at the cover, eyebrows rising. "*The Werewolf in Lore and Legend*?" she reads.

"Um," I say.

"Yeah, we're doing lycanthropy research," Brigid says from behind the counter, as easy as anything. "I mean, we were. I'm pretty sick of it."

"Do you want me to put feelers out for more books?" Hattie asks. Spencer and I meet each other's eyes.

"If you want." Brigid shrugs. "Wolfsbane, too."

Hattie rolls her sleeve up, makes a note on her arm, nodding. "Can do, kiddo."

"You're the weirdest person in this town, Hattie," Brigid says fondly.

"Birds of a feather," Hattie fires back.

I take one last look at them all before I leave, clustered together around the counter's display case. I wonder if I'm forcing myself into their little town in a desperate, lonely attempt to be a part of something for the first time in months—if I'm just hovering at the fringes of another group of people that I don't fully belong to. But then Brigid looks up and snaps her eyes to mine, winking, and I suddenly feel that line of affection that's pulled between us as solidly as if it's made of twine, two tin cans on either side of a childhood friend's backyard. It feels like I've always known her. And just like that, I realize that I'm not sure I can imagine my life without her in it, either.

-------

**oof ouch my bones (ONLINE – 6)**

**al (thorswagnarok):**

> YALL PLEASE LOOK AT WHAT MAX JUST SENT ME
> WE WERE TALKING ABOUT CRYPTIDS AND –
> https://liminal.earth/wolfman?/
> it's not just one person who saw it though, there's literally a local mag that mentions it, too:
> https://back-basin-intelligencer.com/articles/bellows-beast/113727495
> NEW! CRYPTID!!

**Max (quintuplevampire):**

New cryptid, baby!

That took forever, my voice to text does not understand what a cryptid is

**katie (fyodorbrostoevsky):**

ohhhh my GOD

**Seb (mereextravagancy):**

I also do not understand what a cryptid is

**bridge (bigforkhands):**

hang on you two are talking outside the group chat??

that's adorable but also how dare you

**Priya (paranormaldetective):**

............have you clicked the link yet, Brigid?

**al (thorswagnarok):**

YOU DON'T KNOW WHAT A CRYPTID IS???

**katie (fyodorbrostoevsky):**

Seb... honey...

**al (thorswagnarok):**

I'm sorry

HONEY??

**Max (quintuplevampire):**

It's a creature that hasn't been proven to exist yet

Like the loch ness monster

Or mothman

**Seb (mereextravagancy):**

So a mythical creature

**katie (fyodorbrostoevsky):**

no because they do exist, obviously

**Seb (mereextravagancy):**

Obviously

**katie (fyodorbrostoevsky):**

ok holy shit about the bellows beast though

look? At that picture???

**Max (quintuplevampire):**

I know!

**al (thorswagnarok):**

I knowwwwwwwwwwwwwww

**bridge (bigforkhands):**

i

**Max (quintuplevampire):**

I'm usually really skeptical of this kind of stuff. But this looks intimately real

**Seb (mereextravagancy):**

What is it wearing? On its back?

**al (thorswagnarok):**

a shirt, maybe?

**katie (fyodorbrostoevsky):**

guys

come on, that's

like

this is a werewolf?? This is obviously a werewolf

**al (thorswagnarok):**

oh my god

**Max (quintuplevampire):**

Oh come on Katie

**Seb (mereextravagancy):**

Yeah I'm with max, that's insane lol

Someone's dog obviously just got loose

It's in the middle of nowhere, what else would they have to report on in backwoods PA

**al (thorswagnarok):**

hold the hell on, doesn't bridge live in PA?

@bridge (bigforkhands), have you heard anything about this?

bridge (bigforkhands) is offline.

**Max (quintuplevampire):**

Guess not lol

**Priya (paranormaldetective):**

Yeah, she lives close to there!

That's crazy that there's some kind of wild animal loose

**katie (fyodorbrostoevsky):**
oh okay, so no one is on my side about the werewolf thing

**al (thorswagnarok):**
I AM!!!!

what wild animal looks like that?!?

**Priya (paranormaldetective):**
Okay, guys

**Max (quintuplevampire):**
Yeah we can stop Charlie Kelly ing for now

**katie (fyodorbrostoevsky):**
can we talk about the bellows beast, mac? I've been dying to talk about the bellows beast

**al (thorswagnarok):**
[600PX-PEPE_SILVIA.JPG]

**Seb (mereextravagancy):**
Hahahaha

**katie (fyodorbrostoevsky):**
alksjdflksdjskdlf

**al (thorswagnarok):**
ok, we're done, we're done

**Priya (paranormaldetective):**
How's it been going, al?

**al (thorswagnarok):**
it's ok!!

i'm meeting with my school counselor after class now

she's actually really cool

and she told my parents for me

**katie (fyodorbrostoevsky):**
how did they react?

I know you were worried

**al (thorswagnarok):**
my mom was upset but i guess in the regular way, like she's sad i'm feeling this way

my dad didn't say anything

but he's not telling me not to go to therapy so I guess that's good

**Max (quintuplevampire):**

Love you, Al

**Priya (paranormaldetective):**

That's good

I'm sorry your dad wasn't more supportive

**al (thorswagnarok):**

it's what i expected

**Priya (paranormaldetective):**

I'm still sorry

**al (thorswagnarok):**

thank you <3

i mean i still feel like something inside me has been unplugged by accident, like my brain tripped over the router or something

but it's all good in the neighborhood

does anyone else have something to vent about? i don't wanna hog the chat

**Seb (mereextravagancy):**

You aren't hogging it!!

I, on the other hand, did not shut up for our first few meetings

**katie (fyodorbrostoevsky):**

oh, hush

**Seb (mereextravagancy):**

You wish I could!!

**Priya (paranormaldetective):**

You were fine!

**Seb (mereextravagancy):**

I just try to fill the space up

**Max (quintuplevampire):**

You did fam

It made us all feel at home

**Priya (paranormaldetective):**

Yeah, thank you for starting this, Seb

I was feeling pretty alone before

**katie (fyodorbrostoevsky):**

me too

**al (thorswagnarok):**

i'm gonna save something sappy for when we're all here

**Seb (mereextravagancy):**

Good, I didn't need to cry today

(although, guess who just started T, which will make it harder to!)

**Priya (paranormaldetective):**

!!!

**Seb (mereextravagancy):**

Ugh, I was ALSO trying to save that for Tuesday, I just got excited!

**al (thorswagnarok):**

dude!!

**Max (quintuplevampire):**

The others are gonna be mad you didn't wait

**al (thorswagnarok):**

@bridge (bigforkhands)

@Spook (spookyspoony)

@lee (typhoonsss)

get in here

**lee (typhoonsss):**

it is date night so i am shutting down your notifications

but seb and al, that is very exciting, congrats!

okay goodbye, children

**Spook (spookyspoony):**

Nice!

Lee (typhoonsss) is offline.

Spook (spookyspoony) is offline.

**al (thorswagnarok):**

BYE MOM AND MOM

**Priya (paranormaldetective):**

Seb, does testosterone interact with EDS at all?

**Seb (mereextravagancy):**

> I was really worried it would, but I talked to my doctor about it, and she thinks the testosterone might actually help with dislocations and joint stability!

> The injections are giving me crazy bruising though, and my leg hurts like hell, so I've been anxious for the chair to arrive

**katie (fyodorbrostoevsky):**

> you're doing so great, seb

**Seb (mereextravagancy):**

> <3

I open another tab to message Brigid. The article could have been worse, I guess; it could have made national news, or had a clearer photo attached to it. But you can see Brigid in it, her BUS DRIVER shirt a deep-blue blur as she's loping through the woods near Bellows. I watch the view counter ticking up. When I refresh the page, there are already two more comments.

**paranormaldetective:**

> ...hey

**bigforkhands:**

> softly: don't

**paranormaldetective:**

> I didn't even say anything!!!

**bigforkhands:**

> I FEEL LIKE I MIGHT KNOW WHAT YOU WANT TO TALK TO ME ABOUT, THOUGH

**paranormaldetective:**

> Maybe I want to start a conversation about my love life

**bigforkhands:**

> you don't have one of those

**paranormaldetective:**

> >:(

**bigforkhands:**

> do you want to talk about your love life, priya

**paranormaldetective:**

I do not, brigid

**bigforkhands:**

do you want to talk about the picture of me that's currently making its way through the weirdest part of the internet

**paranormaldetective:**

Yes I do

**bigforkhands:**

my face is in my hands

**paranormaldetective:**

I figured you'd be more excited about this, honestly

**bigforkhands:**

i WOULD BE

but they RUINED IT

**paranormaldetective:**

???

**bigforkhands:**

have I always wanted to be a cryptid? YES, of COURSE

that's dope as HELL

mysterious! a creature of urban legend and lore!

**paranormaldetective:**

okay so no part of this is you being worried that this picture exists

**bigforkhands:**

lmao no

**paranormaldetective:**

So what's the problem

**bigforkhands:**

"the bellows beast" ????

**paranormaldetective:**

that's you

**bigforkhands:**

NO!!!

i'm finally a cryptid and I don't even get to be called something cool!??!

"bellows beast"
whatEVER
that's boring as SHIT

**paranormaldetective:**
Hahahaha

**bigforkhands:**
i am furious
Hold on I'm messaging the group

**paranormaldetective:**
I so wouldn't

**bigforkhands:**
i'm asking them if we're really sold on "bellows beast"
i feel like there's a better name here

**paranormaldetective:**
Like what?

**bigforkhands:**
well I don't KNOW, PRIYA

**paranormaldetective:**
Your energy is off the charts right now

**bigforkhands:**
no my vibes are impeccable

**paranormaldetective:**
Oh ok you. You really did message the group

**bigforkhands:**
shrugguy.com
what about "the creature of echo creek"

**paranormaldetective:**
You don't live in echo creek

**bigforkhands:**
they don't know that! i live CLOSE to echo creek!

**paranormaldetective:**
It sounds like a nancy drew pc game
Did you ever play those?

**bigforkhands:**
no??

**paranormaldetective:**
They're amazing

**bigforkhands:**
we should play one sometime then

**paranormaldetective:**
Aw, yeah!
...is it weird to say I miss you?
I know I saw you this morning, but

**bigforkhands:**
I MISS YOU TOO
it's not weird!!
ok it's probably a little weird but I still miss you

**paranormaldetective:**
Are we codependent?

**bigforkhands:**
i mean yeah, obviously

**paranormaldetective:**
Isn't that like? bad?

**bigforkhands:**
well adjusted people wish they had what we have

**paranormaldetective:**
Stop lol

**bigforkhands:**
i shan't
you coming by again soon?

**paranormaldetective:**
Probably not, I should hang at home for a while
I'm kind of wiped out
And also my family needs the car

**bigforkhands:**
excuses, excuses
what about "the wolfwoman"

**paranormaldetective:**
...no comment

**bigforkhands:**
We'll crack it

**paranormaldetective:**
Goodnight, brigid

**bigforkhands:**
xoxo, wolfwoman

# 26

**I'm in the process of googling "werewolf lore cures" when my** father comes into the room, looking over my shoulder. I click over to the window where I've got a Google Doc open, quickly enough that I don't think he notices.

"What are you working on?" he asks me, the same way he's checked in every other hour for the past four months. He and my mother have split things up, tactically: she bothers me about my health, and he bothers me about my schoolwork.

"My independent study," I say, clicking at random.

"Remind me what that is again," he asks. "And why you need to go to Pennsylvania to work on it."

*There's no way he believes me*, I think, looking at him, but I lie anyway. Well. It's not quite lying. It's the truth, with a few holes punched in the middle of it.

"I'm writing about the symptomatic aftereffects of severe bacterial and viral infections, and how that compares to the effects of a genetic disease that gets triggered by something specific," I say.

My dad nods. "You're writing about yourself," he says, as though that's the only solution, and I bristle.

"I'm not," I say sharply. "I don't know why everyone assumes I can only research exactly what happened to me."

"Maybe you should," he says. "It would be a good way to take advantage of it."

"I don't want to take advantage of it," I snap. "I don't want to study it. God, it's like this is the only thing people can see when they look at me now."

"Don't curse," he says sedately.

"God isn't a curse!" I say.

"It's about your tone," he says. "I don't care for it, Priya."

I'm seconds away from grinding my teeth. I know anything I say right now will be *tonally* wrong, so I don't say anything. My dad raises his eyebrows.

"Why don't you look into summer sessions at the community college?" he asks brightly, as though he's helping. I know he's trying to. It's what I tell myself to keep my blood pressure down.

"I probably should," I say.

"It will keep you fresh," he says. "Competitive with the other students."

*It won't, it won't, it won't*, I want to scream. *It's already too late. It won't matter.*

"I was thinking about shadowing someone at a lab," I burst out, suddenly desperate to say something useful. My father's eyes light up.

"That's a great idea!" he says. I can practically feel his excitement. "Let me start looking up local research labs. I can ask around work, too, see if anyone knows anything."

I already wish I hadn't said anything. "You don't have to."

"I want to," he says, patting my leg as he leaves.

"Thank you," I say. I sigh and pull up the tab I was looking at in the first place, typing "myth" instead of "lore."

"Why are you googling werewolves?" Suresh's voice comes over my shoulder.

I jump. "How do you move so quietly, S?"

He shrugs. He's holding a bowl of cereal in his hands, even though it's five in the afternoon. "So are you making up a fake independent study?"

"No, I—"

"To hang out with your internet friends? Gotta say. I don't really see how the werewolves tie in."

"It's . . . a long story."

"Hm," he says. He takes a slurping bite of cereal.

"Are you gonna blackmail me?" I ask.

"Nah," he says. "Too much work. Plus, you don't have anything I want." And then he shuffles back into the kitchen.

"Thanks a lot," I say. My phone buzzes.

### hashtag team werewolf

Spencer:

HOLY SHIT

CRYPTID SPOTTED

[IMG_2711]

I laugh so hard I snort when the picture loads. It's a blurry picture of Brigid, midway through swiping at the camera, making a face somewhere between a frown and a laugh. I save it to my phone.

Whoa, Spencer... that's not just any cryptid

Brigid:

p i will end u

Spencer:

It's not?!?!?!?

That's the bellows beast!!

Spencer:

:O

Brigid:

DON'T CALL ME THAT!!!!

Hahaha

Spencer:

Ok your wolfness

Brigid:

u know... better

Speaking of wolfness

Brigid:

i'd so rather not

Spencer? How's it going?

Spencer:

Still no werewolfing out

It's been... 2 weeks?

Spencer:

Ish

And Brigid hasn't turned either?

Brigid:

nope

Brigid, that's good, right? Maybe the transformations are evening back out

Brigid:

could be

but I feel like shit like. all the time now

:/

What do you mean?

Brigid:

it was easier to tell when I was gonna turn before but now I'm having the same pain like all the time

Not great

Brigid:

no shit

Grandma update?

Brigid:

working on it

How?

Brigid:

thanks for the 20 questions, doc

Didn't your mom grow up in bellows?

Brigid:

close

i'm asking around

hattie was kinda weird abt it, so

Spencer:

Could be something

Brigid:

she also found this book

Oh?

Spencer:

?!?!?!?

What is it?

Brigid:

ingredience

Ingredients? What does that mean?

Brigid:

her friend who runs an occult shop upstate found it for her

Uh...

Brigid:

so spencer i am gonna need ur help

Spencer:

Yeah, shoot

Brigid:

i need a bat

to be specific i need its blood

Spencer:

Yeah that's a hard no

Brigid:

>:(

DO NOT DO THAT

Brigid:

u both suck

Spencer:

Do you want a rare disease

This is how you get a rare disease

Brigid:

stop being responsible

Spencer:

That's my job

Sort of

Brigid:

well I'm sick of it

Brigid, what are you making

Brigid??

Brigid:

hold on

gotta go on the roof

???

Brigid:

i'll facetime u both later

She never replies. I text Spencer a few hours later, the first message I've ever sent just to him. It feels a little weird, but he replies right away.

Do you think it's weird she never responded?

Like do I think she turned?

Yeah

Can you like...

Check in on her?

Yeah, idk

I'm paranoid

You're not

I'm clocking in in like 10 minutes and I don't get home until late, but I can go tomorrow, maybe?

> If she still hasn't texted back

> > That works

> > Thank you haha

> You gonna be up around here next week?

Something almost possesses me to type "why, do you miss me?" into my phone, and I'm struck to my core with embarrassment even though I've only thought it in my head, not texted it to Spencer.

> > We'll see, only if my family can spare the car

> Cool :)

> > Talk to you later?

> Anytime, dude.

-------

**Spencer FaceTimes me the next day.**

"What's up?" I ask. I catch sight of the kitchen behind him and realize he's at Brigid's. One of the cabinet doors has been ripped off its hinges, and the wood is gouged with claw marks. "Oh my God, what happened there?"

"She turned," Spencer says.

I groan.

"Oh, great, tattle on me to Priya," I hear Brigid growl from the background. "Thanks, Mom and Dad. Screw you guys."

"The place is *destroyed*," Spencer says. He turns around the kitchen and the living room to show me. The screen door's been ripped out and shredded. The couch has been torn apart and the stuffing is scattered around the living room, along with the feathers that used to be inside the pillows. One of the chairs in the kitchen is broken, the garbage can is knocked sideways, and the trash is dragged over the floor and out into the backyard.

"Oh . . . no," I say.

"I know," she says miserably. She's lying on the floor against the couch. "Trust me, I know."

"You know how really smart dogs will destroy your house if you don't give them tasks to accomplish?" Spencer asks.

"I didn't," I say. "Really?"

"Yeah, like border collies or blue heelers," he says. "Herding dogs. Brigid, I think you need enrichment. You're too smart."

"No, I'm pretty sure wolf Brigid's a dumbass." She groans. "It felt great at the time."

"And now?" I ask.

"I coughed up a bunch of feathers this morning. It was like a cartoon."

"Fun."

"As fun as a bullet in your skull."

"Alright," Spencer says, swiveling the camera back to his face. "I'm gonna go."

"Bye, guys," I shout. "How's the waiting game?" I ask Spencer.

"Uh," he says. "I forget about the bite like half the time. It looks like it's healing up pretty well."

"Why do I feel like there's a but coming?" I ask, swallowing.

"But . . ." He looks over at Brigid. "I'm, uh. I told Brigid earlier, I'm just starting to feel kind of . . . sick?" He says it like a question.

"What *kind* of sick?" I hiss.

"Like, achy, and—does it actually matter?" he asks. "It won't stop whatever's barreling down the pike."

"Oh, this is so bad," I say before I can stop myself.

"Thanks a million, Priya," he says.

"We'll know for sure in a few more weeks," I say.

"That we will," he says.

"What voice was that?" I laugh.

"I don't know, shut up. Check in on Sunday?"

"Sure."

"Okay, bye." Before he presses the END CALL button, I hear him talking to Brigid. "I don't wanna clean this, maybe we should call for backup." I can hear Brigid mumbling something in the background. "Oh, Hattie's gonna—" Spencer starts, and that's when I get cut off.

# 27

**I'm relieved we're late for church, because I don't have to talk to** anyone on the way in. My family drives half an hour every single Sunday to go to the South Asian church a few towns over, a group of (mostly) first- and second-generation Indian Americans that meet in a tiny old building with that burgundy carpeting I've seen in every small church I've ever set foot in. We used to complain about the drive growing up, once we got old enough to realize we could complain about it, but looking back, it was actually nice to have that community.

I forget it's almost Easter until they hand me a palm frond coming in. I rub my thumb along the thin leaves and end up sandwiched in a pew between Kiki and Suresh, who try to tickle each other's noses with their fronds until my mother shushes them.

"In India we used to scatter marigolds on the ground," she says. My father nods.

"We should tell them to do that instead," says Kiki in a loud whisper, brandishing her palm. "This is uglier."

She gets a death stare. "It is not ugly, Kiki. It's a red carpet. For Jesus."

"Yeah, they're gonna change their tune in a few days, huh."

"Spoilers, Suresh," I whisper, and he pretends he's sneezing into the crook of his elbow to hide his laugh. My chest floods with fondness, light and comforting like a hot breeze.

"Signs and wonders aren't always glamorous," Reverend Chowdary says at the end of his sermon. "They may be painful. They may look like a man on a donkey riding toward his death. Sometimes, it's not until we look back that we realize God's been working a miracle in our lives all along." I lift up my palm frond along with the rest of the congregation, and it feels like I'm a part of something.

When we get outside, Kiki and my dad are teaching the kids to turn their fronds into crosses, Suresh is flirting with the high school girls, and my mom is talking to the other moms. I'd been dreading talking to everyone at church, but when old family friends gather around to press my hands, tell me how worried they'd been, and mention that I'm still in their prayers, I find myself genuinely touched. When my phone buzzes with a video call, I excuse myself to walk around the lawn toward the back of the church.

Spencer's the only one on the screen, nodding to me with bedhead and tired eyes. He's wearing a white tank top and eating a bowl of cereal. I'm momentarily distracted by the sight. I'd known he had to be strong for his job, but seeing that confirmed by the wiry muscle of his arms throws me.

"Uh, hi," I say, clearing my throat.

"'Sup," he says.

"Hanging at church." I nod.

"Oh, so that's why you look so nice," he says.

"I can't tell if that's a compliment or an insult," I say, trying to hide my smile.

"It's a compliment! Aw shit, that didn't come out right, did it."

"You look . . . underdressed."

"It's my day off," he says, pointing his spoon at the camera. "Cut me some slack."

"Okay, should we try to get Brigid on the line?" I ask.

"Man, Brigid's always your numero uno, huh?" he says, his tone light. "You don't want to talk to *me* about anything?"

I purse my lips, trying my hardest to not be charmed. "Okay. How was your week, Spencer? Dearest friend Spencer who I have known for a really long time?"

"We met, like, a whole entire month ago."

"You thought I was crazy."

"Yeah, yeah. Jury's still out on that one."

"Hilarious."

"I know. My week was not nearly as interesting as the one before, but we did break up a dogfighting ring and free *several* possums who were trapped in someone's wall."

"Oh my God."

"What can I say, a day in the life of a hero."

"I'm not sure you can say that."

"Those dogs are not going to get hurt anymore! Well, except the ones who are too violent to get rehabilitated. They might get put down."

"That's awful!"

"People are awful. Dude's goin' to prison, which feels good. But the rest of his gang's still out there."

"His *what*?"

"Yeah, dude. I'm all up in that criminal underbelly. Protecting and serving your local animals."

"*Animal Cop*: this fall on CBS."

"Better than a cop cop."

"Can't argue with that."

My phone buzzes, and the screen splits in two.

"There's our girl," I say, even though that makes it sound like Brigid is our daughter. I crinkle my nose in apology.

"*Where's* our girl?" Spencer asks.

"I'm at Hattie's," Brigid says.

"I thought Hattie's was closed on Sundays."

Brigid holds a ring of keys up to the camera, shaking them and grinning. There's something in her smile that makes my stomach clench. She's showing all her teeth, but there's no joy there. It feels more like a threat.

"Hang on, I'm gonna put you guys down on the counter," she says. "Hattie keeps the witchy stuff behind the register."

"Are you . . . stealing?" I ask cautiously.

"Is it stealing if you work there?" she asks brightly.

"I mean, yeah," says Spencer.

"Materially, yes," I say. "Maybe even double stealing, since Hattie is also paying you."

"You can't double steal something," she calls. "Besides, this shit's expensive." She climbs unsteadily up on a step stool, one of those antique ones that folds down into a tall chair, and starts pulling bottles off the shelf, peering into each of them. Spencer looks into the camera at me and mouths "bruh," eyebrows up.

"Are you doing okay, Bridge?" I ask.

"Never fucking better," she says. "Ah! Sweet!" She grabs a plastic bag and climbs slowly down, coming back to the camera. "Got the cinquefoil and the sweet flag."

"The what?" Spencer asks.

"They're, like, flowers. Used in a lot of medicine."

"Oh, that doesn't seem so bad," I say.

"Up next is . . . deadly nightshade."

"Okay, there it is. Yeah. You can't do this."

"Yes, I can."

"Listen, I'm no expert," says Spencer. "But I feel like having the word 'deadly' in the name isn't a great sign."

"You're still on my hit list, Spencer," she says. "Wouldn't help me catch a bat. I don't think that's so much to ask when the first recipe in the book required human child's fat."

We both stare at her.

"That was for the salve, not the potion," she clarifies.

We keep staring.

"And obviously I want the potion."

"What are you talking about?" I ask. "Is this from that book you found?"

"Are you doing *spells*, dude?" Spencer asks.

"On the Lord's day?" I add.

"Yeah, that's definitely the worst part," he says. "For sure. Am I gonna get cursed here?"

"One way to find out," Brigid says, holding up a thin, cloth-bound book. Its cover is brown, unassuming and plain, and there's gold leaf stamped into the spine. In small letters, the front reads NATURAL REMEDIES FOR UNNATURAL AFFLICTIONS. It looks like something you'd find on the shelf in a college library.

"See? It's natural. That means it's good for you. They translated it from Latin in the 1870s." She opens the book to a section where a receipt has been slotted in, clears her throat, and reads.

"A tonic to choke the wolf and thus to end the curse." She looks up at us, raising her eyebrows excitedly.

"Wait, is that it?" I ask. "Brigid, that could mean *anything*."

Spencer nods.

"Like . . ." I pause. "God, Brigid, what if *you're* the wolf?"

"Okay, I'm a *were*wolf. The human part is the *were*, the part where I turn is the *wolf*. So I want to choke the wolf out, right? It makes perfect sense. This is gonna *fix* me."

There's an undertone to Brigid's voice, fierce and desperate, that stings. "This book came to me at exactly the right time, guys. How is that not a sign of something?"

"I mean—" Spencer starts.

"Because it involves *literal poison*," I say, cutting him off.

"Spencer's on my side," she hisses. "Thanks to me he's turning any second now, so he's gonna want this, too."

"Can we not talk about this right now?" Spencer says, voice high.

"Brigid, you can't take *nightshade*."

She literally rolls her eyes, and frustration rises like bile in my throat.

"If you take too much you will die," I say.

"I'm not going to take too much," she says. "Mostly because it's not here. I'll have to find it somewhere else."

"What else is in this tonic?" I ask.

Brigid looks down at the book again. "It's all normal stuff, really. I've got the sweet flag, cinquefoil, raspberry leaf, licorice, and oil. It says I can use either water parsnips *or* hemlock, so I think I'll go with the water parsnips. It also says *ash gum*, but I think that means sap from an ash tree, not, like, wet ashes? Maybe it means ash ash. Ashes from an ash tree. I don't know, still gotta figure that one out. Then that just leaves the nightshade and the bat blood." She sucks in a breath. "See? It's easy!"

"And you're supposed to . . . brew this?" I ask.

"Yeah, it'll be like drinking a refreshing cup of tea every day. I wonder if I could use another animal's blood," says Brigid thoughtfully.

"Maybe they just needed the iron," I say before I can help myself. "Wait! No! I am not helping you with this!"

"I don't need your help!" she says. "I can order half this stuff right off of Amazon!"

"I thought you hated Jeff Bezos?"

"It's desperate times!"

"Brigid—"

"No! I can't keep *doing* this, okay? This book has the only solution I've seen so far. I don't care if it's dangerous. I have to do something, or I'm going to start turning all the time and die of exhaustion. Or maybe I'll just stay transformed, like, twenty-four seven."

She opens up a backpack and starts tossing in the vials from the shelf, along with the book.

"I've gotta go find some blood," she says. She points at the camera. "Don't try to talk me out of this."

And then she vanishes from the screen, leaving me and Spencer to stare at each other.

"She's gotta. Find some blood," Spencer says blankly.

"Yeah, I heard her."

He tips back his cereal bowl, chugs the milk, then puts it back down. "Well, I'm out."

"Yep, okay."

-------

**Brigid calls me later that night as I'm clearing my dinner plate and** listening to Kiki and Suresh fight over the best worst movie.

"Hey," I say, relieved. "I've got some ideas, if you wanna talk more about all of this. I knew you'd just need some time to think about it, so—"

"I know where my grandmother is," Brigid says.

"Oh," I say. "Oh my God."

"She's been in Philly this whole time," she says.

"How did you find out?"

"Hattie caved," she says. "She knew the whole fucking time. Apparently she's been writing to her to, uh, send her updates on my life. I'm not sure what exactly there is to update, but I guess she wanted to know about me? This whole time I thought she hated me but—but maybe she's been like . . . looking out for me."

"So why wouldn't Hattie tell you the first time?" I ask.

"I don't know," she says, quiet. "She told me to be careful."

"What, like, your grandmother is dangerous?"

"No, dummy, like, emotionally," she says. She pauses. "Well, I think that's what she meant. Maybe Gran *is* dangerous."

"She might be a werewolf, so."

"Thanks a lot."

"You know what I meant—"

"Yeah." She sighs. "I tried calling the number I found on White-pages but no one answered. So I'm thinking it's time to go to Philly."

"Hell yeah," I say, ignoring the glare my father shoots my way across the room. Philly is so close to Brigid. Did her grandmother really never bother to make the trip? Or did her mother stop her from seeing her? "This is huge, Brigid," I say softly.

"Do you want to meet me there?" she asks tentatively. "You don't have to, I just—"

"Yeah, of course," I say. "I'll figure it out, I'll be there."

"Thanks," she says. "I really don't want to go by myself."

"It's our first road trip," I realize, smiling. "Oh—unless Spencer is gonna come, too."

"Nah, he's working," she says. Pauses. "Plus, this feels like more of a me-and-you kind of thing. The OG duo."

"Aw," I say, touched.

She must hear it in my voice because she clicks her tongue. "Did you think I'd leave you out of something like this?" she says. "Come on, kid. You're like . . . my best friend."

"I think you're my best friend, too," I say, and I'm surprised to realize that it's true as I'm saying it. "Not even my best online friend. Just . . ."

"Regular. Yeah."

"Okay, just tell me when and where."

"Yeah, okay." I hear a smile start bleeding into her voice. "I found that book. I'm gonna find more answers from Gran. I think things are looking the fuck up, Priya."

"Me, too," I say. I really hope I'm telling her the truth.

# 28

**I realize I'm going to have to take the bus to Philly. There's one** that comes every hour, but I still need someone to take me to the stop and drop me off. Somehow, I'm not sure either of my parents would be thrilled to do so.

I get up early enough for the morning rush for the first time in months. Suresh has already left, but Kiki is screaming something about her shoes from upstairs. My dad sees me sitting on the kitchen island, and he stops in the doorway to look at me. I frown at him.

"What, *appa*?!"

I can see tears starting to pool in his eyes. Oh, no. My father is a crier, in the specific way that spreads tearfulness like an airborne disease. Whenever he cries, I cry, too.

He walks up to me, patting both my knees, and smiles. "You look better, Priya."

The way he says it startles me. I feel like I've been pushed off-kilter. I've spent the last seven months becoming sick—*being* sick. I've spent the last four months wrestling, like Jacob, with a concept of myself that I knew I was never going to see again. It's taken me such a long time to come to terms with the fact that I'm never going to get better. I never thought that maybe—eventually—I actually would.

"Don't look so surprised." He chuckles.

"I am," I say. "Surprised. I hadn't realized."

"You couldn't have climbed up onto that counter a few months ago," he says.

"I used the step stool."

"Even so." The corners of his eyes crinkle. "I'm proud of you."

"I haven't done anything," I say.

"That isn't true," he says. "You've made the best of a hard situation. You've kept your chin up."

"I guess."

"No guessing. I know it."

"Well, since I look so much better . . ." I say, testing the waters. "Can you drive me to the bus station on your way to work?"

"Which bus station?" he asks.

"I'm going to meet Brigid in Philly today. I told you."

"That's right," he says. "But I have to take Kiki to school, and then I've got book club after work."

Of course, book club, where they drink wine coolers and talk about women's fiction. My father is the only man in the group, but he doesn't seem to notice.

"But you can ask your mother," he says pointedly. I sigh. This is what I'd been hoping to avoid. Things have been tense with us lately. We haven't talked about it, but I know she's upset about the time I've been spending on my "independent study," about the things she senses I haven't been telling her.

But the things I haven't been telling her feel like they're filling my life back up. I don't have to spend another day watching everyone else leave the house to go to school or run errands or hang out with friends or go to sleepovers or picnics or church potlucks or cultural events at the temple while I watch Netflix in my bed or try to avoid social media.

I didn't even take inventory this morning. I just felt the aches and got out of bed anyway.

The sound of the garage door grinding open fills the kitchen, and my father wags his finger in the air, lifting his eyebrows once, quickly. "Perfect timing."

My dad sticks his head out the door to ask my mom what she's doing.

"Trying to carry all these bags alone!" she yells in Tamil.

"Kiki!" my dad yells. I step down onto the stool—hopping is still a little too brave for me—and walk to the garage.

"Priya, that's okay," my dad says.

"No, she can carry something," Mom says.

"I can carry something," I repeat.

"Something light," Dad specifies, handing me paper towels.

"Kiki!" Mom yells this time.

"Oh my God, I'm coming!" she shrieks from inside.

"No cursing!"

"It isn't cursing!"

I walk back into the kitchen with my heavy load, raising my eyebrows at my sister, who has finally appeared. She rolls her eyes at me.

"We're almost finished anyway," Mom says to Kiki.

"Come on, just hand me the bag."

"No, I've got it."

"I didn't come all the way over here just to leave, Mom."

"Well you didn't come over here very quickly."

"Give it to me, please!"

"Okay!"

The door slams, and my father instantly tells my mother, "Priya had something to ask you."

I clench my teeth, trying to shake my head, but he doesn't notice. Mom pushes a few loose-hanging curls out of her face with the back of her hand and looks at me expectantly.

"Can you drive me to the bus station before work?" I ask.

"Oh, another thing for my list." She huffs. "Where are you going this time? Canada? New York City?"

"You already know I'm going to Philadelphia," I say. "You said it was okay yesterday."

"No, I will not drive you to the bus station," she says, staring me dead in the eye. Anger burbles in my chest, but before I can say anything, she sighs. "I'll drive you to the train station. Better than the bus."

"Are you sure?" I ask.

She turns around and opens the back door again. "Do you want a ride or not?"

I pull on my shoes and follow her to the car.

-------

**"How are you feeling, Priya?" my mom asks. It's the first thing** she's said since we've been in the car.

"Uh, I don't know. Okay, I guess. Better than before."

"We're seeing the rheumatologist again on Monday," she says.

"I know."

"I'm just reminding you, you don't have to be annoyed."

"I'm not annoyed," I say, which wasn't a lie five minutes ago but is right now.

"Yeah, okay," my mom says, turning onto Route 202.

"Are you mad at me, Mom?" She darts her gaze to me with wide eyes before looking back at the road. She's surprised. I am, too. We don't talk like this. One of us will be upset about something, but we let it linger until it fades, then pretend it never happened in the first place.

"No, of course not," she finally says. "Why would you say that?"

"You seem like you're mad," I say. "Like the way that I am annoys you."

"No."

"Mom."

She keeps her eyes on the road. "I'm not angry, or annoyed, Priya. I know you've been having a hard time. I know you want to be in California with your friends right now instead of having to spend time with us. Or Pennsylvania. Anywhere else, really."

"I'm trying my best!" It comes out explosive, so I take a breath and try again. "I'm not mad at any of you. You just don't know what it's been like."

She nods, slowly. "That's true."

"Yeah."

"But we're trying our best, too, Priya. You wanted to go away for college so badly instead of applying somewhere close by, like Princeton or Penn, but this is still your home. It can be, anyway."

"I missed you when I was gone," I say. I've surprised myself twice in one conversation, because that's true, too.

"You don't have to say that," my mom says.

"No, I actually mean it," I say. "I just don't think I realized it until I came home."

She smiles, just a little. "Well."

"Well?"

"We missed you, too. We wish you weren't sick. We wish we could take that pain away from you so you didn't have to feel it. But even with all that, it's been nice to have you home. To have you close enough to take care of."

I nod. She keeps saying *we*, but I know she means *I*.

"I love you, *amma*," I say.

She glances at me again, smiling. "I love you, too."

-------

**Still gotta park,** Brigid texts me when I tell her I'm at 30th Street Station. *U ok to walk 5-10 mins or should I come get u?*

I look around the station, crane my neck to look up at the high ceiling and hanging lights. I feel myself in my body. My knees are sore, and my breathing is shallow, and there's a twinge in the muscles in my back, but I feel almost at home in it right now.

*I can walk*, I text back. *Where am I going?*

She texts me a screenshot of Google Maps, which is decidedly less helpful than an address would be, but I plug in her location and start walking. It's a run-down outdoor parking lot, surrounded by chain-link fencing. A train rumbles by, headed for the station.

I catch sight of Brigid outside her nightmare of a car. She's wearing an oversized frat-boy tank top over a sports bra with a flannel tied around her waist. She pulls a long strip of duct tape off the roll with a *skkrrt*, tearing it off with her teeth and attaching it to the place where the passenger window used to be. She's covered it with several layers of what look like Saran Wrap, and it pulls in and out like a vacuum in the breeze.

"Oh my God, Brigid," I say. She turns, sunglasses low on the bridge of her nose, and squints at me. Her hair is different than it was last time I saw her. She's cut it shorter at the sides so a shock of hair, dyed electric blue, flops over in the front.

"What," she says. There's still a rasp in her voice, bruises around her eyes that the sunglasses don't cover.

"I just—"

There's a clunk from the other side of the car, and I follow her around.

"Nuts," she mutters, grabbing the mirror. "Can you hold this?"

I hold it in place, and she wraps duct tape around it four or five times until I can't even see the arm anymore.

"I feel like this isn't safe," I say.

She tears the tape with her teeth again and slides the roll onto her wrist, stepping back to assess her work.

"I think we're good," she says.

"Your window is made of Saran Wrap," I say.

"And?"

"And someone might break into your car."

"Oh. Hm."

She opens the back door, tossing the duct tape in. She's got clothes strewn around the back still, and I spot a bottle of Gatorade that's a color I don't think I knew existed. She grabs a Sharpie and walks over to the cling-wrapped window.

I OWN NOTHING, she writes. She looks at me and raises her eyebrows. I shrug.

BREAK IN AND I'LL EAT YOU, she adds.

"Brigid."

"Hey, I ate a cat. Anyone could be next."

I fold my arms across my chest, giving her a look. She gives it right back to me, and I feel a knot loosen in my chest. I can feel a smile start creeping across my face.

"I like your hair," I say.

"Thanks." She grins. "I did it myself."

"Figured as much."

"Let's catch the bus."

"To?"

"South Philly."

"Right behind you."

-------

**The row houses are squat and connected, two and a half stories** of red brick alongside gray slate with wrought-iron handrails and window bars. The shape of them reminds me of those fake cities you'd play with as a kid, tiny cloth awnings over ice cream shops and vet offices. There's a Catholic church on the corner of the street with a big, circular stained-glass window facing the road. A pair of tennis shoes are hanging over a power line.

Brigid clenches her hands into fists when we find the door, but not before I notice them trembling.

"Hey," I say. "Are you okay?"

"I'm okay," she says. She pushes her sunglasses to the top of her head. "Kind of. No, I'm okay, I'm ready."

She's about to ring the doorbell when a woman opens the door, blinking at both of us in surprise. She's wearing a teal jacket with a pin on the collar, purse slung over her shoulder. She looks both younger and older than I'd imagined—her wrinkles are dug deep into her face, especially on her forehead and around her lips, but she stands ramrod straight, white hair falling to her shoulders.

I can feel the tension build in the air between us as the shock of recognition hits her. "Brigid?" she finally chokes out. It's impossible to read her tone.

"Hey, Gran," says Brigid, too loud, terrifyingly calm. "Can we talk?"

# 29

"Do you want tea?" Brigid's Gran calls from the kitchen. Her politeness wins out over everything else, the rules of hospitality filling the awkward silence. The house is small but homey, yellow drapes and white lace tablecloths over warm, orangey wood. The windows are open and the sun is shining in.

I settle uncomfortably on the couch in the living room next to Brigid. I feel like I shouldn't be here, but Brigid's grandmother seems nice enough. Completely normal, actually. There's a framed poem on the wall, knickknacks on the side tables.

I hear the telltale whistle of a tea kettle and Brigid blinks quickly, like she's forgotten where she is. "She won't be able to carry three cups," she says to herself, pushing up off the couch. I don't miss how hard it is for her to do so.

Brigid and her grandmother come back into the living room, handing off the tea. She settles down across from Brigid and me, raising her eyebrows. The way she does it reminds me suddenly so much of Brigid that I have no doubt they're related.

"It's nice to see you," she says. "It's been a little while."

Brigid purses her lips and nods. "It's been nine years," she says. Her grandmother recoils slightly. "And you knew exactly where to find me." I should have known Brigid wasn't going to beat around the bush. She runs headlong at this the way she does at everything, teeth bared. *She's brave*, I think suddenly, with a swell of pride. I want to take her hand.

Her grandmother doesn't look at her. "You don't understand—" she starts.

"No, I don't," Brigid says. "That's why I'm here."

"Uh—" I say. Two sets of eyes swivel toward me. "I think Brigid wanted to ask you some questions."

"Oh, just one," Brigid says. I can feel her energy building. "Are you a werewolf, Gran?"

Margaret Leahy reacts like she's been slapped. She puts her tea down on the table, mouth pursed.

"Please don't use that word," she says.

"I know you called me unnatural," Brigid says, voice shaking. "I know you called me a monster, and I know you left when I started turning, but I also know Hattie's been sending you letters, and I—I have to know if that's what you wanted."

"I'm not ready to do this right now, Brigid," she whispers. "Please—"

"Tough shit!" Brigid says. "Did you pass this curse to me? Are you like me?"

"I used to be," her grandmother says, voice beginning to shake. *I knew it*, I want to say.

Brigid is quiet beside me.

"This whole time," she finally says. "This whole time, you could have been helping me, and instead you just left? You left my mom to do all of this by herself—"

"I thought I was free of it!" her grandmother says, raising her voice, too. "Your mother was healthy, and *normal*, and I thought—I thought it was *over*, do you see?"

"Do I *see*?" Brigid's voice cracks. "You left me behind when I needed you the most. How could you do something like that? How could you be so selfish?"

"You don't know what it was like!"

"Then tell me."

Her grandmother glances at me. "We don't need to talk about our time of the month," she says. "Especially not in someone else's company. It's impolite."

"Impolite?" Brigid yells. "Are you *shitting* me?"

My skin is starting to crawl. I shouldn't be here.

"I'm not shitting you," her grandmother says. She looks at me again. "Not to be rude . . . what was your name?"

"Priya," I say miserably.

"Not to be rude, Priya, but this is a family matter."

"That *is* rude," Brigid says.

I start to stand. "No, she's right. I can wait outside."

Brigid's hand finds mine, pulling me back down. "No," she says, softly. She pulls my hand onto her lap, covers it with her other one. I lace our fingers together, nodding.

"No," she says again, looking at her grandmother. She squeezes my hand. "I want her here. I trust her."

I see her looking between the two of us as if she's trying to puzzle something together. "You trust her?" she says quietly. "Sometimes that's the worst choice a person can make."

"I am so sick of the cryptic bullshit," Brigid says. "I'm getting worse, Gran. I'm getting worse, and I don't have a single answer, and you are the one person who knows anything about what's wrong with me—with *us*. I don't know how to fix this, but maybe, if we could have a conversation like adults, I'd be able to figure it out!"

"Okay," she says. "Fine. You've twisted my arm. Where do you want me to start?"

"The beginning, I guess," Brigid says. I squeeze her hand back.

Brigid's Gran closes her eyes, takes a deep breath. I'm expecting tears when she opens them again, but instead, there's this profound blankness, smooth and hard like a kitchen knife. "Okay," she says. "The beginning."

-------

**"We had a farm in Iowa, this tiny scrap of land we all had to work.** The chickens were the worst. By the time you'd cleaned out the coop they'd already shit all over it again, covered the floor with it. When I was thirteen, I . . . well. What did you call it? Turning? There's something almost nice to that. I called her the monster.

"I didn't—I never understood why she got her claws in me, why she ruined me like this. They tied me up in the shed behind the barn at first, but I got out one night, killed one of the cows. After that they locked me up for good. And who could blame them?"

Brigid huffs. "Gran—"

"You have to let me finish," she says. "If you want me to talk about this, you have to let me finish."

"I'm sorry," Brigid says.

"They tried everything. You have to understand. It was 1954, they didn't—they thought I'd been possessed. Called me the devil's child until I believed I was, too. They tried to get it out of me, brought in the priest, but nothing worked. And maybe—"

She pauses. "There is something of the devil in me, even now," she says. "The monster, she did something . . . something unspeakable, when my father—"

"Your father?" Brigid asks. "What happened to—"

"I was sixteen when I got away," she says, her tone wrestled back to flatness. "It's a miracle I survived that time, honestly. The monster stole livestock from the farmers. I've still got buckshot in my hip. But I did what I had to do, and I made my way east. I didn't let anyone take advantage of me. And eventually I made friends on the road. My other misfits. They weren't like me—how could anyone be? But they . . . they cared for me. No matter how many times I pushed them away. I just—I couldn't bear to let her hurt them."

"What happened then?" Brigid asks.

"I built a life, I suppose. The only life I could. They all got a house together in Pennsylvania—everyone had their own rooms, there was no impropriety there. It was this hideous wreck of a thing they all had to fix up on their own."

"You didn't live with them?"

"No, I lived nearby. A cottage with a cellar, stone walls. They helped me reinforce the door, and that was that. They took care of me when I couldn't make my own living. I existed on their kindness for years. They were my family, then. And Gene was—Gene was mine, too. Despite everything."

"Grandad?" Brigid says.

"Of course," she nods. "I didn't love him at first, but I knew he was a good man. A kind one. He loved me for ten years before I agreed to marry him. I think it would have been easier if he were crueler, but I was so—I was so afraid of what the monster would do to him. Of how I'd hurt him."

"You didn't hurt him," Brigid says.

"Oh." Her Gran sighs. "I did. Just not the way I thought I was going to."

"You left them," Brigid says. "When my mom was a teenager."

"Yes," her grandmother says, matter-of-fact. "I came here when I stopped turning."

"You stopped?" Brigid says. "You—you figured out how to fix it? Does that mean there's a cure?"

"I didn't figure anything out," she says. "I hit my fifties, and the turning slowed down, and when I was sure it was gone for good, I—I couldn't believe I was free. I knew your mother would be okay, and your grandfather. I didn't allow myself to want things, before. I never allowed myself to want anything—not college, or life in a city, or going to mass, or making my own living. I lived within a thousand feet of that godforsaken cellar for more than thirty years. A lifetime chained underground. I wasn't going to do it a second longer."

"That's—that's it?" Brigid says. She sounds hollow.

"That's everything I can tell you. The only other time I stopped turning was when I was pregnant with your mother. That was an accident. I didn't want to risk passing this to any more children."

"I guess one was enough," Brigid says.

"I thought it was over," her Gran says. "Your mother was perfect, but I was so afraid. I should have known when you were born, but I didn't want it to be real. I wanted to see it as—as a dream, a memory of some other life."

"What—" Brigid sounds angry again. "What do you mean, you should have known?"

"You were born with teeth," she says.

". . . What?"

Her Gran holds her gaze. "A full set of teeth. They all fell out before your baby teeth grew in."

"What the *fuck*," Brigid says. "And you just—what, you just didn't tell my parents? Like, 'hey, watch out! I'm a monster, and your daughter might be one too, so you might wanna live somewhere where you can lock her in the cellar'?"

"I had hoped you would be normal, too," she said.

"Normal?" Brigid barks. "No, no, I'm a freak, just like you, Gran!"

"Brigid," I say, softly.

"No, I'm not done," she says. "So what, you just—you just wanted a normal granddaughter, and when I started turning—when I needed you more than I've ever needed you in my life—you just fuck off? To *Philly*? You have been two hours away this entire time!"

"I told your mother everything she'd need to know to take care of you—"

"That's not the *point*!" Brigid's voice goes shrill. "I didn't need an instruction manual! I needed—I needed to know I wasn't alone! I needed to know that I wasn't the only person in the world going through this!"

"I couldn't face it again, Brigid!" her Gran says, raising her voice again. "I couldn't live through it again!"

"Well, now I have to! For—for thirty more years, I guess. If I even make it that long." She pushes herself up. "I need some air. Great to see you again, Gran."

The door slams behind her. I look at her grandmother, and for the first time, I see the mask slip. There are tears in her eyes.

"I did the best I could with the life I was given," she says to me, hoarsely. "Even if Brigid doesn't believe it."

*You were abused*, I want to say. Or, *what happened to you wasn't fair, but you also used it to hurt the people who loved you the most, and that wasn't fair, either.* But I just nod instead. "I believe you," I say. "Can I—can I ask you one more thing?"

"Might as well," she says tiredly.

"Were you bitten by anything, or did you get sick before you turned that first time?"

"No, it just happened."

I nod. "And did *you* ever bite anyone else, while you were turned?" She's quiet. "Or, uh—did the monster bite anyone?"

"Many times," she says. "My mother. My husband, more than once." She pauses. "I never deserved him."

I know I should say something here like *he sounded lovely*, but I am so close to the answer here that I can't. "And they didn't—they never turned?"

She shakes her head. "Never," she says. "It only lives inside me. That was my only relief, until nine years ago."

Spencer's safe. He's not going to get his werewolf powers after all. I have to call him, so I stand up, as does Brigid's Gran.

"Um," I say. I thrust my hand out toward her awkwardly. "It was nice to meet you."

"I can't imagine that's true," she says, but she shakes it anyway. I'm almost to the door before she speaks again.

"Priya?" I turn. "Can you—would you tell Brigid that I'd like to see her again?"

"I can try," I say.

"Can you tell her I'm sorry?"

"I can." I nod. "But I think you're the person she really wants to hear it from."

She nods. "You're probably right."

I pause, pulling out my phone and scrolling through the contacts. "Do you want her cell phone number?" I ask. I'm not sure if it's the right thing to do, but I want to leave her with a way to reach out. She scrawls it on a notepad and reads it back to me.

"Thank you," she says. "I'm glad she has someone taking care of her."

There are a lot of things I could say—corrections to assumptions that I could make—but I don't. I just say, "I'm trying to."

I spot Brigid across the street and mouth "Spencer." She nods, turning to her phone, and I do the same. He answers right when I start expecting to hear his voicemail.

"Hey," he says, sounding out of breath. "I'm on shift but I just ran outside. Did you guys figure anything out?"

"It's genetic," I say.

"Holy shit," he says. "Are you sure?"

"Her grandma had it, and she bit people, and none of them ever got it. You're okay; you probably just have, like, a cold or something."

He lets out a whoop so loud that I have to hold the phone away from my face. When I put it back to my ear, he's broken down laughing.

"Spencer?"

He's babbling. "Oh my God, thank God."

"What about your werewolf powers? I thought you were excited to get them?"

"I was LYING!" He laughs. "I didn't want Brigid to feel bad! This has been the most stressful month of my entire life! Oh my GOD, oh, I am so relieved I could cry. Marty is looking at me super weird. Oh my God. Thank God. Oh man."

My phone buzzes, then again, and again, and again. I hazard a glance. Brigid's messaging the group chat.

"Spencer?"

"Yeah, got any more news for me? I feel like I could run a marathon right now."

"No, I just think I should go check on Brigid."

"Yeah, yeah, totally. I'll see you guys soon. Love you. Wait, shit. That was weird. I'm sorry, I'm hyped up."

"Don't be sorry," I say. "We love you too."

"See you soon."

I check the chat.

**bridge (bigforkhands):**

> so i'm a werewolf
>
> i have lycanthropy
>
> that's what's wrong with me
>
> the new cryptid you guys were talking about? also me
>
> every month I literally, physically, turn into something else, and it hurts, and i'm very tired
>
> it's getting worse, and I don't know why, but I'm sick of lying to everyone, so
>
> there it is

I fast-walk across the street, but she starts moving before I can catch up to her. "Brigid!" I call. I follow her until we're shoulder to shoulder. I can feel my phone buzzing almost nonstop, so I turn it off.

"Brigid, wait." I grab her hand and pull her to a stop, and she shakes me off, turns to face me.

"What."

"Are you okay?"

"Am I okay?" she huffs. "No, Priya. Not really!"

"I'm sorry," I say. "Dumb question."

"She sure did love saying *monster*, huh!" She forces a smile onto her face, flashes her straight, white teeth and her red gums. "Just couldn't get enough of it! A lot of excuses that really just boil down to 'it was miserable to even look at you,' huh!"

"Brigid—"

"Oh, but hey, she had some great solutions, didn't she! Wait around a few decades! Go out and have some unprotected sex with a man! Get teen pregnant!"

"You can't get teen pregnant," I say.

"No, I'm going to!" she shouts.

"No, I mean, it's impossible. You're twenty."

She freezes for a couple of seconds, and we stare at each other. She lets out a short little laugh that almost sounds like a hiccup. And then she's quiet again, aside from a sniffle and a quick inhale.

I reach up and slide the sunglasses off her face, folding them with two plastic *clicks*.

"Hey," Brigid protests weakly. "Those were so you couldn't tell I was crying."

"I can tell anyway," I say.

"You're supposed to look away and pretend you don't notice!"

I don't say anything. I pull her close instead and she snuffles into my shoulder, grabbing me just as tightly. We stand like that on the street, just breathing together.

"I wanted her to fix everything," she says, quietly. "And even if she couldn't, I wanted her to want to. I wanted her to say, 'no, Brigid, I've cared about you this whole time.'"

"I think she does care," I say, without pulling away. I know she doesn't want me to look at her yet. "But she hurt you trying to protect herself. She told me she wants to see you again."

Brigid hums into my neck, and it tickles, so I squirm. "Stop it." I laugh, pulling away.

"Thief," she says thickly, plucking her sunglasses out of my hands and putting them on top of her head.

"If you say so." I smile, grabbing them back and putting them on.

"I will allow it," says Brigid, "only because you look exactly twenty percent cooler right now."

"C'mon."

We walk until we pass a park next to a playground. It's busy, kids shrieking on the jungle gym and leaping off swing sets. We sit on the grass, staring up at the cloudless sky. There isn't a single shape to identify, nothing to divine.

"Do you wanna talk about it?" I ask.

"In a minute." She nods, lying back and closing her eyes. There's a pause.

"Do you want me to count to sixty, or—"

"Shut up, Priya."

I do.

"A werewolf is born with teeth," she says, eventually. "Which indicates that it is out to consume the world."

"What?"

"That's what the rabbi said about Benjamin. I guess he was right." She squints up into the sky. I wait for her to keep going. "I just . . . everything about the way I turned out has been completely inevitable. This thing has been waiting inside me the whole time, from the second I was born."

"With teeth," I say.

"With *teeth*." She sighs. "It was always gonna be this way. There's nothing I could have done about it."

"It's probably hormone triggered—" I start. She turns her head toward me and glares. "Right. Sorry. Not the time."

She sits up, rips out an entire handful of grass, then another. "I just, like—we moved back to the same exact place my Gran was locked up. It's like we traded or something. And now I stay within twenty square miles of my own cellar, like I'm on a fucking leash. How's that for the circle of life?"

"You're forgetting her ending," I say. "She doesn't turn anymore. She's here now."

"Yeah, after alienating everyone she cared about." Brigid digs her fingers into the earth. "I'm not as patient as my Gran, Priya. I can't do this for another thirty years."

"I know."

"I can't—" Her voice cracks.

"You're already farther outside that radius than she was," I point out. "We're in Philly right now. You came to visit me in New Jersey. You have your dad's whole family, and all of us in the chat. Your world is already so much bigger than hers."

The blood drains from Brigid's face. "Oh, shit."

"What?"

"The chat."

" . . . oh no."

"I'm just . . . I'm just going to . . . Just give me a second . . ." I watch her take out her phone, swipe to ignore the hundred notifications from the chat, and power it off.

"You just told the entire chat you're a werewolf."

"That seems like a later problem."

"I mean—"

"They're not going to believe me anyway."

"They might believe you believe it, though."

"I do believe it."

"Yeah, so do I, because it's true."

"Yeah, exactly."

"But they don't know it's true."

"I reiterate," she says, "that's a problem for future me."

"How's that working out for you?"

"Fucking fantastic." Her voice cracks.

"Hey," I say. I poke her with my foot. "Wanna kick some kids off the swing sets?"

"Is this you trying to cheer me up?"

"Is it working?"

"Yeah," she says. "Yeah, we should do something fun while we're here. I've been meaning to go to this one museum for a little while."

"I was thinking we could go to the library," I say.

She frowns. "I said something fun."

"We know more about what's happening to you than ever, Brigid," I say. "We've made so much progress, it's crazy. We might as well check a few things out while we're here, right?"

I watch the smile drop off her face. "Oh."

"What?"

"I'm tapped out for the day, dude," she says. "I don't want to think about this right now."

I know I should back off, but I hear myself start talking. "You kind of have to think about it, Brigid."

"Gee, thanks, Priya!" she bites back. "You don't say!"

"Brigid—"

"I've got a plan here."

"Oh, the poison plan?"

"Yeah, the poison plan, because it's the only lead we've got, despite all this really, really helpful girl-detectiving we've been doing."

"I'm just trying to help you," I say.

"Oh, I owe you an eternal debt," she snipes. "You know you're not actually a doctor, right?"

A kid screams behind us, and the swing sets creak, and a flock of pigeons flies by. Neither of us says anything.

"I do know," I say, quietly. "I'm never going to be one."

I see her face twitch. "I'm sorry," she finally says.

"It's okay," I mutter.

"I just—can't we go see Einstein's brain?"

"Einstein's *brain*?"

"They have it on slides at the Mütter Museum. I just want to do something normal for once."

"Oh, what's more normal than looking at dead people's brains?"

"It's the *medical oddities museum*, Priya. Look at me and tell me that's not right up both our alleys."

I push her sunglasses onto the top of my head and meet her eyes. She looks serious. I'm waiting for her to break into a loud laugh, but she doesn't.

"You said it, I'm down to one good week now."

"Okay, then." I nod. "Lead the way."

-------

**I'm hoping the Mütter Museum will let us erase the last few** hours. It's the kind of thing that, on any other day, both of us might have loved, but I feel Brigid drifting further from me with every step. I wait for her to crack a Yorick joke when we come across the skulls, but she's silent. I can feel her tense every time we stop at an exhibit, every time I try to point something out to her, cheer her up. She's radiating frustration, and annoyance, and something else that I can't put my finger on. I watch her jaw work as she looks down at the body of the Soap Lady. She's standing a foot away from me, but I have no idea how to reach her.

"Hey," I say. "Are you okay?"

"Can you stop asking me that for five minutes?" she says sharply.

"Fine," I say.

"I'm going to the garden," she says, and I try not to be hurt that she isn't using *we* anymore. I follow her. It's a nice day, so the herb garden is crowded with people sitting on benches or taking pictures of plants. I stop to read the signs, and I lose track of Brigid. When I spot her again, I walk around the path until I can see that she's crouched in front of a bed of purple flowers with drooping, bell-like petals stacked together. My mouth goes dry; I recognize them on sight.

"Brigid," I say. "No."

"No what, Priya?" she says. She's crouched in front of the plant now, and she pulls a gallon-sized freezer bag from her backpack, turning it inside out and putting her hand inside it.

I can feel my heart pounding in my head and in my throat, a more visceral fear than I've ever felt in my life.

"Brigid," I say, evenly. "I swear I will get the guard."

I can't see her eyes behind the sunglasses, but I know that her expression would terrify me.

"Go ahead," she says. Her hand closes around one of the flowers, quick as a snake, and pulls it back. I want to lunge at her, grab it out of her hand, but I know that if either of us touches any part of the plant, we could be poisoned, just like that.

"Brigid, I'm not bluffing, I'm serious," I say, desperately. She's zipping the bag closed, casual as anything. No one has noticed. "People have died of aconite poisoning! Just by *touching* it!"

"Well, I'm not going to be one of them," she says.

"You don't *know* that!" I hiss. I can feel tears pricking my eyes. "God, is that why you wanted to come here? To steal wolfsbane from the garden?"

"I've got almost everything else on the list," she says.

I pull out my phone, reading off the results I find. "You can die if you ingest two *grams* of this, Brigid! Every single part of it is toxic, okay?"

"You can buy it online!"

"That doesn't mean it's safe!" I'm shouting, now. "Plus those have like—like, dosage instructions. It would be so easy to overdose. You make one mistake and—and—"

"And what?"

"And your heart stops! Do you *want* to die, Brigid?"

"No!" she hisses. "I'm actually terrified of it, thanks! But I think I'm going to die if I keep turning like this, and this tonic is an actual, tangible solution! It's going to make it stop!"

"You don't *know* that!"

"It's the only idea any of us have managed to come up with!" she says. "You could *help* me, you know. Get the dosages right, test the formula, all that shit."

"Are you kidding me? I'm not going to help you poison yourself!" I say, loud enough for people to turn and look.

"Priya, shut up," Brigid says.

"No." I turn, looking around frantically for an employee. I spot her, wave my hand when she looks over. "Excuse me!" I shout. "Ma'am, could you come over here?"

Brigid runs. She's gone by the time the woman comes over, out the gate. Her phone goes straight to voicemail when I call her, and by the time I make it back to the parking lot, her car is gone. She's so convinced that this is going to work, so feverish about the idea of a cure. But all I can think about is that phrase at the start of the list of ingredients.

*Choke the wolf. End the curse.*

I feel sick to my stomach. I get on the train and go home.

# 30

**bigforkhands:**

| i'm sorry

**paranormaldetective:**

| Are you okay?

| ...sorry, I know you don't want me to ask

**bigforkhands:**

| no, i

| you know

**paranormaldetective:**

| Yeah, I know

| Sorry for being reckless or sorry we fought?

**bigforkhands:**

| sorry we fought

**paranormaldetective:**

| Me too

**bigforkhands:**

| are we okay?

**paranormaldetective:**

| I love you, and you're freaking me out, but I guess we're
| okay

**bigforkhands:**

| i love you too

-------

## hashtag team werewolf

Brigid:

i've alwavs wanted to get like

scam married

...what??

Brigid:

like fake married but real

Spencer:

Oh like, that green card shit

Brigid:

spencer gets it

like what's the point of marriage if u aren't committing fraud

Love?

Brigid:

hm. Sounds fake

:(

Spencer:

Hey what the hell are you talking about

You'll learn not to question it

Spencer:

This is how I unlock lore though

Brigid:

two of the wackos at hattie's were telling me their tale of love

Spencer:

Oh my god, they're still coming in???

It's. so funny that they're asking you about this

Uh, wanna fill me in, guys?

Brigid:

omg, how did i not tell u???

Spencer:

So cryptid hunters are coming to bellows now

Brigid:

"crvptid hunters"

so dramatic

just call them weirdos

Spencer:

So weirdos are coming to bellows now

To look for ~the bellows beast~

And where are they pulled to, like a beacon?

...hattie's antiques and oddities emporium

Spencer:

Yup

Brigid:

bingo

> Are you telling people about the bellows beast??

Brigid:

> OBVIOUSLV

> Oh my God haha

Brigid:

> i have suggested new names for me

> i have also been doing a lot of untruth-telling

> Lying?

Brigid:

> who knows

> I cannot believe you

Brigid:

> i am creating LEGEND!!!!!

> i'm gonna get a WIKIPEDIA PAGE!!

> I believe in you

> What was the tale of love btw

> From the cryptid hunters

Brigid:

> oh she married him so he could get a green card, then thev fell in LOVE

Spencer:

> Over a mutual love of the unexplained?

> That's kind of romantic

Brigid:

it is

so i told them the beast was a werewolf

Spencer:

You have to stop

Brigid:

u cannot make me

it's fine

i told the last ones it was aliens

It's always aliens

Spencer:

[AjcLIxXnEfWnS.PNG]

-------

**oof ouch my bones (ONLINE – 8)**

**Seb (mereextravagancy):**
So... are we gonna talk about the elephant in the room?

**katie (fyodorbrostoevsky):**
the...werewolf in the room
I guess

**al (thorswagnarok):**
the werewolf in the chat room

**Spook (spookyspoony):**
My favorite bailey school kids book

**Priya (paranormaldetective):**
She's literally right here, guys

**al (thorswagnarok):**
...sorry bridge

**bridge (bigforkhands):**
ah
my later problem is now a now problem

**lee (typhoonsss):**
are you doing okay, bridge?

**katie (fyodorbrostoevsky):**
we've been worried about you

**Max (quintuplevampire):**
Like... really worried

**bridge (bigforkhands):**
oh, you guys think I'm crazy

**katie (fyodorbrostoevsky):**
no!!

**Seb (mereextravagancy):**
I would not use exactly those words

**Spook (spookyspoony):**
I was thinking you might be suffering from a particular delusion

**lee (typhoonsss):**
_spook_

**Spook (spookyspoony):**
What, we're all thinking it, lee

**Priya (paranormaldetective):**
She's telling the truth, guys.
I've seen her in both... states

**katie (fyodorbrostoevsky):**
I

**al (thorswagnarok):**
oh... my god???

**Seb (mereextravagancy):**
Hold on

**katie (fyodorbrostoevsky):**
I just

**Spook (spookyspoony):**
This isn't like... a good practical joke

**Priya (paranormaldetective):**
Hey Brigid, is it ok if I send them a picture
Spencer took some when you were out in the backyard

**bridge (bigforkhands):**
yeah whatever

**Priya (paranormaldetective):**
...are you sure

**bridge (bigforkhands):**
yeah definitely, i already told them! i don't care

**Priya (paranormaldetective):**
Ok
[IMG_3232.JPEG]
[IMG_3234.JPEG]
[IMG_3238.JPEG]

**katie (fyodorbrostoevsky):**
well

**Max (quintuplevampire):**
What the fuck

**lee (typhoonsss):**
wow
WOW

**al (thorswagnarok):**
i'm freaking the fuck out

**katie (fyodorbrostoevsky):**
wel lthat's a werewolf

**Seb (mereextravagancy):**
You're pranking us, right?
Like you photoshopped these

**Spook (spookyspoony):**
Are you seriously telling us that the cryptid in the news was... bridge
A person in this discord chat. That we all know.

**Priya (paranormaldetective):**
I don't know how to prove it but I swear I'm not lying to you.

**al (thorswagnarok):**

this is cool as shit

you look nice in those pics, bridge

**bridge (bigforkhands):**

well thanks, al

this is kind of big for me, so please don't be like, afraid of me or anything

god, i hate doing this

**al (thorswagnarok):**

how could we be afraid of you?

ur one of us

**Seb (mereextravagancy):**

I mean not... exactly like us

But... I guess EDS is different from fibromyalgia and Lyme and migraines and endometriosis

So

So, yeah

Yeah.

**katie (fyodorbrostoevsky):**

oh my God I made a lot of werewolf jokes

that was so insensitive, I'm so sorry

**bridge (bigforkhands):**

no, it's okay!

**Spook (spookyspoony):**

So we're not going to dig into any of this?

We're just moving right along here?

**katie (fyodorbrostoevsky):**

oh no and we totally just did that thing we've been complaining about for months, where we told you your chronic illness was all in your head

I hate when people do that to me and we did it to you

**bridge (bigforkhands):**

breathe, katie! you're being very sweet, it's okay

**lee (typhoonsss):**

how are you feeling?

i'm sure we all have a lot of questions right now

**Max (quintuplevampire):**

A lot of questions

Are you super strong would be my first question

**lee (typhoonsss):**

BUT we should just let brigid tell us about it when she feels ready

**al (thorswagnarok):**

ugh okay

**Max (quintuplevampire):**

Yeah we do want to know how you're doing

And also any powers or abilities you might want to tell us about at all

**lee (typhoonsss):**

MAX

**bridge (bigforkhands):**

i'm... I don't know, it's been tough

man I had more evidence pictures locked and loaded for you guys

but you're just like? good?

**al (thorswagnarok):**

yeah

**Max (quintuplevampire):**

Yeah this rules

**Spook (spookyspoony):**

No! Not really!

**Seb (mereextravagancy):**

Ain't no thang

...I regret that

**al (thorswagnarok):**

katie i feel like we owe you money or something

**Seb (mereextravagancy):**

Yeah you did very much say that the bellows beast was a werewolf

And we blew you off

...Priya? you knew??

**Priya (paranormaldetective):**
...yes

**Max (quintuplevampire):**
Convincing liar

**Priya (paranormaldetective):**
Thank you?

**Spook (spookyspoony):**
Hang on, this was what you were messaging me about, Priya?

The research questions?

Bridge is your independent study?

**Priya (paranormaldetective):**
Well, not

I wouldn't say it like that, exactly

**katie (fyodorbrostoevsky):**
OKAY THANK YOU

I would love money

**al (thorswagnarok):**
i would love more pics

**bridge (bigforkhands):**
ok

[IMG_4711.JPG]

[20200409.MP4]

**katie (fyodorbrostoevsky):**
what... is that

**Seb (mereextravagancy):**
Those look like

...no

Brigid, what are we looking at

**Max (quintuplevampire):**
Well that's a country crock margarine tub

**al (thorswagnarok):**
yes but what's INSIDE it

**bridge (bigforkhands):**
my teeth

**Seb (mereextravagancy):**
NNNNOP3

**Spook (spookyspoony):**
??????????????????????????????????????????????????????
??????

**katie (fyodorbrostoevsky):**
bad

**al (thorswagnarok):**
alsjlsflksfjslfaslfjslfkjsdfl sfjksskfljl sldf ljkdfjdlkfj ?

**Priya (paranormaldetective):**
Honestly brigid I feel like you LIKE freaking people out

**bridge (bigforkhands):**
I mean

...it's a little fun, right

The simple pleasure of grossing out your friends
whenever you can

**lee (typhoonsss):**
okay, so we might have two questions

**bridge (bigforkhands):**
the wolf teeth push them out every time I turn

and then at the end those kind of melt and my regular
teeth are inside of the big teeth

**Priya (paranormaldetective):**
...oh my God

I'm sorry

When you said toothpaste

You meant tooth paste

**bridge (bigforkhands):**
yeah, my body is a miracle, etc etc

it's also public enemy number one rn on account of
trying to murder me in cold blood

but like, you know how it is

**Seb (mereextravagancy):**
We... sort of do...

**lee (typhoonsss):**
there is a lot to unpack here

**bridge (bigforkhands):**

i actually just figured out a solution

i've been turning every few weeks instead of every month

**al (thorswagnarok):**

oof

**katie (fyodorbrostoevsky):**

that's brutal, bridge

**bridge (bigforkhands):**

BUT I've found something to stop that from happening

**al (thorswagnarok):**

!!!

**Max (quintuplevampire):**

Hey

**Seb (mereextravagancy):**

Wow!! That's great!

**bridge (bigforkhands):**

it IS great, thank you all

see, priya?

**Priya (paranormaldetective):**

Okay I just don't think it's a great idea to follow rules from an ancient recipe book with ingredients that might kill you

**bridge (bigforkhands):**

because you have no faith in me

**Priya (paranormaldetective):**

We don't have to get into this right now

**Spook (spookyspoony):**

I'll also throw my hat in the ring and say you should be careful prescribing yourself anything

**bridge (bigforkhands):**

yeah, yeah

**katie (fyodorbrostoevsky):**

hey bridge, are you bulgarian? Or eastern european at all?

**bridge (bigforkhands):**

| my mom's irish but maybe farther back somewhere? why

| that sounds like a setup to a joke

**katie (fyodorbrostoevsky):**

| lol no, it's just

| we have this old family legend on my dad's side about a woman who could turn into a beast

| I thought it was BS but now I'm... wondering...

**bridge (bigforkhands):**

| ARE WE RELATED?????

**katie (fyodorbrostoevsky):**

| MAYBE?????

| I'll DM you haha

**bridge (bigforkhands):**

| how many werewolves could there be, cousin

| you're my cousin now

**katie (fyodorbrostoevsky):**

| awesome!!

| I'll ask my dad if he has more info on it

**bridge (bigforkhands):**

| that'd be super cool! Thanks!

| Man, you guys have been like. Really chill, thank you

**Seb (mereextravagancy):**

| I mean, I'm not sure chill is the right word, exactly

**Max (quintuplevampire):**

| Yeah there was a lot of cursing

**Seb (mereextravagancy):**

| I feel like I probably dreamed this

**bridge (bigforkhands):**

| yeah but you still love me

**lee (typhoonsss):**

| of course we do, honey

**bridge (bigforkhands):**

| i love you guys, too

| i feel pretty lucky

well, on this front

the friendship front

**al (thorswagnarok):**

me too

i said i wouldn't get sappy on saturday but i'll get sappy now

i don't wanna think about where i might be if it wasn't for you guys

honestly

i was in a real bad place and you gave me a safe place to land

**Seb (mereextravagancy):**

That was really beautiful

I love you guys

**Max (quintuplevampire):**

We're moving on from the werewolf stuff?

**katie (fyodorbrostoevsky):**

Yeah

**bridge (bigforkhands):**

please

**Seb (mereextravagancy):**

Alright, let's all get caught up

# 31

**My phone buzzes when I'm at Easter dinner with our extended** family. It's late, and we've taken one car here, which isn't here at all right now because my dad went to go pick up more food from my auntie. I don't check it right away, but when it buzzes again, I slide it out under the table to read the messages.

### hashtag team werewolf

Brigid:

> So two thnig s

> Im banned from olive garden now

Spencer:

> What's happening

Brigid:

> And I think im turni ng in the parking lto

> That wsa the toher thing

Spencer:

> Oh my God

> The one in ryeburg???

Brigid:

Es

Spencer:

Don't go anywhere, okay?

I'm on my way, I'll be there in fifteen

Brigid:

Dkvmsoi

Spencer:

Do not move!!

Shit

Go back inside, lock yourself in the bathroom

The door's like, weirdly heavy in there

I'm going to call you, Brigid, okay?

Brigid?

I bolt up from the table so quickly that it shakes the plates, and twelve pairs of eyes stare at me as I get up.

"Sorry, one second," I say. "I'm just going to clear my plate here."

I go to the kitchen and drop my plate in the sink, but there are too many people in here. I see my mom's friend trying to catch my eye, but I say something about needing some air and make my way as quickly as I can to the front yard. I sit on the porch steps, watching the sun start to go down. I'm probably going to get bit by mosquitos. *Maybe another tick*, says a voice in the back of my head. I stand back up, jittery, and call Spencer. I'm moving slower than my new normal; my joints have been clenched for the past two days like when your jaw gets tight from stress. I need it to rain. He doesn't pick up the first time, so I call him again.

"Priya, yeah, hey," he says. He's got me on speaker. "Sorry, I can't really talk. I don't know any more than you do right now but I'm almost at the restaurant."

"Sorry, I don't know why I called," I say, feeling awkward and helpless.

"You care about your friend," Spencer says.

"Yeah. I just want to help."

"I know, I'll keep you posted."

I watch the leaves roll over to show their underbellies to the wind. I head back inside to my family.

-------

**I can't focus on the movie my cousins pick. My mind's spiraling** into a thousand worst-case scenarios, watching Brigid turn in the restaurant, people screaming as she vomits teeth and bristles fur. I slip into my cousin's room and start scrolling through every social media app I have, searching "Ryeburg" and "Bellows Beast" until I find something.

*uhhh there's a wolf in the olive garden shgslkjfsdlkj??* someone's tweeted. *bellows beast??* someone else commented. I click through to their profile, but there are no more updates. I see a livestream in the Bellows Beast hashtag, but it's already ended. The existing video's a dark blur, then a shot of the floor. *Who carpets their restaurant?* I think.

I finally find a tweet from the local news in Ryeburg. Live video coverage. I suck in a breath and click through to see the news crew is interviewing a police officer outside the Olive Garden. I can't see what's happening inside.

"We had to shut this whole restaurant down," the officer says. "I'm not some kind of tree-hugging PETA idiot. That thing comes out into the parking lot, we're putting a bullet in its skull."

My heart stutters. *Brigid's gonna get her Wikipedia page, alright.*

I call Spencer again, but it goes to voicemail. I call him two more times before he finally picks up.

"Priya," he hisses. "I'm—shit." Something clatters. "I'm a little busy!"

"I'm watching you on the news," I say. He curses loudly into my ear. "Well, not you. The cops outside. They're, uh. They're gonna shoot her if she gets out," I say. "So please don't let her get out."

"We won't," he says. "Any idea how to get her to turn back?"

"No," I say. "It just happens. She usually eats before she turns back, I've noticed? But it takes hours."

"We don't *have* hours," says Spencer. "There's a fucking werewolf in the Olive Garden."

"Spencer—"

"Okay, I said that too loud. Marty's here, too, I brought him for—*Jesus Christ!*—for backup. He's about to figure out a couple of things real quick. I have to go."

When he hangs up, I turn back to the news, but I can't see anything that's happening. Until finally—finally, I see a familiar truck park around the corner, and Marty and Spencer walk into the parking lot. The reporter rushes forward, sticking a microphone into Spencer's face.

"Do you believe you've just captured the creature that's been terrorizing the area? The Bellows Beast?"

"Yeah, this is the animal they've been talking about," Spencer says. He rubs the back of his neck nervously. "It's a wolf-dog hybrid that someone tried to keep as a pet, which is actually illegal if you don't have a permit, so. It's also got mange, and seeing any animal you're not prepared to see can be a scary experience." I give him a mental thumbs-up. I'm suddenly grateful that I called him that first night, grateful Brigid bit him and pulled him into this mess with us.

His eyes flick to the ground, and he grins. "So, uh, that wraps it up, I think! Gotta go, see ya, bye!"

I call him as soon as he's in the car. "Hey, Priya," he says. "Oh man. I am *covered* in sweat, that was so awkward. How'd I do, did they get my good side?"

I can't bear to tease him when he sounds so earnest, so I tell him the truth. "You sounded great. Like, weirdly professional."

"Ha, ha."

"It was unsettling."

"But convincing?"

"Yeah, I think so. What did you grab back there?"

"Brigid's keys," he says. I hear her frantic whine in the background, and my heart clenches. I wish I was there, climbing in next to her, whispering soothing words on the drive back to Bellows.

"How is she?"

"I don't know," he says. "She looks worse. The mange is worse. She's moving slower."

"Okay," I say. "Feed her?"

"Yeah."

"Okay," I say again. I want to take his hand. "Thank you, Spencer. For everything."

I can hear his tired smile across the line. "I care about her. Both of you, actually."

"Aw."

"Yeah, yeah."

"Call me when she turns back?"

"Obviously. Bye."

"Bye."

I watch the video on my tiny screen until the footage cuts, feeling strangely empty when it finally goes blank.

# 32

**I don't drive over until a few days later, after I get the okay from** Brigid. I knock three times before I text her, and she just replies *it's open*. I let myself in.

"Brigid?" I call.

"Kitchen," she rasps back, leaning briefly into my line of sight.

I walk past a pile of discarded cardboard boxes. The house is still destroyed from when Brigid turned, and the kitchen is a war zone of spilled herbs and stacks of Tupperware. There are plates piled in the sink and something is boiling over on the stove. There's blood splattered across the countertop, soaking into the grout. I start to point at it, but the pot on the stove sizzles angrily.

"Ugh, shut up," Brigid says, dead eyed, dragging the pot to another burner. She leaves the flame on, and it dances orange after licking up whatever spilled over before turning blue again.

I turn the stove off and slowly face her. Her hair is shaggy now, the strip of color grown out a few inches after her ill-fated Olive Garden Incident. She brushes it out of her eyes with the back of her hand, and I realize her hands are shaking. There's an angry red rash creeping up her arm, a bald spot where her arm hair should be.

"Hey . . ." I say carefully, holding eye contact. I approach her now the way I approach her when she's turned: slowly, hands outstretched. "Do you want to sit?"

"I can't," she says. "I've gotta finish this."

"This, being . . . ?"

"You know exactly what this is, Priya."

"Yeah, I do. I just think it's a really bad idea."

"Yeah, you've made that pretty clear. You also haven't given me any other suggestions, so."

"I'm working on it."

"Yeah, okay."

"Okay, what do your parents think about all of this?" I take in the kitchen again, nervousness building. "You did call them, right?"

"Yeah, definitely," she says, but it's dripping with sarcasm.

"I don't understand—"

"Yeah, of course you don't fucking understand!"

Brigid's cursing feels sharper when it's directed at you, a firework going off right beside your ear.

"You made the local news," I say instead. I know it's the wrong thing to say the second it comes out of my mouth.

"I don't—"

"—want to talk about it! I know, you never do! But people *saw* you."

"Oh, you mean when I had a meltdown when they tried to cut off my free breadsticks, or when I turned into a werewolf in the kitchen?"

". . . Yes."

"I just . . . Listen."

"I'm listening."

"I think it's pretty fucking cool of me to have gone this long without having a breakdown. It was overdue, and now I've gotten it out of the way, so it's fine. It's fine."

"I heard you climbed on top of your table."

"I may have climbed on top of my table."

"Okay."

"And then I did puke on the table, and slip on it, and fall onto the ground."

"Yep. That's it."

"It's been a bad year."

"I know. I'm sorry."

"You didn't have to come," she says. "Today, or when I turned in the car. You're not my babysitter, or my doctor, or whatever else you think you're supposed to be."

"Your friend, maybe?" I say, sharply.

"If you're my friend, I don't get how you aren't trying to help me right now! You do a whole lot of shit that I never asked for, but the second I ask for your help, specifically—on this *one* thing—you're like, nope, sorry, no can do!"

"It's *dangerous*! You *know* it's dangerous, but you keep doing all of these things lately that are really, genuinely scaring me!" She scoffs, but I keep going. "No, I'm serious. Driving when you know you're gonna turn? That thing with the broken glass from the jelly jar? That was *scary*, Brigid. You keep putting this stuff into your body that could really hurt you!"

"That ship has already sailed!" she shouts. "My *body* is really hurting me! You know I'm getting worse. This is going to kill me anyway, so why does it matter if something else does?"

Maybe she doesn't want to die. Maybe she really does just want to walk right up to the edge of death in order to stay alive.

"Brigid," I start.

"Wait, hold on—I'm sorry, did you look through my sketchbook? My sick journal?"

"I—you left it in your car. I found it by your teeth."

"And you just *read it*? You had no right to do that."

She's getting louder, so I answer louder, too.

"We're friends, Brigid! We've told each other our deepest, darkest thoughts anyway."

"It's not the same and you know it," she snaps.

"I don't—"

"*Friends*," she says. "You keep saying that. But I don't think that's what I am to you at all."

"Oh, come on," I scoff. "What does *that* mean? How can you even say that, after—"

"After everything you've done to try to fix me? To—to *study* me?"

She looks at me like she's expecting an answer, but she doesn't give me time to think of one.

"Yeah, I didn't miss that, in the group chat. You calling me your independent study. I'm really glad that I'm so useful to you. Maybe you can use me to get back into college across the country, when this fun little adventure is over for you."

"I'm just trying to help."

"This is my *life*, Priya. You know what I think?" Her nostrils flare, and I know that whatever she says next is going to hurt. "I think that you needed something to fill up your time. I think that you needed me to be your personal project so you didn't have to think about how shitty your own life is. Like, yeah, I'm sick, but at least I'm not a monster like Brigid is!"

"I've never called you a monster. I would never."

"But you *think* it! I can see it on your face! You've turned me into your own personal Mütter Museum freakshow! You're going to put me under a microscope until you don't need me anymore, and then you're going to leave."

"That is not fair."

"Nothing is fair, Priya! Look at us! It's not fair that you got sick, and it's not fair I was born with this shit hardwired into me, but we just have to deal with it! So stop playing doctor with me just because you have no idea what to do with your life anymore! I am sick of it! Try turning that microscope the other way for one miserable second!"

I clench my jaw, anger bubbling up from a well deep inside of me. "You know what I think, Brigid?"

"Yeah, I really do."

"I think that we—we bonded over being sick, and you're angry that you're getting worse, and I—"

"You what? Say it."

"You're getting worse, and I'm getting better! You're *jealous* of me!"

She balls her shaking hands into fists like she's thinking about fighting me.

"I can't stay sick just to keep you company!" I yell.

For the first time, I see real rage on her face. And I think I'm more afraid of her like this than when she's a wolf.

"Then don't," she says.

She grabs a glass from the counter and walks over to the pot on the stove. She dips her whole hand in with it, scooping out a cupful of liquid that runs down her arm, drips onto the burner. It's a murky red-brown, the color of rust, with steam rising up from it. I instinctively move toward her to see if she's burned herself, but she steps back from me.

"Don't do this," I say. "We—we'll figure out something else."

"What do you mean, *we*?" she says. "It's not your fucking body, okay?"

"It is literally poison!"

"Well. Only one way to find out," she says. And she tips the wolfs-bane back down her throat.

# 33

**After our fight, I refused to leave Brigid's house until I saw that** she wasn't having a reaction. We sat in uncomfortable silence on either side of the table, and every time I'd asked her how she was feeling, she shot me a jagged look. I think that sometimes this is what caring about someone looks like in real life: a stubborn refusal to leave them alone, even when they say they want you to.

When I got home I googled deadly nightshade and found a case where a girl didn't have a reaction until the next day, so I texted Spencer to make sure he'd swing by and check in on her before his shift.

*what, am i under house arrest*, Brigid texted me.

It's the only text I've gotten from her in over a week. She's started posting more art lately, and I catch one of the sketchbook doodles, cleaned up digitally. I look at the green dot next to her username, open the chat window only to close it again. At least I know she's okay. That's what I keep telling myself.

-------

**I can tally a list of the most painful moments of my life, illumi-**nated in my past like a burst from a flashbulb. When I fell playing soccer and heard my wrist snap a second before I felt that searing poker of pain. When I got on an airplane with a raging sinus infection that felt like it was going to burst my head open as the plane landed. One period when I forgot painkillers and my cramps were so excruciating that I threw up in a Starbucks bathroom.

Last fall, after months of puzzling every doctor and ignoring every worsening symptom and white-knuckling my way through finals week, when my chest got tight like a fist and I saw stars and passed out during my Calc exam. When they took me to the hospital and stabilized me but couldn't figure out what was happening. When they brought me home just to spend Christmas in the hospital, an IV snaking into the crook in my arm for weeks and weeks and weeks.

The way I feel right now doesn't make the top five. It doesn't physically hurt as much as any of these things did, but it feels more like a betrayal than any of them. I'd thought that getting better was a linear thing, but now I remember that *chronic* means "over and over" at the same time as it means "always" or "forever." Sometimes, forever.

I wake up at four in the morning feeling the way I did in February, swollen joints and cloudy brain and shaky limbs. I'm hot, but it hurts to push the blanket off. My skin feels like it's bruised solid, aching and tender. For a second I wonder if it's the flu, try to convince myself that this isn't happening again, but I know better. This kind of pain is an old friend.

I can't remember the word for this until my mom comes up to see why I'm still in bed and I screw my eyes shut and let out what can only, pitifully, be described as a whimper.

"Oh, Priya," she says softly. I can tell she's upset. "Are you having a flare-up?"

*Relapse* had seemed like a better word. Back to square zero. But *flare* is the word for something that continues to rear its head when you don't expect it to. It's happening again. It's always going to happen again, no matter how careful I am, no matter how good I start to feel.

I want to scream. I want to throw things that break. I want to shatter glass and cry. Instead, I let my mom help me into the bath again. I swallow my pride, along with as many ibuprofen as I'm allowed to take.

I don't leave my room for three days. I don't want to make my way down the stairs. I don't want to face my family. I know, logically, that getting sick again is not a moral failing, and I know they care about me, but I can't bear to see my own disappointment reflected back on their faces. I'm mad at myself for getting sick again; I'm mad at myself for thinking that I was actually getting better in the first place. I finally come down after my mother tells me, sternly, that she's not going to bring any more food into my room.

My dad comes into the living room as I'm watching TV. I'm mainlining *True or False* again from the beginning, and I'm already at the end of season one. I'm coming up on the episodes I watched with Brigid, and I think about whether or not I should skip them.

My dad looks at the screen and chuckles, sitting down next to me. "How many times have you seen this, Priya?"

"Lots," I mutter. My brain is too tired to latch onto something new or follow any kind of complicated plot. Carlos and Evie follow the same beats every episode: Carlos finds the first criminal, which leads them to the red herring; Evie breaks several laws, which Carlos loudly objects to; and finally, they crack the case together. (*you know, none of this would be admissible in court*, Brigid had messaged me, years ago. *They address that in season two!!* I'd written back.)

"How are you feeling today?"

"Not great, Dad," I croak, keeping my eyes on the screen.

"You're going to get better again, Priya. This is just a temporary setback."

"It's not!" I say, louder than I mean to. It comes out cruel. "I get that you're trying to be positive. But I'm never going to get better. Positivity isn't going to fix me. I know you and Mom are obsessed with finding a cure, but sometimes there isn't one. Have you ever thought that this might be as good as it gets?"

"Priya—" he tries.

"No, I don't want to talk about it."

"Maybe you'll feel well enough to work on your independent study later," he says.

"That's over," I say. "It doesn't matter anymore."

"Don't say that."

"There was never any independent study. Not one I could turn into anything useful. Trying to do that cost me someone I care about."

I'm not making any sense. I can tell he has no idea what I'm talking about. "Do you want to talk about it?" he asks, softly.

"I'm just going to have to learn to let a lot of things go, okay?" I try not to let a tremor creep into my voice. "I'm never going to be a doctor. I wouldn't be able to handle the hours, med school, any of it. And—and Brigid doesn't even want to talk to me. It's—it's over."

"It's never over, Priya."

"Stop it, *appa*!" I shout, clenching my jaw. "Just stop! I don't want to talk about this! Could you just leave me alone for one second?"

"Okay," he says, putting his hands on his knees and pushing himself up off the couch. I almost call out to him as he's leaving, but I can't make my mouth form the words. I watch the rest of the episode alone.

-------

**oof ouch my bones (ONLINE – 8)**

**katie (fyodorbrostoevsky):**
Seb, show em your new wheels

**Seb (mereextravagancy):**
[IMG_4478.JPEG]
Kachow

**al (thorswagnarok):**
lookin good, lightning mcqueen

**Spook (spookyspoony):**
Ahh, you landed on the one we talked about! That's exciting!

**Max (quintuplevampire):**
Crazy fast on insurance's timeline congrats dude

**Seb (mereextravagancy):**
I know, I feel like my dad bribed someone or something

**Max (quintuplevampire):**
How's the adjustment

**Seb (mereextravagancy):**
Good, mostly
I don't use it all the time, just on special occasions
But like... my energy levels, you guys
It's helping so much

**lee (typhoonsss):**

i am so glad to hear that <3

**Seb (mereextravagancy):**

<3

Also... the saga of the bellows beast continues, huh?
www.ryeburg-chronicle.com/article/04873/local-restaurant-evacuated/

**al (thorswagnarok):**

I SAW THIS

...bridge did you... turn into a werewolf in an olive garden...?

**bridge (bigforkhands):**

and? what about it?

**lee (typhoonsss):**

oh... no

**bridge (bigforkhands):**

listen it's,,, fine,,,

**katie (fyodorbrostoevsky):**

omg wait, does this mean you know the hot animal control guy???

**bridge (bigforkhands):**

the WHAT

HAHAHA

**Seb (mereextravagancy):**

yeah, the what?

**katie (fyodorbrostoevsky):**

oh hush, sebastian, you know I only have eyes for you

**Seb (mereextravagancy):**

:)

**al (thorswagnarok):**

i am going to scream. please make out already

**katie (fyodorbrostoevsky):**

:))))

**Priya (paranormaldetective):**

We cannot tell spencer anyone has called him hot

**katie (fyodorbrostoevsky):**
is that his name????
and it's not just ME calling him hot, people on twitter are literally calling him "hot animal control guy"

**bridge (bigforkhands):**
this is amazing lmao

**Priya (paranormaldetective):**
He's not /not/ hot but we can't let this go to his head

**al (thorswagnarok):**
people are also saying that the whole thing is a conspiracy to cover up the actual bellows beast

**lee (typhoonsss):**
well...

**bridge (bigforkhands):**
you got me there dot png!!!

**Max (quintuplevampire):**
Bridge side note are you like okay

**bridge (bigforkhands):**
i'm actually feeling good
trying the new medicine and I haven't turned yet
it's been a few weeks so i think that's a good sign
but i'm keeping an eye out this week, that's kind of when we'll find out

**al (thorswagnarok):**
that's awesome!

**bridge (bigforkhands):**
what's new with everyone else?

**Max (quintuplevampire):**
I'm graduating which is weird but exciting
Had to point out that the steps in the auditorium aren't wheelchair accessible because my school is full of idiots
And I'm working on my plan for college. It's pretty exhausting but the school I picked Houston is one of the only colleges in the US that actually provide accessible accommodations for like people with CP so I can't imagine trying to go somewhere else

**al (thorswagnarok):**
| ugh
| yeah I feel like I probably don't know what "accessible" means either, though
| other than ramps?

**Seb (mereextravagancy):**
| There's so much you don't realize at first

**Spook (spookyspoony):**
| So many restaurants say they're accessible and then don't have any room for you to maneuver between tables

**Max (quintuplevampire):**
| Or they won't bring out lids or straws so I can actually drink my drink
| Anyway it'll be fun to go to college and have to explain accessibility to strangers in a whole new location
| Ok I'm done someone else go

**Seb (mereextravagancy):**
| I think if Katie doesn't tell you guys the news, she's going to vibrate out of her skin

**al (thorswagnarok):**
| ?!?!?

**katie (fyodorbrostoevsky):**
| HEY EVERYONE
| [IMG_1429.JPEG]

It's a selfie of who I can only assume are Katie and Sebastian; her eyes are scrunched small from smiling so wide, showing the gap between her front teeth. He's smiling affectionately with his mouth closed, but his eyes are happy in the way you're happy when you can't quite believe you're allowed to be. It looks like they're in someone's bedroom, and Katie's resting her head on Seb's shoulder.

**lee (typhoonsss):**
| this is absolutely PRECIOUS
| LOOK AT YOU TWO

**Max (quintuplevampire):**
Cute!

**bridge (bigforkhands):**
did you guys legit one-up us making fun of you DMing each other by hanging out in person

**al (thorswagnarok):**
oh my God
absolute LEGENDS

**Priya (paranormaldetective):**
<3

**Spook (spookyspoony):**
Where are you guys?

**katie (fyodorbrostoevsky):**
i'm done for the semester and I'm visiting Seb in seattle!!

**Seb (mereextravagancy):**
I do want you all to know that Katie workshopped that selfie extensively

**katie (fyodorbrostoevsky):**
sebastian do not shame me

**Seb (mereextravagancy):**
"It would be cute if I sat on your lap" "Yeah, but then you might dislocate my hips"

**katie (fyodorbrostoevsky):**
SEB

**bridge (bigforkhands):**
hahahhahahha

**al (thorswagnarok):**
sjsdklsdflk
foiled

**Seb (mereextravagancy):**
I did say I could just pop them back in
Might have been worth it

**al (thorswagnarok):**
so are you two beautiful kids... an item now

**katie (fyodorbrostoevsky):**
that's PRIVATE, al

**Seb (mereextravagancy):**
Yes
............. I mean...

**al (thorswagnarok):**
FINALLYYYYY

**lee (typhoonsss):**
YES!

**al (thorswagnarok):**
i thought I was going to have to intervene

**Seb (mereextravagancy):**
You did intervene
Several times

**al (thorswagnarok):**
yeah, ur welcome

**lee (typhoonsss):**
I HAVE BEEN ROOTING FOR YOU TWO FROM THE START!!!

**Spook (spookyspoony):**
Mazel!

**katie (fyodorbrostoevsky):**
we are seeing if we might be able to give it a go
long distance, etc

**Max (quintuplevampire):**
Oh right
Katie you're in Chicago right

**katie (fyodorbrostoevsky):**
for school, yep
I am taking this week to not worry about feeling crappy or the stuff I have to submit to my insurance AGAIN
and just have a GOOD TIME with someone i CARE ABOUT

**Seb (mereextravagancy):**
Oh hey
It me :)

**al (thorswagnarok):**

sickeningly sweet, as always

have fun, you crazy kids

**Spook (spookyspoony):**

You are the youngest person in this chat, al

**al (thorswagnarok):**

it's hard out here for a teen parent

whose children are all older than they are

**bridge (bigforkhands):**

kid is universal, kid

**lee (typhoonsss):**

whatever you say, children

**al (thorswagnarok):**

hey, btw

how are you doing, priya?

you've been really quiet this week

@Priya (paranormaldetective)

**lee (typhoonsss):**

i was going to ask the same!

**Priya (paranormaldetective):**

Thank you guys

That's

That's sweet, thank you

**Spook (spookyspoony):**

That's not an answer

**Priya (paranormaldetective):**

I didn't want to be a downer! Everyone else had such great news

I didn't want to be the one to say I was having a bad week :/

**Seb (mereextravagancy):**

Oh no :(

**Priya (paranormaldetective):**

Yeah, it's a pretty bad flare up

Everything hurts, my brain's slow, etc

**bridge (bigforkhands):**
| shit

**lee (typhoonsss):**
| oh, hon, I'm sorry

**Priya (paranormaldetective):**
| The worst part is, I feel so stupid?

**katie (fyodorbrostoevsky):**
| what do you mean?

**al (thorswagnarok):**
| you're not stupid.

**Priya (paranormaldetective):**
| For a while I actually thought that I might be done with this
| That I might get better
| Like, back to the way I was before the tick bite, better
| But I... don't think that's ever going to happen
| And I shouldn't be so disappointed, but I am
| I just am

**lee (typhoonsss):**
| you're allowed to be!
| i remember just hoping that i would get better on my own, somehow
| and it just didn't happen
| we just have to manage as best as we can

**Spook (spookyspoony):**
| And honestly, flares happen, but you're doing better than you were, right?
| Overall?

**Priya (paranormaldetective):**
| I guess that's true
| Just hard to remember right now

**Spook (spookyspoony):**
| If it helps I had an awful week, too

**Priya (paranormaldetective):**
| No, I don't want you guys to feel bad, either!

**Spook (spookyspoony):**
| Ah, I thought it would help
| Solidarity, and all of that

**lee (typhoonsss):**
| i also had a rough week
| you aren't alone!
| but, my hysterectomy is finally scheduled! i'm getting this thing out in a few weeks!!

**Priya (paranormaldetective):**
| Yay!

**al (thorswagnarok):**
| woohoo!

**bridge (bigforkhands):**
| adios uteroso!

**Max (quintuplevampire):**
| The word is útero

**bridge (bigforkhands):**
| hey maybe I should get rid of MY uterus

**lee (typhoonsss):**
| one drastic thing at a time, bridge

**bridge (bigforkhands):**
| you sound like priya

**Priya (paranormaldetective):**
| I didn't say a word

**bridge (bigforkhands):**
| shrugguy.com

**lee (typhoonsss):**
| well regardless of bad days or good days, we have got each other's backs, right?

**Priya (paranormaldetective):**
| ...right

**bridge (bigforkhands):**
| you'd think so, wouldn't you

**Priya (paranormaldetective):**
| Okay, don't start

**bridge (bigforkhands):**
I saw that ellipsis, I could say the same thing

**Spook (spookyspoony):**
Hang on, are you two fighting?

**lee (typhoonsss):**
spook!

**Spook (spookyspoony):**
Asking is the quickest way to get a simple yes or no answer

**bridge (bigforkhands):**
...

**Priya (paranormaldetective):**
...

**al (thorswagnarok):**
i cannot take these kinds of emotional ups and downs

**lee (typhoonsss):**
:/

**al (thorswagnarok):**
do we need to do an intervention

**bridge (bigforkhands):**
no

**Priya (paranormaldetective):**
No!

**al (thorswagnarok):**
but i'm so good at those
i'm an intervention expert, seb said so

**Max (quintuplevampire):**
Katie and Sebastian aren't paying attention anymore are they

**Spook (spookyspoony):**
This is just like thanksgiving

**lee (typhoonsss):**
one big happy family

-------

hashtag team werewolf

Brigid:

p thinks you're hot spencer

...oh my God

Why would you say that

Spencer:

Haha thanks??

Technically I said you weren't not hot

Spencer:

Same THING

Thanks a lot, Brigid

I thought we weren't going to tell him about twitter

Spencer:

I know what twitter is

Brigid:

they're referring to you as "hot animal control guy"

Spencer:

WHAT!!!!!!!!!!

Literally what did I say

Brigid:

i don't know, i didn't retain that

Thanks

Spencer:

> You have to make that my contact in your phones now

Brigid:

> no

> Absolutely not

I hate trying to pretend everything is okay in these groups but not being able to reach out to her one-on-one. She doesn't respond to the messages I send just to her, so I stop trying. Two days later, though, I get a package of dandelion tea in the mail. There's no return address, but I think I know who it's from. At least, I hope I do.

# 34

I carve out my schedule over the next week, adding back one thing at a time as I start to feel like myself again. I listen to my mom rattle off ingredients, agree to cut out gluten for a few weeks to see if it makes a difference even though the thought of going without bread products makes me almost as depressed as everything else does. "The MSG got you, Priya," she says. "It was that orange chicken. I knew I didn't trust that restaurant."

I open up my school email for the first time in two months to find hundreds of unread messages, and I finally start combing through them to find the work that I was supposed to have finished already. It's strange, poking through the detritus like this—I've gotten emails from clubs that I forgot to unsubscribe from, college bulletins, community service opportunities, class bonding activities. There are actually a couple emails from people on my floor, friends from some of the classes I took checking in on me. There's one from my Human Bio professor, too, encouraging me to reach out if I need help finishing the work from last semester.

It's a lot, to be reminded of that whole other life all at once, to put it on top of this one like tracing paper on a backlight. I'm starting to realize that there are a lot of ways to build a life, in so many different directions.

I email my professor back. I open all the PowerPoint slides, start making my way through the projects and quizzes that I missed. It's miserably slow going, and I'm aware of how many more times I have to read the text to retain any of the knowledge, how quickly my head starts to ache or the words swim in my vision. But I start the work anyway. I let myself be proud of that.

I'm still in bed on Saturday when my dad knocks softly on my door. I've gone and ruined my sleep schedule again, my pain keeping me awake until I finally give in and sleep until noon. I push myself up onto my pillows and he sits down beside me. I notice he's got a small stack of papers in his hands, and I raise my eyebrows.

"What is that?"

"I want to say something first," he says.

"Can I?" I say. He nods. "I didn't mean to snap at you like I did. It's not your fault that this is happening to me."

"It's alright," he says. "I don't think any of us are very good at arguing, or the part that comes after where you talk about it."

"Okay, your turn."

"Okay." He faces me. "I don't want you to feel pressure from me. I'm so proud of everything you've done, this year and before that. You're strong, Priya. You tough things out. And I don't want to tell you what to do, but I feel like being a doctor was something that you really wanted."

I nod.

"And it's not like you to just give up on things."

I can't hold my tongue any longer. "I don't *want* to! But what am I supposed to do? Isn't being an adult just realizing that you have to give up the things you really wanted in order to survive?"

"Oh, Priya," he says quietly. "Sometimes. Sacrifice is important."

"Then this is the one that I am going to have to make," I say. "I'll find something else. But I've been sleeping for twelve hours a night. What if I have a flare-up during med school? How could I do a residency when I have to keep sitting down, or sleeping that much?"

"Your health is the most important thing," he says. "But I don't know if you have to choose between that and being a doctor."

It sounds ridiculous. "No one wants to go to a doctor who isn't healthy," I say. "That's like . . . well, I don't know what it's like. My brain isn't working right now."

"I've been doing some reading," he says, as if that isn't the thing he does most. He shuffles the papers, and I can see that they're articles from different websites. I find the fact that he's printed them out for me so endearing that I feel myself tearing up. I catch a few headlines as he looks through the pages: DOCTORS WITH DISABILITIES ARE CHANGING THE FUTURE OF MEDICINE; I'M A DOCTOR WITH CHRONIC ILLNESS; TOWARD A WORLD WHERE A PHYSICIAN IN A WHEELCHAIR IS NO BIG DEAL.

"A lot of people are talking about system reform," he says. "But—ah, there it is!" He pulls out an article called CAREER ADVICE FOR DOCTORS WITH A CHRONIC ILLNESS, right behind HOW TO SURVIVE MED SCHOOL WITH A CHRONIC ILLNESS AND/OR DISABILITY. "People have advice on how to do it. And a lot of people say these doctors understand their patients in a way no one else possibly could. Empathy is important, but you have really been in the patients' shoes, Priya."

"I am the patient," I say.

"Maybe you could be both?" He stacks the papers again, leaving them on my bedside table. "Just something to think about. I just want you to see that you have options. The world is still open to you."

"Maybe."

"Yes."

He leans in to kiss me on the forehead, and I pull him in for a hug. I love him for doing this, for caring about me in the best way he knows how: exhaustive research.

"Thank you, *appa*," I say.

"Come get your lunch," he says.

He's at the door before I speak again. "Do you—" I start. He turns to look at me, raising his eyebrows. "Do you think you could help me find researchers in the area to shadow or . . . or intern with?"

"Sure!" he says, visibly excited.

"I want to find out if I'd like it."

He nods. "I'll look it up this afternoon."

-------

Hey, Spencer

Sorry, I only answer to "hot animal control guy" now

Or maybe "local hero"?

How about "dumbass"?

Hmm... lol

How is she doing?

Brigid, I mean

Who else would you have meant

That's fair

I think she's okay

I swung by earlier this week to check in

She still hasn't turned?

Nope

And I'd know

No weird phone calls to animal control

Aside from the usual kind of weird

15ft python in a children's play place, etc

...what is the etc

Do you actually want to know?

Not really, no

Why don't you two just like

Talk to each other

You don't get it

Why, because I'm a guy

I didn't SAY that

Explain it to me

We had a huge fight

Friends fight

Play some mario kart and get over it

That is EXACTLY what my sister said

Minus the mario kart part

She sounds smart

She's 14

I guess she's pretty smart

But it was this horrible, ugly, knock-down, drag-out fight

We said awful things to each other

And nothing has changed

She's still taking the potion

Potion?? Lol

Sorry

I mean... it's working

She's alive, and she's human

Well, I guess she's always human

But it's been a month and she hasn't turned

So this is just what works for her, right?

...you think I should apologize?

Idk...

Ugh

Hahaha

I mean

It's not all selfless, I miss you around here too

Thanks :)

Anytime

# 35

"Where's my *apron*?" Kiki shrieks, sprinting past me with one sock on and half of her costume. "Mom, did you wash it?"

"No!" Mom yells from the other room. "Go check your room!"

"I checked already!"

"Check again!"

"Ugh!" I hear her thudding up the stairs. It's the opening night of her musical. I'd love for her energy level to be about half what it is right now.

"We have to drop you off in five minutes, are you sure you need the apron?" I shout. I hear footsteps again, then Kiki appears halfway up the stairs, staring at me.

"Do you even hear yourself? How am I supposed to be a peasant without the *apron*, Priya?"

"Maybe you were too poor to afford one?"

"It's in the car!" Mom shouts. "Let's go."

My sister runs by me again, and I haul myself up off the couch.

"Priya, are you coming or not?" Kiki yells.

"Yes, just give me a second."

"I have to help the others do makeup, the boys have no idea what they're doing. I'm really good at the fake dirt. That's, like, my specialty."

"Impressive," I say.

Suresh meets us at the auditorium. Three songs in he feigns surprise and whispers, loudly, "Wait, is the whole *thing* singing?"

He checks his phone afterward as we wait for Kiki, which reminds me to turn mine back on.

"We don't have to go to all four shows, do we?" he asks. Mom and Dad both give him a look, and he rolls his eyes. "Come on, we were all thinking it."

"Your mother and I will be going to all of them," Dad says. Then, after a beat, "But you can talk to your sister."

"Sweet, we're free," Suresh mutters.

Kiki comes bounding over, all smiles. "What did you think?" she asks, and it's impossible for me to tell her that I fell asleep for the entire back half of the musical.

"You were great, kiddo," I say, hugging her. My mom gives her some roses that we picked up at the supermarket before the show, and it's all very cheesy, but she seems happy.

"We were so high-energy tonight," she says, her grin stretched wide. "I think we really nailed it, except when Christian dropped the candlesticks. But that was at the very beginning, so we had plenty of time to bounce back."

I notice a blonde girl hovering behind my sister, and I raise my eyebrows, nodding in her direction. Kiki turns, and her smile freezes on her face.

"Sophie," she says. "Hi."

"Hey, Kiki," the other girl says. She fidgets. "I just wanted to come over to say good job. You did—well, uh, you did a good job."

Kiki's smile turns genuine, wiping the confusion off her face. "Oh, thanks! You did a good job, too. Your solo was amazing, I can't believe you hit that note every time."

"Thanks," Sophie says. "It's a little awkward doing 'Lovely Ladies' in front of everyone, but at least I get to wear a ballgown at the end."

"Yeah, totally." Kiki laughs. I can't look away. I'm fascinated by their dynamic. They're so awkward that I can't stand it.

"So, uh." Sophie clears her throat. "A few of us were headed over to IHOP for some late-night pancakes, if you wanted to come? Sarah's big sister is driving, and they have room for one more in their car."

"Oh, that'd be cool!" Kiki says. "I mean, great choice. They are open twenty-four hours."

"Actually, I think they close at midnight."

"Oh."

"Sorry, I don't know why I corrected you."

"No, it's fine. Let me go talk to my parents." As soon as Kiki turns back to me, I give her a look, trying to stifle my laughter.

"So was that your nemesis?" I ask.

"I mean, who knows what her angle is," Kiki says.

"Yeah, she seems horrible," I say.

She frowns. "Shut up."

I check my phone for the first time in hours, and a jolt of adrenaline hits me right in the chest. All the amusement drains out of me, and I can hear my heartbeat in my ears. I've got three missed calls from Spencer and four texts. The message in the preview is the name and address of a hospital in Echo Creek.

I don't read anything else. I just hit DIAL.

"Hey," he says when he picks up. I don't let him say anything else.

"What's going on, what's happening?"

"Did you get my texts?"

"I didn't read them. I was at my sister's school musical."

"Okay, Brigid's in the ER now, we're still waiting on more information."

I'm silent for so long that I hear Spencer say, "Priya, are you still there?"

"Yeah, I'm here," I say. "What—what happened?"

"I, uh, I don't know exactly. Apparently she collapsed this afternoon and Hattie drove her here. I only know because Hattie and Marty had plans later, and Marty ended up telling me when Hattie canceled."

"Are you there right now?"

"Yeah, I'm letting Hattie go home for the night. I'm in the waiting room, they're still trying to stabilize her."

That word, *stabilize*, hits a nerve inside of me, and the fear I was already feeling ratchets up. "Oh my God."

"The doctor said she went into shock?"

"Oh my God."

"Adrenal shock, something like that? I don't know, I don't know this stuff."

"Okay, I'm on my way."

"Okay, good, I texted you the address."

"I'll see you in, like, an hour," I say.

"Try to speed?"

"Yeah. Thank you for calling me."

"Yeah, of course. Of course."

"Hey, Spencer, do you have her phone?"

"Yeah, Hattie gave me her backpack before she left."

"Call her parents."

"Will do." I hear the fear in his voice, too, and my heart cracks open a little more. "Get here soon, Priya."

"I will."

I start walking toward the parking lot, but Suresh catches me. "Whoa whoa whoa, what's going on?"

"My friend—Brigid's in—she's in the hospital, I have to go."

"Priya, can you even drive right now?"

"I'll be fine, Suresh, I just have to get there."

He grabs the lanyard with the keys out of his pocket. "Okay," he says, nodding. "I'll drive you. Let's go."

-------

**I keep checking my phone in the car. Suresh glances over at me a** couple of times before turning some music on low. I feel completely useless, so I text Spencer again.

> Anything new?

> Nope, sorry

> I'll let you know right away, I promise

> Sorry

> Don't be

I open Discord, but I'm not sure if it's an invasion of her privacy to let the group know what's going on. *I* don't even know what's going on. I close the app.

"She means a lot to you, huh?" Suresh says quietly. I'm not entirely sure what he's asking.

"She's my best friend," I say. It doesn't feel strong enough. "I would do anything for her."

He glances over at me quickly. "You know I'd do anything for *you*, right?"

It's so grown-up of him to say, but I can hear his old little-kid sweetness right underneath it. It makes me think about the way he used to crawl on top of the covers next to me when he heard me crying in the middle of the night, not saying a word. I watch the lights pass over Suresh's face as he taps the steering wheel with his musician's fingers in a steady rhythm.

"I feel like you've been wanting to go through this whole thing alone," he says. "And I get that. Like. I don't, how could I, right. And I didn't want to, like, push you. But . . . you know I've been waiting here the whole time, right? You know you're allowed to tell me what's going on with you?"

I don't realize I'm crying until Suresh says, "Priya, sorry, it's okay."

"I'm sorry," I say. "I'm sorry, I don't know what's wrong with me."

"Nothing's wrong with you, Priya," he says. "Well, other than the Lyme disease stuff. Like. Emotionally, I mean."

That makes me snuffle a wet laugh. "Okay," I say. "This is going to sound insane, but I want to tell you what's going on with Brigid before we get there. Just stick with me."

"Yeah, we've got time," he says.

I start talking. None of it's in order, and none of it makes sense, but Suresh listens.

It's 11:30 p.m. by the time we get to Echo Creek Medical Center, and I'm already exhausted. I scan the ER lobby but I don't see a single familiar face under the stark fluorescent lights. Just standing in a hospital is familiar in a way that curdles my stomach, but I'm not here for me.

"Who are we looking for?" Suresh asks me.

"My friend Spencer," I say. "But he's not here. One second."

Spencer picks up on the third ring. "Hey, sorry," he says. "I was about to call."

"It's okay. I'm here but I don't see you."

"They just moved her up to a room in the ICU."

"The ICU?" I'm hit with another spike of anxiety. "I thought she was stable?"

"She is, she just needs something for her blood pressure and stuff. They want to keep an eye on her while they try to figure out what's wrong."

"Which room is she in?"

"Room 237. Do you want me to come down?"

"No, stay put. I'll find you."

We ask the nurse on the second floor to point us to the right room. I spot Spencer right when we round the corner, still wearing his uniform, slumped against the wall in the hallway outside the room. He walks toward me as soon as he sees me and, to my surprise, pulls me into a tight hug before I can even say hello. I tense for a second, but he holds on until I take a breath, feel my muscles start to uncoil. My eyes fill with tears.

"Hey," he says into my ear.

"Hey," I return, looping my arms around him, too.

"Uh, hey to both of you," Suresh says, waving a hand.

"Oh my God, Suresh," I say. "Spencer, this is my brother. S, this is Spencer."

"Hey, man," Spencer says with a nod. "Good to meet you."

"You, too." Suresh nods back.

"Can I see her?" I ask.

"Yeah, go ahead," Spencer says. "But just, uh—she looks worse than she is. That's what the doctor told me."

I swallow. "Okay, you're freaking me out even more."

"No, I just wanted to give you a heads-up."

I go into the room. It's quiet in the hospital this late at night, but her room is louder than I expected, between the steady, slow beep of the heart monitor and the rumble of the air conditioner. The room is heavily shadowed, like something out of a Renaissance painting. There's a wheelchair in the corner, shades drawn over the window. Brigid is thrown into sharp relief on the bed in the center of the room, the light shining directly on her.

The first thing I notice are all the tubes bundled onto her arm, feeding into her bloodstream. She's got more than one IV in her arm and another in her hand, one of those heartbeat sensors clamped onto her thumb, patches stuck to her chest.

Spencer wasn't kidding. She looks bad—scary bad. She's pale and drawn. Her skin is sallow, almost gray, and she's breathing quickly and shallowly. There's a sheen of sweat on her face and chest, like she's fighting something really, really hard. She probably is.

I want to walk over to the bed, but I can't get my feet to move. This was me, I realize. When my family came into my hospital room a few months ago, they looked at me and saw me exactly like this, fragile and broken down, IV antibiotics pumping into my system.

There's a knock at the door, and the doctor walks in, trailed by a girl a few years older than me with a badge that says MEDICAL STUDENT.

"Hi, I'm Dr. Nowak," she says.

"Hi," I return, feeling stupid and small.

"We're going to take blood for a few more tests right now, see if we can keep ruling things out," she says.

The med student goes over to Brigid, and I look at her nervously. I want to say something intelligent, something useful, but all that comes out is, "Is she okay?"

"Well," Dr. Nowak says. I hate the way she pauses. "We've stabilized her. She's lucky she came in when she did. She was going into hypovolemic shock. Any longer and her organs would have started shutting down. She's got a fever, and she's severely dehydrated, so we're giving her fluids and steroids to get her levels back up while we try to figure out the root cause of this."

I nod after every sentence, like I know exactly what she's talking about.

"We're going to give it a few more hours to see if she starts responding, and if not, we keep running tests."

"What are you testing for right now?" I ask.

"We're going to look at her cortisol levels to see if she's got adrenal insufficiency," she says. "It's a hormone-producing gland, and if those levels get too low, there can be some pretty nasty side effects."

"Is she going to make it?" I surprise myself with the question. I didn't want to ask it. It just slips out.

Dr. Nowak softens. "Yes, honey, we'll figure out what's wrong with her. It may take some time, though."

"But, uh . . . but people die of this?"

She looks uncomfortable, but she answers me. "Yes, they do."

"I, uh . . . I know she was taking a lot of supplements, could that be the problem?"

"Hard to say. Get me a list of her medications, though."

"Okay," I say. "Can I stay here for a while?"

"Yes, of course."

"Thanks."

I pull a chair over to the side of the bed when they leave, studying Brigid. I'm afraid to touch her. I can see a spot on her head, behind her ear, where her hair looks like it's falling out. Her hands look pale, too, and her fingernails are purple, almost blue, ridged on the surface.

The light above her flickers. It reminds me of that first night, seeing her transformed for the first time. For a second, I feel what everyone else who's ever seen something like this must feel, thinking of that unexplained, alien thing happening inside her. An enchantment, maybe. A spell. But then I look at her again. She's human. Her problem is medical, not magical.

"What are you doing, Brigid?" I whisper. "How are we gonna solve this one?"

Her hands twitch. I look at the heart monitor. It's slow, sluggish.

"Hey," Suresh says from the door. "This isn't a great time for this, but I just talked to Mom on the phone. She wants us to come home."

"No," I say. "Absolutely not."

"Yeah, I figured you'd say that," he says.

"You should go back, S, but I'm staying."

"I don't want to just leave you here."

I shake my head. "No, I'll be okay, I promise."

"Are you sure?"

I'm not. "Yeah, I'm sure."

"Okay." He comes over to give me a hug and rests his cheek on my head. "Tell me what happens. I can have Mom and Dad add her to the prayer chain."

"Yes, please. Thank you for driving me here. And for everything else."

"It's whatever."

"It's not whatever." I turn to look up at him. "You're a good brother."

He smiles. "I'm gonna need that in writing, P."

"Yeah, yeah," I say, smiling back. "I love you."

"Love you too," he says.

I let my expression fall when he leaves. Spencer comes in, dragging the other chair to sit next to me.

"You okay?" he asks.

"Yeah, I'm okay," I say. My throat is tight. "But Brigid isn't."

"I called her parents," he says. "Three guesses as to where they are."

"Brazil?" I ask.

"Hey, you only needed one," he says. "They're on the next flight."

"I knew she never told them," I say. "She doesn't know how to ask for help."

"Well, we're gonna help her anyway," he says. "It'll be okay, Priya."

I shake my head as I look at the monitor, watching her heart rate drop another five beats per minute. "I—Spencer—"

"What?" he asks. I don't look at him. I look at her.

"Spencer, what if she's dying?"

# 36

**"It's too late for wolfsbane poisoning, right?" Spencer asks, lean-**ing back. He looks as tired as I feel.

"Unless she suddenly took a huge dose, I think so?" I say. "The doctor doesn't seem to think her symptoms line up with poisoning."

"So what the hell is wrong with her?" Spencer asks.

"I don't know." I rub my eyes behind my glasses, sighing. We're sitting in the back of the room on the padded bench beneath the window, brainstorming everything we can think of that might help.

"Walk me through what we know," Spencer says. "Again."

"Okay." I sigh. "Brigid is a werewolf. She's supposed to turn once a month but she's turning every few weeks instead. She started taking the wolfsbane a month ago—"

"Thirty-three days," Spencer corrects me, looking at his phone.

"Have you been keeping count this entire time?" I ask, frowning.

"Yeah, dude," he says, turning the screen of his phone toward me. "I downloaded a period tracker app."

I blurt out a laugh, covering my mouth. "Oh my God."

"Nothing funny about it." He shrugs. "This is scientific info."

"No, it's charming," I say. "Okay, okay. She hasn't turned since she started the wolfsbane."

"Nope."

"And we know that her illness is genetic, too."

"Thank goodness."

I zero in on the red lines of the period tracker app. It kicks an idea into my head. I message Spook, who replies right away.

**spookyspoony:**

Werewolf stuff?

**paranormaldetective:**

Yeah, werewolf stuff

**spookyspoony:**

It's past midnight

**paranormaldetective:**

Do you need to go to sleep?

Please say no

**spookyspoony:**

...I can stay up a few more minutes

What's up

**paranormaldetective:**

Can a genetic disease also be hormonal?

**spookyspoony:**

Yeah, totally

Lots of genetic endocrine disorders affect hormone production

MEN I and II, some cases of gigantism or something more common like PCOS

**paranormaldetective:**

Okay, that's what I thought

**spookyspoony:**

Hirsutism is actually a hormonal thing

(Excessive hair growth)

So tbh you're probably onto something with that

**paranormaldetective:**

Plus the onset was puberty

And her grandmother stopped turning in her 50s

**spookyspoony:**

Huh

So it's cyclical, like a menstrual cycle

**paranormaldetective:**

And herbal remedies can mess with your hormones, too?

**spookyspoony:**

In high enough doses, they can do some damage, yeah

I mean what we call supplements now used to just be called medicine, they have real side effects

Like st. john's wort is an anti-anxiety supplement, but it can also disrupt the effectiveness of chemical medication, like birth control

**paranormaldetective:**

Ok, thank you

**spookyspoony:**

Np

Going to bed now, goodnight

"I was right before. It's hormonal," I say.

"What?" Spencer asks.

"Whatever's happening is hormonal—not just genetic. But I don't know what that *means*." My body is aching, and my eyes are starting to blur. I blink to clear my vision. I'm exhausted. "I don't think this is helping."

"Don't think what is helping?"

"This. Any of this, us being here. We aren't going to figure it out."

Spencer looks at me for a few seconds before he says anything. "This isn't all on you, Priya. You know that, right?"

"Her doctor doesn't have all the information."

"Oh, you wanna tell her?"

"Somehow I don't see that going over well."

"You can mention the hormone thing."

"Yeah."

"She's gonna be okay."

I clench my jaw. "You don't know that."

"Yeah, I totally do," he says. "For sure for sure."

"Liar."

"Optimist."

It's weird talking about her like this when she's lying a few feet away from us, heart monitor beeping. I'm trying to look at her like a doctor or a researcher would, put the puzzle pieces together. But I just keep remembering the way she snapped at me for analyzing her. I wish I could talk to her right now, as a friend.

"Hold on," I say. "Do you have her backpack?"

"Shit, yeah. Yes."

Spencer dumps the contents of Brigid's bag out unceremoniously between us. I see *Natural Remedies for Unnatural Afflictions,* her car keys, seventeen crumpled receipts, a roll of duct tape, a shower of what looks like loose birdseed, and something black and shriveled that might have been an apple at one point.

Her sketchbook is in there, too, lodged in an inside pocket. Rereading her sick journal is as close as we're going to get to talking to her right now, so I flip back through it, offering Brigid a silent apology for looking again.

"Bingo," I say, scooting over so Spencer can read over my shoulder.

"God," he says, eyes flicking over some of the words.

"I know," I say. I point to the entry I read two months ago, when I found this in her car. *I get more tired all month . . . tingling, leg cramping, weird bruises . . .* One thread knots itself around another in the back of my head.

"Oh my God," I say.

"What?" Spencer asks.

"What if—what if there's more than one thing going on inside her body?"

"I think that's true of everyone."

"No, like—like, she feels worse and worse all month, right, until she turns."

"She feels bad after she turns, too," Spencer says. "She always looks like she's half dead."

"No, but that's because she's tired, like after a workout."

"Okay?"

"So what if—what if turning isn't the sickness at all? I mean, it is, but . . . What if it's . . . what if it's what's keeping her alive?"

"So you think she's like this now because she *hasn't* turned?"

"That's the thing that changed, right?"

"So the wolfsbane actually worked. It stopped her from turning into a werewolf."

"Right."

"But now that she hasn't turned, something's gone wrong."

"Right." I pause. "So . . . we have to get her to turn."

"That's the one thing we couldn't figure out how to do," Spencer says. "We just goofed around in the backyard."

"Hold on a second," I say. "Is there anything in the book?"

He pages through, frowning. "A tonic to choke the wolf and thus end the curse," he reads. "That's all it says. I can look for a tonic to un-choke the wolf?"

I plug my phone into Brigid's charger, which is—of course—frayed, split open so you can see all the wires inside. *Oh, Brigid.*

**oof ouch my bones (ONLINE – 4)**

**Priya (paranormaldetective):**

Hey guys

I know it's late but Brigid's in the hospital right now

I just

Do any of you have any ideas about how to get her to turn?

We think that's what would help

**lee (typhoonsss):**

oh no, i am so sorry

what's going on?

i don't have any ideas, but i would love to keep you company right now

**Priya (paranormaldetective):**

You're up late

**lee (typhoonsss):**

early, dear

**Priya (paranormaldetective):**

Oh, right.

**al (thorswagnarok):**

is she ok????? what happened???!??

**Priya (paranormaldetective):**

not sure, she went into shock and they're giving her fluids and steroids right now

I'm not sure if she'd want me to tell you guys or not, but I thought you should know

**katie (fyodorbrostoevsky):**

oh my God

this is the worst :/

Seb says he loves both of you, he can't find his phone

For the record, I also love you guys

**Priya (paranormaldetective):**

<3

You guys don't have to stay up with me

**katie (fyodorbrostoevsky):**

yeah, but we're gonna

**lee (typhoonsss):**

we'll stay as long as we can manage

**al (thorswagnarok):**

how is she right now?

:/

**Priya (paranormaldetective):**

Uh, I don't know, exactly

The doctor says she's gonna be okay though

It's mostly just kind of scary seeing her like this

**al (thorswagnarok):**

do you think it was that stuff she was taking?

i thought it was working

**Priya (paranormaldetective):**

Well, it is working

She hasn't turned in more than a month, I don't think

But maybe that's the problem

**katie (fyodorbrostoevsky):**

i... might have something?

I mean, old family story, something

I'm not sure it means anything for real

**Priya (paranormaldetective):**

Tell me anyway

**katie (fyodorbrostoevsky):**

ok

it's short, but my dad told me this legend about two sisters

when they would go into battle together, one was a girl

and the other was a wolf

and when the girl wanted to turn into a wolf, she'd gather a bouquet of white flowers and breathe them in to become the wolf-warrior

**Priya (paranormaldetective):**

Huh

Do you know what kind of flower?

**katie (fyodorbrostoevsky):**

no, it's just called "the white flower"

:/

That doesn't seem helpful

**Priya (paranormaldetective):**

No it might be

Thank you

I love you guys, I'll keep you posted.

"Did you read anything about a white flower that turns you into a werewolf?"

Spencer raises his eyebrows, scanning the pages. "Hold on."

"Is that a yes or a no?"

"It's a give me two seconds, oh my God."

"It's a—"

"Hold on," he hisses. "Shit, yes, right here. Right here." He clears his throat. "The white flower of the Balkans does not have a name. It is poison to the touch, lethal to the taste. Vivid white, it produces a viscous sap and a sickly odor." He looks up at me. "Gross."

"Is that it?"

"One more line," he says. "The scent of the flower, when inhaled deeply, will shock the system and begin the transformation."

"Can I see?"

He nods, passing me the book, and pulls Brigid's sketchbook back onto his lap. I flip through the pages, but I can't find anything else. "Great. Let's go to Europe. Spencer, I don't know what else—"

"Jesus," Spencer says. "Did she tell you she broke her arm?"

"She what?"

"There's an entry about it."

"What do you mean there's an entry?"

"There are comics in between but she wrote more, here in the back."

I grab it from him and start reading.

> I fell off the roof. And here's the weird part—I swear I broke my arm. Like, bone snapping, arm bent into a whole new joint. There was a second while I was falling, and it felt like I was falling forever, and I just thought, this is it. You know. Like, this is it, it, I'm finally gonna break my neck, and Spencer's gonna find my body back here. And this spike of fear shot through me, and my arm broke, and I threw up, and I turned. And when I turned back my arm was fine. I think that's the first thing this dumbass body has ever fucking done for me. I'll take it.

"Oh my God," I say. Brigid's heart monitor beeps softly.

"You look like you're having an idea," Spencer says. "Come on, keep going."

"The flower, the roof, the hormones. It's adrenaline."

"What?"

"Adrenaline is a hormone. A protective mechanism."

"But we tested for that, right?" Spencer says. "When I shot her in the backyard?"

"She wasn't *scared* then," I say. "She was expecting it. It didn't give her a large enough jolt of adrenaline to trigger an off-cycle transformation."

"But falling off the roof did," Spencer says.

"Exactly," I say. I feel like I'm sprinting a hundred-yard dash. "Exactly. So what if—"

"Bring it home, chief."

"What if an influx of adrenaline can turn her?"

Spencer doesn't say anything, just drums his fingers against his knee.

"Do you think I'm wrong?"

"I think you're right," he says. "We could tell the doctors."

"We could," I say. "We—we should."

"Do you think they'd do it?"

"No, I don't."

"Priya . . ." he trails off. "Man. I can't believe I'm saying this. It feels like a bad idea. Like. I don't know. Not regular bad. *Bad* bad."

"Tell me," I say.

"I have an EpiPen," Spencer says.

I can hear my heartbeat in my ears. "Seriously?"

"Yeah, in the car."

"Oh, I could kiss you," I say before I hear myself.

"You . . . could?" Spencer says.

"I won't. Do that. Uh—"

"I gotta say, this isn't how people usually respond to my shellfish allergy."

"Oh my God, stop," I say. "Focus up."

"I'll be right back." he says. "Two minutes."

He isn't gone long, but it's long enough for me to start to ask myself questions. Questions like, *what the hell?* And *are you seriously going to do this?* And *do you think you know better than the medical professionals?* And *isn't this completely inappropriate?* And *wait, aren't you supposed to keep your EpiPen on you, not in your car?*

But he's back before I can answer any of them.

"Are you sure about this?" he asks.

*No,* I think.

"Yes," I say. My hands feel like they're moving on their own as I take the EpiPen from him. "The doctor said adrenal insufficiency, right? That means she doesn't have enough adrenaline."

"Do you want me to do it?" he asks, looking nervous.

I look at Brigid. Her breathing is more labored than it was a few hours ago. We don't have time to wait for the wolfsbane to leave her system, for the IV to try to flush it out. It's going to choke her first.

I shake my head. "No, I—I'll do it."

My hands start to tremble. I think about Katie's story, the girl and the wolf. How each of them was brave in their own way, but tied to each other, stronger together.

Maybe all of this was a little bit magic, after all. Maybe there was something miraculous about the way we found each other in the first place, the push and pull of our relationship. My grandmother told me once that when you love someone, you can feel their pain in your body, take some of it for yourself. And this is what I find myself praying for as I remove the blue safety release from the EpiPen, watch the needle shoot out of the orange tip.

"Sorry, Brigid," I whisper.

And then I drive the needle straight into her thigh.

# 37

**The beep of the heart monitor ratchets up, double time. My eyes** seek out Spencer's frantically.

"Nothing's happening," he says. I can hear him starting to panic, too. "Priya, why is nothing happening?" Oh my God. I just injected my best friend with epinephrine. Oh my *God*.

The heart monitor beeps faster. *Come on, Brigid*, I think, looking at her face. *Come on*.

She sucks in a gasp like she's been holding her breath for longer than she can bear, her whole body arching up. Her eyes fly open, pupils blown wide. She starts to cough, bunching the sheets into her hands, her eyes darting around the room.

"Brigid, Brigid, it's okay, I'm so sorry," I say, sliding my hand into the junction of her shoulder and her neck. Her eyes find mine and they look hazy and confused.

"Priya?" she chokes out. And then she grits her teeth, pushing her head back against the hospital bed, and groans. She screws her eyes shut, breathing heavily.

"What's going on?" I hear a voice at the door and look up to see the med student look at Spencer, then at me, then at the used EpiPen still clenched in my hand. I see shock on her face, then horror, then rage.

"Get out of here," she says.

"I can't, you don't understand—"

"I'm getting the doctor," she says. Then, pointing at me: "And I'm calling security to escort you out."

Brigid lets out another yell. She grabs blindly at the bar by her bed, gripping it until her knuckles turn white. She pulls herself up just enough to throw up over the side of the bed, clear and yellowish and slimy. There's a trail of spittle stretching down from her mouth, and she wipes it slowly with the back of her hand, squinting down at the IV. She seems confused to see it in her hand. She looks back at me.

"I'm turning?" she says, eyes narrowing. I notice the soft fuzz on her face getting thicker and darker before my eyes. The hair starts to push itself more densely through her arms, her legs. My gut roils. "Why am I turning?"

"Oh my God," Spencer says from across the room. "I don't have any of my gear. I didn't bring the truck."

Brigid pushes herself up unsteadily, swinging her bare feet over the edge of the bed. The IV stand falls onto its side and she rips the needle out of her elbow like it's nothing. An alarm starts to go off.

"I don't think we thought this through," Spencer says.

Brigid hunches over, gripping the bed for support, and spits out blood, opening her mouth. A front tooth hits the ground near my feet, then an incisor, a molar. The ground stains pink as more blood drips down, mixed with saliva. I'm frozen in place.

A nurse runs into the room. "You need to get back in the bed!" she shouts, starting to move toward us.

"I wouldn't do that!" I shout. Brigid turns her head toward the nurse, sharp teeth bared and blood welling as her mouth elongates, pulling itself into a snout. The nurse drops her clipboard and stumbles out of the room.

There's a ripping sound and I realize Brigid's claws have pushed themselves through, tearing through the bedsheets and down into the foam of the mattress.

"Priya, get back," I hear Spencer say, and enough fear wells up in my throat for me to start backing away from her. It's strange, though. Before he said anything, my first impulse was to help her stand, think about putting her arm around my shoulders.

Brigid screams again, but it's not a human scream anymore. I can hear it echoing down the halls, low and urgent. The fur is covering her body now in a thin layer, getting longer and thicker by the second.

It's horrible to watch. Her mouth moving to make room for her new teeth, her limbs growing longer and thinner, cracking and bending back. Every part of my brain, rational and primal, is telling me it's not something I was ever supposed to see. I hear a ripping as her hospital gown tears, the patterned fabric hanging loosely off her.

I hear a scream, this time distinctly human, and turn to see Dr. Nowak with her hand over her mouth. A security guard is there, too, eyes wild with fear. The med student is the only one who looks nonplussed, staring dead-eyed at the scene in front of her.

"I hate this rotation," she says.

Out of the corner of my eye I see the security guard reach slowly for his handcuffs, then drop them again.

"Give her some space," I hear Spencer say, surprisingly calm for the situation. I glance over as he rummages through his pockets. "Animal control officer. I am one, I mean. I swear I have a badge somewhere, but just look at the uniform, alright?"

"Where's the patient?" Dr. Nowak says.

"Um," I say.

"She ran when she saw the animal," Spencer says.

"She woke up earlier," I tack on.

"You guys go look for her, we'll take care of the animal," Spencer says. He's trying to use his I'm-a-professional voice.

"Alone?" the security guard asks.

"Good point," Spencer says, nodding at him. "We might need you. Wait outside the door."

We wait for Brigid to finish turning. She's still for a few moments, chest and back rising and falling as she heaves in each breath. I sink down slowly into the plastic chair by the bed, watching her. I don't know how much she remembers between forms, if she's forgotten that we're here or if wolf-Brigid has even noticed us in the first place. I don't want her to panic the way she did in her car, or in the restaurant.

"Do you have another tracker?" I whisper without turning to look at Spencer.

"I don't have *anything*," he says.

"How are we gonna get her out of here?"

"One problem at a time. Her parents gave me a couple of tips on the phone. I'm gonna MacGyver this shit."

"How traumatic would you say last time was for her?"

"Uh . . ." I hear rustling. "I don't think she had a great time, no.

Fingers crossed she remembers she likes me when she's human."

Brigid blinks slowly, shaking herself. She rises on wobbly legs that become more certain of themselves the longer she stands. She looks right at me with her uncanny eyes and noses forward toward my scent.

I turn my hands palm up, and she sniffs along my legs up to my forearms. Her breath is hot against my skin, her ears back against her head.

I don't dare move. I tell myself that there's nothing to be afraid of and, strangely, for the first time, I find myself believing it. The animal in front of me is as much Brigid as my friend is. I trust her.

Her mouth lolls open, tongue hanging beside her row of gleaming new teeth. Her ears perk back up, one swiveling toward the noise that Spencer is making, and her tail makes a tentative sweep across the hospital floor. I feel myself grinning, but then something shakes itself loose in my chest and a few tears start leaking out. I should be giddy right now, relieved, triumphant. Instead, my exhaustion hits me all at once. It's past two in the morning. I'm on the second floor of a rural hospital with a werewolf.

Brigid snuffles and licks my wrist, and I sniff loudly, letting out a short laugh.

"Welcome back, Brigid," I say, rubbing a spot under her jaw before I lose the nerve. Her tail wags more forcefully.

"I've got a leash," Spencer says over my shoulder.

"How do you have a leash?" I say, glancing back. He's tying his belt to a couple of IV tubes.

"I was a Boy Scout," he says, edging closer. Brigid is moving toward the door now.

"Were you."

"I was a Cub Scout."

He tosses the loop around Brigid's neck, and as soon as she feels it tighten, she looks at me, betrayed.

"I know, I'm sorry," I say. She yanks herself backward and Spencer lurches.

"Shit," he says. "Brigid, it's fine, we just have to get outside—" he says. But Brigid growls, the slippery IV tube slides right through Spencer's fingers, and she bolts for the open door.

Spencer lets out a string of curses. "Can you run?" he says.

"No, just go."

He shakes his head, running for the wheelchair. "Sit down," he says. I push off the parking brake, pull my feet in, and he pushes me through the door.

It's not hard to figure out where Brigid's gone, a streak of mangey, brown-black fur across the stark white of the hospital hallway. The security guard looks like he's wet his pants, and I hear screams echoing down the hallway.

"Go, go, go!" I shout, and Spencer runs to the right, shoes squeaking on the Formica. We whiz past the nurse's station and I hear one of them calling the police, frantically describing the animal running loose in the hospital.

"And there's another entry for the Wikipedia page," I say. "The cops are coming."

"Great! Fantastic!" Spencer shouts. Brigid barrels past a nurse, out of the ICU, and we follow behind. The chair judders as we turn a sharp corner. Some kind of machine has been knocked sideways, totally destroyed, glass smashed and hundreds of pills spilling out across the floor.

"Watch it," I shout.

"I see it, God, have a little faith here."

"You're the one driving, I'm trying to help!"

"I don't need—"

There's another crash, more screaming. I wince.

"We've gotta get her off this floor before someone has a heart attack," Spencer says.

"They're gonna have to disinfect . . . everything."

"Yeah, that's the least of their—Brigid! Hey, buddy, over here!"

We've chased her into a dead end, one of those sets of double doors that require pushing a button to open. I see a nurse approaching from the other side, looking down at a chart, and I start waving my arms.

"Stop!" I shout.

"Don't come in here!" Spencer yells.

The nurse looks up, surprised, and then blinks, trips, and falls over in shock.

"How smart do you think Brigid is like this?" I ask. At the mention of her name, her ears prick up, and she steps toward us again. I hope she's distracted enough not to start panicking.

"Like, do I think she's going to open the door herself, *Jurassic Park* velociraptor style?" he asks.

I watch Brigid's head swivel back to the double doors. She jumps, scrabbling against the glass, and howls. There are screams from the other side, and her bushy tail wags back and forth.

"Too smart for her own good," I say. "Brigid!" I call. "Brigid, come here!"

She doesn't make a move. "Do you have any food?" I ask.

"Why would I have food on me?" Spencer snipes. "I—oh wait, hold on, I had beef jerky in my pocket earlier."

"Is it still there?"

He feels around. "No, one second."

"Spencer!" I swivel in the chair. He's running down the hallway. "Where are you going?"

Brigid's losing interest in the people on the other side of the door, and she bounds back toward me. "That's it!" I say. "Come here, girl!" She sniffles into my neck, sneezing. It's disgusting. *She could tear your throat out,* I think, distantly. I put my hand into her fur. *Yes, she could. But she won't.*

I hear an enormous crash, followed by the sound of tinkling glass. Spencer skids back into view, wild-eyed. He's bleeding from a cut on his arm, and his hands are absolutely filled with bags of chips.

"What are you doing!" I scream.

"I had to get her food!" he yells back.

"I have money! You could have just asked me for a dollar instead of—what, destroying the vending machine?"

"I *panicked*!" he shouts, ripping open a packet. "Brigid! How do you feel about . . . backyard barbecue?"

She darts forward, knocking me out of the wheelchair, and Spencer helps me to my feet. I can feel my hip starting to bruise, and my wrist. He opens more chips, tossing them to her.

"People definitely saw me throw a chair at the vending machine," Spencer says. "I figure we've got three minutes before security finds us."

"Where's the stairwell?"

Spencer points. It's not far. We just have to coax her down.

"What's the plan if she runs?" I ask, watching her lick the hospital floor clean.

"Let her?" says Spencer.

"I don't want her to wake up in the middle of the woods with no way to get home or contact anyone," I say. I imagine her, shivering and naked, too exhausted to move after turning back.

"Do you think there's tape around here?" Spencer asks.

"Yeah, check the nurse's station," I say. He emerges, triumphant, with a roll of packing tape. He pulls the cap of a Sharpie off with his teeth and writes something across the tape, two words I can't make out. He fishes his cell phone out of his pocket, pulls off a strip of tape with his teeth, and approaches Brigid.

"Spencer," I say.

"No, this is a good idea," he whispers.

I toss Brigid another open bag, grabbing ahold of her IV leash and feeding the end through the handle of the door to secure it. "Two minutes."

He tapes his phone around her front leg, looping twice for good measure. She bites at him, but he dodges.

"Problem solved," he says, propping open the door to the stairwell. "Let's get outta here."

It's cool when we walk out into the night. There are more stars here. I always forget that. The crickets are loud and demanding, a constant hum behind the rest of the nighttime sounds. An owl hoots in the distance, followed by a low, almost human croaking, a few clicks I can't identify but that almost sound like summer. Brigid closes her eyes contentedly when the breeze hits us, lifting herself up onto two legs to sniff the air. She's taller than me and Spencer like this, casting a terrifying shadow onto the asphalt. I notice that she's still wearing her patient bracelet and hope that no one in the hospital did.

"She has to come back when she turns back," I say.

"Yeah, obviously. They're gonna issue a missing patient alert."

"Oh God," I say. "Oh, this went so badly."

Spencer shrugs. "She's alive, isn't she?"

I look over to see her watching us. "Yeah. Yeah, she is."

Her ears swivel, and I see the red-and-blue flashing lights in the parking lot ahead. She tenses. One of the sirens whoops, piercing the night air, and she tries to run, straining at the makeshift leash.

"Spencer, you're gonna choke her," I say.

"*I'm* gonna choke her?" He leans back on his heels, widening his stance. "C'mon, Brigid, it's fine, it's—"

The knot holding his belt to the IVs snaps, and she bolts off into the night. Just like that, she's gone.

I'm too tired to be worried. I wonder if she's ever gotten to run like this before. I wonder if she's ever been able to cover this much ground, wind in her fur, pulling puffs of air into her lungs. I hope she feels like herself. I hope she feels free.

# 38

**We sleep at Brigid's in case she comes home, but she doesn't.**
Spencer uses my phone to call Marty and ask him to be on the lookout
for her, but no calls come in. My phone buzzes with a missing patient
alert sometime in the afternoon, and Spencer and I share a look.

Brigid's parents burst through the door late the next night, looking harried and frightened, and I almost burst into tears when I see
them in the foyer. Brigid's mom has wild brown curls and tired eyes,
her dad tanned skin, uneven teeth, and a shaved head. We tell them
everything, from start to finish. For the first time I feel like we have a
safety net, like Brigid is actually going to be okay.

My phone buzzes with a call from Spencer's number on day two,
and all four of us crowd around it, desperate to hear Brigid's voice.

"Hey," she croaks. "'Sup?"

"Hi," I say on speakerphone. "Where are you?"

"Uh . . . woods, I guess? Leaves? Trees? Mud?"

"Brigid Maria," her mother says.

There's a long silence. "Shit," Brigid says.

Spencer tells her step-by-step how to turn on her location. In a
few minutes, we discover she's just two towns over, near Miners Gap.
Brigid's parents leave immediately to pick her up.

Brigid's mom squeezes both our hands before she goes, nodding.
"You can go home now," she says. "I promise we'll keep you posted."
She looks back at us from the car, rolling the window down. "Thank
you both. For everything."

I don't want to leave. I want to sit in the rocking chair on the porch until they bring Brigid home. But Spencer takes me by the arm and leads me to his car. "C'mon, Priya. I'll drive you home."

Halfway back to Jersey, I finally speak.

"What did you write across the tape?" I ask him.

He glances at me with a furrow in his brow, like it should be obvious. "Call Priya," he says. "What else?"

- - - - - - -

**I go back a week later. I rap my knuckles softly against the door** to Brigid's room. It's covered in peeling stickers: the David statue blowing bubble gum, a skeleton dancing, a UFO with the words I WANT TO LEAVE, a speech bubble that just says YIKES. At the top, it says DON'T DEAD OPEN INSIDE. Out of all the times I've been to this house, I've never made it up the stairs. Her room is the only thing up here besides the landing that looks over the living room, where I can see her parents sitting, deep in conversation. It's still strange to see them answer the door, thank me for coming by, and offer me something to drink.

"Who knocks?" Brigid shouts hoarsely.

"Priya," I say.

There's a pause. Then: "Oh my God, what are you waiting for, an invitation?"

"Yeah, kind of," I say.

"I invite you to come into my room," I hear her say. "Vampire."

I push the door open. Her room is a nuclear dump site, piles of clothes and loose papers covering the floor so completely that I can't see underneath them. I spot a large, plastic gas station cup on her dresser, filled to the brim with teeth. Brigid's on her bed, wearing sweats and mismatched socks. Her hair is almost chin-length again, her eyes tired and bloodshot. There's an enormous bruise on the back of her hand, purple and yellow at the edges.

"Happy hospital release," I say. "Well. The official one."

"The one where the doctor actually discharged me, not the one where my friend turned me into a werewolf."

I don't say anything. I'm just glad she used the word *friend*.

366

"I heard you got a diagnosis."

"I heard you stabbed me with an EpiPen."

"I . . . did do that."

She looks at me, relenting a little. "Turns out my thyroid levels are crazy low. The doctor asked me if my periods have been irregular lately, and I was like, yeah."

"So this whole time, we should have . . . just told you to go to the doctor?"

"Crazy, huh?"

"Huh."

"I'm on levothyroxine now for hypothyroidism. They think it should level me out."

"Cool. That's really great."

We stare at each other. The seconds drag by.

"I'm sorry," we both burst out at the same time. Relief hits me.

"No, *I'm* sorry," we both say again, then laugh. Brigid pats the bed beside her and I wade through her laundry and crawl onto the mattress, turning to face her.

"Hey," I say.

She lays an arm across her stomach and breathes in slowly, turning her head so we're face-to-face. "Hey," she says finally.

"You were right," I tell her.

"I love to hear that," she rasps.

"I didn't want to have to deal with any of my own stuff. I have . . . no idea what I'm doing. At all." I pause. "But I think I'm starting to feel more okay about that."

"Hell yeah," she says. "I mean, no one really knows anything, right? Being sick just forces you to stop pretending you're in control."

"How's the thyroid medicine?"

"So far so good. It's making me a little jittery. I don't think my body knows what to do with . . . energy."

"Does this mean you'll stop turning every other week?"

"Yeah, I think so," she says.

I don't see the relief in her face that I thought I would. "Brigid, that's amazing."

"Yeah, I guess it is," she says. She searches my face, and I'm not sure what she's looking for until she speaks again. "I kind of can't believe you did it, looking at you right now."

"The EpiPen thing?"

"It was ballsy. Were you not worried about killing me?"

"The dose of epinephrine in an EpiPen is not enough to kill someone!" I burst out. "I was trying to do the opposite!"

Her face turns serious. She kicks at my legs. "You thought I was going to die?"

"I don't know," I say. "I don't know. I was just scared."

"I'm sorry for scaring you," she says.

"I'm sorry for stabbing you," I say. "I mean, I'm not. But, I feel like I should say sorry, anyway."

She looks up at her ceiling. There are glow-in-the-dark stars stuck up there, greenish-yellow with age.

"I was really mean to you," she says. "It doesn't matter if I was right. It was mean to say it like that. I know you care about me, for real, and I just kept pushing you away. I was just . . ." She chews her lip. "I just wanted it to *work*, you know? I needed it to. I was so desperate that I told myself it was *going* to. But I . . . I can't stop this. There's nothing I can do to fix it. Even if the thyroid medicine works."

"It will."

"Even if it does, I—I *failed*, Priya," she says, voice cracking. She looks devastated. It makes me ache. "This big experiment of living on my own, telling my parents that I can manage it by myself? You should see the way they've been looking at me."

"They love you."

"They're never going to let me out of their sight again. I'm never going to be able to live alone."

Her hand curls into a fist between us. I tap each of her knuckles until she opens it again for me.

"Being alone isn't all it's cracked up to be," I say.

"Priya—"

"I'm serious. So you need other people to look out for you. So what. We all do, I—" I think about my family's patience over the last five months, how I'd gotten it all wrong. How this whole time, they were just waiting for me to be ready to tell them what I needed from them. "*I* need other people. And I think that's okay."

"I could have roommates, one day," she says, looking a little brighter. "People who know what happens to me."

I crack a smile. "Could you imagine me, you, and Spencer all living together?"

"I can now!" She smiles, but it's tissue-paper fragile. "But—"

"But?"

"But I still have to turn every month, forever. For the next thirty-something years. That's a whole lifetime."

"Yeah, you do. I think . . ." I try to figure out how to phrase what I'm saying. "I think your body is trying its best, you know?"

She looks at me again. "It doesn't feel like it."

"Turning is really horrible," I say, "and it hurts you every time. I know it sucks to not have any control over that. But I think it's also, like, a defense mechanism? Your body trying to keep you safe."

"From what?"

"I'm not sure yet," I say. "I was telling Spencer I think it's a hormone. A separate one."

"A werewolf hormone?" She smiles. "You've gotta call it that when you make the discovery."

"It would explain why it interacted with your thyroid," I say. "Or vice versa. It's all connected."

"How about wolf juice?"

"We're not calling it wolf juice."

"Aren't we?"

"No."

"So." She pushes herself onto her side, too, wincing from the pain. "You're saying the same body that's trying to kill me is also trying to keep me alive."

"Yeah."

"Yeah."

"I get why you tried to chase down a cure," I say. "Trust me, I get it more than anyone."

"I'm sorry you got worse again," she says.

"Yeah. Me too."

We sit for a few minutes like that, with our aching bones and muscles, our hazy minds and tired bodies.

"Thank you," she says, so softly I almost miss it.

"For what?" I ask.

"For what," she scoffs. "For everything. For saving my life."

"Eh, it was nothing," I say. And then, by way of explanation: "I love you."

She grins, wide enough to split her lip. "I love you, too." She tugs on a strand of my hair. "Can I say something cheesy?"

"You have to now."

"Okay," she says. She softens around the eyes. I half expect her to burst out laughing, but she doesn't. She just keeps looking at me like that, solid and warm. "This is coming from someone who does a lot of online shopping . . ."

"Okay?"

"But you're the best thing the internet's ever brought me."

A lump lodges itself in my throat. "Brigid—"

"You, and that life-sized cutout of Doctor Phil that I sent to my high school math teacher's house."

"Oh my God!" I say, shoving at her. "I knew you were going to ruin it!"

"He never knew it was me!" She chortles. "To this day, the mystery continues!"

"Stop it!" I say. She bats at me but I catch her hands in mine, hold them steady. "I'm so glad you messaged me," I say, and I watch her eyes start to fill with tears.

"Priya, I am not emotionally mature enough for this," she says.

"Oh, you can dish it out, but you can't take it?" I ask. "I haven't even said anything yet! You have to let me be cheesy, now!"

"Okay," she says, breathing out and smiling. I can't look at her directly. I talk to her wall, just past her shoulder.

"I'm so glad you knocked my whole life off course this year. You're strange and funny and adventurous and a total force of nature. And you were there for me when I felt like I was . . . completely alone."

"So were you," she says. "Shit. I love you so much."

I just squeeze her hands, and she squeezes back, but it feels like sealing a pact, like spit in palms or mingled blood. She's mine. I'm hers. That's that.

A throat clears at the bedroom door. "Why are you both crying?" Spencer asks.

"Spencer, you ruined the moment," Brigid says, pulling back to look at him.

"Hey, Property Damage," I say.

"Hello, Pseudoscience," he says to me. "My Enormous, Continuing PR Nightmare," he says to Brigid.

She pats the bed beside her. "Come on down." He drapes himself across the foot of the bed, looking up at both of us. It's silent for a few seconds.

"So," he finally says. "That was batshit, huh."

And I can't pinpoint who starts laughing first, but once one of us starts, the rest of us tumble after, marbles spilling out of a bag, kids rolling down a grassy hill.

-------

**When we grab Brigid's laptop after Spencer leaves, we mean to** watch another episode of *True or False*, but we end up Skyping the whole group instead. It's Katie's idea; when she hears that Brigid is back home, she sets the whole thing up before I can even thank her for it.

I don't know how to put into words the feeling that freezes the words in my throat at seeing all of them in the flesh, the warmth that settles in my chest. Lee has short black hair, her curls cut close to her head, and tired, warm eyes. She's in her bed with the covers up. Katie and Seb aren't in the same place anymore; she's outside somewhere, sunlight flaring at the corner of the image, and he's on his couch. Spook has wire-rimmed glasses and freckly skin, and her expression is as deadpan as I'd thought it would be. It feels a bit strange to see her face and still not know her real name. Al is squinting at the screen wearing enormous over-ear headphones and their aforementioned piss-yellow glasses like some sort of futuristic video game character. And Max is somewhere loud, fumbling with the camera. Once it steadies, we can see a graduation cap on his head and a maroon gown around his shoulders. They're beautiful, every single one of them.

"Oh my God, Max!" Katie shrieks. "Are you GRADUATING?"

"I just did," he says with a grin.

The cheer that erupts from the rest of the group is so loud that I reach over and toggle the volume down on Brigid's computer.

His eyes focus on something beyond the screen, and he shouts, "*un momento, mamá!*"

"Congrats," Spook says.

"I'm sorry I couldn't make it," Al says.

Max shakes his head. "I'm seeing you next week, buddy."

"Oh, so everyone's hanging out in person now!" Spook says.

"We started a trend," Brigid stage-whispers. I grin sideways at her.

"Thank you for sharing this moment with us, Max," Lee says.

"Your accent!" we all chorus, and she huffs, rolling her eyes fondly.

"Americans," she says.

"I'm Canadian," says Spook.

"And Brigid!" Al says. "Welcome home!"

Everyone lets out another cheer, and I start laughing.

"This is fun," Seb says. "Does anyone have anything else to cheer about? Like, Katie, perhaps?"

"Oh my God, Seb," she says, fondly.

"What's up?" Brigid rasps. She gestures to her throat. "This is why I liked texting, I sound like a corpse."

"The cutest corpse around," Katie says.

"Definitely our favorite werewolf, out of all the werewolves we know," Al says.

"Katie, go ahead," I say.

"Yeah, okay," she says. "I have a diagnosis. I finally know what's wrong with me."

On cue, everyone cheers again, and she laughs a little, softly. "Thanks, gang. I don't know, it's weird. The not knowing has been a part of me for so long."

"Are you planning on leaving us in suspense?" Lee asks.

"Uh, I have celiac disease," she says. "I had a really nerve-wracking week after the ANA bloodwork was off the charts but I just got the genetic tests back. It's celiac."

"I feel supremely guilty about feeding you bread," Seb says.

"How are you feeling?" Lee asks.

"Hm . . ." Katie says. "Well, uh. Honestly, pretty overwhelmed. I'm gonna have to change my whole diet. But also, kind of dumb? Like, I've been struggling for such a long time and the solution is like . . . don't eat bread. How stupid is that."

"Not stupid," Spook says.

"None stupid," says Al.

"Left smart," Brigid says.

"Left valid," Seb adds.

"It sounds like . . . a big adjustment," Max says.

"Yeah, it's a lot," she says. "And it's not like—it's not like this is going to fix me. They think I'm at risk for another autoimmune disease, too. But . . . I don't know. It feels like I actually have something to work toward, for once."

"I'm so happy for you," I say.

She smiles. "Thanks, Priya. And thanks for checking in, everyone. Someone else go, any final cheers?"

"My thesis just got approved!" Seb shouts. Everyone cheers.

"I don't know what I'm doing with my life, and I think that's okay!" I say. Everyone cheers.

"I impulse-bought a snake!" Spook shouts. Everyone cheers.

"I got my hysterectomy," Lee says, and the cheers are louder than ever.

"Lee, why didn't you say something earlier?!" Seb says.

"I'm tired," Lee says.

"Are you healing okay?" Brigid asks.

"I think so," she says. "I don't know, I . . . Can I be honest with all of you?"

"Of course," Spook says.

"You can tell us anything," Al says. "We sure have overshared enough."

"Okay," Lee says. "Well. I knew I didn't want kids, and I was so tired of being in pain. And the doctor told me they had to unstick my intestines, so it—it had to happen. I just assumed I'd have nothing to mourn afterwards?"

"Do you?" Katie asks.

Lee clears her throat. "Um, yes, I think I do. My hormones are going nuts right now, and I can't replace them because of the endo, so it's like I'm an old woman. I feel like I've lost my youth. Like, on some basic level, I am a different person now. And it's happened twenty-odd years too soon, you know?"

"Where's the technology that lets me hug you through the screen?" asks Al. "Why hasn't that been invented yet?"

"It's coming," says Max. "I'm going to invent it."

"We love you, Lee," Katie says. "And we're so sorry."

"Thank you, chickadee," Lee says. "But I think that this is just life."

"What is?" I ask.

"Oh, you know. You celebrate. You mourn. And most of the time it's about the exact same thing. It usually cuts two ways."

"Wow," says Seb.

"So I think it's good to celebrate as much as we can. Even the little things." Lee pauses. "Hold on, have I become wise in my old age?"

"You've always been wise, Lee," Brigid says.

"That was beautiful," Al says. "I just wanted to send a specific gif, of that woman nodding and crying."

"Yikes," Spook says.

"This is real conversation. I think my brain is broken. Guys, did the internet break my brain?"

"The internet has already broken a-all our brains," Max says.

"If you look inside my ear it's just brain soup, sloshin' around," says Brigid. She nudges me with her arm. "Isn't that right, Priya? Isn't that medically correct?"

I lean forward. "Yes, Brigid, that's how brains work."

"I knew it!" she crows.

"Maybe we're all stupid, none smart," Al says.

I fall back against Brigid's throw pillow, laughing as I watch the conversation devolve. I'm grateful for all of them, these people that I never talked to before I got sick. I used to think that Lyme disease was the worst thing that had ever happened to me, the event the rest of my failures would pivot on. I used to think that it was the one misstep that shot me into the wrong dimension, where I'd be lost forever.

And it is all of those things, in a lot of ways. It's my new reality, no matter how hard I try to shake it. But it's also the thing that led me to all of them.

My body stops me from driving, from going up stairs, from going to school the way I'd planned. It clouds my mind and cracks my joints and takes ten hours to rest and swells my knee and wrists.

But my body keeps fighting to keep me alive. My lungs take in breath and push it back out. My eyes see and my ears hear and my tongue tastes and my hands hold, most of the time, and my mouth speaks, regardless of if the words are the right ones or not.

Mourn and celebrate.

I can feel Brigid's solid warmth beside me. I watch our friends on the other side of her screen, and I decide to celebrate.

# 39

**"Okay. Snacks?"**

"Check."

"License?"

"Check."

"Are you sure?"

"Oh my God, do you want to strip-search me? Yeah, I got it."

"Sunglasses?"

"It is a two-hour drive, Priya. We're not going to California."

"I just want us to be prepared."

Brigid slides her sunglasses down her nose. "Well, your checklist sucks. You left off the most important stuff."

"Such as?"

She hauls her backpack up from the backseat and plops it down between us with a *clunk*, raising her eyebrows.

It's summer. Brigid's parents have forced her to replace her car window and broken seatbelt, but she refused to get rid of the car, even though they called it a "death trap" and "an accident waiting to happen." "Too much history," she had said wistfully. There are still claw marks gouged into the driver's seat and a small bloodstain on the passenger side. You know. History.

She pulls out a truly hideous pair of sunglasses, as ugly as hers but neon yellow instead of neon orange.

"A backup?" I ask.

"Priya, Priya, Priya," she says. "These, my bosom friend, are a gift."

"Aw," I say, smiling. "I'm not loving 'bosom friend,' though."

"Apple of my eye? My tennis partner, but emotionally? My biolu-minescent bacteria?"

"Stop!"

"I'll workshop something else."

"Thank you." I pause. "It's bacterium, technically."

"Oh my God."

"If there's just one of them."

"You're bullying me now," she says. "I'm being bullied by a nerd."

"Did I ever tell you that the gene in angel's glow that acts as a toxin is called 'makes caterpillars floppy'?

"What?" she snorts. "Like, the scientific name for it is *makes cater-pillars floppy*?"

"They abbreviate it to mcf," I say. I slide the sunglasses on and turn to look at her. This time last year I would have been too embarrassed to wear them. They are embarrassing, but somehow, I don't care. She grins at me, clapping, and it's infectious. I can't help grinning right back at her.

"You look amazing," she says. "We have to take a selfie for the group."

"When we get there."

"Okay, doc, when we get there."

"What else is in your bag?" I ask.

"Hmm?"

"Brigid, I know you heard me."

"It'll be a fun surprise."

I unzip the bag the rest of the way and frown at her when I see what's inside. "Brigid!"

"What!"

"Why is this bag full of spray paint?"

"I figure that's something you can probably piece together on your own."

"I'm not a vandal!"

"No, of course not. You'll stab people, but you draw the line at putting paint on an abandoned highway."

"How long are you going to keep bringing that up?"

"Probably forever."

She backs the car out my driveway, turning onto the road. We both wave to Suresh, who waves goodbye. Brigid has somehow become a worse driver since the last time I was in the car with her: too fast, taking the curves in the road at breakneck speed, lounged back in the seat.

"Okay," I say, holding tight to the handrail. "Give me the low-down about where we're headed."

I can feel the excitement coming off her in waves. "Centralia, Pennsylvania, has been on fire for over fifty years." She starts talking like she's practiced what she's going to say. Knowing her, she probably has. "It's largely abandoned at this point, but you can still see the place that used to be a mining town."

"Largely abandoned?" I ask. "Do people still live there?"

"Yeah, I think so," she says. "Like, ten of them."

"Wow."

"The church is still standing, and the graveyard."

"Poetic."

"I thought so."

"So is it like . . . safe?"

"Ugh, classic Priya question."

"I would like to know if we're driving to our deaths via mine shaft right now, yes."

"I think it's fine. The highway is, anyway. People have left their marks all over it for years. And we're gonna be next. Start thinking about what you want to spray-paint."

"You're the artist, not me."

"Nah, you have to contribute, too. Fifty-fifty."

"Okay, I'll let you know when we get there."

She holds the steering wheel with one hand while trying to open a bag of popcorn. I see her shift her knee toward the wheel, and I grab the bag from her before she has the chance to attempt driving hands-free. Brigid rolls the windows down and I put the open bag between us, rest my arm on the lip of the window and let the sunlight hit my skin.

"So, have you decided yet?" Brigid asks, popping a kernel into her mouth. I grab a handful, too.

"What I'm going to paint?"

"Don't dodge my question."

"No," I say. "I have not."

"Two weeks until the deadline, pal."

"Yeah, I know," I say. "I'm working on it."

I've been splitting my time this summer between my family, weekend trips to Pennsylvania, and a part-time internship at a local lab about fifteen minutes from my house. It turns out that one Dr. Silva has been studying the systemic, lasting effects of tick-borne illness. Now I'm studying them, too.

My parents have helped me fill out all the readmission paperwork to Stanford, gotten me notes from my GP and my rheumatologist. But I haven't hit SEND yet. I'm not the same person who left for Stanford; I can't figure out if I'm the person who should go back. Somehow, I think that's okay.

"So why is the town still on fire?" I ask.

"I know you're trying to change the subject," she says, switching lanes, "but lucky for you I would love to answer that. I have no idea."

"Riveting."

"The fire is actually underground, but they think it's going to keep burning for two hundred and fifty more years."

"That's insane."

"Insane."

I stretch out my knee. I started to think of it as my "bad knee," and then tried to be a little nicer to myself. "Trick knee" might be a little more fun.

"It's almost like . . . one of those fires in old-fashioned temples that you could never let go out, but something else is sustaining it."

"An eternal flame."

"Right. I don't know, it's horrible to think about having to leave your home, but it feels like some kind of memorial, almost. To an evacuation."

"Mm," Brigid nods, serious. Then, after a pause: "they also based *Silent Hill* on it."

We'll get there in just shy of two hours, park too close to the river of mud outside the cemetery and get it caked onto our shoes, steadying each other as we walk up the road. We'll follow a path where the tall grass has been trampled, over a tiny hill, to see the highway stretching for miles in front of us, no end in sight. We'll pass a handful of people taking pictures and remember to take one for the group, and for Spencer. We'll walk until we don't feel like walking any farther and sit down on the ground, shaking out the backpack and shaking the cans and covering our mouths and noses with the crooks of our elbows. I don't know what we'll paint on the highway, but it'll stay there long after we leave. It'll remember us.

But for now, Brigid is driving badly. She cranks up the radio and forces me to sing along with her. One of us spills the popcorn and it scatters all over the car floor. I remember what it felt like to see teeth there, and I catalogue the feeling of seeing the kernels instead, white and burst open. If the teeth were seeds, they look like flowers now, fully bloomed. I crunch them under my feet. I let my hand ride the wind. And I look over at Brigid, and she looks over at me through her matching sunglasses, and for once, we don't have to say anything at all.

# Acknowledgments

I can't believe I actually get to write these. Here goes nothing, folks. Thank you, thank you, thank you:

Jessie—my platonic life partner, for all of it. Thank you for listening while I fleshed out the characters, reading every draft, mourning when I needed to mourn, celebrating when it was time to celebrate. I didn't realize I was writing about the two of us until halfway through the first draft, but who else could it have been. There's more, of course, but you already know it.

Hannah—my first reader, my proto-agent, my dearest friend. Thank you for telling me it was time to start my next novel, for rolling your eyes when I said, "I don't have any ideas—except this one about a girl and a werewolf," for stopping me right there in the street and saying, "that's the one." You were right—you always are. This book wouldn't exist without you.

Mom and Dad—thank you for reading that novel I wrote when I was fifteen and telling me it was good. I know now that you were lying, but it kept me writing. You've been so supportive the whole way through, from five-year-old ramblings up to twenty-seven-year-old ones. You believed I could make this happen, even when I didn't.

Kyle—you're the best brother in the world, mystery twin. I wonder every day how I got so lucky. Thanks for pointing out plot holes, interrogating premises, and telling me that I already have the pieces I need to figure out what happens next. Thanks for talking with me about short stories, novels, and D&D campaigns for pretty much our entire lives.

Jhanteigh—you must have sensed something in the ether. Thank you for reaching out to me, and for seeing exactly what I wanted to say with this novel, and for falling in love with Priya and Brigid, too. You've made this book so much better than it was when it first reached you, and I'm so lucky to have gotten to work with you.

Dana—thank you for understanding me right down to my bones (oof, ouch), for listening to all my worries, big and small, and for giving me guidance. I knew from that first two-hour coffee meet that you were the right agent. I'm so excited to see what happens next.

Mary Ellen Wilson, Jane Morley, John McGurk, Ryan Hayes, Nicole De Jackmo, Kelsey Hoffman, Christina Tatulli, and the rest of the Quirk team—thank you for working so diligently on this book, from proofreads to copy edits to design to production to marketing and publicity. I'm sorry for all the moving parts and text elements! You did such beautiful work.

Everyone who's ever had the misfortune of being in a group chat with me—the chats in this book could have been a lot more cursed. I'm looking at you, worm can and Nancy Drew crew. <3

My Tumblr and Twitter friends—thank you for reaching across the divide of many, many miles to take my hand. I love you guys so much. If any of you are werewolves, you're legally obligated to tell me.

Dr. Larne—thank you for talking to me, at length, about werewolf hormones. I'm sorry for asking so many insane questions, but I'm absolutely delighted that you answered every single one of them so thoughtfully. Remember me when you're famous.

Sam Holtzen, for letting me pick your brain about molecular biology research; Tracy Engle, for telling me exactly what Lyme disease and its fallout felt like, and for being one of my very first online friends; Amelie, for explaining what migraines with aura are; Rebecca, for telling me about the antique store taxidermy bathroom that scarred you; Pria, for lending me your name, your thoughts about the New Jersey first-gen experience, and your enthusiasm.

Strangers on reddit—for educating me on everything from Lyme to Ehlers-Danlos to working at animal control. Reddit user mamidragon, your animal control stories were legendary—thanks for telling me exactly how you'd trap a werewolf.

The shiftythrifting Tumblr, for an endless well of Brigid shirts; Typhoon, the McElroys, and Jon Bois for making content I wanted to spotlight in the kids' usernames.

My very first readers—Mary, Steph, Shelbi, and Em. Thank you for hyping me up so much and for writing "oh my god??" in the margins of the haircut scene.

Christine, Melanie, Loan, Erin, Caroline, Katie Gould, Katie Henry, and Jess Zimmerman, for your support.

Everyone who encouraged my writing along the way—Barbara and Grandma, for listening to my little-kid stories; Aunt Denise, for the story prompt flashcards; Mrs. Legband, for listening to me talk about my novel after English class; Mr. Acker, for patiently and seriously answering all my physics questions about how superpowers would work in real life; Pastor Andy, for telling me to drop chemistry and try to do the thing God created me to do, even though it was risky; Dr. Finneran, for giving me a C on my first writing assignment and challenging me to become a better writer; Sandra Newman, for reading this first chapter and writing THIS IS GOOD in the margins.

God—thanks for giving me the chance to write this. And thanks for letting me yell at you for giving me this body that I am still working on loving. All of these things put together have been an act of worship.

# About the Author

**Kristen O'Neal** is a freelance writer who has written for sites like Buzzfeed Reader, Christianity Today, Birth.Movies.Death, LitHub, and Electric Literature. She lives on the internet. You can find her at @Kristen_ONeal on Twitter and kristenoneal on Tumblr. *Lycanthropy and Other Chronic Illnesses* is her first novel.